Cathryn Grant

MADISON KEITH

Ghost Story Collection - Volume 3

LAST CHANCE
EATEN ALIVE
EMPTY HOME

D2C Perspectives

About Madison Keith

Both the living and the dead like to reveal their secrets to Madison. As the administrative assistant in the basement office of a suburban church, she gets plenty of opportunity to hear from both. Through it all, Madison offers up a steady stream of opinions on everything from the subject of religion and ghosts to finding a soul mate.

The Madison Keith series includes:
FATAL CUT (#1)
SHALLOW WATER (#2)
UNHOLY CHILD (#3)
STONE COLD (#4)
DEADLY STREETS (#5)
LONELY GHOSTS (#6)
LAST CHANCE (#7)
EATEN ALIVE (#8)
EMPTY HOME (#9)
UGLY TRUTH (#10)
BELOVED GHOSTS (#11)

Cathryn Grant

LAST CHANCE

A Suburban Noir Ghost Story

Published by D2C Perspectives

One

MYRA, THE ETHEREAL, almost other-worldly wife of one of the church deacons had delivered her first child while I was in Australia with JD. The baby was five weeks premature, which wasn't surprising since Myra was so thin and delicate she'd given me the impression she was barely holding onto life. When Myra finally brought little Pamela home from the hospital, Pastor Kate went to stay with them to help out with meals and stuff.

Two days later, Kate was waiting in the church office when I arrived at work. Instead of relaxing in one of the armchairs across from my desk like she normally does, she was standing right near my computer. Her face was almost the color of her pale blonde hair, made more blank-looking by the oatmeal-colored shirt she wore, and not helped at all by her usual covering of make-up. "I need your help," she said.

The office door closed on its own behind me. I set my messenger bag on the desk. "I don't smell any coffee."

I went to the pot and saw it hadn't been emptied from the day before. "Let me go rinse this first."

"I'll go with you," she said.

This was entirely unlike Kate. Standoffish, moody, sharp-tongued Kate, following me like the proverbial puppy, anxious to talk to me? Asking for my help?

We clumped through the basement area to the restroom on the opposite side. "Why are you here so early?" I said.

Kate turned on the alcove light and we went into the women's restroom. I poured the old coffee down the drain and twisted the faucet. As water hissed against the inside of the glass carafe, Kate hovered near the door, holding it open.

"There's something scary at Myra and Dave's."

"I bet it's scary having a baby so tiny. She's six pounds now?"

In the mirror above the sink, I saw Kate nod. "Yes, but that's not what I'm talking about. There's an, uhm, a … presence in their house."

"What kind of presence?"

"I guess I'm not sure."

I turned off the faucet and dried the outside of the pot with paper towels. "Do you mean a ghost?" I turned the faucet on again and filled the pot to the top line.

She glanced away. "Sometimes there's a heaviness in the air, the feeling you have when someone sneaks up behind you, and a moment before they make themselves known, you feel something change, a weight in the air. Or you go into a room you thought was empty and someone is sitting in a huge armchair looking out the window. The chair is so large you can't see them, then you feel something there, and all of a sudden they start talking."

That was a very specific explanation. I wondered if those things had happened to Kate or if she'd thought it up on the spot. "Are you saying the house is haunted?"

We walked out of the alcove. I held the pot with both hands to keep the water from sloshing out. We started across the large, empty space, the ceiling too low for a room that size, which makes it feel scarier, as if the ceiling gets lower every day and soon you'll be crushed, like I saw once in a horror movie. It's always dark unless the doors to the two offices and the conference room are open, which they were not.

"I think it might be." Her voice was low, as if she was scared even now. Although maybe it was the basement getting to her. It usually only gets to me when I'm by myself.

"I thought you didn't believe in ghosts." I poured the water into the coffee maker, added ten scoops plus a bit more so it would be dark and strong. Pastor Joe always wrinkles his nose when he tastes my coffee, but Kate gulps it down as often and as fast as I do.

"I don't."

"Then how can you say a place is haunted?"

"I don't know what else to call it."

"So you do believe in ghosts now?"

"I didn't say that."

"You can't have it both ways." I went to my desk and pulled out the chair. It was our usual formation, me behind the desk, Kate seated in one of the armchairs, more often than not, playing with the carved sea lion that sits on the small table between the chairs.

"Can I explain what happened? And get your take on it?"

I settled in my chair. "Go for it." I shouldn't have been quite so harsh. Even though Kate had challenged me on my ghostly experiences, she didn't completely disregard them. She asked questions. Not like Joe who forbid me to talk about them and didn't want to hear a word about it. His attitude wasn't a problem when I encountered spirits on my own time, but tricky when it involved the church. I usually veered toward throwing caution and directives aside, and so far it had worked. Joe was annoyed, but all he did was constantly remind me to stop discussing the subject.

"I don't even know how to start."

"Just jump in."

Instead, she went to the coffee pot and pulled it off the hot plate. Because it was still brewing, coffee hissed onto the burner. She stuck one mug under the still dripping coffee and poured a second mug from the pot. She pulled the mug off the hot plate and quickly stuck the pot back into the machine. For someone who was hovering when I first came in and followed me all the way to the restroom, she was taking a long time to tell me what she was so anxious about. Or had been anxious about. Maybe she was having second thoughts, maybe even admitting something could be haunted made her feel she'd betrayed her beliefs, or made herself look gullible.

She put one of the mugs on my desk and sat down facing me. She held her mug with both hands but didn't blow on the coffee or try a tentative, tongue-burning sip. "I spent the weekend there. I'm helping with meals because the baby is so small she's waking every two hours for feedings. Sometimes more."

"I know. You told me."

"Okay. Well anyway, Dave was on duty — he's been working a lot of double shifts because a few cops retired and some have taken jobs in other cities, and with pay cuts, it's hard to recruit new officers. There's been a lot more burglaries and vandalism lately."

Sunlight cut through the large window to my left. There are only a few minutes a day where we get direct sun in the office because it's below ground level with a narrow area carved out around the building, so you have windows looking at an ivy-covered slope. Besides, the drapes are usually closed, so the sun has to hit just right to get through the center area where they don't meet up correctly. The light made it difficult to see Kate's face and maybe she knew that because she started talking very fast, as if she wanted to take advantage of the fact that I couldn't see her eyes for a moment.

"Most of the time Myra gets up with the baby. All the time, obviously, since she has to feed her. But last night the baby woke every hour. By 3 a.m., Myra couldn't even stand up and she was worried she'd drop the baby she was so exhausted. She had a few bottles of frozen breast milk, so I told her to sleep and I'd feed the baby. Pammy didn't eat much and she fell asleep with her mouth half on the nipple. It was so precious. Anyway, I put her back in her bassinet. I was hungry so I went down to the basement. Since the house is tiny they use the basement as a pantry. It smells like mildew, which would make me nervous about keeping food down there, but they said it's just because it's old and it's nothing to worry about. I grabbed a box of crackers and turned out the light."

"Why would you walk up the stairs in the dark?"

"There was still a light upstairs near the stove."

"So it wasn't totally dark?"

She shook her head. She sipped her coffee and I could see that she didn't like telling me this, but couldn't not tell me.

"I felt something brush past me."

"Okay. That doesn't sound too dramatic. It could be . . ."

"I'm not done. I thought I imagined it, but I stopped. It felt so ... I don't know, I guess chilling. I started shivering and couldn't stop. Then, I ... I sort of ... something pushed me. Hard."

"Pushed?"

Now I could see her eyes again. They glittered with tears. She took another sip of coffee. "I smacked against the wall and fell down two or three steps. I hurt my knee. There's no railing, so there was nothing to grab onto."

"Maybe you were tired. It sounds like you woke up every time Myra did."

"I didn't imagine it."

I bit on my tongue and pressed my lips together. I wasn't going to point out how hard it had been for me when I tried to describe ghostly encounters in the face of her almost complete disbelief. "Is that all?"

"No. I saw a … a thing at the top of the stairs."

"What kind of thing?"

"Shadowy. With long hair. I couldn't see a face. I started shaking so hard. It was . . . to be honest . . . I was scared. I can't describe it."

"How do you know it wasn't Myra?"

"It wasn't a person, it was a shadow, almost transparent."

"What color?"

"I don't know what *color*. What does that matter?"

"It doesn't. Just curious. And trying to figure out how you can be sure it wasn't Myra."

"When I went up, Myra was in her bed. Besides, I know the difference between a human being and a . . . a thing."

"So you saw a ghost."

"I don't know. I can't think in those terms."

"Why are you telling me?"

She glared at me, her eyes outlined in a color that looked like chocolate and her lids shaded with taupe and a hint of beige.

"Okay, I know why you're telling me, but you had this

experience and you still can't acknowledge the possibility of spirits revealing themselves to us?"

"I might have imagined it."

"Is that what you think? You just said you didn't imagine it."

"I don't know what I think." Her voice trembled. She stood and gulped her coffee. "What do you think it was? The shoving?" Her voice shook harder. "It scared me to death. More than it should have, I think."

"It sounds like a ghost."

"I don't know what to do. Maybe I was dreaming, or hallucinating."

"If you didn't believe it was real, I don't think you would have told me."

"It's hard to think things like that exist. But I'm afraid it will come back . . . and try to hurt me."

"It might have been a one-time event."

"I know you're just saying that."

"Did you tell Myra?"

"I didn't want to scare her."

"What about Dave? If it wasn't a ghost, shouldn't he know someone was in the house? Or were you afraid he'd shoot her and when nothing happened, you'd know for sure it was a ghost?"

She glanced at the door leading to the basement area as if she was worried the church basement was also inhabited by other beings. Or that the ghost had followed her.

"You didn't tell them because you're afraid they'll think you're nuts? I'm the only one who won't laugh at you."

"Is this payback for me not believing your supernatural experiences?" She stood and walked to the coffee pot. She refilled her mug. "I should get to work."

"Wait. I just want to see if you're going to admit you saw a ghost."

She turned. "Okay. I saw a ghost. And something tried to push me. Something that wasn't human." Her eyes filled with tears, but they stayed put.

Maybe it was a skill she'd developed in order to prevent eye makeup from running down her cheeks. I'd never seen her teary-eyed. I'd seen her mad, insulted, irritated, self-righteous. She's tough and strong and even though I know how she'll react to most things, and I know a bit about her past — raised in a super-religious family and went to religious schools all the way through college and beyond — I know nothing about her life outside of Central Avenue Church. Possibly that's because she's so dedicated to her job. She's passionate about helping people who are low income, helping children, teenagers, and old people, but not caring much for the big swath in the middle between ages seventeen and seventy. Or maybe I don't know much about her because she deliberately hides it. Sort of like me. Which also might be why we could be kindred spirits in some weird, aloof way.

"Are you gloating?" she said.

"No."

"What should I do?"

"Why do you have to do anything?"

"I'm scared to stay there. And I promised I'd help. At least until the baby is stabilized enough to only require one or two feedings a night."

"Why are you scared?"

"Why do you think?"

"Did you feel like it wanted to push you down the stairs? Or that you were just in the way? What I'm saying is, were you scared of it trying to hurt you or scared because it's something from another realm, or something that makes you think of the reality of being dead?"

"I honestly don't know. I'm just scared. I was shaking. I couldn't eat the crackers. I'm scared now."

The room was quiet for a moment, and while we sat there, a shadow passed behind the drapes — a human shadow, not a ghost. The office door opened and Pastor Joe stepped inside. "Good morning," he said. "How's the baby doing?"

"Eating more every day," Kate said. She took a sip of coffee.

He looked at me. "Do you have the minutes from the business meeting typed up?"

"Not yet."

He glanced at the clock, calculating how long I'd been there and wondering why they weren't weren't done yet. Normally he wouldn't be so hot to get the notes, but he'd told me after the meeting the night before that he wanted them *asap* in the morning. He needed to refresh his memory about all the things people had said regarding supporting an educational effort in Africa that the church was considering. As always, there was disagreement. In this case, it was because the organization running the program wasn't affiliated with the church and some people thought only programs that delivered religious messages should be supported. It constantly amazes me how a group of people who all look at the world through a similar lens can have such wildly different opinions about every single thing they do. They never have a unanimous vote about anything, yet they're all basing their lives and choices on the same book.

He looked at me, then Kate. "What's the serious conversation about?"

"It's not serious," Kate said.

"I walked into the middle of something." He winked. "I can feel it." He went to the coffee pot and filled a mug. He stood in the doorway to his office, which is opposite from my desk, and leaned against the frame.

Kate put her mug on the coffee stand and topped it off.

I knew she wanted Joe to go into his office and close the door like he usually did when he first arrived so he could have privacy for returning phone calls. She really hadn't said what she wanted me to help with, unless it was just to validate she'd seen a ghost.

"What's the big secret?" he said.

"There's no secret," Kate said. "You're imagining things."

"Girl talk?"

Kate curled her lips into a slight frown.

Joe smiled. His eyes crinkled like he was going to laugh and his teeth glistened white, in sharp contrast to his dark mustache and goatee. For a minister who supposedly loathes gossip, it sure seemed like he thought we were gossiping and he wanted to get the inside scoop. If needling Kate, pushing her feminist buttons to get her to include him wasn't working, he was at least going to enjoy watching her simmer.

"Kate saw a ghost." Immediately I felt bad. Really bad. She hadn't said it was a secret or that she was telling me in confidence, but clearly it wasn't going to help her reputation with Joe. I looked at her and was shocked at what I saw.

I expected her face to be red, which happens quite easily when she's angry. Or maybe there would be a glint of hurt, but what I saw was utter shame. I don't know how I knew this. I think it was mostly because she was looking at the floor, watching the toe of her cowboy boot draw a line on the edge of the other boot. She put her hand over her face. When she uncovered her face again, it didn't seem like she was looking at me or thinking about me at all, wondering why I'd betrayed her. There was just a blank, empty expression that said she wished she'd never admitted, even to herself, what she'd experienced.

Joe laughed — one short, abrupt sound of disbelief.

He looked at me. "How many times do I have to remind you not to talk about the occult?" See, this is his problem. He thinks ghosts are the same as soliciting power from the dead, or dabbling with the forces of darkness. Aside from God and angels, he puts all supernatural things in one big box and wants to duct tape it closed and store it in a locked closet, as if it's Pandora's box and he can put all the knowledge and any bad things back inside. Although what he might not know, or has forgotten, is that the one thing left in Pandora's box was the spirit of hope, and maybe that's what ghosts provide — hope that there's something or someone waiting for us on the other side of death. I didn't want to argue with him. He'd never see my point of view, at least not until he encountered a ghost.

I was much more interested in why Kate looked so ashamed, as if she wasn't just sorry she'd told me, but truly ashamed that she'd seen the apparition of someone who had died. I didn't understand how you could feel ashamed of something completely outside your control.

When neither of us spoke, Joe gave up. He sipped some coffee, carried his mug to the stand, and left it there, presumably for me to wash out. Sometimes he washes the mugs, but not often. It's more a gesture to show he doesn't expect me to do it as part of my job, just enough to show he's helping out, but not enough to make it truly balanced. From my desk, I could see the mug was almost full. Like I said, he thinks I make the coffee too strong.

Kate walked out of the room at the same time Joe went into his office. I got busy typing up the minutes. I printed them and took them into his office. It seemed he'd forgotten all about the occult and Kate seeing a ghost, because he gave me a list of other things to do, then asked me to close the door on my way out so he could return his calls. Less than two minutes later, Kate was back in the main office. Her face was still pale, but that shadow of shame was gone — or whatever it was that I knew was shame, while still thinking it was impossible to read such a specific feeling on someone's face. She glanced at Joe's door. Her shoulders relaxed when she saw it was closed, although I'm pretty sure she heard it close or she wouldn't have shot out there so quickly.

"Look." She walked up to my desk, pressed her thighs against it, and leaned forward. Her lips were dry, sticking to her teeth as she spoke. "I was thinking you could stay at Myra and Dave's with me."

"Really?"

She nodded. "If it comes back, you'll know what to do."

"How would I know that?"

"It's more familiar to you."

"Every situation is different."

Although she had the same nearly white hair, the same expensive and perfectly applied makeup, the same short neck and broad shoulders and large breasts of the Kate I'd been working for all this time, I felt like I was talking to a stranger. I'd never seen her look uncertain, or behave as if she needed anything from anyone, especially not me.

"I don't know. What will you tell them? That I'm there to protect you from a ghost?"

She smirked.

"I'm serious."

"Let me think about it. I'm not only scared for myself, I'm afraid for the baby."

"Why?"

She closed her eyes, letting me see the grandeur of the smooth shadowed contours of her eyelids. "What if I'd been holding Pamela when I was pushed?"

I waited for her to open her eyes. When she finally did, her pupils were pinpricks, and even with the fluorescent lights, the office wasn't that bright.

"I'll think about it," I said.

"Are you trying to torture me? Do you want me to lie awake all night, scared out of my mind?"

"I already told you, no. But I hardly know them. I've met Dave once, and I've seen Myra with him. That's it. I can't just show up at their house and say I'm the backup team for baby care."

"I'm not asking you to take care of the baby."

It was becoming clear she was so scared she didn't care if it looked odd to drag in a near stranger. I felt sorry for her, and I wasn't trying to say I wouldn't help her, although I wasn't sure how I'd actually do that. It's not like I'm some expert in communicating with scary ghosts.

They do what they want, but no ghost has ever tried to hurt me, no matter how much they scared me. Although there was that ghost in Australia who wanted to take JD with her to the other side.

"Will you say yes, if I can figure out what to tell Myra?"

"Sure. Okay."

"You're a true friend."

Her eyes got all teary and red when she said that, and then I really felt like I was talking to a total stranger. The ghost must have scared her personality to a back corner of her brain.

Two

I DIDN'T HEAR until late that night how Kate explained to Myra and Dave Hicks my sudden appearance at their front door with my sleeping bag and pillow. Whatever it was, they were welcoming, at first, and seemed to take my presence in stride, so I was pretty sure they didn't think I was there to figure out why their tiny home was haunted.

The house was built in 1937. It was caramel-colored adobe with a flat Spanish tile roof. The front door had glass panels set in a wood frame which was really cool, but they'd covered them with drapes. I don't know if the windows were blocked by drapes from the beginning, or if people in 1937 were less concerned about neighbors and strangers peering into their living room. The house had a small, dining room adjoining the living room and a kitchen with a bar for eating, but no room for a table and chairs. There were two bedrooms and one bathroom. Steep, narrow stairs led from the kitchen to the basement, which contained open shelves, cupboards, and an alcove cut into the wall with a bed no one ever used. There were some boxes and stuff stacked near the back. The basement extended under the living room but not under the full foundation of the house.

The single car garage was detached from the house and it contained the washer and dryer, so there was no room for a car. There was also another small building at the back of the property — large enough for an old desk and a small bookcase.

The basement indeed smelled of mildew. I noticed the heavy feeling Kate had mentioned and wasn't sure if it was damp, still air, or something else. Although I didn't think it was the same feeling you had when someone was in the room and you suddenly become aware of their presence.

I wondered how they could stand storing food down there. Maybe the odor wasn't as intense for them. Some people pick up every little hint of odor, and others glide through life with their noses plugged, unless their senses get flooded by spilled gasoline or pungent cigar smoke. Kate and I are in the former category.

It was a Wednesday, and Dave was working a double shift. Myra suggested I could sleep on the bed in the basement, but I knew I'd never sleep with that smell.

"I can put my sleeping bag on the floor in the baby's room. I'll be fine."

"I don't think that will work. I don't want all these people in there when I bring her in for her feeding." She was small and thin, and despite having delivered a child less than two months earlier, her hips were narrow and her belly looked flat under a loose linen blouse with pleats that flowed around her hips. Her hair was cut to her shoulders, light brown, and wavy. She had brown eyes and a larger than average mouth. She was very serene, seeming to drift on the fringes of life. I didn't know if that was the result of new motherhood or her permanent state.

Kate had said they were expecting me to stay three nights, which was fine with me. JD and I had plans for Sunday, so I'd still get Saturday to clean and run errands and have time to myself. I'd left two containers of seed and extra water for my parakeets, Simon and Sarah. I planned to stop by on Friday to check on them again.

I put my sleeping things and duffel bag in the baby's future bedroom where Kate had been sleeping. Apparently one person sleeping in there while Myra fed the baby was fine, but two was a huge crowd she couldn't accommodate. Not that I blamed her, I sort of wondered why Kate had been sleeping there. The baby stayed in a bassinet in her parents' room, but Myra didn't want to wake Dave when she was nursing.

Kate had brought stuff to make tacos for dinner. We set to work grating cheese and chopping tomatoes and sautéing tiny strips of chicken breast. Kate also had a tortilla warmer with her. In fact, she brought everything, even Tabasco sauce. She'd made sure she would not have to go down to the basement for any supplies.

While we cooked, Myra turned the iPod to 60s rock, including the Stones, which I love. Then she left to feed Pamela. I danced around the kitchen, trying not to grate my knuckles. Kate complimented my dance moves which made me feel self-conscious for half a second, but then I kept moving. There's something about that era of rock that forces you to dance. I guess it's the solid beat, more drum, or more insistent drums than you hear in most pop songs now, where lots of them have an electronic sound.

Kate seemed to be able to resist the urge to dance, which was good, because she doesn't really have a body designed for dance, and I don't know if I could have watched her without laughing. That's not very nice, but true. And it's not just her body. Maybe people get bodies that fit their personalities, because nothing about Kate is light-hearted or inclined to let go and dance.

She slid the sharpest knife I'd ever seen through the last tomato. It sliced through the skin with the clean cut of a razor blade. Tomato skin usually resists like it's a piece of plastic, and watching a non-serrated knife make that sharp cut was frightening and fascinating. The music had changed to disco, so I'd stopped dancing.

"You should have taken the bed in the pantry," Kate said.

"It stinks. How can they keep food down there?"

"I don't know. I guess they figure it's just mildew. It doesn't seem to bother them. Lots of old houses have damp or musty smells. It's part of the charm of a place that's been around for a long time."

"Musty and mildew are not the same thing. Musty might be charming, but mildew smells like a disease."

"Don't say that to Myra."

"I wouldn't."

"I can never be sure with you. Anyway, if you took that bed, you'd have a better chance of encountering the … the thing."

"The ghost."

"Right."

"I'm not sleeping with that smell. I'd be awake all night."

"Myra said she doesn't want both of us sleeping in the baby's room." She lowered her voice. "If you don't sleep down there, how are you going to see it? How are you going to help?"

"This was your idea, I thought you had something in mind."

"I want to know what it is. I want it to go away. The smell isn't that bad. And you'd be asleep."

"Not if the ghost woke me."

"It doesn't smell like sewage or something toxic. You could stand it for a few nights."

"Why don't you sleep down there and come get me if you see the ghost?"

She laughed and ran that deliciously sharp knife through a wedge of tomato. She made a few more cuts and began dicing the pieces into tiny spears. She was very careful about everything she did. These were going to be awesome tacos.

"I thought you weren't afraid of encountering

something supernatural," she said.

"I'm not. This is about the smell."

"Can't you overlook your own finickiness to help me out?"

I scooped the grated cheese into a bowl and started slicing a stalk of green onion into tiny, transparent disks. "I'll stay down there if you sleep with me."

"In the same bed?" Her voice was thin and strained, uncertain.

"I'll use my sleeping bag, you can have the bed. Although I hope my bag doesn't pick up that smell. And I need some kind of padding."

"I don't know."

"Are you that scared? You thought I'd take care of it and you wouldn't have to see it again?"

"Yes."

"It would have been nice to know that before I agreed to stay here."

"I thought it was understood."

"What was understood?" Myra was in the doorway. There were damp spots on her shirt from the baby and I noticed in the brighter lights of the kitchen that her eyes were bloodshot and her lids puffy.

"Nothing," Kate said. "We were just talking."

"It smells good," Myra said.

"Five more minutes. Maybe ten." Kate plugged in the tortilla warmer and handed me a stack of three blue plates to arrange on the eating bar.

"Let's eat in the dining room," Myra said. "It gets

crowded with three people at the bar."

When we were seated around an array of bowls filled with cheese and tomatoes and guacamole and chicken, I asked Myra how long they'd owned the house.

"Dave had it before we were married."

That didn't answer my question at all, but she folded her taco and took a large bite, so I didn't want to fire another question at her while she was trying to chew. The poor woman looked like she was starving, yet wasn't quite sure if she'd prefer to be eating or taking a nap.

After she'd scarfed down her first taco, she talked about the baby, wondered how long until she slept more than an hour or two at a time, and complained a bit about Dave working so many double shifts, spending the small amount of free time he had doing tasks related to his duties as a church deacon.

Kate made sympathetic noises. She pulled the cheese bowl to the side of her plate and sprinkled more shreds on top of her chicken.

The room was dim. The lights in the chandelier appeared to be the lowest wattage available. The table and chairs were mahogany and the walls were cranberry red, which made everything even darker. The windows were long and narrow, covered with drapes the same color as the wall paint. The floor was hardwood.

It felt very civilized eating in a dining room. My condo has an eating area that connects to the kitchen and also opens to the living room, so it feels like one big, bland room. Myra's dining room made me feel as if I'd gone back in time. Houses that have separate dining rooms and parlors are somehow more practical — everything has a definite purpose. When all the rooms run together, it makes everything seem open and connected, but maybe it also makes everyone feel like they're floating around without moorings.

Eating tacos and making small talk was a little surreal when I wanted to find out more about what Kate was thinking. This was the first time we'd spent time together away from the church property, not at a church event, and I was curious about the rest of her life. The ghost must have really freaked her out to make her willing to admit she needed my help, to even admit that she'd seen and felt something. I wanted to hear her tell the story again, but even more, I wanted to find out why she had so much trouble calling it a ghost and what she was thinking of her beliefs and her views of me now that something had come in and forced her to see the world from an entirely different perspective.

I knew so little about her personal life. I didn't even know where she lived. I didn't know if she had a boyfriend or what she did in her free time. Sometimes it seemed like her whole life belonged to the church.

Instead, we were forced to talk about babies, and I know nothing about babies, and with what I gathered from Kate's comments, she didn't know a lot either.

I decided to have another go at getting more information on the history of the house. If there was a ghost, it most likely came from someone who lived there.

Or died there.

"I love old houses. Kate said this was built in 1937?"

Myra nodded. Three pieces of chicken and a few tomatoes fell out the back end of her taco. "Surprising, isn't it?"

"Why?"

"I always assumed that in the middle of the Depression they weren't building new homes. I guess it shows that all the photographs of soup lines you see were only part of the story."

I know nothing about the Depression, although I guess I would have assumed the same thing, if I'd thought about it. "So, how long have you owned it?"

"Dave bought it in 2002, before we were married."

"How long have you lived here?"

"Since 2010."

"Are there any stories?"

Even though I wasn't looking directly at Kate, I could feel her glaring at me, worried I was on the verge of mentioning the ghost. But I don't think my question hinted at the subject of ghosts at all. Every old house has stories. If Myra had heard of any ghost stories, it would help. If she hadn't, then it wouldn't matter and she'd think I was talking about stories like the house getting damaged in an earthquake, or one of the previous owners painting all the walls that bloody-looking cranberry red and they painted over all of them except the dining room.

Myra popped the rest of the taco in her mouth and chewed. She took a sip of water and pinched up one of the fallen pieces of chicken off her plate. She put it in her mouth. "Not really, not that I know of. Dave might know some. The same family owned it for the first sixty-five years. A couple bought it when they were young and lived here until they died in their nineties."

"That's romantic," I said.

Kate grabbed the tomato bowl and started eating tomato pieces like she was snacking from a bowl of mixed nuts. "I suppose they died of old age," she said.

Myra furrowed her brow.

Kate blushed slightly. She wasn't very adept at asking casual questions. When someone lives into their nineties, it's pretty obvious they died from old age, although I suppose they could fall down the stairs or have a car accident and then it's not technically old age. Or they could get pushed down the stairs.

"If someone lives in the same house their entire life, the house has seen a lot of things — babies being born, sadness, parties, grief," I said.

Myra laughed. "You make it sound like the house is a living thing."

As she laughed, I noticed her wide mouth again. Perfectly straight teeth drew my attention to it and I found myself observing their precise alignment more than I normally would. "Don't you think a house takes on a personality?"

"I don't know what that means. This isn't a Disney film, with talking furniture."

Kate glared at me again. As I watched her scowl twist

with even greater intensity, I realized it was silly not to tell Myra what I was doing there, silly not to come right out and ask whether she'd ever seen a ghost.

Although her laughter made me lean toward thinking she hadn't. Did that mean the ghost made its first appearance to Kate, or did it mean it tried to appear to Myra, or Dave, and they weren't capable of seeing ghosts? Or wrote it off as a bad dream?

"I think houses, and really, all buildings, have an atmosphere, or something — a presence. Like the church basement gives off a creepy feeling, and when you go into a museum it's calming because looking at art makes people feel reflective. I think that mood gets absorbed into the walls and the floors."

Myra pushed out her chair and stood. "I never really thought about it, but you sound like a very sensitive, spiritual person." She smiled. "I hear Pamela fussing, I'll be right back." She walked out of the room. It felt darker, somehow, the plates and bowls looked abandoned. The heaviness Kate had mentioned settled over the table. Maybe I imagine all this stuff, I don't know. But if I do, then Kate was starting to imagine it also.

Clearly we weren't going to hear any stories about the house, and it was obvious Myra had never seen or felt any kind of spirit. Or else she was afraid and didn't want us to know what was wrong with her house, and so she'd become a very good liar.

"Why did you bring that up?" Kate said. She stood and picked up her plate. She stacked it on mine and went to Myra's place where she did the same.

"A house this old must have stories."

"You almost told her the place is haunted."

"No I didn't."

"You did."

"I said houses have an atmosphere from the things that happened there."

"Like people dying and ghosts taking over the place."

"Not just that."

"It's what you meant."

"It would help to know if someone was murdered here. Or committed suicide."

"How would that help?" She glanced toward the living room and the hallway leading to the bedrooms, then walked around the table and went into the kitchen. The plates clattered against the hard plastic prongs as she inserted them into the dishwasher rack. She returned and picked up two of the bowls.

"If there's a ghost, I'm willing to bet someone had an unpleasant death here," I said.

"You didn't mention that before."

"I thought it was understood."

The fact that I'd repeated her words seemed lost on her. Maybe she was too annoyed with me, or maybe she wasn't really listening.

"You shouldn't have asked her those questions."

"Why am I here if you don't want my help? And I'd really like to know if either one of them has seen it."

She glanced at the hallway again. "We shouldn't be

talking about it, she might hear us. Come in the kitchen."

I picked up three bowls and followed her.

She turned on the water and stuck the frying pan under it. She squirted a long, pink stream of soap at the pan, enough to wash an entire tub of dishes.

"Why did you invite me here? It feels awkward."

"I don't even know. I just can't sleep, knowing I might see that spirit or whatever you call it."

"Why can't you call it a ghost?"

"Because they don't exist. Or if they do, they're ungodly. Evil."

"If they're human spirits, how could they be evil?"

"I don't even know. I've seen something that supposedly doesn't exist. Or if it does, a Godly person shouldn't be involved with it. This makes me question everything."

"It's not like you went looking for it. You had nothing to do with it."

"I know." She scrubbed the pan, her arm jerking violently as if she was trying to scrub her mind free of everything that didn't make sense to her.

"Me being here won't prevent it from appearing."

She shut off the water, picked up the sponge, and turned to face me. "I invited you for comfort, okay? I'm scared and I don't know what to do and with all your talk about ghosts, you were the logical choice."

For some reason, that hurt my feelings. She didn't feel any friendship or affection toward me after all. In her mind, I was simply a ghost expert. I'm sure I'm the only person she knows who's ever seen a ghost, or at least the only one who admits it. Most people wouldn't find that admission difficult, it's one of those unusual, far outside the norm experiences you're compelled to talk about. But when the people you hang out with believe that ghosts come from the devil or hell or some such rigid view, telling everyone you've seen one probably doesn't help you connect with your friends and fellow believers.

The whole time we cleaned up the kitchen, Myra stayed in the back with the baby. I wondered whether she'd fallen asleep or didn't want to answer any more questions about the history of the house. And that made me think maybe there was some history she hadn't mentioned. The more I turned it over in my mind, the more I thought her answers were deliberately vague, dodging questions that weren't difficult. They were just part of a casual conversation that was appropriate in any house that had been around for seventy-five years. Houses that old have stories to tell.

Three

WITHOUT DISCUSSING IT further, Kate yielded. Once Myra and the baby were asleep, she grabbed some sheets and a blanket out of the hall closet, dragged the quilt off the bed where she'd been sleeping in the baby's future room, and led the way through the kitchen and down the stairs to the putrid basement.

We left the light turned on over the kitchen sink so it wouldn't be utter darkness once we turned out the basement light. Kate made up the bed and I spread two folded blankets on the ground. The carpet felt as if it was glued directly on the concrete. Kate said, "You're young, you can handle it."

The odor, not really putrid, I exaggerated that because I like pleasant smells — fresh air and food cooking — would probably keep me awake half the night. That, and adrenaline, because I was so curious about the ghost. Plus, I knew I'd be staring into the darkness, trying to think of a way to get Myra talking. Maybe I'd sneak upstairs when I heard the baby cry and if Myra were in a half-dream state, she'd tell me what she was holding back. And I knew she was holding back.

Kate sat on the bed, tugged off her thick pink socks, and swung her legs up. She pulled the blankets over herself and curled on her side facing me. "Will you turn off the light?"

I felt like I was babysitting. Any minute I expected to see her hugging a flashlight against her stomach, prepared to turn it on under the covers the minute the overhead light went out.

I walked to the foot of the stairs and flicked the switch down. The darkness was solid, and the light over the sink really only faintly illuminated the top two steps. The rest of the stairway was in thick shadows, and in the basement itself it was impossible to see the shelves or even the glistening of the silver handles on the cabinets.

Sliding my feet so I wouldn't stumble in the darkness, I felt my way back to the foot of my sleeping bag.

"Are you okay?" Kate said.

"I'm fine." I wanted to laugh. The tough girl act I'd known since I met her had evaporated. Even the quality of her voice was different. Not all the time, but right then, and when she talked about the ghost.

"Sleep good," she said. The bed squeaked as she shifted her position.

I tucked myself into my sleeping bag and pulled the zipper halfway up. The air was still and tight and I knew I was going to end up sleeping on top of the bag because with the two of us breathing and no air flow and the mildew odor, the room was going to get warm and damp.

To be honest, the odor of mildew was less intense and I was less fixated on it. Or maybe it was just that my curiosity had taken the front seat.

I don't know what time I fell asleep or what time I was woken by the baby's screaming. It was the most un-ghostly thing I'd ever heard. The noise was shrill, penetrating every corner of the house. How did parents tolerate it? I couldn't imagine caring for a new baby and being woken by screams that sounded as if the poor little thing was being tortured. It was a terrifying sound and made me feel like crying myself. I unzipped my bag and crawled out. Getting on my hands and knees, I felt my way to the stairs.

I suppose it was rude of me to decide to burst in on her feeding time with her baby, mother-daughter bonding and all of that, but I thought I'd be able to find a way to help. Although doing what, I had no idea. I'd never changed a diaper, so I doubted I'd be much use there. I could dispose of the diaper. Or I could bring her a glass of water.

Once I reached the foot of the stairs, I stood and walked up a few steps. I paused, waiting to see if some unseen presence tried to push me down, but I felt nothing. The heavy feeling in the air I'd noticed earlier was gone. I looked up toward the kitchen and saw only the faint pool of light on the linoleum.

I climbed to the top. I got two glasses out of the

cabinet and filled them at the spigot built into the refrigerator, but not too full, so it would be easy to walk through the dining room and living room without spilling. Muted light from the street came through the curtains fitted over the front door. The couch and the recliner looked like boulders. Only the outlines of the framed paintings — one of the Pacific Ocean and another of Lake Tahoe surrounded by the snow-capped Sierras — were visible, making them appear to be windows looking out at the night sky.

The soft carpet in the hallway felt good on my bare feet after the cold hardwood floor. It occurred to me that Myra or Dave might not want a virtual stranger walking barefoot on what looked like new carpet, but it was too late. I wasn't going to juggle the water glasses back through two dark rooms and go downstairs for my socks.

The baby had stopped screaming. The house was silent. I had no idea whether Dave was home from his shift.

"Myra?" I kept my voice low so I wouldn't startle the baby, but possibly too low because after waiting a few seconds, there was no response.

"Myra? It's Madison. I brought you a glass of water. Can I come in?"

"Sure. No problem."

I went into the bedroom. The only light was from a small shaded lamp at one end of the antique marble-topped dresser. Myra was seated in the armchair nursing the baby.

"She's adorable." I held out the glass of water.

Without looking up, she shook her head. I carried it across the room and set it on the dresser. I took a sip of my water.

"How many times has she been up tonight? You must get really tired."

"This is only the second time. Did she wake you."

"Yes, but that's okay."

She glanced at me. Her hair fell back from her face and her lips were pulled into a slight grimace. I guessed she was thinking of course it was okay, this was the baby's house not mine, and if my sleep was disturbed, that was too bad.

"It must have been hard having her stay in the hospital for so long."

She nodded.

"Is anyone else coming to help you, or just Kate?"

"Just Kate. My mother lives in Kentucky and she's not in good health. Once the baby is older, we'll go visit her."

I waited, expecting to hear a report on Dave's mother, any sisters, or friends, but she didn't add any more information. It was kind of disturbing to hear myself assume any help would come from females, but I guess that's how it is.

"Kate's an angel. I don't know what I would have done without her."

I nodded. Angelic was the last word I'd use to describe Kate, but obviously Kate was a huge help since Dave had such crazy hours, and apparently, there was no one else.

"It was nice of you to offer relief to Kate, if she has to work late," she said.

"No problem." So, that's why I was here. It sounded lame, but overall it made sense. And it made me feel less obvious as I inserted myself into her baby's feeding time, poking around for a history lesson on her house.

"Sorry you have to sleep in the basement. I know it smells a little off down there."

"It sort of fades after you're there for a while."

"I noticed that. I'm usually not in there any longer than it takes to unload groceries, but it gets to me sometimes. It's kind of embarrassing."

"Why?"

"It makes it seem like the house isn't clean."

"It's just old."

"Still. I had the last housekeeper work on deep cleaning it every few weeks, but it didn't help."

"The last housekeeper?"

"She quit. We just hired a new one and I haven't talked to her about the mildew yet."

The baby had stopped sucking, but her tiny, pale pink lips were still wrapped around Myra's breast. Her eyes were half open, seeming to gaze in the direction of her mother's face. Myra was running her finger across the baby's brow and down her nose.

"Is she done eating?"

"Yes, but I don't like to put her back in her bassinet until she falls asleep."

I didn't see how she was going to fall asleep with her mother tracing lines on her face, smiling at her, capturing her attention, but maybe Myra didn't care. Maybe she didn't want to miss a single minute of her child's first months on earth and she figured she could sleep later, in another year.

"So you and Dave have been married almost three years?"

"Yes."

"Did you plan to have a child so soon?"

"Of course."

I could see I'd insulted her, implied the baby wasn't wanted, or something worse. This wasn't going well between putting her on the defensive during dinner and now this.

"Why do you have all those tattoos?" she said.

"I like them, I like the colors. The vines remind me to be connected to the earth." Even as I said that, I realized I'd kind of forgotten that was why I'd chosen the vines for my ankles and my left wrist, and the ladybugs across the back of my neck. I'd had them for several years now, and no one had asked what they meant since I first started working at the church. In the rest of the world, tattoos are fairly common, but around the church-going crowd, they're still a bit of an oddity, although that's mostly an age thing.

"I don't want my daughter to ever mutilate her body like that." She took the baby away from her breast and pulled her top down. She pressed the baby close, tucking the tiny head against her neck. She drew the baby's hand close to her face and kissed it. Her lips lingered across the backs of the little fingers. The baby gurgled and wriggled in her arms.

"I don't think I mutilated my body."

"You marred it forever. Look how perfect her skin is."

"It doesn't stay perfect. Think what happens to your skin by the time you're old."

"But you should cherish your body. And it belongs to God, it's not ours to color up with ink. Or to stab holes through our flesh."

"You have pierced ears."

She didn't seem to have a comeback for that. I guess it's only lots of holes in your flesh that's objectionable, not two holes like she had. So it's really about fitting in with everyone else, not concern with offending God. I didn't point that out because I wanted to get the conversation off my supposedly damaged skin and back to her house. "The stairs to your basement are steep. Have you ever fallen down them?"

"No."

"It would be easy to do. Especially in the dark."

"Why would you walk down the stairs in the dark?"

"If the power was out. And the switch is at the bottom."

"The power hasn't gone out the whole time I've lived here, and if it did, I'd probably manage to not go into the basement."

"Did your housekeeper ever fall?"

"No."

"So no one ever fell down and broke a bone . . . or . . . died?"

She stood. She shifted the baby to her shoulder. She spread her feet slightly and swayed, rubbing the baby's back. "I shouldn't be talking. It's going to keep her from falling asleep."

I stood up and pointed to her glass of water. "Do you want this?"

"Yes, thanks. Just leave it there."

If the suggestion that I leave wasn't clear a moment earlier, it was now. "Sorry to disturb you. I'm wide awake and I wasn't thinking."

"No worries." Her voice was a whisper. She closed her eyes and continued swaying.

AFTER BEING SO focused on how dangerous the stairs were, I was extra cautious when I went back down to the basement. I kept my left hand on the wall. It struck me odd that Dave hadn't made the effort to add a railing. I couldn't imagine Myra going up and down the narrow staircase when she was pregnant, especially the final few months when her balance would have been completely off. That was another question I should have asked her, although it wasn't likely she'd want to hear any more of my insistent, senseless questions.

I crawled into my sleeping bag and lay there listening to Kate breathe, once again hyper-aware of the mildew odor, hoping it would fade so I could sleep. Instead, it felt like the spores had crept inside my brain and washed away every inclination toward sleep.

It seemed a very long time that I remained awake, staring into the darkness. Listening. I heard nothing from upstairs, not Myra carrying the baby back to the bassinet in her room, or Dave coming home from his late shift, if he hadn't already been in bed while I was talking to Myra. The conversation accomplished nothing. I hoped I'd have a chance to talk to Dave, but it looked like he was either on duty or sleeping.

The more I thought about it, the more I wondered whether I was there to find out what was going on, or my sole purpose was to calm Kate's fears. She was acting like a big baby herself, afraid to say what she was thinking, afraid of the dark, afraid to explore things outside what she'd always been taught or chosen to believe. I suppose I shouldn't have been so harsh. I probably have my own fears, they're just different. Although wrapped up in my sleeping bag, waiting for sleep, I couldn't think of anything I was afraid of.

I turned on my side, even though it was a painful position with the unyielding concrete beneath the carpet, but I needed to move around or my muscles would get stiff and I'd never fall asleep.

The bag was constricting because my cotton pants and t-shirt caught on the flannel liner and the various pieces of fabric grabbed onto each other. I pushed out the bag. I turned to my other side. A little while later, I'm not sure how long, I felt a tug at the foot of my bag. I jerked up onto my elbows and realized I'd been asleep after all. My bag was being yanked toward the staircase, not dragged, but short, quick pulls. I might have whimpered, but if I did, it wasn't very loud because I heard nothing from Kate, not even the creak of her shifting position and no sound of her breathing.

The tugging repeated every few seconds. I couldn't see anything, certainly not the figure Kate had described. There was nothing frightening, and the tugs were light enough that after a few minutes, I wondered if it was still my bag twisting around, catching on my clothes. Or a dream. The smell had faded and the room was so dark I was disoriented.

After a bit, the tugging stopped. I drifted back to sleep and when I woke again, I was equally split between thinking I'd dreamt everything and thinking a presence had entered the room and was trying to get my attention.

The basement was filled with gray, watery light, so I assumed the sun was up and coming through the back door of the kitchen.

"Did you see anything? Hear anything?" Kate said.

I turned over. She was on her back, not moving, looking as if she was still asleep.

"Are you awake?" I said.

"How else would I be talking?"

"You could be talking in your sleep."

"I'm not. Did you?"

"No."

"Nothing? You wouldn't lie, to keep me from

worrying, would you?"

"No. I might have felt something, but I'm not sure."

She sat up and pushed the blankets away. Sitting on the slightly sagging mattress, she looked like a soft ball of flesh, all curled around herself. It was strange seeing her like that, when I'm used to her all made-up and her hair styled and her large breasts well-secured, and her feet covered. I realized I'd never seen her in sandals.

"What happened?" She sat up straighter and looked less like a ball.

"I went upstairs and talked to Myra for a while. I'm not sure if I dreamt it, or my bag was just twisted around, but when I came back to bed, it felt like something tugging on my sleeping bag."

She shivered and pulled the blankets up, forming a tent around her body. "What should we do?"

"We don't need to do anything."

"Do you think the house is haunted?"

"I don't know. I don't usually think in those terms."

"Why not?"

"It sounds like a myth when you say it like that."

She nodded. "What should we do?" Her voice sounded as if tears were pressing to come out and she was using all her breath and strength to hold them inside. "What if it tries to hurt the baby?"

"If there was something here, which I'm still not sure about, it didn't try to hurt me at all. And if Myra had encountered anything that was a threat to the baby, don't you think she would have mentioned it?"

"I'm so scared," Kate said. "I can't believe this is happening to me. I have no idea what to do. I always thought this was all in your imagination, I thought if it was even real, it only happened to people who messed around with the occult."

"Nothing is happening to you."

"Something tried to push me down the stairs!" Her voice was shrill and loud enough to carry up the stairs.

"Shhh. You don't want to wake up the baby, or Myra. Don't panic."

She got out of bed and hurried to the foot of the stairs. She flipped on the light switch. "I'm not panicking. We need to do something."

"We don't know anything. I don't even know if there was actually something in the room. Calm down."

She shivered and rubbed her bare arms. "Don't be so casual. This is scary for me. And I feel ridiculous for being one of those people who sees things."

I unzipped my bag and folded it back. I sat up and hugged my knees. "Let's make some coffee and toast and get ready for work."

"I think I need to tell them. It was a mistake to invite you here without telling them what's going on. I could have risked Pamela's life!"

I stood. "Come on. Get a grip. Nothing happened."

She shuffled back to her bed, pulled up the blankets, and patted the pillow into place. I wondered if she made her bed with a quick yank and a smack at home or if her anxiety made her not care.

"This is all normal to you, but it's not to me," she said.

I rolled up my sleeping bag and secured the elastic strap around it. I put it between some boxes in the corner, stacked the blankets and my pillow on top of one of the boxes, and went upstairs.

As if by agreement, we didn't talk about it anymore. Myra and Dave were asleep, so we kept our voices low, but I think neither of us wanted them to overhear until we decided what to do. I knew what to do — wait. There was nothing to say and nothing that scary. If something had tugged at my bag, it was so mild it made me think Kate had over-reacted.

Four

DURING MY DRIVE to work, I tried to think of how to get Myra to open up. Usually I have the opposite problem — people tell me more than I want to hear. Standing off by myself smoking is one reason I think I attract people telling me their secrets. They might not realize they're revealing secrets, but they are. If you listen carefully enough, everyone does, showing you what upsets them, trying to justify their behavior; complaining, so you can tell they're hurt or scared, they just won't admit it. They know I'm not going anywhere before my cigarette is finished, and I think that gets them talking. It seems we're all used to other people cutting us off, walking away, doing something else when we want someone to look us in the eye and listen.

They also talk to me because I tend to say most of what's on my mind, and that has a way of loosening others' inhibitions. They realize it's not so bad to reveal the truth.

Myra didn't want to talk to me and I don't know if it's because I was pushing too hard instead of just being there, or if she didn't like having her house invaded by a stranger. Or if she had something to hide. I know I was coming across like an interrogator. What a way to stop the flow of words. I regretted being so impatient but it was too late now.

The whole situation was awkward, playing a silly game, not wanting to tell Myra and Dave their house was haunted. I didn't even know for sure it *was* haunted. Maybe Kate *wanted* to see a ghost.

Let's be honest. Seeing a ghost is not just scary. It's exciting. It's an experience outside the norm, it wakes you up from the physical, easily explainable world, and proves there may be a whole other layer of reality. Several layers. It's almost as if ghosts are saying — *things are not what they seem. Life is not what it seems.*

The sky was cloudy and there was a twenty percent chance of rain. I always wonder how they come up with those precise forecasts — ten percent, twenty percent, eighty percent. And often it rains when there's a ten percent chance and the sky is dark and spongey but nothing comes of it when there's eighty percent.

In this case, I was hoping for no rain. Sleeping in that mildew-encrusted basement would be far worse if a huge storm let loose, or even a steady dripping rain.

The parking strip in front of the church was empty. Kate and I had left the Hicks' at the same time, but Kate planned to stop by her house, feed her cat and her fish, and then pick up some lattes for us.

We'd had two cups of coffee each, and I would make more at the church, but after not sleeping much, I wanted the treat of a latte and Kate offered to get me one.

Before I opened the car door, my phone rang — JD.

"How was the haunted house?" he said.

"Not very haunted."

"Give it time. Did you get any sleep?"

"Some."

"I was thinking of coming by for lunch. Can you get away for an hour or two?"

Lunch with JD is always high on my priority list, nearly at the top. In fact, seeing him at all is at the top of the list. But the thought of escaping from Kate and her odd blend of panic and denial made lunch sound even more appealing. Plus, it was lunch out. Usually I eat a sandwich in the church garden or soup at one of the long tables in the empty, echoing multi-purpose room across from the sanctuary.

"No problem. I can take at least an hour, I've saved up quite a bit." Pastor Joe, and Kate, for that matter, didn't always like me looking at it that way, thinking I could bank my lunch minutes and take two hours away every few weeks. Since half my job is to greet visitors and answer the phone, leaving the office unattended for an hour or two was viewed as not actually doing my job. But I figured I earned it. And there were days when the phone didn't ring for hours and then I'd go to the restroom and three people would call by the time I walked back and forth across the basement.

Joe and Kate didn't tell me to stop hoarding the extra minutes, and they didn't complain directly, they just made little comments about how important it was to have someone present whenever possible. Well I was present whenever possible. They just didn't think lunch hours should be viewed as cash in the bank. But people called at night too, did that mean it was my job to be there at two in the morning?

JD said he'd pick me up at 11:45 and we'd go to an Italian place downtown called La Pastaia. They have fresh pasta, obviously, and pizza. There are lots of tables for two that are nicely separated from the large group tables so you're not thrown together with bunches of co-workers out to lunch, all trying to talk over each other, slamming into your ears from every direction.

At 11:41 JD walked into the office, looking yummy as always in stone-washed jeans and a dark purple shirt that buttoned — highly unusual since he normally wears t-shirts. His hair was dry and his ponytail silky, so obviously he'd taken time to get ready.

We went outside and got into his SUV. We kissed for a while before he started the engine and headed away from the church to the expressway.

"Missed you," he said.

I put my hand on his leg and squeezed it slightly. "Me too."

The SUV rocketed along the expressway, creeping close to sixty. I took my hand back and gripped the shoulder strap of my seatbelt, as if I could hold myself in place. I know he isn't the only guy who drives too fast, in fact a guy who doesn't drive too fast is probably more unusual, but sometimes I felt as if we were going to take flight. The funny thing is, I like to drive fast. It's thrilling to stomp on the gas and shoot forward, drive for five or six blocks without hitting a traffic light, to feel as if the world is racing past, to accelerate down an onramp and fly along an uncrowded freeway. I love going fast when I'm in the driver's seat.

When someone else is driving it's not so exciting. It must be something about being the one in control, you know when you're taking that little extra risk or when you are perfectly managing the vehicle. But when someone else is driving, you have no idea when they feel that. I suppose I should trust him, but mostly I wish he'd drive even three or four miles an hour slower. I don't mean to make it sound as if he goes eighty in a fifty-mile-an-hour zone, but he's almost always ten miles over, and on the freeway, sometimes more. He's only had two speeding tickets, so maybe if his luck changes, he'll slow down. Until then, I don't say much because he looks at me and smiles and then I have the added worry that his eyes are off the road, and we're still going just as fast.

The parking lot at La Pastaia was full, but we circled twice.

"The lot across the street is half empty," I said. "We could be sitting at our table instead of racing around like a Tasmanian devil."

We started around a third time and at the second row,

a Honda was backing out just as we rounded the curve. I'd just as soon park further away and walk, but JD views it as a game, to see how close he can get, how good his luck and timing are.

"See, I'm always lucky. You just have to be patient."

I didn't think it was about patience at all. It makes no sense to drive around and around, usually with other luck-seeking drivers, so you end up in a battle of first-come-first-serve stalking.

JD ordered lasagna and coke, I ordered gnocchi in pesto sauce. I never order lasagna in restaurants, and I don't know why. It could be that I can make it myself, even though I don't very often, or it could be it always seems to have so much more than what I make myself — more tomato sauce, more meat, more layers, and it all just seems like you're eating a brick.

Our table was one of the best ones, in a section that only had three tables, and we had the one near a bay window that looked out on the street and felt extra spacious.

I told him about Myra and Dave and my failed attempt to find out if there'd been a murder or some other violent death at the house. I told him about the tugging on my bag and Kate's near panic.

"I don't know what you're going to accomplish by staying there."

"It makes her feel better."

"If the place is haunted, I'm sure they've already experienced strange events."

"Then why wouldn't Myra mention it?"

"Not everyone is as eager as you are to admit they see things that supposedly don't exist." He winked. He picked up his coke and took a long swallow. The glass was sweating and his fingers left streaks in the moisture. He wiped his fingertips on the napkin, then put it on his lap, still folded. He always sets the napkin on his leg, knowing that's what's required, but acting as if it's some kind of assault to his male ego to spread it out so it can actually do its job.

"I really want to see what Dave says about it. If there's been a ghost since the former occupants lived there, he must have seen it at some point."

"It's not your job to investigate."

"I'm not investigating. I'm curious. And wouldn't he have told Myra? That seems like sort of an important thing to mention to someone before you get married."

"Maybe Kate dreamt it all."

"I thought of that. But she's genuinely scared."

"Dreams can be scary. Or maybe she thought she saw something because she's jealous of you, that your life is more exciting because you've seen all these ghosts."

"So she imagined it because she *wanted* to see one? I sort of wondered about that too. But jealous? Really?"

"Think about it. She's religious, they want to have a personal connection with some greater being, feel like something out there is stronger than them, or taking care of them. But it's all based on believing, not actual experience. Then you pop up and start seeing and hearing from all these ghosts. They almost prove there's more to existence than just the physical world."

Our food came, which was good, because I wanted to think about what he said before blurting out the first thing that came to my mind, which was — *you think God and ghosts are the same thing?"*

I stabbed a piece of gnocchi and popped it in my mouth. Big mistake. It was steaming hot and instantly seared my tongue and the roof of my mouth. I spit it out.

"Nice," JD said.

"It's hot."

"What did you expect?"

"I'm hungry. I didn't think it would be that hot. Sorry for being disgusting."

"It was kind of cute. You looked like you were coughing up an organ." He pointed his fork at the plate of plump white dumplings. "Those things are weird looking, especially with all that green gunk."

He had a point, but who cares what food looks like if it's delicious? "You really think Kate is jealous?"

He nodded.

"But even if she's a little jealous, it doesn't mean she didn't encounter a spirit. I'm almost positive I felt something too. Which is right back to the question of whether Myra knows and if she does, why she wouldn't want us to know."

"Like I said, most people don't brag about their house being haunted."

"How can you be so sure?"

"Okay, some people probably would. People who

want attention."

"But you really think Kate and I had a similar dream?"

"I'm just saying it's a possibility. Power of suggestion."

"She was pretty definite that she was standing on the stairs."

"You know how dreams can be."

I did. But I didn't think her fear would linger for so long after a dream. I think it would have faded and she never would have mentioned it to me unless it was a real experience. And she seemed reluctant to admit what she'd seen. If she was jealous, wouldn't she be excited to tell me?

I cut a piece of gnocchi in two and touched one half to my tongue. It was a more pleasant temperature. I took a sip of water and then a drink of my iced coffee. That cooled everything off, but the skin was still raw. It made me wonder how old I'll be when I learn to stop shoving hot food in my mouth when I can see the steam. I know that restaurant food is always hotter than food at home. Isn't the point of nerves, getting burned, bruising your legs by running into tables in the dark, to teach you to be more careful?

"Hopefully tonight Dave will be home and I can find out more about the original owners."

"Or what happened when he lived in the house before Myra."

I looked up. So he was with me after all, no longer

thinking I was putting myself in the middle of a situation that had nothing to do with me. It wasn't as if I'd sought it out. Kate asked me. Begged me.

"It could have been something that happened when they were building the house," he said.

"Do you think all houses have ghosts?"

He chose that moment to put a huge forkful of lasagna in his mouth. While he chewed he glanced to his left and I wasn't sure if he was thinking or distracted or wishing he hadn't encouraged me. Since our trip to Australia, I'd felt like I had a harder time figuring him out than I did before we went, which made no sense. We were together all day every day for two weeks. I should have known him better. Maybe the more you get to know a person, the less you really know because you realize how vast they are. Like looking at space and seeing one planet and some stars, but you learn about the solar system and the galaxy and everything else and you realize there's so much, you'll never see or know all of it.

Before he'd completely finished chewing, he put another bite of lasagna in his mouth. I guess that answered my question. He wasn't thinking of an answer, he was trying to avoid giving an answer. Or maybe it had nothing to do with me. Who knew what he was thinking. Like when we were in Hamilton Island and he'd asked if I wanted to live together, completely out of nowhere. I never saw that coming. And then when I hesitated, which anyone would when she was caught off guard, he backed away. He hadn't said a word about it since. Had he forgotten all about it? Was it just tropical-induced romance? Did he decide I wasn't thinking like him at all and so he wasn't going to push it? All questions I should have asked him, but I didn't. For someone who is always saying what's on her mind, I was feeling like I was saying less and less.

"Do you?" I said.

"Do I what?"

Maybe he was playing games. Or just being a guy.

"I asked you if you think all houses have ghosts, but they don't always reveal themselves."

"Good question. Probably not. If they linger because they have something to wrap up, or they want to torment people left behind, or whatever they're after, why would they stay hidden? If they didn't have specific business, they would have passed over to the other side."

"So you believe there's another side?"

"How can you not, if you've seen a ghost?"

"Maybe you die for good, once your ghost resolves your issues."

"I really don't know," he said.

"Don't you ever think about things like that?"

He drank his coke and pushed his plate a bit to the side, even though half the lasagna remained.

"Aren't you hungry?"

"It's rich. It fills you up. And it was enormous. I don't think about things like that as much as you do. Of course, I haven't had as many weird experiences as you, so I can understand why you think about it all the time."

"I don't think about it all the time." I popped a piece of gnocchi into my mouth. Not only do I love the taste and texture of gnocchi, I love their shape. They're like perfect, compact modules of food, fun to chew, tasty and so filling. Yet I could never stop eating halfway through like JD. I knew I wouldn't be finished until all that remained were puddles of green and a few pine nuts.

"Why did you invite me to lunch?"

"No reason. I missed you."

I smiled.

We were both quiet for a few minutes. He pulled his plate back and ate a few small bites of lasagna while I savored each ovoid of pasta. When I was finished I took a long drink of iced latte. "I was wondering about all houses being haunted because I've been thinking about something."

"Wondering if your condo is full of ghosts?" He laughed, but must have seen something on my face or in my eyes because he stopped suddenly.

"I've wondered lately if my parents' ghosts are in the house where I grew up."

He put down his fork. He placed his forearm on the table and opened his hand for me to put my hand on his. I didn't, but he kept his hand there, waiting for mine.

"Shouldn't you let that go? I'm sure it's hard. Really hard. But it's been a long time."

"Yes. Half my life. Almost." As I said that, it suddenly occurred to me that maybe I'm only living half a life.

"What are you thinking of doing?" he said.

Just when I think he doesn't know me that well, he says something like that, and I know that he knows me very well. He realized instantly that I wasn't just speculating, that thinking about it meant more than simply mulling things over.

"I want to go see the house."

"Someone else lives there?"

"Yes."

"Do you know if it's the same people who bought it after . . . ?"

"I don't know. But that doesn't matter. The sellers have to let the buyers know there was a murder."

"The first time, but if it's sold again?" he said.

"They would have to pass on the information to the next owners."

"Even if they know, will they want you poking around?"

"I have to try. I know I can't just walk in the door and expect my parents' spirits to emerge. But what if they've been waiting for me all this time? What if they were there and I never knew because my Aunt and Uncle never let me go back?"

Even though I was very upset inside, no tears were coming, and my voice didn't flutter. You would think I might start crying, thinking about all the time I'd lost, the total failure of the police to find anyone to seriously question about their murders. It was so unjust I could hardly breathe whenever I spent any amount of time thinking about it. I didn't think about it much, but it was always there, as if I'd grown an extra heart, a secret one that was hidden away, that I couldn't see into, didn't want to see into.

"Why do you have to try?"

"I just told you."

"I thought you said ghosts appear when they have something to say?"

"But I'm not there for them to appear to," I said.

"If you think they're going to give you suggestions about their killer, wouldn't they have done that to the people who moved in after?"

"I don't know what they would do. I don't know anything. Maybe they *have* haunted the area, maybe the people who live there now are blind to that sort of thing, or . . . I don't know. I have to do it. I have to try. What if they could speak to me and tell me who killed them?"

"It doesn't always have to be you."

"What do you mean?"

"You're not the only person on the planet who's had supernatural encounters."

"I know that." It seemed like he was trying to hurt me. What did it matter to him if I went back to the house where I grew up? I didn't even have to tell him what I was planning, but I did because we were in a relationship and that's what you do. It wasn't as if I needed his agreement or his support. Although that would have been nice.

I nudged my plate to the side, only a few inches, but just enough to show I was done eating. It turned out there would be five pale gnocchis swimming in green and a bit of yellow oil after all. Suddenly they didn't look so delicious, they did look like I had coughed up several organs. I moved the plate closer to the edge of the table. "It's important for me to find out. I can't live the rest of my life knowing I didn't even try."

"What if they don't communicate with you or they can't? What if they've moved on?"

"Then I'll know."

The waiter glided by with the check. JD took the folder out of the waiter's hand, flipped it open, and laid cash inside. He closed it and set it on the edge of the table so the waiter could catch it on his return trip.

I took a sip of water and pushed my chair back. "Are we leaving? I should get back to work."

"Don't be angry."

"I'm not."

"Don't be upset. I'm telling you what I think," he said.

"And I appreciate that."

"Let's not fight."

"We're not fighting. I'm going to do something and you don't agree. That's not fighting. It's not like you have to give me the okay."

"I didn't say that. You seem upset."

"I thought you'd see it differently, that's all."

"I think you'll be disappointed."

"I can handle it."

He stood and came around the table. He put his hand on the back of my neck and rubbed it lightly. It felt good but it didn't change anything. I shouldn't have been so bitchy, it wasn't as if we have to see everything the same way. I guess I thought he knew how hard it had been for me, finding my dead parents with those holes in the middle of their foreheads. I thought he'd want me to do it, to find some closure, as they say. It was more disappointing that he couldn't see how it was for me than it would be if I'm never able to connect with my parents' ghosts.

Five

THAT NIGHT WHILE Kate and I were clearing the dining room table, the front door swung open, hard and fast. Both of us jumped a little because we didn't immediately see Dave standing there. I guess we had ghosts on our minds. His dark hair and dark blue uniform were buried in the shadows on the front porch. Myra hadn't turned on the outside light and the living room was dark.

Dave had extremely broad shoulders. The muscles in his upper arms and chest screamed — *I lift weights . . . extremely heavy weights.* I imagined that lawbreakers who ran into him were intimidated even though his height was average.

He stepped inside and shut the door. The window panes rattled and I realized how flimsy it was for a front door. Not exactly flimsy, but not giving a secure feeling either, with all those windows and not much wood holding them together. A friendly door, but when you're in a house that might have a ghost, being friendly to anyone or anything that passes by isn't your first instinct.

"Pastor Kate. Hi. And I forgot you were here . . . uh, Madison?"

Unlike his front door, it wasn't the friendliest greeting in the world. He walked to the center of the living room and stopped. He unbuckled his belt and pulled off all the equipment including a rather large and ominous looking gun. "Let me put this stuff away."

"We have lots of spaghetti," Kate said. "Are you hungry?"

"Sure." He turned and walked to the hallway.

I thought he might stop in to see Myra and his daughter, but he went immediately to the back bedroom. I heard him thumping around in there for several minutes.

When he returned, the table was cleared and Kate had set a new place for him, complete with a bowl of salad, two pieces of bread, the nearby butter plate, and a heaping pile of spaghetti with meatballs that we'd rolled ourselves. The meatballs were tiny, not much bigger than large marbles, and I thought we'd done a very nice job.

He immediately chopped up everything on the plate — the spaghetti into stubby strands and the meatballs into bits of ground beef, as if we hadn't rolled all those perfect spheres.

"What do you want to drink?" Kate said.

"Coke, please."

She went into the kitchen and returned with a can and

a glass. She placed them in front of him. I wanted to laugh at how she was waiting on him. I'm not sure why. Maybe because she doesn't seem like the type of woman who would serve a man his dinner. She was trotting back and forth to meet his needs like a female from another era.

I leaned against the curve of the arched opening between the dining room and living room. "You work long hours," I said. "Plus all the things you have to do as a deacon. It must be hard to juggle it."

He nodded.

"How long have you been a cop?"

"Fifteen years."

"Do you like it?"

"Not when I'm working doubles."

"But otherwise you like it?"

He looked up. He squinted as the light from the chandelier hit directly into his eyes. "Why don't you sit down?"

"I already ate."

"I know, but it's unsettling having you stand while I sit, and you're hidden in the dark."

I pulled out the chair at the end of the table and sat down. Kate was back in the kitchen, whipping up a pan of brownies for all I knew.

"Does Myra worry, knowing you're in dangerous situations?"

"She's not a worrier."

"That's good."

"Why are you staying here too? It seemed like Kate had everything covered."

I shrugged.

"You don't know?"

"To help out."

As if she had a wire connected from my shrugging shoulders to a little bell on the kitchen counter, Kate plowed through the swinging door into the dining room. "I didn't sleep much the other night and with you working so much, I thought Myra needed extra backup," she said.

"Lots of women for one little baby," he said.

Kate laughed. "I suppose. Madison's only staying for two more nights."

"The house is small. Not a lot of room."

"We slept in the basement last night," I said. "There's the extra bed . . . "

"Guess that little girl can keep the whole house and half the block from getting any sleep." He grinned. He took a bite of bread and chewed slowly. He ran the bread through his spaghetti sauce. The chandelier light glistened on his hair, making it almost black. When he looked up again his pupils were dilated, black as onyx. "She's a screamer. Likes to make her presence known."

It seemed he'd forgotten about how odd it was that I was there. It also seemed like he kept his cool and the fact we were sleeping in the basement didn't register more than if we were sleeping in a tent in the backyard. Either he'd never seen the ghost or he had a very solid facade to show the world. I suppose cops are trained to not show what they're thinking.

Kate went back into the kitchen and turned the water on full force. I guess she figured the danger had passed, although it made me think again that being so secretive was ridiculous. Why not just come out and say it? Of course, with the way most, if not all, members of the church thought about supernatural events, she probably knew what she was doing. It's just that I felt more conspicuous than ever, spending three nights in the home of people I hardly knew, cooking their dinners, hanging out with Kate. The only good part was that being in a strange place took my mind off JD and how he'd reacted to my plans. I was still upset, maybe a little shocked that he wasn't as in tune with me as I'd thought. Or me with him.

"I love old houses." I paused for a minute or two. I felt a hint of that heaviness in the air again. I shifted to the side in the chair and it faded. "Yours is really unique. Myra said you're only the second person to own it."

"That's right."

"How did you find it?"

"What do you mean, how did I find it? I got a realtor and asked to see houses within a five- mile radius of both the church and the police station that fell into my price range."

"How did you know this was the one?"

He put his fork on the placemat. It left a smear of spaghetti sauce. He inched his chair back from the table and folded his arms across his chest which was no small feat. "You make it sound as if you're talking about finding a wife. There isn't just one house that works."

"Then why did you choose this one?"

"Why are you so interested?"

"Like I said, I love old houses. And yours is unusual. The front door, the color of the adobe."

He laughed. "Really?"

I knew that was a reach, but there was something very unusual about the front door. In fact now that I thought about it, the door was more like something you would see opening into the backyard or a private side garden. The whole charm of it was spoiled with the drapes covering the glass, so what was the point?

I couldn't decide whether both his and Myra's reluctance to talk about the house was because I was so determined to learn about its history or because they were hiding something. Sometimes when you desperately want to know something, the other person can seem obstructionist, when it's only that they're simply not interested in the topic. Although in my experience, most people are excited to talk about their homes. They tell stories like the ones you tell of a baby's birth, going into unwanted and excessive detail about the process of buying it, or what they changed after they bought it, how they improved it, and yes, even how they knew, just *knew* it was *the* house for them.

He continued staring at me. It was so intense, I almost hoped Myra would come out with the baby and break the mood, or Kate would pop out of the kitchen with a plate of brownies, even though I knew she wasn't actually making brownies. Thinking about them made my mouth water and I decided I'd make a pan over the weekend. Maybe two, then I could give a plate to JD.

Dave smiled, displaying teeth that, despite looking like they'd been straightened with braces, had a small gap on the upper left between his center tooth and the next one over. He unfolded his arms and picked up the last piece of bread. The salad bowl was empty. "I've never had anyone ask me that, but you're right. I did get a sense that this was the right house. I think I liked that it was small. Monster houses make no sense to me. How much space do you need? It just encourages you to buy more stuff. I don't like big parties so I don't need all kinds of rooms and space for entertaining. A few people at a time is plenty."

"Did the people who lived here before you die in the house?"

"That's a morbid question."

"Just curious. Myra said they lived here their whole lives."

"I really don't know how they died."

That was a lie. I could tell it was a lie because he said it with disgust. And I didn't ask how they died, I asked if they died here. Maybe there was something unplanned about their deaths. I'd assumed because they were old, it was natural. But maybe not.

I'd come to the end of my conversational tools. The

only other way to find out what I wanted was to flat out ask if he'd seen a ghost, or if anyone died in the house while he owned it. Trying to elicit information was hard. I had a sudden appreciation for cops and detectives and I wondered if he realized what I was up to. Everything about the situation felt forced — me staying in the house, Kate asking me what happened at night like I was a bug under a microscope, trying to pry information out of an obviously reluctant Myra and Dave. Or maybe there was nothing to pry. Maybe it was a dull house with only a few occupants over the years, all living out their days happily, and dying ordinary deaths. Maybe there was no ghost, just Kate dreaming because she was conflicted about the subject, and me getting twisted in my sleeping bag.

He pushed his chair out further and stood. "Great dinner. Thanks. I assume you had a hand in it?"

I nodded. I was annoyed with myself. Why did I even care? I'd seen nothing, felt only the slightest tug on my bag, which was so vague I was now convinced it had been a dream. So Kate was scared. What was I supposed to do? Suddenly, I was dying for a cigarette.

Dave carried his dishes to the kitchen and I followed. When he left, presumably to check on Myra and the baby, I grabbed my messenger bag off the bar and told Kate I was going outside for a smoke.

"I don't think that's a good idea."

"Why not?"

"You'll come back reeking of smoke."

"I don't reek."

"You do."

"Okay. I'll go for a walk."

She made a face. "And leave me here alone?"

"It's only seven-thirty. Dave and Myra are right in the other room."

"But it's dark."

"So it's not that I smell like smoke, you just don't want to be alone in case the ghost appears?"

"Plus, I have to sleep with you. I don't know if I can handle the smell of smoke when I'm trying to sleep."

"It's better than the smell of mildew. I need a break and I'm going outside for a bit. I'll go for a walk when I'm done, so the smoke blows off me."

The kitchen was spotless. Kate had sponged off the white tile counters, washed and dried the large pots we'd used, and loaded all the plates and utensils into the dishwasher.

"Maybe I'll go with you. I'm done here." She grabbed a blue and white striped towel off a hook at the end of the center island and dried her hands. She walked around the island and pulled her over-sized fluffy blue sweater off the back of the stool.

I took a few steps toward the door until my spine was pressed against the doorknob. "I need some time alone. The smoke will bother you and I can't relax if you're wrinkling your nose and batting it away. I'll be back in half an hour."

I opened the door and stepped outside. I didn't look back to see the expression on her face.

Six

WHEN I RETURNED from my walk around the neighborhood, I didn't have any more clarity than when I'd left. As I turned up the front path toward that friendly and unfriendly front door, I was feeling tempted to walk into the house and tell Kate I was going home to my condo.

But after all this time working at Central Avenue Church, I finally had a chance to get to know her on a more personal level. Why that mattered, since she was more or less my boss, I don't know. And it might be the *more or less* part that made me want to get to know her. Pastor Joe hired me without any input from Kate. He was the one who gave me performance reviews, with some input from Kate, and he was the one who told me what I should be focusing on. So in a lot of ways, she wasn't my boss.

I don't have many friends. The kids I knew when I was growing up drifted away when my parents were murdered. No one knows what to say or do when something that horrible happens, so they say nothing. Soon you feel as if you're living in a bubble, watching the world go by, but not really connecting with anyone. You smile and talk and everything looks normal on the outside.

It's not like I was depressed or falling apart on the inside, but everything around me looked so different, as if the world was covered with a dark orange film and it shifted my perception so I could see things no one else saw.

In high school, I made a few friends after my parents were killed, but since I'd been homeschooled through my freshman year, we hadn't had four years to bond. I stayed friends with Renee and we're still close, but with her living in Oregon, it's mostly a virtual relationship.

I have a few friends from my former job, but I can tell the longer I'm away from the high tech environment and all the gossip of the company, the less we have in common. Plus, two of the three have gotten married and had kids, which gives us next to nothing in common.

So I guess I'd like to make some new friends. Kate is almost fifteen years older than me, but she's opinionated, which I like. And even though she's quite specific about what she's thinking, it's hard to know her as a real person.

That sounds strange, but that's how I see it. I think we could be friends. I think we could have more fun working together, and now that her strict view of the supernatural had been shaken up, she'd suddenly become a lot more interesting. Maybe we would see a few more things the same way.

I guess my walk did give me clarity after all.

I went around the side of the house and through the gate into the backyard.

The kitchen was dark. The door between the kitchen and the dining room was closed but a thin strip of light underneath was enough for me to find the light switch that was freakishly far from the back door, making it difficult to just feel around for it.

I turned on the light. I got a red glass with a short stem, almost like a wine glass, but beveled and much thicker. I pressed it to the water spigot on the fridge. Water gushed into it and I took a few sips before going into the dining room.

Kate and Dave were sitting at the table. Kate's laptop was on a placemat and she was typing furiously. Dave was playing a game on his smartphone. His thumbs hit the screen at a speed faster than Kate's multi-finger typing. They hit so hard, I could hear the sound of his flesh on plastic as well as the soft bleeps and explosions coming from the speaker. Neither one of them looked up. Myra was in the living room reading on her tablet.

I felt like a ghost myself as none of them acknowledged my presence. Had Kate told them I was smoking and they were all disgusted with me so they thought they could shame me into quitting? I realized that was making a huge leap in logic from Kate's comments to thinking they were talking about me, as if they had nothing else in their lives to discuss. My iPad was in the basement. I thought about getting it, but I really wanted to watch a movie on it, not surf the web or read, and the silence in the room, except for the bleeps and tapping fingers and thumbs, told me they might not welcome a movie soundtrack.

The smartphone emitted a crashing sound, indicating the game was over. Dave thunked the phone onto the table. He looked up at me. "We don't want you near the baby since you've been smoking, so don't go into the living room or the front bedroom."

No matter how much I understood their concern, the sharp words hurt my feelings. It wasn't as if I was carrying a cloud of smoke around me. I know I should quit. I know that. And I will. Someday. Smoking calms me. It was the one thing that helped make me strong after my parents' deaths. It's hard to let go of it because for some reason, that feels like I'm letting go of my independence and my self-reliance. I know that makes no sense, but lots of things we do and feel make no sense. That's what makes us human beings. "What about using the bathroom?"

He looked surprised. He picked up the phone and swept his finger across the screen. Without looking at me, he said, "Let Myra know when you need to use it and she'll shut the baby's door and our bedroom door."

"Maybe I should leave."

Kate's fingers stopped tapping. If I'd thought she was lost in whatever she was typing, I was wrong.

"That's not necessary."

"It seems like I'm in the way."

Myra was lost in her reading. She hadn't looked toward the dining room since I'd come in. I was amazed at her power of concentration, especially as sleep-deprived as she was.

Kate closed her laptop. She pushed back her chair. "Everyone's tired. Dave didn't mean to sound harsh. Just don't go in the baby's bedroom right after you've been smoking."

"He said the living room. And he said don't go in there period."

Dave kept his head down, studying the phone. It's a great device for ignoring other people, for escaping from uncomfortable conversations. What an invention.

His face was reflected in the glossy tabletop, but it was far too blurry to read the expression in his eyes.

"I shouldn't have mentioned the smoking," Kate said. Her fingers shook on the edge of her laptop. Her left eyelid trembled slightly.

Dave set his phone on the table again. "Kate's right. I'm dead tired. It was an over-reaction."

Nice way to dodge saying he was sorry, but I decided not to push it. I was only staying two more nights, and the evening was gone. "I'm going to wash up now and go downstairs."

"Sounds good," Kate said. Her voice was so chirpy she made me think of Simon and Sara.

Myra still hadn't looked up and I wondered if she'd

even been part of the smoking conversation or if she'd been lost in whatever she was reading the whole time and it was all Dave.

I'D BEEN IN my sleeping bag for over forty minutes before I heard Kate descending the stairs to the basement, which now smelled worse than ever. Maybe it was the bad taste from Dave's rudeness. Although I understand the danger of second-hand smoke, it seemed odd that they were concerned with the baby breathing a hint of smoke off my clothes from four or five feet away but not worried about that awful mildew smell. And it really was awful. I was angry at myself for agreeing to sleep here. Hadn't I read somewhere that mildew spores can cause depression? I think I read some kinds can even kill you.

"Are you awake?" Kate whispered.

I let out a small, fake-sounding shriek. "Are you the ghost?"

Kate shrieked in reply, much louder than I had, and much more natural sounding. "That's not funny. Not at all." She flicked on the light. She wore an ankle-length nightshirt, tennis socks, and a zippered sweatshirt.

"I don't think there's a ghost here."

"You said you felt something last night."

"I'm not so sure."

"Don't do this to me, Madison."

"Do what?"

"Make me sound crazy." She walked to her bed,

yanked the quilt down, and folded back the sheet and blanket.

"Why didn't you turn out the light?"

"I'm nervous, okay?"

"I can't sleep with the light on."

"Then turn it off." She sat on the bed, shoved her legs under the blankets, and pulled the bedding up to her chin.

"You're sleeping in your sweatshirt?"

"Yes."

I got up and went to the foot of the stairs. I snapped the light switch down and moved slowly in the sudden darkness back to my sleeping bag. "Sorry I scared you."

"Is it payback for me telling Dave you were smoking?"

"I don't really care. I guess I understand their concern."

"Liar."

"No . . . I do understand."

"I meant that you don't care."

"I really don't. It's not like it's a popular habit. I'm used to harsh comments and dirty looks and threats."

"Threats?"

"People warning me that I'm killing myself."

"That's not a threat. It's the truth."

"I suppose. You do know that even though there's a correlation between smoking and cancer and emphysema, science can't really prove anything definitive. There's always some uncertainty."

"It's pretty clear."

"Not everyone who smokes gets cancer."

"But your risk goes up."

"Your risk goes up if you eat red meat. I don't see people forcing red meat eaters out onto the street in the middle of winter. In fact, steak houses are practically worshipped."

She laughed. She was quiet for a few minutes. "Do you think it will show up tonight? Or do you really think I dreamt the whole thing?"

"We'll see."

After that, we were quiet.

I think I fell asleep quickly because when I woke, I didn't remember either of us saying goodnight or anything else. I don't know if it was the conversation about smoking seeping into my brain, reminding me that I was no more at risk than every single person grabbing a burger every few days, but I had a strong craving for a cigarette. Maybe I hadn't enjoyed the earlier one because Kate made me feel I'd abandoned her. Maybe it was the mildew smell, or still feeling agitated about the evasiveness of Dave and Myra. What was the big deal about asking for stories about their house? I was just being friendly. Unless they felt the unspoken agenda.

The zipper of my bag sounded like someone tearing cardboard even though I pulled it slowly and quietly. Trying to be quiet made it sound louder. I heard Kate's breath, deep and smooth, almost peaceful.

I sat up and felt around for my messenger bag, then I remembered I'd left it in the kitchen. I hoped Dave wasn't so aggressive he'd gone through it and gotten rid of my cigarettes. Maybe he would assume he had a right to search a bag left lying around inside his own house.

But I was wrong. My bag was where I'd left it and the cigarettes and my lighter were right inside. I grabbed my jacket and slowly turned the deadbolt while I shoved my left arm into the sleeve. I opened the door and shrugged the rest of the jacket into place.

The concrete back steps were cold. I stepped down onto the grass, which wasn't much warmer. The blades scraped my feet like tiny icicles. I should have put on shoes, but it was too late now. Not actually too late, I suppose, but I was too lazy to go back inside, down the stairs, fumble around for the ballet slipper shoes I'd worn that day, and come back outside.

A glow from the streetlight hit the steps. There was a bare dirt patch under the hose attached to the side of the garage. I could drop my ashes there, but I was sure Dave wouldn't be pleased to find them. I walked toward the building that housed the office and tried the door. It was locked, of course. Near the step was a clay flowerpot half filled with dirt. It also contained a few gum wrappers and what looked like charred stuff scraped off a barbecue grill. I figured a few cigarette ashes wouldn't hurt.

It's a constant problem, trying not to leave a mess everywhere I go. Even if I have a bad habit, as most would say, that doesn't mean I have to be a litterbug too. I usually squash the butt and carry it away in a baggie, which I think is going above and beyond what's required.

As I smoked, I didn't think about much, just enjoyed the quiet and the cold. My mind drifted in a nearly empty space. It's like meditating, but easier, because for some reason, when I meditate, the act of sitting down and trying to be still makes thoughts zing around like fireworks, but smoking, I focus on inhaling and exhaling, which meditation is also supposed to do. The smoke and the taste of the cigarette have a way of getting the brain more situated in one quiet spot. People who don't smoke don't understand that. They think it's a nervous habit, that it makes you jittery. And maybe after the nicotine, it does, but the act itself is calming. Almost like being in a spiritual state. Maybe that's why Native Americans smoked peace pipes. I really don't know. I should look into that.

When I was finished, I stabbed the end of my cigarette in the dirt. After the tip was good and dead, I folded my hand around it and went back to the house. I tucked the butt into the baggie.

The house was silent, so silent it felt there was no one there but me. Obviously the baby was sleeping. The microwave clock glowed one-twenty-three. The baby usually woke at two, which would explain the soundless rooms around me. Suddenly I was overcome with a desire to be in my own condo. I was tired of the smell and didn't look forward to descending the stairs, as if I were entering some kind of dungeon. I didn't like the iciness from Dave and Myra and didn't like that Kate was gripping me so hard I almost felt like it was part of my administrative assistant's job to help her feel calm. She was acting a bit like the boss, hinting that I was required to do this. I know that was post-midnight twisting of my thoughts, which are less logical when I wake up, no matter how alert I feel. There's always a sense of unreality to the world when you're woken from a deep sleep and you don't even know why. I'd hoped smoking would put me into a dreamy state, but it hadn't. At least my sleeping bag would warm my icy feet, and that thought got me moving toward the stairs.

I stepped around the wall that formed one side of the stairwell. A figure stood just past the bottom step. It had flaming red eyeballs that looked like the whites were soaked with blood, with black pinprick centers. My mouth opened into a scream, but no sound came out. I closed my eyes and sank down. My tailbone hit the edge of the step. Pain shot up my spine. I looked again and saw the bleeding, oozing eyes. The figure was charcoal gray. I couldn't tell if it was a man or woman. I shivered and tried to stand.

It screamed, howling almost, and then I knew it was a woman. I started to cry. Surely the whole household would wake up, but there were no other sounds. I opened my mouth, straining again to scream, but I couldn't. The vibration in my throat, the pressure inside my head felt like I was in a dream, screaming inside, sound wanting to escape, begging for help, but there was nothing. Those eyeballs, the blood so disgusting it made my stomach twist into a hard lump. I felt certain I was going to die.

Without warning, without any sign of effort, the thing rushed up the stairs, straight at me. Fists hammered my back and arms. Feet as hard as those wearing steel-toed boots battered my shins. Every bone in my body felt as if it was splintering. My skin tore and I felt blood dripping down my legs. She screamed and howled, half-sobbing, "I loved you. I gave you every part of me. I thought we had something special! How stupid I was. How stupid! We had nothing. You looked me in the eye and said you loved me, a hundred times, a thousand times, and you didn't! You never loved me!"

She continued to scream and pound my body. I curled into a ball, tucked my head under my arms, and squeezed my legs as hard as I could. I clenched my feet and hunched my shoulders.

As suddenly as she'd rushed at me, she was gone.

I remained folded like an egg, hugging myself. My heart pounded against my ribs. It felt huge, pushing its way up into my throat.

After a while I opened my eyes. It was difficult to loosen my grip on my legs, but when I finally extended my arms, my skin was smooth and unbroken. I pulled up my yoga pants. There was no swelling, no welts or blood on my legs. Still, I knew it hadn't been a dream because my bones ached and my stomach was bruised and pulpy. I pressed my hands against the wall and dragged myself to a standing position. I peered into the darkness past the bottom of the stairs but there was nothing. I don't know why I strained, looking for that gray shadow because with those eyes, it would be impossible not to see it.

I slid one foot after the other to each successive step. The basement was silent and damp and stunk like something rotten. When I reached the bottom, I heard Kate's regular breathing. It had all seemed so loud, the howling, the kicking and clawing. How could Kate have slept through all of that noise? I must have grunted, I must have fallen against the wall. I turned on the light. She was undisturbed in her bed, lying on her right side as she'd been hours earlier.

After quite a few a minutes, I finally pressed the light switch down. Darkness rushed over me.

I scurried to my sleeping bag and flopped down. I rolled over, shoved my lower body inside, and yanked the bag around me, zipping it closed with one quick tug. The bag was like a cocoon, soft and warm, holding me close, but lying with only the thin carpet and the folded blankets beneath me made everything ache more. I wondered if I'd have bruises or I was feeling some kind of phantom pain. It was all so real while she was attacking me. Not seeing the evidence of her assault had been unnerving. It wasn't that I wanted to walk around covered in bruises and cuts, but it felt disconnected that the pain and the memory were so real while there was nothing visible.

After a few minutes, I stopped shaking and started thinking about the ghost.

Obviously a woman had been betrayed. The original owner, or someone else? If they'd lived here throughout their long lives, was she betrayed but eventually forgave her husband and stayed with him? In those days, women did that more. I assumed it was her husband, but maybe not.

Either Myra and Dave didn't want anyone to know about the ghost, or they hadn't seen it. If they hadn't seen it, why was she making herself known so violently to me, and less so, to Kate?

Seven

I DECIDED NOT to tell Kate what had happened. What was the point? I didn't need to stir up her terror all over again. I suppose it would have helped her with the doubts she was having now, but she didn't truly have any doubts — she wished she did. She wanted it to be a dream, a hallucination, even, but she knew it wasn't. Telling her would not get rid of it and would not help explain who it was. The only thing it might accomplish would be getting her so wound up she'd put forth some effort to get Myra and Dave talking about the history of their house.

We left for work in our own cars, Kate in her Camry, me in my Volkswagon bug.

The day was crazy hectic, one phone call after another for Pastor Joe so that I even had to put a few people on hold, which is rare. In between there were quite a few calls for Kate about an upcoming weekend camping trip she was planning for the high school kids.

It kind of made me jealous. I'd only been camping once, when I was eight. I hardly remember it. I don't remember where we went, and of course my parents aren't here to ask. All I remember is how cozy the tent was with our sleeping bags and pillows and duffel bags, as if that was all we really needed in the world. Our food was compact too, stored in a large cooler and in boxes in the back of the car to keep the bears from eating it. So I guess we went somewhere with bears. Most likely the Sierras. We'd gone to Lake Tahoe and stayed in a cabin twice —once when I was ten and once when I was eleven, so obviously my parents liked the mountains.

Camping seems like a great way to stop racing around, to pause and think about the earth and how little you can get by with. Of course, you're only getting by for two or three days, maybe two or three weeks if you're a hard-core backpacker, so maybe it's an illusion.

At five-fifteen when I was ready to leave work, Kate was still making buddy lists and chore schedules. She told me to head over to the Hicks' without her.

When I turned onto their street, a white minivan was parked in front of the house. Myra kept her little SUV in the garage. Dave usually parked his BMW pressed up close to the garage door, as if his car was protecting Myra's. I parked behind the white minivan.

I walked up the front path, dragging the heels of my boots which was not good because it wears them down. Now, more than ever, I wanted to know the history of the house, but I couldn't stop feeling like some kind of invader, a friend of Kate's that they didn't want around, that they only tolerated because they were so grateful to Kate for her cooking and cleaning up the kitchen, and dealing with diaper disposal.

Before I could knock, the door opened. A woman close to my age stood in the doorway holding a dust rag and an aerosol can of wood polish with a label featuring a big lemon and a block of words announcing how fresh it smelled.

"Hola. Can I help you?"

"Hi. I'm Madison. I'm staying here to help with . . ." There was that awkwardness again. I couldn't say, *I'm staying here to make sure the baby-helper doesn't get attacked by a ghost.*

She opened the door and stepped back. "Myra said you were coming."

I followed her inside, through the living room and dining room. She had the door to the kitchen propped open. She stopped in the dining room and sprayed polish on the hutch. I went into the kitchen and over to the stairs, planning to take my messenger bag down and leave it by my sleeping bag.

"Don't go downstairs," she called.

I walked back. "Why not?"

"It's bad down there."

"What do you mean?" My heart thumped harder. I almost held my breath. "That's where I've been sleeping."

Her eyes practically popped out of her skull. "It's a nasty place to sleep." She pinched her nostrils with her thumb and index finger.

"Oh. The mildew."

"It makes you sick. Myra asked me to clean it, but I don't know where it's coming from."

"It might be somewhere you can't get to. Where did you try to clean?"

She shrugged and wiped at the stuff she'd sprayed on the hutch.

"Well I need to put my stuff away."

"How can you sleep with that smell? And so scary."

"It's the only place. You don't notice it as much after a while. And when I'm asleep, I don't notice at all."

She nodded. "I don't like it down there."

"I'm only here for one more night."

"There's no way out," she said.

"That's always how it is with basements."

She shivered. She sprayed stuff all over the table, walking the length of it. Then she worked her way back, dragging the rag through the moisture and buffing it hard.

"This one's *limoso*."

"What does that mean?"

"Like slime? Not good." She shuddered.

"Because of the smell or something else?"

She straightened and set the can on top of the rag. "I'm cleaning and I look up and Mr. Hicks is standing in the doorway."

"Cops can be scary. They're supposed to be there to keep you safe, but when you see one, it's easy to get nervous, or think they're going to catch us doing something wrong, even when you didn't. It feels like they're sizing you up and categorizing you."

She laughed, but her voice trembled slightly. "He looks . . . *cachondo*. There's no way out."

I should have asked her what that meant, but I focused on the lack of escape. I could imagine being busy trying to chase elusive mildew and looking up to see a big guy like Dave, a huge gun on one hip and a radio and all that other stuff, the stick hanging from his belt. It would be very intimidating. I held up my bag. "Anyway, I'll go put this away. I was going to start dinner. Are you done in the kitchen?"

She nodded. She picked up the can and sprayed the rest of the table. She started rubbing hard, looking down, watching her hand. She'd been so friendly for a minute, but now she seemed like she was suddenly done talking. Her hair fell over her face and she didn't toss it back and I wondered if it was hard to clean with it in the way. I always tie mine back or braid it when I'm cleaning the house. She wore a tight pink t-shirt and black jeans and pink and white tennis shoes. Muscles moved in her shoulders and upper arms when she rubbed and her hand was tightened into a half fist as she gripped the dust cloth.

I left her alone and put away my bag.

Kate had said we'd make stir fry for dinner. It was turning out to be an ethnic food extravaganza with tacos, spaghetti, and now stir fry — mushrooms, bamboo shoots, bean sprouts, broccoli, tofu, and chicken. She was planning to make rice noodles to go with it.

I washed my hands and pulled apart three cloves of garlic. I peeled them and sliced each one into thin strips and chopped those into little bits. I rinsed the broccoli and started cutting it into bite-sized pieces. I was nearly done, tiny green pebbles of broccoli flower littered all over the cutting board, when the housekeeper came into the kitchen.

"I forgot to ask your name," I said.

"Liz."

"Nice to meet you. Myra said you just started working for her and Dave?"

"Uh huh." She glanced at the door to the dining room and then the kitchen door leading to the yard.

"Are you looking for something."

She shook her head.

"You seem nervous."

She glanced at me but didn't look directly at me, more at my shoulder, or maybe over my shoulder.

"Did you see something?"

She frowned. "No." She went to the corner near the stairs and put the wood polish and rag in a laundry basket filled with cleaning supplies. She glanced down the stairs and looked back at me, still not meeting my eyes. "Be careful down there. Sleeping."

"Why?" Now I was sure she must have seen the ghost. Did it appear during daylight? For some reason, I expect them in the dark, even though I know that's not always the case.

"No way out."

"Did you see something down there?"

"Something?"

"Did something frighten you?"

She picked up her basket. "I need to go."

"What happened?"

"It's not a good place to be in the dark. To sleep."

"Kate, a woman I work with, is sleeping there with me."

She nodded. "Good."

"What's wrong?"

"Nada. Nice talking to you." She went to the door and turned sideways to carry the basket into the dining room and over to the front door.

I hurried after her and opened the door.

"Gracias." She stepped outside, smiled, and lifted her shoulder as a farewell greeting.

"Please tell me what you saw."

"I need this job. It was a bad mistake to talk."

She turned and walked to her van.

I didn't close the door until she pulled away from the curb. Now I knew something, but really, nothing.

ALL THE VEGGIES were chopped and sitting on the cutting board in colorful piles and Kate still hadn't arrived. I sliced the tofu in delicate strips and the chicken into bite-sized squares — at least as square as you can get with chicken. I put the chicken in a bowl, washed my hands, and stuck the bowl in the fridge.

I hadn't had a smoke all day and sort of wanted to

head out to the backyard to enjoy one, but then I'd be constrained to the back rooms, and since Myra and I were the only ones there, it was a perfect opportunity to talk to her, so I resisted the desire for a smoke.

The sun was long gone and the dining room and living room were dark. I flicked on the porch light as I went past on my way to the baby's room. Myra stood near the changing table, her back to the door. Her hair looked like it needed a wash and her long, purple sweater hung like it was draped over a hanger. Black leggings made her legs look almost invisible. Her feet were bare. She'd painted her toes cherry red, but the polish was chipped off the corner of her left big toe.

I knocked on the doorframe. This time I'd take a different approach. I'd obviously alienated her and Dave with my constant questions, and forgotten the fact that when I just chat, other people start doing the same. The pressure of Kate wanting me to figure out who the ghost was and the implied request that I would then be able to get rid of it, had twisted me in knots. I needed to relax. I was still curious, even more interested after Liz's hint that she'd encountered something frightening, but like JD said, it wasn't as if I had to figure this thing out.

"Come on in," Myra said. "You have to see Pamela's outfit. She looks like a doll!" She stepped to the side. Pamela wore miniature black patent leather shoes and white socks with lace trim. She kicked her legs and although I'd seen her do that before, I wondered if she was trying to remove the shoes, her first show of independence. Myra grinned, gazing at her daughter as if she was the first child ever to get dressed up. The rest of the outfit consisted of a blue and white striped dress with a white peter pan collar and a matching bonnet. I was surprised the baby's effort was concentrated on getting rid of the shoes because the bonnet looked much more uncomfortable, covering her forehead and cheeks so only a tiny oval of her face was visible.

"She's adorable," I said.

Myra picked up the baby and held her out so she was facing me.

"What's the occasion?"

"To surprise Dave."

I smiled. From what I'd observed of Dave so far, I doubted he'd notice.

"Did you get any sleep today?"

"Yes. She slept for three and a half hours and so did I. And after her eleven o'clock feeding, she was calm, so I got to sit and eat a tuna sandwich."

"Nice."

"I never did make it into the shower though. Do you mind keeping an eye on her while I jump in real quick?"

"I don't mind at all, but I'm not that familiar with babies. And Dave seemed worried about me being around her. Because I smoke."

She shook her head and carried the baby to her plastic seat. "He's very picky. Don't worry about it. I'll just put her in her carrier and she'll be fine. I'll only be ten minutes, and I'll leave the bathroom door open, so if she starts to fuss, I'll hear her."

"Okay, sure."

The baby stared at me the entire time Myra was in the shower. I stared back at her but she didn't seem to be bothered by it, didn't seem to care that she really had no idea who I was.

When Myra returned, smelling like coconut, her hair glistening, wearing the same purple sweater over a white t-shirt. She'd changed into white leggings. The tight lines had faded from around her eyes and along her forehead and jaw. She smiled. "I'm glad you two got along so well."

"She's very friendly," I said.

Myra laughed.

"When is Dave getting home?"

"Not until eight-thirty or so. It'll be just us girls again for dinner. I'm starving."

"I can make tea."

"Sounds good. Lunch seems forever ago."

While I filled the kettle and got out mugs and tea bags, cinnamon for Myra, peppermint for me, she rocked the baby seat and smiled at Pamela. She asked how I liked working at the church and I told her all the uninteresting clerical parts as well as the extremely interesting angle I'd never expected when I was hired — figuring out who had killed some of the people that were murdered on the church property. It was tricky explaining that part without bringing in the ghosts. It wasn't that I really figured out anything at all, the ghosts pointed the way. Maybe that was a mistake not giving her the full picture, but I still felt sort of obligated to follow Kate's lead on that. After talking about work, I babbled on about JD for a bit.

"Have you had lots of boyfriends?" she said.

"Only one other before him."

"Where did you grow up?"

"In Marin County."

"Do you have any sisters or brothers?"

"No." I poured the boiling water into the mugs. I set the kettle on a cold burner and picked up the tab at the end of each tea bag, dipping them up and down in the water. That probably doesn't make it steep any faster, but it's a habit. I think I got it from my mother.

"Did you go to public school or private? Dave's for private, but I'm leaning toward public."

It seemed a bit early to be planning Pamela's education, but a few times I've heard parents talking about schools before the baby is even born, so maybe Myra and Dave were behind schedule compared to their friends.

"I was homeschooled."

"Really?"

"Yes."

"Did you like it?"

"I don't have anything to compare with, but I was a happy kid, so I must have."

"Did you ever go to a regular school?"

"When I was fifteen I started going to a public high school."

She nodded. I stuck a spoon in the mug and pressed out the liquid from her tea bag. I set the mug on the bar next to the baby carrier, quite a few inches away from Pamela's wildly kicking black patent leather-clad feet.

"Dave and I never discussed homeschooling. I bet he'd like that even more, but I'm not sure how I feel about it."

"Why would he like it?"

"Cops, you know. They're paranoid. They see all the bad stuff. He wants her to grow up safe. He thinks even nice suburbs are getting dangerous. School shootings, bullying, drugs."

"None of that happens at private schools?"

"Not as much."

"I suppose those things don't happen at all if you're homeschooled."

She laughed. Then she turned serious. "I think after what happened to his first wife, he's even more anxious about how bad things can find their way into a safe neighborhood, into any family."

"He was married before?"

She blew on her tea. "His wife disappeared. She was murdered. She got into smoking pot and they think she had a bad situation with a dealer. They found her car in downtown San Jose in a crummy area."

"They didn't find her?"

"No."

"How awful. They didn't find her body?"

She shook her head.

"He didn't mention it."

"Why would he?"

"I don't know. I guess he wouldn't."

"It's in the past."

"Is the case still open?"

"Yes, but open doesn't mean anyone actually does anything."

I knew all about that. "How long ago was it?"

"Five or six years." She picked up her mug and put her lips to the rim, but pulled back suddenly and set the mug on the counter. Pamela twisted in her chair, wrapping her dress around her like a dishtowel being rung out. She let out a little cry followed quickly by a shriek. Myra pushed the mug to the end of the counter, unstrapped Pamela from her seat, and lifted her out. She straightened the dress and untied the bonnet and removed it. She stood and put Pamela against her shoulder. She walked a few steps to the top of the stairs.

Could the ghost be his first wife? But if she'd disappeared, why would she come back to this house? Although, it wasn't as if I knew all about the behavior patterns of ghosts. I just assumed they lingered in the place where they died, but maybe not. I sort of wanted it to be that way. Because if they traveled, went to different locations, why hadn't my parents' spirits found me? It wasn't as if I moved thousands or even hundreds of miles away. My Aunt and Uncle lived right in the next town.

"Have you ever seen a ghost?" I said. I quickly swallowed some tea.

"That's a random question."

"I guess thinking about someone being murdered made me think of it."

"Ghosts aren't real, they're just invented for scary stories."

"Lots of people say they've seen them. About thirty percent of the US population."

"Thirty percent of the population will say anything." She shifted the baby to her other shoulder. The baby was quiet now, but Myra continued rubbing her back, as if she couldn't stop.

"That's a lot of people, all saying the same thing."

"So? Why are you asking me that?"

"Just curious. Are you going to drink your tea?"

"Yes, as soon as she's calm." She walked back across the kitchen and into the dining room. She circled the table and then went into the living room.

Pamela seemed calm to me, but I'd heard her quiet down before and the minute Myra put her in her bassinet or the baby seat, she started up again. I drank some more tea and waited for her to complete her circuit of the house.

It really confused me that Kate had such a rough encounter with the ghost, that I'd had an even more violent experience, yet Myra and Dave had never seen or heard anything. Well, I didn't know about Dave. Maybe he had. But wouldn't Myra know? Were they so in denial about the possibility of people appearing from beyond the grave, that they were incapable of seeing or hearing an angry, aggressive spirit? Or was the ghost was afraid of them and hadn't felt comfortable making herself known.

I laughed to myself. It sounded as if she might have appeared to Liz. So visitors saw her, but the owners had no idea?

There was a knock on the front door. Myra opened it and I heard Kate's voice.

A minute later they came into the kitchen together. I stood, swallowed the rest of my tea, and put the wok and the pot for the noodles on the stove.

"Thanks for getting everything ready," Kate said. She went to work, pouring a puddle of oil into the pan and retrieving the chicken from the fridge.

I filled the large pot with water and turned up the heat on the back burner.

Myra decided the baby was hungry and asked me to bring the carrier to the bedroom. Her mug of tea sat on the counter, surely cold by now.

After Myra was settled and Kate was busy with dinner, I went outside and called JD. I walked down the street and told him about the ghost.

He pointed out that maybe Dave had seen the spirit but was too macho to admit he was scared, or maybe too religious to admit he'd seen something that wasn't supposed to exist.

There's nothing like a guy's viewpoint to help you focus your thoughts. It seems like most guys, not all, have a way of cutting through all the extraneous thoughts and impressions to the basics.

DAVE ARRIVED HOME, all blue uniform and heavy

black shoes, weapons and instruments of security strung around his waist. He went through the same routine, removing his belt in the living room and carrying it to the bedroom. He came out a few minutes later, barefoot, wearing jeans and a gray sweatshirt. He kissed the top of Myra's head.

She pouted. "Pamela was all dressed up for you but she got hungry and after she ate, she spit up all over her dress."

He patted her head, leaving his hand there, weaving his fingers through her hair. "That's what babies do."

She nodded and his hand kept time with the rhythm of her head. She made no move to get up, so after a moment, Kate stood and went into the kitchen to serve noodles and stir fry onto a plate for him.

After talking to JD, I'd decided I was going to stop being coy and come right out and ask him if he'd ever experienced supernatural events in his house. What did I have to lose? If he complained to Pastor Joe, I might get in trouble, but so far, I hadn't been told I'd be fired. I was pretty sure I'd be given a warning before that happened. Besides, is that legal? To fire someone for talking about the supernatural, when your business is talking to people about the supernatural, comforting them in their griefs and fears with promises of the supernatural?

It worked out perfectly. Pamela started crying before Dave slurped up his last noodle. Kate said she would do the dishes since I'd done most of the prep work. A super polite person might have insisted on helping. After all, chopping vegetables and cutting up chicken and tofu is fun, scrubbing pots and pans isn't quite as enjoyable. But I didn't. I'm not super polite anyway — why demand to help when someone has already offered? I hate silly games, like arguing over who's going to pay for a cup of coffee or a dinner out, or what movie to see. If someone offers, I accept, and if they ask me what movie I prefer, I tell them. I don't provide a list so that, in reality, they're choosing the movie. Maybe I'm selfish. Or maybe I just don't like to be superficial, except when I am . . . superficial.

Dave had already told us two stories about his day, with quite a bit of detail. The first was about a drunk woman sleeping in one of the easy chairs at the public library. Usually they allow the one or two homeless people that gravitate to the library to hang out there. Although most of the other patrons don't like it, it's a public building, and if they're just sitting in a chair, the librarians can't really do much. But this woman reeked of alcohol and then she started talking, loudly, to an older man who was trying to read the newspaper. They finally called the police and when Dave arrived, the woman screamed at him like she was possessed by the devil — Dave's term, not mine.

The second incident involved a ten-year-old boy at one of the elementary schools who had pulled a pocket knife on another boy. It was a tiny knife, but with all the rules about weapons on school property, they're required to call the police. This kid got quite aggressive and I guess they actually had to grab him to take the knife away, which is pretty upsetting and a little bit shocking for a kid that age. Dave was very wound up about it and I imagined it fueled his determination that his sweet baby girl was going to a private school.

Asking about his day seemed redundant after that.

I asked about his plans for the weekend and he said he had to work. "How long is Kate staying to help out?" I said.

"As long as Myra wants."

That was rather bold of him. What about what Kate wanted? He acted as if Kate had no life of her own that they might be keeping her from. Of course, maybe she didn't have much of a personal life, but it was still rude to treat her as if she didn't.

"A better question is how long are you staying?"

"Tonight's my last night."

He pushed his chair away from the table and picked up his glass of coke.

"You mentioned the homeless woman being possessed by the devil, is that what you really think?"

"Naw, it's just alcohol poisoning."

"Have you ever seen anyone possessed by the devil?"

He shook his head.

"Do you think there are other spirits out there?"

He shrugged.

"Have you ever seen anything strange in this house?"

He sipped his coke, staring at me with expressionless blue eyes.

"No." He tipped his chair back so the front legs were

an inch or two off the floor. He rocked it slightly, continuing to stare at me. I couldn't escape the feeling that he was challenging me. Waiting to see if I'd ask what I really wanted to know.

It was not the answer I'd expected. I thought he'd ask me to define strange. But I was probably being too coy, still. I was more worried about him telling Joe, about getting in trouble, maybe even Kate getting upset, than I'd realized. "You've never seen a ghost?"

He laughed.

"Does that mean no?"

"You think you saw a ghost?"

"Yes. And I think your housekeeper did too."

He brought the chair forward. The front legs hit the ground with a thud.

"She seems scared."

"Why would you be talking to the housekeeper? You're here to help Kate, not stick your nose into our lives. All you do is ask questions and try to stir up trouble."

"I haven't tried to stir up trouble at all. I'm just curious."

He stood. "Mind your own business."

"Why are you so upset? Did someone die on the stairs to the basement?"

"Of course not."

"There were no stories about a murder when you bought this house?"

"No. The family lived here peacefully for years. When

they passed, the house went on the market."

"So what happened with your housekeeper? She's scared about something."

"I have no idea. People like that tell stories."

"People like what?"

"From a lower socio-economic class. I see it all the time."

Wow. Was I right in thinking that's how cops view things? Slotting people into file folders? Good and bad, criminal and law-abiding, liars and honest, upper class and lower class? "She didn't tell me any stories. In fact, I got the impression she didn't want to talk about it."

"Don't fall for that. Ignore her."

"But she . . ."

"I told you to ignore her. You're a guest and I don't like your attitude. You come in here thinking you can smoke and ask my wife all kinds of questions that are none of your business. I don't know what you're after, but I don't like it." He walked to the doorway. Without turning to look at me, he said, "You're only here because Kate seems to think she needs your support. And because you work at the church."

Now I was a little scared. He was definitely holding back some anger, but barely. I wasn't scared he'd lose his temper, but I was worried he'd complain to Joe. And not just a casual complaint, but a long diatribe about whatever was upsetting him. He seemed like the type who would try to get me fired. I guess I *was* being nosey, but it didn't start out that way. I was asking friendly questions about the house, not prying. At least I don't think I was. Pastor Joe and I had a good relationship, didn't we?

Dave took a few steps into the living room, turned on the light near the couch, then came back to the dining room. His face had completely changed. His jaw was relaxed and his lips soft, as if he was smiling but not as if he was laughing or trying to force an expression. Even his eyes seemed changed, the glare was gone. "Ghosts are nothing but superstition. You probably had a bad dream because you were in a strange place. Sleeping on that concrete floor would give anyone bad dreams."

"It wasn't a dream."

"Then you're hallucinating. Or telling stories. Ghosts are not real."

"I saw a ghost."

"No you didn't."

I think I gasped a little.

He laughed. "Don't look so offended. And do whatever it is you're here for, helping Kate fix meals for Myra."

"I'm not your employee."

"You're the church's employee."

"I don't know what you're so angry about," I said. "I wasn't trying to be rude."

"I'm not angry."

I stood and put his silverware on his plate and picked it up. "There's something strange in your basement, and you can try to intimidate me into forgetting about it, but it won't work."

"If you're so worried about the basement being haunted, why don't you go home tonight?"

"Because I told Kate I'd stay."

"Whatever." He stepped into the hallway. Instead of turning toward the baby's room, he went to his bedroom. An instant later, the door closed, firmly.

I pushed open the kitchen door and carried his dishes to the sink. Kate had earbuds in and her iPod tucked into her pocket. Her head was tilted up and she was softly singing along with the music being piped inside her skull. She moved her shoulders and swayed in time with the beat, which looked blood-pumping from what I could see in her body.

I waited, hoping she'd turn because if I tapped her shoulder, she'd scream. She was blissfully unaware of me. She bobbed her head, her short pale hair drifting gently like she was under water. Her feet were bare, solid on the tile floor, confident. Despite the cold air, she wore a black sleeveless shirt that gave her a more sophisticated image than she usually portrayed, often favoring colors that veered toward garish, and too many of them — pale blue tops with purple pants, jeans with bright green or red or yellow tops and intricately decorated cowboy boots, the occasional orange or bright green dress with navy blue shoes. She was like an energetic bowl of Skittles.

After two or three minutes, she hadn't turned. It amazed me she could be so unaware of my presence. Usually I feel a change in the atmosphere when someone walks up behind me. But I don't often have earbuds and music going in public, so maybe that sense of someone being there includes sound, even if you can't identify the exact noise.

I tapped her shoulder. As I predicted, she screeched, lurched forward, and yanked out her earbuds. She turned. Her face looked hollowed out — her mouth open and her cheeks sucked in.

"Why did you do that?"

"I've been standing here for a few minutes, I hoped you'd notice me."

Her cheeks turned red and she breathed deeply. "You scared me to *death*."

"I know, but there was no way around it."

She pressed the pause button and tucked the cord and earbuds into her pocket.

"I'm going to have a smoke and then go to bed and watch a movie."

"Okay. I'll finish this up. If Myra doesn't need anything, I'll probably join you and read for a while."

I went to the door. I put my hand on the knob and turned. She'd put her iPod on the counter. I guessed she wouldn't be listening to music while I was gone. Her cheeks were still red and I'm sure she wondered what I thought of her dance moves. They were actually quite good.

THE BASEMENT SMELLED worse than ever after I'd scrubbed my teeth and face, and changed into sleeping clothes. Maybe because I felt so clean in a fresh t-shirt and yoga pants with my hair brushed silky smooth. The stench seemed to cling to my skin, making my face grimy again and my feet feel as if they were sunk in gooey mud.

Kate was already in bed, the blankets pulled up to her neck, reading. She acknowledged me with a nod. I popped in my earbuds and scrolled through the movies on my iPad. I started four different ones, but couldn't seem to settle on watching any to the end. After an hour or so, I turned over and pulled out my earbuds.

Kate placed her magazine on the floor. "What were you and Dave talking about?"

I got up and turned off the light and wriggled back into my sleeping bag. It felt damp. Not actually wet, but giving off that same not-clean sensation I felt on my face and neck and hands. I shivered. "I'm glad this is my last night."

"Oh. Can't you stay one more? Just to be sure?"

I sighed. But softly, so she wouldn't hear me.

"Why are you sighing? What's the big deal?"

"I'm tired of the smell, tired of not being welcome, and my back is stiff from sleeping on the floor."

"Please."

"I can't stay here forever."

"But what if it shows up again?"

I knew I should tell her. I took a deep breath. The problem was, when I told her, she'd be even more scared, and more insistent that I stay. I don't know why I felt I owed her anything. Part of the time, she acted like we were friends and she wanted to hang out, other times, as if I was just her assistant. At this point, I was holding back a lot of information, like Dave's secretive first marriage. I'm sure that's not fair to call it secretive, but he sure avoided mentioning it when he said how long he'd lived in the house. The deliberate talking around it made it feel secretive, at least to me. She didn't know about Liz's fear or how rude Dave had been to me earlier that evening.

"So what were you and Dave talking about?"

"I asked him if he'd seen a ghost."

She sat up. Of course I couldn't see her, but I heard the bed creak and her breathing, hard and fast, coming from a different spot.

"Why?"

"I feel like we're playing games. You saw a ghost and you're worried it might hurt them, and we're dancing around like it's not appropriate to mention."

"It's not. I think I saw a ghost. I don't know for sure."

"Yes, you do. You were scared to death and you never would have asked me here if you weren't convinced."

She was quiet. I heard the bed creak, but she was only shifting her position, turning to face me probably, as if that would make her words have more impact. "You shouldn't have done that. They'll think I'm crazy, that I'm not fit to be the youth minister."

"I didn't say anything about you."

"Then what did you say?"

"I saw the ghost, Kate."

"When? Why didn't you tell me?" She was no longer

making any attempt to speak softly.

I was sure Dave and Myra, upstairs and on the opposite side of the house, couldn't hear us. Unless one of them went into the kitchen without us being aware of their presence.

"It was scary, to be honest. I didn't want to freak you out."

"I'm not a child. I asked you to stay with me because of the ghost, to confirm that's what I'd seen, and you don't think it's important to tell me? I'm really disappointed in you. And a little angry."

Although her tone was sharp, it was kind of funny to hear her tell me she was angry. Usually people count on their voice and their words to let you know how they feel, instead of pasting a name tag on it.

"I don't understand why you wouldn't tell me."

I turned onto my back and pointed my toes to stretch my legs. "I'm telling you now."

"What happened?"

"I went outside for a smoke. When I started back down the stairs, I saw it."

"What did it look like?"

"It was grayish, with terrible red eyes — like they were soaked with blood."

I could feel the stillness, a cooling in the air as if Kate's fear had seeped out of her body and filled the room.

"What else?"

"It was terrifying. She attacked me. She screamed,

almost howled. She was crying that someone betrayed her."

Kate was silent for a moment. Then she said, "Why aren't you afraid?"

"I just said it was terrifying."

"But not enough that you needed to tell me."

She sounded hurt. I stared into the darkness, trying to get my head around that. Unless I misinterpreted.

"Why didn't you tell me?"

"I don't know. Sometimes I need to think things through first."

"And what did you think through?"

"Nothing, really. But something else happened."

"Something Dave said? How did he react?"

"Before that. When I got here this afternoon, the housekeeper was here."

"Okay. So?"

The stink of mildew was making me queasy. I turned on my side and pressed my nose into my pillow for a few seconds, then turned my head so she could hear me, keeping my voice soft, because now I had a creeping feeling that someone was listening. Either Dave, or something else, was nearby. "She was afraid. She'd seen something down here, but she wouldn't tell me what."

"So I'm not crazy."

"No one ever said you were."

"I've never believed in ghosts. It goes against everything I know about the spiritual world. It's very upsetting to have your whole foundation shaken like that.

You should be more understanding."

"No one really knows anything about the spirit world. It's a mystery. Death, life. Everything."

"We know what God communicated. In His Word."

I wasn't going to step onto that innocent-looking strip of dirt, with a land mine buried below the surface, even though the hint of *God's Final Word* was always floating around the edges of Joe's and Kate's and Cindee's attitude about ghosts, and their attitude toward me. It seemed like their devotion to a book never left any room for God to be an actual living being, just an entity who revealed his thoughts a few thousand years ago and then never spoke up again. It made no sense to me. "You saw what you saw, and felt what you felt. No one can deny that."

"I don't want anyone to know," she whispered. "Can you not talk to him about it anymore? Please?"

"Okay. I won't. I wish I could talk to the housekeeper again. But I'm sure she won't be back until next week."

"You're staying another night though, right?"

"I can't keep staying another night."

"Just one more."

"I guess."

"Promise."

"You want me to promise? Are we twelve?"

She laughed. "I appreciate your support."

"I know."

"What did Dave say?"

"He got sort of angry and he never answered the question."

"What was he angry about?"

"That I'm nosey. That I talked to the housekeeper. He said I shouldn't believe *someone like that.*"

"Oh."

She didn't ask what he meant — I guess it was clear from my tone. She was quiet for a long time after that. My mind drifted, half-turning toward sleep, but still thinking about Liz and wondering if she'd seen the ghost or only felt something. I wished she hadn't been afraid to tell me more, and I wasn't really sure why she was afraid. I suppose if you work for someone, and especially as a housekeeper, which seems to be considered one of the least impressive jobs you can have, which isn't really fair because cleaning a house nicely requires a lot of artistic sensibility in my opinion . . . you have to care and be proud of what you do. Sure, some of it's dirty and greasy and all that, but every job has those aspects . . . anyway, maybe if you talk about seeing a ghost in your employer's house, it feels like you're telling their secrets, betraying the trust they gave you when they invited you to come into their home and touch their things.

"There's something else," I said.

"What's that?"

"Did you know Dave was married before?"

"No."

"I wonder if the ghost is his wife. I guess she was into drugs, and they think something happened to her when she was meeting a dealer. They found her car, but have never found her, or her body."

"When was this?"

"About five or six years ago."

"It sounds painful. And I can see why it isn't something that would naturally come up."

"Then why does it feel like he's hiding it?"

"You can't go by feelings. You're drawing a conclusion based on nothing. Hearing something unexpected doesn't make it a secret, or sinister."

I closed my eyes. I was tired of talking and wanted to sleep. I wanted to be away from that smell and away from whatever was going on in that house, even if it was nothing. It was strange that Kate was defending what felt like a deliberate secret. She didn't seem to connect the ghost, the aggression it had toward her and me, with anything related to Dave or Myra.

But it was their house, and if it wasn't related to the original family, then it was intimately related to Dave, for sure, and maybe Myra. But in Kate's mind, it seemed to have nothing to do with them.

"It's not a secret," she said, "Or he wouldn't have told Myra."

"Maybe."

"You really think it's his first wife?"

"I don't know. If she died in some unknown spot, I suppose she might return. I really have no idea. But I do wonder what Myra thinks of it. If she worries that he still loves her."

"Who knows. Marriage is strange. Who knows what kinds of deals couples make with each other."

She made it sound like marriage was a pact with the devil.

"Do you think you'll ever get married?"
"It's not likely, but never say never."
After that, we both drifted to sleep.

Eight

KATE WAS STILL asleep, snoring a bit, when I crawled out of my sleeping bag. I zipped my bag closed. There was a dim, grayish light, the color you would expect from mildew filling the basement. It seemed like I'd been there forever. I was starting to feel as if I'd been relegated to a dungeon, tied to Kate by something that she'd now made even more clear she wanted kept a secret, even though I'd blurted it out to Joe. And of course I'd already told JD. I wondered if telling JD counted in her mind.

I pulled my jeans and a long-sleeved yellow t-shirt out of my duffel bag, picked up my messenger bag, and walked to the stairs. Light, but no sunshine, indicating a cloudy sky, spilled through the kitchen windows above. The house was silent. I went upstairs and thought about making coffee, but decided I'd rather relax at my condo. I used the bathroom, returned to the basement, and wrote a note for Kate that I left on her thick socks, folded in half at the side of her bed.

It was only seven-thirty when I unlocked my front door. The entryway was cold. After not seeing them much for several days, all my things looked like they belonged to someone else. I'd left Simon and Sara upstairs in my bedroom since it stayed warmer up there. They seemed a bit cranky, maybe because they hadn't been covered at night, and they were confused. Perhaps they'd stayed up all night partying, without the usual signal of a sheet going over their cage to tell them it was time to sleep.

The sun was expected out shortly and they were forecasting spring-like weather. JD was coming over later that morning and we were going hiking in the Palo Alto foothills and then out to lunch, hopefully at a place with outdoor seating so we could enjoy the spectacular weather, and then shopping for another parakeet. Now that Sara had come into my life unexpectedly, I wanted a few more birds. I thought I might eventually want seven or eight. I don't know why birds fascinate me, and why one, or even two, isn't enough, but it just seems like a fun idea to have all kinds of colors and personalities. And they do have different personalities — chatty or quiet, varying looks in their eyes as if they want to communicate with humans but aren't quite sure how to go about that. Simon is blue and Sara is green and yellow. I was thinking of another green bird, but hadn't completely decided yet.

I watered my orchid and the potted plants on my back deck and went through the mail — pointless because it's all junk I don't want. I pay my bills online, so sometimes I wonder what the point is of having a mailbox. Half the time I forget to check and then it gets overstuffed.

JD rang the bell at nine-twenty-seven, three minutes early. It's very cute to me how he's always on time or a little early. For some reason, I have the impression of guys being late, not really tuned in with clocks, or calendars for that matter. At least that was the impression I had with guys I worked with, and Joe tends to be that way, always asking me to remind him what date an event is. Maybe that's because he has an administrative assistant so he doesn't have to fill his brain with stuff like that, but since he has a smartphone loaded with a calendar and you can't help but have your whole life mapped out and clipped to your belt, I don't understand why he asks me.

I opened the door. JD grabbed me and kissed me hard. After a few minutes he said maybe we should stay at my condo and forget the hike. I pushed him away. "We can make love after we get my new bird. It's a perfect day for hiking."

He pulled me back and wrapped one arm around my waist, grabbing my hips and pulling me close so that I could feel the warmth of him spreading down my legs and through my belly and up to my chest. He put his other hand on the back of my head and started kissing me again, slow and soft. His hand on my head does something to me, makes me feel as if he wants all of me, not just my body, but all of my thoughts as well. I wonder if I'll ever mention that to him. Right then, my thoughts were about whether we *should* forget the hike.

After a while, he stepped back onto my miniature front porch. "You look good."

I smiled. "Thanks." I was wearing denim Capri pants and a white tank top, a navy blue sweatshirt and hiking boots. My hair was in a French braid. I hadn't had it trimmed since before Australia, and even braided, it reached the middle of my back.

RANCHO SAN ANTONIO is an open space preserve. It's about five miles from Stanford University and includes a choice of trails that wind through the foothills. It gets really crowded on spring and summer weekends, but on an unexpected spring-like Saturday in February, it was fairly empty. There's always a week or two during late January or February when the Bay Area weather turns to spring — the sky is clear blue, the temperature climbs to seventy, sometimes higher. The fruit trees go crazy sprouting their blossoms, fooled into thinking it's Spring. The daffodils come up and the birds reappear with their morning songs. It's such a tease and every single year it makes me think Spring truly has arrived. And then the cold returns.

We walked past a barn and a fenced area with goats and chickens. Several families were clumped around a baby goat. A boy with a buzz cut so his dark hair looked like a guy's stubbly face was chasing a chicken. One mother, wearing jeans and a turtleneck sweater, had a very red face. She obviously hadn't expected it to be quite so warm, especially early in the day. As JD and I walked past, holding hands, moving quickly, getting our blood pumping for the trail, she stared at our hands as if she wished she and her husband could disappear on a quiet walk through the forest. From the shrieks of her son and daughter, it looked like they were going to be spending quite a bit more time in the unshaded pen, petting goats and chasing chickens.

The trail is wide and flat at the start and we continued to hold hands as we started out. JD was wearing army green cargo shorts and an orange t-shirt. I glanced over every few steps to admire the muscles in his calves as he walked, matching his stride to mine.

After about a quarter of a mile, the trail narrows and begins to climb the hillside. We unlaced our fingers but there was still enough room to walk more or less side by side. The trees, pine and eucalyptus and oak, were tall and thick, covering the trail with total shade, but I still kept my sweatshirt tied around my waist because the air was as soft and cool as a slightly heated swimming pool, not like the iciness of the creek that meandered along the same route, sometimes visible, and sometimes at the bottom of an incline, still revealing itself with gurgles of water splashing around rocks. The ground was damp from rain with a few muddy spots, but they were easy to avoid.

I told JD the latest about my conversation with Kate.

"I don't understand why you're staying another night. What's the point?"

"She gets so upset."

"Well are you going to move in there? It sounds like

Dave doesn't really want you there, so who are you going to please? You don't owe her. It's not part of your job."

"I know."

"Then why are you staying? You could stay for two months and not see the ghost again."

"It's been there twice in one week. Somehow I think it will be back."

"Well how are you going to help them? If they've seen it, they don't seem to be afraid of it. And if it is the spirit of his first wife, and the police couldn't solve her murder, what can you do?"

"Maybe she'll tell me."

"Maybe."

"But if Dave really doesn't want you there, you could be putting your job on the line."

"You think I shouldn't sleep there tonight?"

"I think you should sleep with me tonight." He slowed his pace so he dropped slightly behind me. He put his hand on my neck. He stroked it up behind my ear and then brushed his fingers along my hairline. Shivers raced across my back and I almost stopped to put on my sweatshirt.

The trail got narrower so I walked in front. Now we were on more of an incline, but not enough to make us breathe hard, to keep us from talking. A woodpecker rapped against a tree, hollow and echoing. The hillside to our left was covered with tangled vines. I wondered what was beneath, vegetation growing over it and hiding things almost forever.

"You can't stand it," JD said from behind me. "You just have to know." He tugged my braid gently.

"You're right. I know the housekeeper is frightened, and I know what I saw and heard. And I know Dave is hiding something."

"Not everyone who reacts badly to questions or doesn't believe in ghosts is hiding something."

"He must know the house is haunted. He's either afraid I'll find out something from the ghost, or he's afraid Pastor Joe will think living in a haunted house makes him unqualified to be a deacon."

"Maybe he doesn't know. Why can't you leave it alone."

"Because the housekeeper was so scared. I thought she was going to start crying. Not to mention the fury of that ghost." Thinking about it made my stomach wiggle and tighten.

"Odds are you'll never see her again. It isn't a good idea to go snooping into a cop's personal life."

"Why not?"

"Cops are weird dudes."

"You can't say one thing about an entire profession." Even though I was guilty for stereotyping cops, I was surprised by how definite he was, as if he was warning me.

"In this case, I can."

"Why are you such an expert on cops?" I stooped and picked up an acorn with a hat and stuck it in my pocket.

"I'm not an expert. Okay, maybe they aren't all the same . . . "

"I'm absolutely sure they aren't all the same. No one is."

"They have certain characteristics."

"Like what?"

"First of all, they don't trust anyone, which I understand, since I'm sure they hear more lies than the general population, and they know more about the negative side of the human race. But they go into every conversation not believing you."

"How do you know?"

"I have a few friends who are cops. And I've had some encounters with them."

"For speeding tickets."

"Yes, that. But also a woman who used to live a few doors down from me whose husband beat up on her."

"Oh. How sad."

"I called the cops on him once. She didn't want to do anything because the one time she called, they asked what he'd done. She said he shoved her and slapped her arm. This one guy said, *At least he didn't hit you with a closed fist.*"

"That's terrible. I thought they took that stuff seriously? I thought they were required to arrest a guy if he assaulted his wife or girlfriend."

"They are, but they tried to talk her out of it being that bad. They made her feel like it wasn't serious enough to call it domestic violence."

"Really?" I felt naive. I'd thought it was the exact

opposite, that men got more upset because the police were too quick to make an arrest. Maybe JD didn't know the whole story.

"You sound skeptical. I'm telling you, it was kind of disgusting."

"I'm sure it's not always like that. Maybe they had an off night."

"I didn't finish the story. Her husband was a highway patrol officer."

"Oh."

"They'll do anything for each other. And some of them act like the laws don't apply to them, that they have valid excuses for breaking the law, and the average person doesn't."

"You seem really negative. They want to help people, keep us safe."

"They absolutely do not. They think everyone is one step away from committing a crime, that it wouldn't take much for any one of us to lose control."

"Maybe it wouldn't."

"They're self-righteous and they're on ego trips. They want to make everyone squirm, they like the feeling of power, of knowing they're in charge and no one can mess with them. It's like a drug. You can see it in their eyes, burning with this arrogant look that says, *Just try and argue with me*. I'll show you who's the boss. It's a total power trip. Don't kid yourself that someone becomes a cop to help people or to protect society. They're cowboys. They love having a gun on their belts. No one else gets to do that. They love knowing people are afraid of them, love it that you can't argue with them because you know it will get you in worse trouble."

"I don't know how you know all this from one incident where one cop said the wrong thing." It flashed through my head that I'd thought along the same lines when Dave dismissed housekeepers as "lower class" — assumed it was a cop thing instead of a Dave thing. I guess that's how stereotypes take root. You observe something outrageous and you tie it to a classification — lawyer, cop, politician; Asian, Hispanic, Anglo; male, female. But why? I don't understand why we seem compelled to classify people's behavior.

He put both his hands on my shoulders, still walking behind me. We climbed in silence for a few minutes, then he said, "I didn't mean to make you mad."

"I'm not mad. I just don't know if I believe that's true. You sound so cynical."

"Have you ever been stopped for speeding, or running a light?"

I shook my head.

"Have you ever had to call the cops for anything?"

"When I found the dead bodies at the church."

"That's different. You were reporting a crime. It wasn't an incident where it's your word against another person's."

"Speeding isn't your word against someone else. Neither is running a red light."

"True, but they never want to hear that you might

have a reason. Sure it's wrong, but when they're in a hurry, they do it without even thinking."

"It's different."

"Is it?"

"They're chasing someone who broke the law."

"How do you know?"

I didn't know, but I think you sort of have to trust the people who are in charge of keeping you safe.

"They never want to believe anything you say."

"Did something happen that made you think like this?"

"My neighbor."

"It wasn't that they didn't believe *you*. So what else happened?"

He squeezed my shoulders and let go. He came alongside me and put his arm around my waist, even though he was walking in heaps of pine needles and wild plants, more off the trail than on.

I took a deep breath. It felt as if I hadn't been outside in forever. The mildew odor in the basement had wound its way through my brain, like the vines threading their way around tree trunks and up through branches, dangling like uncombed hair off some of the branches overhead. I really had no idea how Myra and Dave lived with that smell. It was strange that it didn't find its way into their kitchen or any of the other rooms. Maybe it wasn't as strong as I made it out to be, a faint odor that because of the concrete walls and floor and the small space, felt thick and damp and more powerful than it was.

I would never keep my food, even though it was boxed and canned, in a place that smelled like that. For a couple so concerned about their baby's every breath, you'd think they would either get a professional in to figure out how to get rid of it, or sell the house and move to someplace new and clean. It might be a good way to be rid of a ghost as well . . . if they knew about the ghost.

"Did anything else happen to make you think this way about cops?"

"I know some cops. I hear them joke around. There are two highway patrol guys who come into The Distillery bar every few weeks. Another good example. They slam back three or four beers and hit the road. Okay for them to drink and drive because they're superior drivers."

"They said that? They said, *we're superior drivers?*"

"Look, it's just my experience that cops are a different breed and I don't think you're going to get anywhere snooping into his personal life."

I stopped walking. "I'm not snooping."

"Okay. Wrong word. I just think you should let it go. If they have a ghost living there and they don't like it, they can move."

Exactly what I'd already thought. We were arguing over nothing.

"Between his cop ego and the general macho guy attitude and the strict views at that church, even if he's experienced some kind of phenomenon, he's never going to talk to you about it."

I knew he was right. But I couldn't let it go. Even

though it had nothing to do with me. If Dave wasn't frightened by it, why should I care? And if Myra knew, she seemed blissfully unconcerned, more worried about her infant's future education than the potential health effects of mildew or a ghost. Maybe I couldn't let it go because of Kate, because of a sense of loyalty requiring me to support her. Or maybe simply because ghosts fascinate me and I have to find out why they're showing up.

The woodpecker, which had paused for a few minutes, started rapping his beak into a tree. It felt as if he was pounding his pointed beak into my skull, drilling a hole, searching for something that kept eluding him.

"Maybe they've both seen the ghost and want to keep it a secret. Kate said couples make dark deals with each other."

JD laughed.

"What's so funny?"

"She has a pessimistic view of marriage. But probably accurate in a lot of cases."

"What do you think she meant?"

"Isn't it obvious?"

"I want to hear what you think."

"Well the obvious one is women who stay with a cheating guy for financial security. They tell themselves they have a whole life together, but it's a lie. They're basically taking cash for the illusion of being loved."

I shivered. The air wasn't any cooler but goosebumps covered my arms and all the hairs stood up, making my forearms look like a miniature field of wheat. It wasn't just the words he said, but the emptiness in his voice, a sadness that was so deep it had wiped out every other feeling or thought inside of him. So far, JD hadn't come across like a very emotional guy, which I guess most of them aren't, and hearing that echoing sadness felt like an unexpected kick in my stomach.

"But couples make other deals — *I won't tell people how much you drink when we're alone if you let me watch all the football and baseball I want. Or I won't tell anyone about your kinky fantasies if you go to all these social events with me, even though you hate them.*"

Now the chill was deep in my bones. It seemed as if all the marrow had seeped out and they were hollow, the woodpecker pecking his way into them, like the bones of a dead person. I hadn't expected him to have such specific ideas about the subject of deal-making in marriage. Did he know people in situations like that, or had he just observed a lot? I suppose it's the cliche of bartenders hearing everyone's secrets, because the patrons feel safe talking to a stranger, and they're more prone to talk without inhibition when they're sitting at a bar with nothing to do but keep sipping alcohol.

"How could anyone live like that?" I said.

"People do."

"Could you?"

"Every relationship has compromises. It's a slippery slope from normal give and take to a soul-numbing deal that turns your relationship into something fake."

He'd obviously thought about the subject quite a bit. I don't think of guys putting that much analysis into relationships. But maybe they do, and they just don't talk about it. Or maybe I was making another stereotype. Guys have traits in common, but they certainly aren't all the same. Not even close. Just like cops aren't all the same.

I didn't know what to say, and luckily, the trail narrowed further and started to climb more steeply, so we hiked in silence. The woodpecker had stopped hammering. After a while, my mind calmed down, soothed by focusing on nothing but where I was putting my feet, and the blood surging through my muscles, and the oxygen moving in and out of my lungs.

AFTER A DELICIOUS lunch of spinach salad with mandarin oranges, bits of soft, fresh mozzarella cheese, and vinaigrette dressing, and tons of pasta, too much pasta, really, with tomatoes and thinly sliced triangles of Italian sausage, we drove to the pet shop.

Because I was now going to have three birds, I needed a larger cage. When I brought the new bird home I would put her in the old cage, move Simon and Sara to their palatial new home, and once they'd had time to get acquainted through the bars of their cages, the new bird would join them.

Parakeets are actually pretty friendly with each other, but they need to get socialized gradually. If I were moving into a house with other people, especially if they were already well-established with each other, I'd definitely want some time to get acclimated.

The new bird would be called Sierra, which seemed like a girl's name to me. I know that's kind of stupid to have all the birds' names starting with the same letter, but the names popped into my head and once I had the idea, it was hard to let go of it. And *S* is a beautiful letter. It has an unusual sound compared to the other letters, except *C*, of course, for a name like Celia. The sound lingers and brushes across the back of your teeth.

The pet shop — Arvie's — sold birds, reptiles, and fish. There were no puppies or cats. The shop was in an old building with several rooms. The main part had supplies and fish on the left. There were terrariums with turtles and lizards and Gila monsters and several small snakes in the back right corner. A few steps down was another room with birds. A built-in floor to ceiling cage in the back right corner of that level was the home of a macaw named Morris. His brilliant blue feathers looked almost unreal. He chatted with everyone who came within a few feet of his cage, and sometimes he yelled across the shop. I desperately wanted a bird like that, but he cost $2100. Besides, I really felt he should be in a house with plenty of room, not a confined place like my condo.

I think I was born loving birds. I remember lying under a tree in the backyard when I was four, staring up and watching juncos hop from branch to branch, chirping softly. I truly believed they were talking to me, telling me why they liked that tree, letting me know what they saw when they flew off to other yards or parks or even outside of suburbia. But they built nests in that tree, so I knew they preferred suburbia to farm life or a home in a wooded area. Sometimes I think we're all smarter when we're children. Maybe the birds and other animals are talking to us, but when we grow up, we stop listening.

After saying hello to Morris, telling JD for the tenth or twelfth time that I wanted a macaw, and listening to Morris ask me how I was doing today, we wandered over to the cages filled with parakeets and finches and canaries.

There were about fifteen parakeets. They were all equally adorable and part of me wanted to take them all home, but I couldn't afford a large enough cage. Yet.

"Shouldn't you pick out the cage first? That way once you pick the bird, we can take it right away," JD said.

One blue and white parakeet sat at the end of a branch. It looked at me and cocked its head. I pursed my lips and made a kissing sound. It bobbed its head and looked so excited like it wanted to jump onto my shoulder right then. I knew that was the bird.

I followed JD to the cages. Most were designed for one or two birds. On the next aisle there were four cages that looked like they had a decent amount of space for three birds. The best one was over four feet high with a domed top, which I liked. It had a large branch in the center, two perches, and two easy-to-open doors. It came with two water dishes and two seed containers.

I lifted the cage off the shelf.

"Let me carry it." JD grabbed both sides with his hands flat.

"It's not heavy."

"I'll carry it and you find someone to help with the bird."

I released the cage into his arms. He walked toward the end of the aisle, turning sideways to get around a stack of boxes with bird toys. I heard his footsteps heading to the front of the shop, and his voice, low and calm, asking the cashier to keep the cage while I picked out a bird.

I wandered back past Morris, said *hello*, and waited. After a few seconds, he cocked his head, grabbed a bite of apple, and said, "How's it going?"

"Good. It's a perfect day outside. I'm sorry you can't see it. If you lived with me, I'd take you outside almost every day for at least a few minutes."

"Lovely," he said.

I smiled and resisted the urge to stick my finger through the bars of the cage to stroke his feathers. I felt someone behind me and turned.

"Can I help you?" A guy, probably six-four, stood a few feet away from me. He had blonde hair in a long, thin ponytail, and a frail mustache that was almost invisible when he shifted away from the direct glare of the fluorescent lights. He wore a t-shirt with the Escher bird design printed on it.

Behind me, Morris said, "Can I help you?" That made him sound a little less intelligent than he had a minute earlier, but I gave him the benefit of the doubt. I'm sure he heard that phrase hundreds of times every week. I know if the clerk hadn't come up, Morris and I could have continued an actual conversation. In fact, for a brief moment, I'd been tempted to ask him what I should do about the ghost at Myra and Dave's and whether I should give up trying to talk to Dave, as JD advised. Insisted is more like it. Not that he was telling me what to do, but he sure didn't understand why I couldn't let go. I think it's because I can never let go, of anything.

"I'd like to get a parakeet," I said.

"Have you picked one out?"

Somehow, for no rational reason, I felt that he knew I had, that it was a rhetorical question, and what I really wanted was someone to unlock the cage.

"Yes."

He turned and walked to the cage full of parakeets.

"Is this your first one?" He pulled a plastic cord out of his pocket. It had about fifteen keys swinging wildly along the length of it.

"I have two others."

"So I don't need to give you care instructions. These all have RFIDs in case they escape."

"I'd never let a bird escape."

"It happens. Despite best intentions."

"I found one of my birds in the green belt behind my condo."

"See what I mean?" He poked his key into the lock and turned it. He'd already set a small cardboard box on a nearby shelf. "Which one?"

I pointed to the blue and white one that had smiled at me. "Is it male or female?"

"Female."

With a quick but not aggressive thrust of his arm, he reached for the bird, enfolded it in his hand so that all that showed was the white top of her head, making her look small and fragile. His hands were larger than normal and suddenly the bird looked helpless and afraid, even though I couldn't see her eyes. My throat tightened and I looked away, trying to draw in a slow breath.

JD was walking down the stairs.

I turned back.

The guy had put Sierra into the box, layered the flaps closed, and locked the cage. He handed the box to me. "There you go."

I carried the box in both hands. It shuddered as Sierra flapped wildly, then paused, deathly still, then flapped again. She did this repeatedly while I paid and as we walked out of the shop.

Once the cage was stowed in the back of JD's SUV and Sierra was settled on my lap, he closed the passenger door, went around, and climbed in his side. He put the key in the ignition but didn't turn it. Staring at the windshield, not smiling, almost as if he were talking to himself, he said, "You know it seems like you're hunkering down for the long haul."

"What does that mean?"

"Putting down roots."

"Because I bought a bird?"

He nodded. "I asked you when we were in Australia if you wanted to move in together. You didn't answer, and now it feels like your answer is, *I'm doubling down where I am.*"

"I told you a while ago I wanted more birds."

"This isn't about birds."

"It seems like it is about birds. Because I bought another bird I'm settling in long-term?"

"Does that mean you do want to talk about living together?"

I stroked the cardboard box, as if I could feel Sierra's feathers. She was quiet inside. I imagined her round glistening, curious eyes, staring at the sides of the box, wondering if she'd see daylight again, scared and feeling as if her whole world had shrunk to four walls and a dark, tiny space. I picked at one of the flaps, wanting to look at her, but knowing if I weren't careful, she'd find a way to escape. Having a parakeet flying around inside the SUV would not be fun. I pressed it back in place. She would survive. But JD didn't seem ready to get us home so she could start discovering her new place.

I really didn't know what I wanted. I was pretty sure I didn't want to move in together. I didn't want to quit my job. Despite their anti-ghost attitude, I liked working at the church. And I didn't want to commute forty-five minutes from Half Moon Bay to work. JD hadn't said a word about looking for a new job or whether he was up for that kind of daily drive if he moved into my condo.

And the whole hunkering down comment didn't make it sound like he was thinking of my condo at all. Did he expect me to sell it?

"It sounds like you're not interested." He turned the key and started the engine.

"I don't know what I want. It's too soon."

"We've been together for a year."

I wasn't sure what to say. It wasn't really about the distance to work, although my mind kept returning to that. It wasn't about jobs and driving and selling a condo. I was almost sure I loved him, but I was almost equally sure I didn't really know how you could tell if you loved someone. Maybe there's something broken inside of me because my childhood was cut short, because my parents abandoned me, which makes me not sure how to recognize love, or makes me afraid, or makes me not think about the future very much. I really don't know. It's not that my parents deliberately abandoned me. It's not like it's their fault they were murdered. But that's how I feel. And it bothered me that JD couldn't see that. Of course, had I really told him that? Those are big things, huge things, and they're hard to explain. I could explain it in my head, but I wasn't sure I could make the words come out correctly. So I said nothing.

"Can you at least say *yes* or *no* instead of just sitting there?" JD said.

"Not yet."

"Why can't you say *no*? Don't try to protect my feelings."

"I'm not."

"What's the problem then?"

One problem was he didn't say, *I love you and really want to be with you.* But there was another problem. "I need to try to find out about my parents."

"You mean chase their ghosts?"

"You make it sound stupid."

"You should let the past go."

"Why?"

"Because it's healthier."

"*Your* parents are alive. You have a brother. I'm all alone."

"You don't have to be."

"I have to try to find out. I have to."

"Why now? All of a sudden? Why didn't you think of this years ago?"

"Because I never saw a ghost. I thought I had to rely on the police to investigate, which they apparently decided not to do anymore."

"You think you can investigate?"

"I think I have to try to do something."

He pulled into one of the guest parking spots in my condo complex.

"And what does any of that have to do with moving in together?"

I picked up Sierra's box and pressed it to my chest. "You aren't with me in this. You don't understand why I have to do it." I glanced at him.

For the first time, he looked hurt. His eyelids were

lowered. His lips looked soft, like they wanted to say something but wouldn't be able to match what was in his heart.

"It's okay that you don't understand. Probably no one who hasn't experienced it could understand."

He turned off the engine and opened his door.

"Let's get your new bird out of that box." He climbed out and shut the door. He disappeared from view and a moment later the back of the SUV opened.

I got out and went around to the back. "Even if you don't understand, please understand." I tucked Sierra's box under my right arm. I put my hand on his waist and squeezed it gently.

He covered my hand with his.

EVERYTHING FELT EMPTY and false, as if JD and I were rehearsing for a play. I hoped the next time I saw him it would be different. We didn't really finish the conversation, but I guess neither one of us knew what to say. It was all too complicated and unfamiliar. It's not like we had practice talking about stuff like death and how to know when it was right to live together. In some ways, I felt like he wasn't really sure himself, that he was just bringing it up because it made sense as some sort of next step.

After Sierra was in her new home, and Simon and Sara were back to hopping around and being busy instead of sitting on one of their perches, staring at Sierra, JD and I kissed each other good-bye. It was a long, lingering kiss that felt sad, almost as if we were saying good-bye to something more than just a beautiful day and a glorious hike and lunch in the sunshine, and making love and eating turkey sandwiches in my bedroom while we watched the birds. But maybe I was turning it into something it wasn't.

We made plans to eat dinner in Half Moon Bay on Sunday night.

"This is your last night staying with Kate, right?"

"Yes."

"Even if nothing gets resolved?"

"Yes." I hated saying that. Something inside me tightened up, not wanting to walk away with unanswered questions, but I couldn't stay there forever. And I didn't want to.

"Remember what I said about cops."

"I will."

"Even if you don't agree, he's made it clear he thinks you're invading his life."

"I know."

I felt like I'd messed up. I was trying too hard. Always before, ghosts whispered their secrets to me for whatever reason, whether they thought I was sympathetic, or a good listener, or open, I don't know. But I don't think I'd been any of those things. Tonight I would keep Kate company one last time, but I wouldn't ask any more questions, I'd go to sleep and if Kate asked me to stay again I would tell her I just couldn't. That was all.

Nine

KATE'S CAMRY SAT at the end of the walkway leading up to the Hicks' tiny adobe house. For the first time, I noticed there were grayish streaks where the rain had run off the tile roof onto the caramel-colored adobe. It looked like mildew, but I was overly fixated on things growing in damp, dark places, smelling it everywhere, making it worse than it was. So what if the basement smelled old? Most basements probably do. It's not like I had a lot of familiarity with them because not many houses in California have basements. It's a housing feature that belongs to other parts of the country. Places that are less open and sunny and carefree. There's something about a basement that makes you feel as if you're being pulled into the earth.

I knocked on one of the glass panes in the front door and Myra opened it immediately. The baby, attached to her in a front pack, was screaming. Pamela's face and the top of her head under the fine sprinkling of wheat-

Madison Keith Ghost Story Collection

colored hair were dark red.

Gray shadows stained the area under Myra's eyes, making the skin look old, a bit mildewed, if that's not too much of an exaggeration. She looked smaller and thinner than ever. As if she was disappearing.

"I'll let you close and lock the door." Her voice was a whisper. Maybe she thought if she spoke louder, she'd start screaming too. She hurried across the living room and disappeared into the hallway.

I closed and locked the door and went to look for Kate. She wasn't in the kitchen or down in the basement. I went to the drawer closest to the back door and opened it. JD's suggestion that I not snoop had planted the exact opposite idea in my mind. The drawer was one you expect to be full of junk, the drawer that's in every kitchen in America, and maybe all around the world — filled with loose keys, tacks, screws, receipts, coupons, and all that other stuff you mean to file away but don't get around to.

The Hicks' drawer was not like that. It was fitted with a white plastic tray about an inch deep. The tray was divided into six sections. Nestled beside it was a narrow container the same length as the tray, holding a screwdriver and a wrench. The tray contained screws, tacks, coins, a ring with five keys, a ball of that gummy stuff that holds picture frames to the wall, and three books of matches. There were no coupons, but I was sure they had another well-organized container for those. Staring into the drawer, I realized the whole house was like that. In the drawer with cooking utensils, each one was placed straight, not tossed in. Ditto for the linen closet where I'd gone to get a hand towel the day I arrived, as well as the silverware drawer and all the kitchen cabinets.

I didn't let my sudden awareness of the neatness distract me from snooping. I picked up the keys and slipped them into my pocket. Just in time, because as the drawer zipped closed I saw Kate outside the back door holding an empty plastic tub. I opened it for her and she stepped inside.

"I took the recycling out." She closed the door with her shoulder, walked around me, and put the tub in the cabinet under the sink. "Why are you just standing there?"

"I was wondering where you were."

"Well here I am. I thought we'd make beef and barley soup for dinner. I picked up some sourdough bread on the way over."

"Sounds delicious."

"Did you get your bird?"

"Yes. She's blue and her name is Sierra."

"That's a lot of S'es — Simon, Sara, Sierra."

"Yes, but it's not like they're children — I won't be calling all their names in a row."

She nodded. "Can you chop veggies?"

"I was going out for a smoke first."

She sighed.

"I'll only be ten minutes."

"I'm not sighing because I can't handle cooking the

meal. I think you should be more concerned about your health."

"Next year."

She made a face.

I went outside and crossed the yard. I stood near the small building that housed the office and lit my cigarette. The building was the same color as the house and also had a dark red tile roof. There were windows on three of the four sides but they were covered by wood blinds, closed tight. A cable ran into a hole in the side, carrying the world wide web into the tiny space. I wondered what it had originally been used for. It was too small to have served as a guest house — I didn't think it had a bathroom.

After I finished half my cigarette, I put it out and went to the door. There was one step up, a small rectangle of concrete. It had a French door like the main house, covered with blinds. I pulled out the keys and tried the first one. The deadbolt turned. The fourth key I tried opened the lock on the handle. I pressed it down and opened the door.

Along the wall to my left was a plain wood table with a computer keyboard and a huge monitor. The chair looked like it belonged in an executive office. On the wall facing the door was a closet door. All the desk drawers were locked and none of the keys worked. The excitement I had about gaining access to Dave's secrets evaporated. The area surrounding the computer was bare. A bookcase stood under the window opposite the desk.

All the books were about law enforcement, weapons, and investigation and interview techniques. I thought about borrowing one, maybe I could use some interview skills to get Dave talking.

I pulled a book off the shelf — *Eliciting Information*. I let those words roll around on my tongue, even though I was alone. They were very melodic. I flipped through it and put it back. Then I reminded myself of my vow to stop trying so hard. It was better to stick with being myself. I'd never had a problem finding out more than I wanted to know in the past and it wasn't as if I had aspirations to become a police officer or a private detective.

That made me start thinking about the fact that I have very few aspirations, period. I know I want more than what I have, that I don't want to be a church administrative assistant forever, or any kind of administrative assistant. But I'm not really sure what I do want to be when I grow up. I suppose by your late twenties you should already be grown up, but most of the time, I don't feel that much different than I did when I was seventeen or eighteen, and I haven't figured out how to start out on my adult life. In some ways, my real life.

Just because I'm stubborn, I pulled on all the desk drawers again. Maybe one had been stuck and it would suddenly open. But none of them did.

I went to the closet. It had the kind of knob that doesn't lock. The knob was thin and small, a relic from the nineteen forties or fifties, instead of the more bulbous doorknobs we have now. It was stiff and difficult to turn. Finally it twisted and the door came open. The closet ran the length of the back wall. The interior was as tidy as everything else. There were shelves on the left that contained construction tools, two hammers, a hand saw, jars of nails, and one of those flat metal tools used for smoothing cement. In the opposite corner was a shovel, a pick, a few buckets, a bunch of rope and cables wound into tidy bundles, and two bags of cement, one opened and half empty with the top folded down over what remained. It seemed strange that tools and cement were stored in the office rather than the garage, but I suppose when you have a small house with a fairly small garage, you keep things where you can find the space — such as using the basement as a pantry.

I closed the closet door, walked out of the office, and secured the two locks. I had no idea what I'd expected to find. Once I was outside, I realized I might have trailed in the odor of cigarette smoke with me. I hoped it would be a day or two before Dave used the office so he wouldn't notice if it didn't smell quite right. I doubted Myra would be using it in the near future. Her life revolved around the short hallway from her bedroom to the baby's room with the occasional trip to the dining room.

When Kate went into the dining room to put placements and utensils on the table, I put the keys back in the kitchen drawer. Dave was working late again. While we ate our soup, Myra talked about baby things. It was amazing how she could consume a half hour or more detailing the process of breast feeding and the baby's sleeping and diaper filling habits. She went on and on and *on*, wrapped in utter fascination with her own descriptions while Kate and I smiled and murmured and finished our soup long before she did.

Kate stayed and listened to Myra some more while I cleaned up. To be honest, I was thankful to escape the descriptions of baby poop and breast milk and sore nipples and spit-up. Rinsing bowls and storing soup and washing the pot was much more satisfying. At least there was an end. There was something to show for my work — glistening counters and faucet, food stored for another meal. Maybe that's why Myra couldn't stop talking about infant care. Her life was an endless cycle, every hour the same, every day the same. The all-consuming odors and immersion in the human body seeped through every part of her mind and made it impossible to think about anything else. Not that she wasn't enjoying her baby. You could tell she adored the little darling. It was almost like she was in love, kissing Pamela's nose and cheeks and even her lips, sniffing her head, cuddling her, and cooing.

Through the closed door to the dining room, I could still hear her talking. Kate encouraged her with questions and expressions of sympathy. I escaped to the basement. The mildew didn't seem so bad after the descriptions of diapers.

Shelves and some covered cabinets lined the wall at the foot of the stairs. The open shelves were lined with cans and boxes of soup and cereal and packages of pasta. The bottom shelf had two large baskets, one filled with potatoes and another with snacks — granola bars, individual boxes of powdered soup, and styrofoam cups of dried noodles.

I opened one of the cabinets. It was filled with CD cases — music and a bunch that were labeled with dates and vacation locations, presumably with photos on them, from years past, before everything started getting stored in the cloud. There were boxes and a few racks that held file folders. I suppose I could have continued my snooping, but everything looked as if they hadn't been touched in years. If there were anything interesting, it would be on Dave's computer, and I had no doubt that was protected with a password, so I hadn't even bothered to turn it on.

Below the cabinets, the edge of the carpet curled up and away from the concrete. I poked it back, but it curled right up again. Whatever dampness was causing the mildew must have made the carpet come unstuck from the concrete. I tried pressing it down again but it refused to stay.

I went to the corner where I'd tucked my sleeping bag between the wall and the boxes. I picked up the blankets and my pillow lying on the top box. The carpet was curling up in the corner as well. I put down my blankets and sleeping bag a few feet from Kate's bed. I pulled at the carpet. Sure enough, there was moisture on the concrete. If the former housekeepers had tried to eradicate the smell of mildew, they hadn't looked very hard for the source. Of course, they probably didn't want to be pulling up the carpet because they were afraid Myra would be annoyed. I'm sure it was a balance between a directive to get rid of an impossible smell trapped in the almost airless space, and not wanting to damage your employer's property by ripping up the carpet.

I didn't care about that, at least not that much. It wasn't as if they could fire me from being Kate's helper.

A whole section of carpet came up easily and I could see the glue in that area had never quite grabbed onto the concrete the way it was supposed to. I pushed it back down and moved the boxes slightly to hold it in place.

WHEN KATE CAME downstairs, I was already burrowed into my sleeping bag, my face pressed down inside so I could breathe in the smell of the clean flannel lining. I poked my head out of my sleeping bag. "You forgot the light."

She went back to the stairs and turned it off, then nearly ran to her bed and hopped onto it. The bed creaked as she arranged herself.

"Do you think it will show up tonight?" she said.

"You sound like you want it to. I thought you were scared."

"I am. I don't want to ever see it again. But I'm staying until next Friday. Are you sure you can't stay with me?"

"I can, but I don't want to. This is ridiculous."

"You saw how terrifying it is."

"Yes, but you know she can't hurt you."

"How on earth can I know that?"

"She didn't."

"She tried to push me down the stairs."

"Okay. But if she really could, or really wanted to, wouldn't she have done more?"

"I don't know. I just wish this hadn't happened to me."

"But it did."

I heard her shift her position, presumably turning away from me to face the wall.

I WOKE A few hours later. At least I think it was a few hours. The basement was so dark I couldn't even see a variation of gray near the stairs. It almost felt like I was in an unfamiliar place, as if I'd never smelled the mildew before, never slept on the stack of blankets that didn't prevent the cold earth below from creeping up through the layers into my bones.

I twisted around and rearranged myself inside my bag. I closed my eyes.

A voice tore through the darkness. *You God damned son of a bitch! You liar. You lying fucking creep! I hate you! You ruined my life! You lying, fucking cheater!* A woman's voice screaming, sobbing like nothing I'd ever heard. The string of curse words continued, as if the more she cried, her options shriveled to three or four words, connected by *lying* and *cheating*. After a few minutes, the hysteria and growling rage seeped out of her voice. It became weak, pitiful, whimpering, like a chained dog. *I thought we had something special. I thought we were soul mates.*

I opened my eyes and saw the shadowy figure with her blood-infused eyeballs. She stood at the foot of the stairs. Red liquid ran down her arms and the front of her, as if all her tears were turned to blood.

The figure moved up two steps, but I could still see her. I started to shiver, but I was still convinced of what I'd told Kate — if the ghost wanted to hurt one of us, she would have already done it. At least I thought I believed my own words.

The bloody-eyed woman was silent now. Staring. I wondered if she could see me, if she knew either one of us were there. It was strange that Kate hadn't woken, unless she was so scared she couldn't speak.

I sat up and pulled my sleeping bag up toward my neck. "Can you hear me?" I spoke in a normal tone, but low, so I wouldn't wake Kate. So far, I had the impression I was the only one who heard the woman screaming and cursing.

"I gave him one last chance."

"What happened?"

She moved closer until the eyeballs were all I could see, glowing and pulsing, like there was something living behind them, but there wasn't, not exactly. Maybe pain living on.

The dark color slowly drained out. The red became transparent so that I saw images moving around inside her head. As I watched, I forgot I was peering behind the bone of her forehead — or what would have been the bone of her forehead when she was a living person.

I saw a woman with brown and blonde-streaked hair, walking down the basement steps. She called out so softly I had to strain to hear, "Is someone there?"

As I watched, she paused on the last step. A young woman, completely naked, with long thick hair and large, perfectly formed breasts knelt near the bed tucked into the wall. She was half-turned, looking at a man behind her. Her clothes were piled on the bed and her fist was clenched in the center of the clothes, as if she was hanging onto them to prevent a bad fall. The man was also naked. His left hand was tangled in her hair, pulling gently so her head tipped back and up, and she was forced to look only at him.

He ran the fingers of his right hand down her face and along her jaw. His hand paused on her neck, his fingers stroking her throat. Her shoulders trembled, but he kept touching the most tender part of her neck, down into the hollow of her collarbone. After a minute, his hand continued across her shoulder, then moved forward and down over her breast. She closed her eyes.

"You're gorgeous," the man said, his voice rough and cracked. "I need you."

In a whisper that filled the room, the ghost said, "I thought you loved me."

The man and woman faded from my view. Again, I saw the woman on the stairs. Her fist was pressed against her mouth, her face crumpled like a wadded up piece of paper, slowly unfolding. She faded from view and all that remained was the ghostly figure. She collapsed on the ground. Her body trembled with violent convulsions. She began sobbing again. Between gasps for air, she whimpered softly.

"Who are you?" I said. "Who are you talking about? Who were those people?"

Kate's bed creaked.

"Madison?" Kate's voice was hoarse, confused. "Are you talking to someone?"

"I must have been talking in my sleep." The lie slipped out so smoothly. I don't know why I didn't tell her the truth. I guess because if she didn't see the spirit, why get her all worked up? And if she realized the ghost was in the room, she'd freak out and then I wouldn't find out anything. And the ghost seemed to be quite eager to talk, now that she'd stopped screaming.

Kate laughed. "Well turn over or something. You woke me up."

I looked back to where the ghost had been. She'd disappeared.

For quite a long time I tried to stay awake. My eyes ached from forcing my lids open. Every few minutes I would feel them fall closed. My body would spasm as my muscles suddenly tensed. I peered into the darkness but I don't know why I was straining to see. It wasn't as if those eyes filled with blood were difficult to make out.

Finally I drifted to sleep.

When I woke again, the ghost was there, silent this time, right next to me, staring down, but not really seeing.

I sat up.

"My husband."

"Dave?"

"Yes."

"Why are you here?"

"The housekeepers. One quits and they hire another one. I'll never rest. And his new wife. She's so dumb, thinking he loves her, that she has anything with him. No woman will ever satisfy him. No single woman. He needs every female he can get his hands on."

"Has Myra seen you?"

"I don't know. She looks right through me. I don't know."

"Has the new housekeeper seen you?"

"Not the newest one."

Suddenly Kate sat up in her bed. "Madison! I can't sleep. Wake up and turn over."

The glossy red eyes disappeared as quickly as they'd materialized.

"Are you awake?" Kate said.

"Yes."

"Good. Then hopefully you won't start talking again."

I laughed a little to myself. She must be half asleep herself because her comment made no sense.

I stayed awake until morning. The spirit didn't reappear.

Ten

AT SEVEN, KATE got up and started getting ready for church. I told her I'd fix breakfast for Myra and Dave, but then I'd be heading home for good. She pouted like an eight-year-old and I ignored her.

As Kate was walking out the door, Myra came into the living room. Dave had gotten home late and then had an early shift. Watching his brief passes through the house before he was back out on duty again was kind of shocking. I wondered if all the cops were burned out. Not that I had much sympathy for him anymore. Either his first wife had killed herself, or he'd killed her. She clearly hadn't been kidnapped or attacked by drug dealers or whatever.

I dressed in jeans and boots and a white turtleneck shirt. I took my coffee and cigarettes out back. The day would be pumped full of coffee since I hadn't slept more than three or four hours, closer to three. The flame from the lighter grabbed the end of my cigarette and burned a bit of the paper. I blew out the smoke slowly in a thin, lazy stream.

It was cloudy, the sky solid white which always makes me feel claustrophobic. Smoking helped a little. It took my mind off the gloom and warmed me and calmed my mind. I thought about what JD had said about cops thinking they were above the law. It was such a harsh view, and completely unfair to lump all cops into a single bucket on the basis of one or two bad experiences. Still, I could see how being in charge of enforcing the law might make you feel powerful and able to rationalize things. But murder? Of course, it would be so easy for a cop to make it look like one thing had happened — a woman killed in a drug deal gone sideways, for instance. And all those tools for mixing and spreading cement in his office. Such a strange place to keep things like that — as if they were too important to be stored in the garage.

My mind drifted. I tried not to let the thick layer of clouds press down on me and make my mood as damp and spongey as the sky. Sure, I was weaving together several unrelated threads — a ghost consumed by the pain of betrayal, a bag of cement and a smoothing tool, and a basement that reeked of mildew. Even though having your wife kidnapped, presumably murdered, by guys selling a bag of pot to her, sounds far-fetched, who would doubt the word of a police officer?

I don't know why the ghost hadn't revealed herself to Kate again. I almost wondered if she used Kate to get me there, but that made no sense, because how on earth, or in heaven, would the ghost know I even existed? Besides, that's sort of arrogant, to think she was looking for me in particular, like I have some inside track with the spirit world. Maybe she only revealed herself to one person at a time. Or maybe Kate got so freaked out and the ghost wanted to let loose her rage and pain, and she needed someone who could take it.

Do ghosts do that? Just want to pour out the pain in their souls? Was she doomed to having her heart ripped out repeatedly, re-living the worst day of her life over and over again? If I had to live the worst day of my life over and over again, walking into my parents' bedroom and seeing them cold and motionless on their bed, if I had to keep experiencing that repeatedly, I don't know how I'd survive. Part of what makes the bad parts of life bearable is the piling up of new experiences after something terrible. At first you're nothing but pure, burning pain, not eating or sleeping or thinking or able to do anything useful. Eventually get an appetite and find yourself enjoying a nice hamburger and salty fries, or you start smoking and find out how relaxing that can be, how numbing to the brain. And then you get caught up in a crochet project, or going to the beach with your best friend, and eventually, finally, the bad thing gets smoothed over. Sort of like smoothing cement over a grave.

If you never got to have those good things, and the bad thing was keeping you from moving on to another realm, the agony would be unbearable. No wonder ghosts are so scary. No wonder her eyes dripped with blood, as if her heart was bleeding, pouring out of her body.

FOR BREAKFAST I made scrambled eggs with cheese, mixing in chopped tomatoes and sliced green onions. I toasted whole wheat bread and covered it to keep it warm. When the eggs were almost cooked and I could leave them for a minute, I went into the living room. Myra was already up. Pamela was in her carrier, dressed in a soft and comfy-looking pale green one-piece suit. Why do babies get all the snuggly clothes? The outfit looked like it would keep you very warm if you were sitting in the living room on a bone-chilling winter night.

Myra brought the carrier into the dining room and put it on the table. Pamela's eyelids were drooping as if she were drunk on her belly full of milk.

Myra's hair was clean and the grayish tinge on the skin under her eyes was less noticeable. She appeared to be recovering from non-stop feeding and diapers and rocking the baby, as if she'd emerged from a tunnel and was ready to start living again. The tails of her crisp white shirt hung out over her faded jeans. Her feet were bare and she'd re-painted her toenails — dark red. I suppose she wanted to show them off. I hated what I was going to tell her, but I knew I had to, even if she didn't believe me.

I carried two mugs of coffee to the table and went back for the butter and jam and the plate of toast. Then I served the eggs, huge piles of them, onto blue plates. They looked gorgeous — orangey yellow from the cheese, with glossy spots of red against the amethyst blue.

Myra didn't talk about the baby as much as she had the night before. Maybe her need to go over all the details of infant care had been temporarily satisfied. Or maybe she thought Kate had a more sympathetic ear than I did.

I buttered a slice of toast. After taking a bite and chewing it, I said, "Have you ever felt this house is haunted?"

She laughed. "Why do you keep going on about that?"

"Have you?"

"No."

"I've seen a ghost in your basement. Twice."

She laughed. "You were dreaming."

"No I wasn't."

She stabbed a chunk of egg with her fork. She put it in her mouth and swallowed without chewing. "What do you think you saw?"

"I don't think, I know."

She squinted, which she managed to do without creasing her brow.

"I saw a spirit that had eyes like pools of blood. She screamed and howled like I can't even describe. She was sobbing that she'd been betrayed."

"Haven't we all."

"What do you mean?"

"Nothing, it's fairly common for a woman to feel betrayed, don't you think?"

"So you believe me? That I saw a ghost in your basement?"

"If you say so."

It seemed as if she wanted me to keep talking until I backed myself into a corner. It was possible she had an agenda of her own. But she was so nonchalant, not really caring what I had to say or what I'd seen in her basement. "And there's that mildew odor."

She laughed. "You think a ghost is causing mildew?"

"I don't know, I'm asking you."

"I have no idea. I thought ghosts were supposedly vapor, not tangible, no voices, no smells, no touch or anything like that." She laughed again. It sounded as if she was going to punctuate every statement with a laugh. I hadn't noticed it when I talked to her before and I wasn't sure if it was nerves, or a bit of madness brought on by sleep deprivation. Maybe she wasn't emerging from that tunnel after all. Or maybe, she was lying and the laugh was her tell. If you're married to a guy who's a deacon in a church that firmly believes the supernatural does not exist, except for their version of the supernatural, but one that excludes ghosts, or rather excludes the ghosts of human beings, but not the ghost of God, then you might lie about having seen one. And what if that ghost told you something you didn't want to hear, something that shook the foundation of your home, when you were pregnant, and thought you had a perfect marriage, that you were together forever with your one true love?

"This ghost definitely spoke," I said. I was going to push as hard as I could and I was going to make her squirm until the lie popped out with more evidence than just a silly, repetitive laugh. "She was crying with this soul-ripping rage. I almost couldn't breathe. It was as if I was hearing her on the day she caught her husband and another woman, naked and wrapped around each other. It felt like having your skin rubbed off so the only thing you feel is burning, stinging pain that won't stop."

"Don't create drama." She put her hand on the edge of Pamela's chair and rocked it slowly, even though Pamela was sound asleep and didn't need rocking.

"I'm just trying to describe what I heard, and felt. I don't understand why no one else has encountered her. Unless the housekeeper saw something, or heard something." Even though Liz said she hadn't seen the ghost, I thought I'd throw it out there to see how Myra reacted.

"Housekeepers are flakes."

"That's not fair."

"It is. I've had six of them quit since Dave and I got married."

"Really?"

"And they don't give notice, they just stop showing up. They don't answer their phones. That's it." She snapped her fingers. "They disappear."

"Strange."

Myra laughed and rocked the baby chair harder. Pamela snuffled and I wondered if her mother was planning to rock her awake.

"Maybe the ghost has scared them all away. She's quite terrifying."

"Then why aren't you scared?"

"I've seen several ghosts, I suppose I'm used to it. And I'm very curious — it helps me not think about being scared."

"You really believe you've seen ghosts? You think they exist?"

"I know they do."

"How do you know? How can you be sure you're not dreaming, or hallucinating?"

"I just know."

"What if I don't believe you?"

"It doesn't really matter. I believe myself."

She pushed her plate away and took a sip of coffee. It was lukewarm by now and I felt that she wanted to leave, yet also wanted to hear anything else I might say. As if she didn't really want to talk about any of this, but on some deeper level, a frightened, knowing, non-denial level, she did.

"I don't think she's going to leave your home until she warns you."

"Warns me?" She laughed, but not the belly laugh that matched the tone of her words, it was that same nervous, slightly unaware giggle.

"Does your husband have sex with your housekeepers? Is that why they all leave?"

She shoved out her chair and stood. "That's disgusting. Of course not."

I waited for her to giggle, or yell, or grab the baby and rush out of the room, but she just stood there.

"Apologize. You can't be a guest in my house and say things like that."

"I'm not really a guest."

"I want an apology."

"For what?"

"For accusing my husband of doing despicable things. For being a cheater. For . . ."

"Why do your housekeepers keep quitting? That's not normal."

"Of course it's normal. That class of person has no stability. And most of them are Hispanic, quite a few are probably here illegally. If they're worried they've gotten on the radar of INS, they disappear underground."

I thought that was an interesting choice of words. It's funny how people will say things without realizing what they've said. First of all, how would she know what it's like to be in the country illegally, but more importantly, why couldn't she stop at the word *disappear*? Why add *underground*? It sounded sinister. It made me think about her basement and Liz's fear — no way out, and whatever she said in Spanish — and the wife who disappeared into thin air. Maybe on some level, Myra knew what was going on in her basement, and it was far worse than an infestation of mildew.

She backed away from the table. "You're way out of line. You need to apologize. Right now."

"Don't you want to know the truth?"

"I know the truth. My husband loves me and our daughter."

"But what about his first wife?"

"What about her? All she wanted to do was smoke pot."

"Really? Why would a cop marry a woman who smoked pot all the time?"

"I don't think she smoked when he met her."

"But you don't really know. And it seems unusual for a person who isn't into pot to suddenly take up the habit. Most people, if they want to unwind, have a few drinks, maybe drink too much, but they don't normally start smoking pot unless they've done it since they were teenagers. It's not like you can just pop into the grocery store and buy a few ounces."

She put her hands on her head and pushed them hard across her scalp. Her hair danced up in fine strands, pulled by static electricity, as if it was gasping for air.

"Why are you doing this? I'm not going to stand here and listen to these lies."

"But you are listening. So maybe you don't really think they're lies."

She did that thing with her hands again, pulling the skin of her forehead tight, so her eyebrows rose and her eyes opened wider, making her look shocked — as if she'd seen a ghost.

"I'm not trying to hurt you," I said. "Or your daughter. But I thought you would want to know the truth, and the truth is that your house is haunted. The truth is this ghost wants to save you from suffering what she suffered — your husband lying to your face, giving himself to other women . . ."

"I want you to leave."

I stood. I stacked my plate on hers because her eggs were gone, the plate wiped clean, not even a tomato seed spotting the surface, while my plate had several bites of egg and cheese, and little rings of green onion scattered across like pebbles on the beach.

I picked up the plates and backed toward the kitchen door, keeping my eyes on her face, hoping she'd stop blaming me for what was wrong in her house. Hoping she'd realize her husband not only slept with every woman that passed through, he killed his wife and buried her in the basement. The more I thought about that, the more I knew it was true, even if the ghost hadn't come right out and said it.

It was stunning to me that Myra didn't want to know the truth. I couldn't understand wanting to live a life that looked like one thing on the outside but was rotten below the surface, like floorboards decaying beneath beautiful Italian tile, or mildew that couldn't be seen, couldn't be sprayed and scrubbed away by an army of housekeepers, flourishing in your basement, giving off its rank odor. Eventually it would creep up the stairs and permeate the entire house.

Maybe she thought she was special and somehow she'd lure him back to her arms, so that he'd never look at another woman, never even think about another woman, and certainly not assault them right in her house. She would grow her hair long, trade in her turtleneck shirts and tailored blouses for low-cut tops, tighter jeans. Although, does any of that really work? If a guy isn't satisfied with one woman, it doesn't really matter what the woman does. It's the variety he craves. Or maybe the idea of winning, seeing if he can capture someone's interest, overpower them with such intensity they'll close their minds to the fact he's married, that he would never love them. Of course, he hasn't really won anything if the woman he's pursuing works in his house and is afraid of losing her job. He might as well hire someone to have sex with him. I don't see the satisfaction in that at all, but what do I know? My experience of guys is limited at best, and I know they think differently in a lot of ways. Or maybe they don't, maybe you just hear about it with guys and you don't hear about it as much with women.

My back bumped against the kitchen door. It popped partway open, then swung the other way and tapped my shoulder. I jumped, feeling for a moment the ghost was just behind the door, filling the kitchen now that she'd consumed the basement, pushing me toward Myra, insisting I make her understand that her life might be in danger.

"You have no right to come in here and try to destroy my family."

"I didn't destroy your family. Not at all. I'm trying to help."

"I wonder what Kate would think of your behavior. Or Pastor Joe?"

I wanted to tell her Kate had seen the ghost, but now

that the experience was fading, would she admit what had happened? And if Joe found out I'd been talking to his parishioners about it again, he'd be pissed. I loved my job. And getting fired is never a good thing, it makes it so much harder to find another job. Or I assume it does, I've never been fired, but it leaves a big hole in your resume, or you would have to make your former employer look like a whacko, and I don't imagine that would go over well with someone hiring you, if you're willing to spill your guts about weird or unprofessional things your former employer had done.

Still, am I the kind of person who runs away from what's true because I'm afraid of losing my job? And would he really fire me? He'd gotten annoyed with me for talking about ghosts but hasn't ever done anything except complain. This was a lot worse though, accusing a church deacon of cheating on his wives, of murdering a woman.

I decided to give it one last effort to convince her she should save her self respect and any chance of a truly happy life, being loved by someone else. If she chased me out, then there wasn't anything I could do. It's not like the police were going to dig up the basement of one of their buddies based on the word of some girl who said she talked to a ghost.

I put the plates on the table and stuck my hands in my pockets, hoping it made me look firm and approachable at the same time, if that's possible. From the corner of my eye, I saw a strand of hair that had fallen out, coppery red against my white shirt. Without thinking, I pulled my hand out of my pocket and plucked the hair off my sleeve. It hung from my fingers, nearly invisible now that it didn't have the white background. I could put it on the plate, but Myra might think I'd carelessly wash it down the drain. I couldn't drop it on her dining room floor. I lowered my hand, hoping she'd glance away and I could let it fall on the plate for now. No such luck. Finally, my fingers aching from pinching something so insubstantial, I pushed it into my pocket.

"Have you seen the ghost? Or heard a woman shrieking and crying?" I said.

"When you're sleep deprived, you see and hear all kinds of things. But the truth is, when people die, they go to heaven or hell, they don't stay on the earth where we can see them. I don't know why you're trying to scare me, or make me upset, or turn me against my husband." She reached into the carrier and pulled out her sleeping baby. She held Pamela close, still curled up, sound asleep. She pressed her nose and mouth against the baby's head. She took a deep breath.

I lowered my voice to a whisper. "What did she say to you?"

"Who?"

"The ghost."

"I told you…"

"I know what you told me." I stepped around the corner of the table and walked to where she stood.

She squeezed the baby, pulling her in closer as if they were melting into a single person. The serene look I'd noticed the first time I met her had shrunk to a pinprick at the center of her eyes. Now, her face looked tired and old, her cheekbones hard and fierce, her jaw locked tight.

"You think your lack of sleep made you hallucinate. But it didn't. The spirit of Dave's first wife is inside this house and I don't think she's leaving until you see what he's doing to you."

"Dave loves me."

"Isn't it better to know the truth?"

"Not always." She stepped past me and walked into the living room.

I thought she'd turn and tell me to leave, or say good-bye, or mention that she might see me around the church, but she walked to the hallway and turned the corner toward the baby's room. A moment later the door closed with a soft thud and a click of the latch.

The house was silent, no sounds of crying from either the baby or the wounded, bleeding ghost, or even Myra, for that matter. When I thought about all the sounds I might have heard at that moment, the silence grew deeper until I was afraid to take a step for fear of disturbing it. Sunday mornings are always quiet no matter where you are, but the heavy blanket of noiselessness grew until it felt like the silence of death.

How could you live, knowing your husband was touching other women, desiring other women? How could you live if there was even the tiniest chance there was a body buried in your basement?

Eleven

THE DAY WAS like crystal — bright blue sky and glittering sun — when I walked out through that beautiful but thickly covered front door. I'd left the kitchen clean, the dishwasher running, and the peeled up carpet in the basement tucked back into place.

Even though I was walking away from a murder, and leaving a ghost to her continuous misery, I didn't see what else I could do. Myra wanted me out of there, Dave was done talking to me. It was possible things might change in the future, that Myra would wake up, or that she'd get enough sleep to realize how she was betraying herself and her daughter. Or maybe the ghost would let loose. I could only hope. Maybe she would force them to listen, force Myra to recognize what happened and start preferring the truth over whatever weird half-dead life she was choosing right now.

I don't know that much about ghosts, I'm learning as I go. But if she was in enough pain, and she wanted to escape the in-between space where she was condemned to experiencing the discovery of her husband's betrayal over and over again, maybe she would stop being so cautious about who she revealed herself to. I'm not even sure why she was being cautious. I'm not sure why she only revealed herself to Kate once.

I knew I was letting her down.

After I cleaned the bird cages and gave Sara, Simon, and Sierra more seed, a treat, and fresh water, I vacuumed and scrubbed my bathrooms. It felt great to be on my knees scraping the sponge across tile and porcelain. Usually I hate cleaning the bathrooms, but because they smelled so fresh, not a hint of mildew, I actually enjoyed it. Then I made a quick run to the grocery store for eggs so I could make two pans of brownies. One was for JD, but of course, I'd probably eat a few of his as well as the pan I was keeping for myself. I took a shower and got dressed for dinner.

I wore dark brown leggings and high-heeled chocolate brown boots that come up to just below my calf. I put on a white tank top like I almost always do in case I get hot and want to un-layer my clothes. On top of that I wore a huge sweater, pink and white, that hung to the middle of my thighs, kind of droopy, but so comfortable. Pink doesn't look that great with my red hair, but it was pale enough, and with all the white, I thought it worked. I even put on mascara and lip gloss.

We were meeting at a chowder house that serves fresh seafood and has an outdoor patio with a view of Half

Moon Bay. I was spending the night at JD's place, but I'd have to get up early to drive back in time for work the next day. It seemed as if I hadn't slept in my own bed in weeks, and I felt bad leaving Sierra and Simon and Sara alone another night, but it was the last one for a while. And sleeping in JD's bed was a whole lot better than a sleeping bag on a concrete floor with nothing but blankets and a thin carpet for padding, and the stench of something eating away at the floor beneath me, and Kate breathing nearby, and a ghost lurking in the corners. I was definitely looking forward to a dinner not talking about baby bodily functions, and watching the sunset with my guy.

When we were seated at a corner table, both of us angled to look at the water, JD ordered a glass of white wine. When it came, he left it untouched and took my hand. "I didn't mean to pressure you about moving in together."

I was so startled, I almost grabbed a sip of his wine.

"Are you okay?"

"Sure. I'm just not expecting it, every time you mention it."

"Why?" He removed one hand from mine and picked up his glass.

I was a little hurt that he couldn't wait to drink his wine until we were finished talking and holding hands. He was the one who brought it up, and now it felt like he was pulling away from me. Literally.

I shrugged and slid my hand out of his. I turned and

looked at the opposite side of the bay. The water in the harbor area was smooth and still. Tiny waves lapped at the shore like eyelashes fluttering on the sand. Beyond the breakfront, the waves were calm, gentle swells. Only two or three surfers sat near the shore, waiting for nothing.

"Why are you surprised?"

"I guess I'm just thinking about dinner and being with you, not making other plans."

He smiled. "Aren't you the Zen princess."

"What's that supposed to mean?"

He sipped his wine.

I picked up a piece of sourdough bread and smeared it with butter.

"Nothing. That's one of the cool things about you. You focus on what's right in front of you."

"What else is there?"

"The future."

"You're right. I don't think about the future a lot."

"That's a good thing. Most of the time."

"Why only most of the time?"

"Once in awhile you have to."

"Maybe when I'm older."

"You're twenty-eight."

"I know how old I am. I don't feel like it though. I don't feel grown up."

The sun was moving fast toward the water. There was a fog bank, thick gray and white clouds, solid along the horizon. We weren't going to have a very interesting sunset. Just a gradual sinking, since there weren't any thin, scattered clouds to reflect the light.

"Why don't you feel grown up?"

The server came to the table. JD ordered a cup of clam chowder and the salmon. I ordered clam chowder and halibut. This place makes the best clam chowder on earth. Or at least the best I've ever had, so it seems like the best on earth.

I know if we're a couple I should want to tell him what I'm thinking and feeling. And I do, most of the time. But I was suddenly tired. I hadn't slept a lot. The ghost drained most of my energy and Myra gobbled up the rest. I took a long drink of water. "I don't know why I don't think much about the future or feel grown up. Maybe because wanting to know why my parents were killed is always hovering in the back of my mind, always there. And maybe having them die like that, I'm still just drifting along, sort of numb. Still a kid."

He took my hand again. "Whatever you need to do, I'm with you. Okay?"

I smiled. I didn't feel as tired.

I wonder what a soul mate is, and how you can be sure when you've found one. I still don't know, but feeling like I had a really good friend right now made me think that this was one piece of knowing what a soul mate is, and one piece of knowing when you've found one.

SOMETHING STRANGE HAPPENED on Tuesday morning when I got to the office.

The coffee was just finishing brewing as Kate walked in the door. I ended up telling her everything I'd been planning to keep to myself. Words rushed out of my mouth like my brain was on fire. I told her about looking through Dave and Myra's office, what the ghost had done and said, about the peeled up carpet, and about Myra's reaction when I told her the house was haunted and that Dave was betraying her.

I told her I asked one of the groundskeepers at my condo what *cachondo* means. He said it meant *horny*. But I didn't really need to know that, the ghost had made it clear. Still, I was curious what the word meant, so I asked.

While I talked, Kate's lips parted slowly. Her mouth opened wider and wider until I can say her jaw dropped, and I'm not exaggerating. She didn't speak, just stared at me with her mouth hanging open, not making a move to the coffee pot.

The coffee smelled strong and woodsy and so alluring, but we stood there a few feet from my desk, staring at each other.

"What are you going to do?" she said.

"I did everything I can think of."

"That's not enough."

"I can't go tell the police a ghost hinted to me that a church deacon murdered his wife and buried her in the basement and set up some phony crime scene. That he's having sex with every woman who cleans his house."

"It's so horrible, I can't even . . ."

"You believe me?"

"Of course I believe you. And it seems obvious that he killed her."

It was unnerving that Kate had such a hard time believing I'd seen ghosts in the past, and now she swallowed everything I said without any of her normal skepticism.

She folded her arms and closed her eyes. She opened them and stared up at the ceiling. She looked back at me. "We could leave an anonymous tip."

"Do they pay attention to those?"

She shrugged. "It's worth trying."

"*Then* what? If that doesn't work?"

"Let's wait and see."

"They won't search his house based on nothing."

"Maybe it will be enough to have them talk to him. And maybe that will go somewhere. And maybe someone he works with is already suspicious and this would push them to look into it."

"That's a lot of maybes. And all from a ghost?"

"You don't need to mention the ghost. Just create doubt."

We were quiet for a few minutes. A jay screeched outside, its voice so harsh it gave me the shivers.

"I think you should call," she said.

"Okay."

"I'll buy one of those throwaway phones."

She filled two mugs with coffee. We sat side by side in the armchairs and talked some more and sipped our coffees. When she finally got up to go to her office, I realized I might have found a second good friend.

IT TOOK A while, several weeks, but on Friday, Kate told me Myra had called her. Two detectives had come by to talk to Dave. They were guys he knew, but they didn't let that get in the way. They just did their jobs and asked him questions over and over and over again. Then they made Myra give them the name and contact info for their new housekeeper.

Myra's stereotype that their Hispanic housekeepers were working illegally was wrong, of course. Liz had already quit, but the newest woman was more than happy to talk to the detectives about Mr. Hicks brushing the back of his hand across her breast the second day she worked there. And then cornering her in the basement, coming up too close, whispering to her, and playing with her hair.

Bit by bit, they put pressure on him, but he never caved. Myra did.

It turned out she *had* seen the ghost — several times. At first, she convinced herself it was the hallucination of a sleep-deprived, anxious new mother. She was scared, and didn't want to believe what the ghost was saying. She didn't want to lose the man she loved. She hadn't wanted to face the shame — showing up at church, having everyone know what her husband was doing, right in her own basement.

One night when she was feeding Pamela, she looked at her daughter's trusting face and finally realized she was swallowing lies and sleeping with a murderer. She'd been afraid the ghost would hurt Pamela, but she realized her own life was in danger, and not from a wailing spirit trapped in the basement.

She invited the police to search the house, and when they dug up the basement floor, they found a woman's body. It hadn't caused the mildew smell, that really was just from an aging house, and maybe not letting the cement dry completely on the rough, hard grave Dave had given to his wife.

I remembered what Myra said, that sometimes it's better not to know the truth. I don't believe that. And finally, neither did she.

Cathryn Grant

EATEN ALIVE

A Suburban Noir Ghost Story

Published by D2C Perspectives

One

PASTOR JOE'S OFFICE is too dark. He keeps the
curtains closed so that church members who come in for
counseling have privacy. How many people does he think
are going to stroll along a narrow concrete walkway,
flanked by an ivy-covered slope on one side, that dead
ends near the back of the building in an overgrown tangle
of more ivy, then peek in through his office window to
see the back of someone sitting on the couch?

Keeping the drapes closed is creepy. All the mis-
matched browns on the upholstery of the couch and two
armchairs, and the ancient, but not antique desk look
drabbier than they are. Even worse, because of all the
bookcases, an old fashioned coat rack, and the way the
curtains buckle behind one of the armchairs, it feels as if
someone is in the room. I usually sit on the couch and
every few minutes I'm glancing to the left, absolutely
certain there's a person standing just over my shoulder,
watching. Listening.

Whenever I go into his office I want to yank the cord to pull open the drapes. I did that once. He didn't say a word. He got up from behind his desk, walked around, leaned behind the couch where I was sitting, and slowly pulled the cord to close them.

When he was seated at his desk again, he commented on the need for privacy for counseling and how he didn't want to be opening and closing them all day.

On a Tuesday in early May, as I stood just inside his office door thinking about the creepiness, he said, "What's up?"

"I need a few days off," I said.

He lifted his right eyebrow.

"I know I used up my vacation when I went to Australia, but this is important. A week, probably. I'll take it without pay, obviously."

As he leaned back in his chair, the spring squeaked. He sat forward again and looked at me as if he was waiting for me to say more.

He could stare with that slightly raised eyebrow for the rest of the morning and all afternoon and I wasn't going to say more than what I had.

Finally he spoke. "Are you committed to this job?"

"Of course. I love working here. Don't you know that?"

"It's difficult to keep the office running smoothly when you're out. We managed during your trip, but you can't take off whenever you feel like it."

"I don't take off whenever I feel like it. I asked for a

few days, for personal business. I guess I should have said that."

"What kind of personal business?"

"It's personal." My plan, which I was not going to tell Pastor Joe, was to spend a week in a motel in my home town in Marin County. I was going to visit the detective who investigated my parents' murder, and check out my childhood home. I was nervous and excited. Nervous because it had been so long, and because I'd never gone back to that house after they removed my parents' bodies. After they took me away from the house, my aunt and uncle packed up all my things.

I had this weird, keyed up excitement because the more I thought about it, the more I was sure this was the right thing to do and the right time in my life. I knew I shouldn't hope for it, but with all the ghosts I've seen over the past year or two, I was getting more and more sure there might be a way to get in touch with the ghosts of my parents.

"It's difficult to consider giving you extra time off if I don't know why it's important," Joe said.

"I wouldn't ask if it wasn't important."

He stood and walked around the desk. He sat on the edge with one leg bent over the desktop, and the other shoved out straight, keeping him propped in place. "Is everything okay?"

"Yes." That was the truth. It's been fourteen years since my parents were murdered, and if life weren't okay, then it wouldn't have been okay every single day I'd worked for him. So I figured that wasn't a lie, even though nothing was okay because I'd wanted to know who killed them for such a long time. Recently the need was growing so strong it was taking me over. I wanted the detective who was working halfheartedly on the case to put forth more effort before it was too late. Although I'm not sure what *too late* meant.

"Why are you so secretive?" Joe said.

"I'm not. It's *personal* business." I almost walked out, but decided to give him one more chance, even though he was being nosey, and possibly controlling. It was no big deal to take time off. Cindee had covered for me the last time, and she loved it. I suppose Joe wasn't quite as thrilled. Things ran smoothly, but having his wife greet visitors was the exact opposite of what he wanted — someone disconnected from the church, an automatic barrier to gossip. If you don't know the people coming into the office to see him, you can't tell any juicy stories. Although I could see over time I was going to get to know people, so maybe my value would fade.

He slid the leg that was dangling over the side of the desk to the front and lowered his foot to the floor. "Then I have to say *no*. Sorry."

"I can only take personal time off if I tell you every detail of my life?" This was important to me, more important than anything in my life right now. It wasn't fair he wanted me to tell my secrets just to get some days off. It had to be illegal, or something. He isn't a cruel or manipulative person, he's a really nice guy, but he was being a jerk just because he could. Like he had all the power, which I suppose he does. "What if I had to attend a funeral? Or go out of town because someone was in the hospital?"

"Then we'd have to work something out."

"So why can't I have some time off? It's only five days!"

"You sound like one of my daughters."

"Maybe because you're treating me like a kid."

He stood, as if he was meeting me head on. He took a few steps to the edge of his desk. He glanced at the bookcase and back at me. "I'm sorry. I didn't mean to come across that way. Do you need to go to a funeral?"

"No." I stepped backwards into the doorway.

"That's all?"

"I need some time to take care of personal things. I don't think it's any of your business."

He coughed.

"I guess that's a *no*," I said. I went out to the main office area and around my desk. I pulled out my chair but didn't sit down. The only other option was to wait for a three-day weekend. I could leave on Thursday night and come back on Monday night, but I wasn't sure how easy it would be to talk to the detective on a weekend. I should call first, but I was leaning toward showing up without any warning. If I called, he might tell me to forget it, there was nothing new, which is the same thing he'd told me every year for the past eleven years since I'd become a legal adult — *Sorry, nothing new. No suspects. We depleted all the people who might be connected a long time ago. The evidence was gone through right at the beginning. Unless we get a tip, there won't be anything new.* Yeah, I had to just show up.

I sat down at my desk. There were plenty of things to do. I had the bulletin to type up for the Sunday service, articles to edit for the newsletter, flyers to design for a senior citizen luncheon in three weeks, but I didn't feel like doing anything. Joe should realize I could have lied and said I had a funeral, or a relative in the hospital. I wasn't going to invent a story. It made me mad that he would have given me time off if I lied.

There was no sound coming from his office. The door remained half open. I stared at it, waiting for him to come out and apologize, to tell me I should take the time I needed, to assure me that he trusted me and that I wasn't some slacker who just wanted to take days off whenever I decided I'd worked too many weeks in a row, or felt like vegging around watching TV or hanging out with JD.

The outer office door opened and Pastor Kate walked in. She glanced at me. "Hi." She went to the coffee pot, pulled it off the burner, sniffed what was inside, and poured some into one of the mugs clustered to the side. "Why are you sitting there staring at the wall?"

"Just thinking."

"About what?"

I shrugged.

She sipped her coffee. "Is something wrong?"

I nodded my head at Joe's office door. She smiled. She

took another sip of coffee then went into the basement area. Her cowboy boots thunked across the floor, echoing in the empty space until she reached her office, then it was quiet.

I knew her smile was an invitation to go back to her office and tell her why I was upset, but it seemed like too much trouble. I'd end up in the same situation because I didn't want to tell Kate about my parents' murder either, even though we're sort of becoming better friends. I know you don't get close to someone by keeping everything to yourself, but this is such a huge thing, and I have to be ready for people to change how they treat me once they find out.

I'll admit, JD hadn't treated me any differently after I told him. Maybe that's one reason things are pretty easy with him. He's not super excited about me focusing on something that happened so long ago, or about talking to the detective and trying to find a way to spend some time at my childhood house to see if my parents' ghosts will make themselves known. Not at all excited, especially about the ghosts. He said he'd support me, but what does that mean? It means I can see in his eyes that he thinks I'm pinning my hopes and my sanity on something that will never happen. Still, aside from that, things are as good as can be expected with us, and he never treated me differently after I told him they were murdered.

But he's the exception. I don't normally like to tell people. I hate seeing their drifting eyeballs, pupils shrinking to tiny dots, gazing past me, feeling sorry for me, thinking I'm so helpless, and not wanting to upset me, saying nothing so I end up feeling alone. Which doesn't matter one way or another, because if they did say something, I know I'd feel equally alone. Living through a tragedy is a very alienating experience. At least it was for me. Maybe I expect too much. Maybe most people can talk about terrible things that happened to them and they don't care if the other person understands or grasps what it's like, they just want to talk, and as long as they get to do that, they're happy. I don't want to listen to myself talk, I want to connect and have people grasp how I feel, as if they'd crawled inside my brain and read my thoughts, and inside my heart and felt what's burning there. And they don't.

But then I was curious. Maybe Kate would see it my way. She's a private person. She wouldn't want to explain all the details of her life to her boss. I got up, poured my own cup of coffee, and went through the basement to her office.

When I stepped into her doorway, she was looking right at me, as if she'd been waiting all that time for me to show up.

"What's going on?" she said.

"I asked Joe for a week off, without pay, and he said no."

"Why?"

"Because I already took extra time off. And I'm giving the impression I don't take my job very seriously."

"No, why do you want the time off?" Kate plucked at

the shoulders of her shirt, a turquoise, flowy thing that looked great next to her pale hair. The color gave a shimmer to her hair as if the two were reflecting off each other.

"I don't think I should have to explain. It's personal business."

"That sounds evasive."

I took a sip of coffee. "Keeping my personal life private is evasive?"

"It shouldn't be, but it is."

"I thought you'd understand."

"I understand why you don't want to tell him details about your life, but since it's not vacation, since you're putting an extra burden on the church, you sort of have to."

"It's not any different from vacation. And how is it a burden? I said I'd take it without pay."

"Someone has to cover for you."

The conversation was going nowhere and I wasn't sure if it was because she's my semi-boss or she couldn't imagine herself in my situation.

"Tell him why you need the time, you don't have to explain every detail," she said.

"It's very personal. And I don't want to and I don't think I should have to." I backed out of the doorway.

"Wait. Is everything okay?" she said.

"I'm fine. I'll figure out how to take care of things on the weekends."

The pressing sensation that lets you know you might start crying filled my sinuses and rushed against the backs of my eyes. I walked quickly across the basement to the restrooms. I set my coffee mug next to the sink faucet. It teetered because the surface isn't flat. I turned on the water and bent over. I cupped my hands under the water and splashed it on my cheeks and eyes. The coolness took away the swollen, everything-is-going-to-spill-out feeling. It was ridiculous that I was crying over this. If I drove up on a Saturday, I could stop by the house, introduce myself to the current owners, spend the weekend nearby. I could even call in sick on a Monday, which I suppose they wouldn't believe for a minute after I'd asked for unpaid time off. And whoever believes it when someone is sick on a Friday or Monday anyway? Still, there was a decent chance the detective would be around on a Saturday.

More time was preferable, but there was no reason I couldn't take several trips. I didn't actually have a plan as to what I'd do when I got there. Was I thinking I'd ask the owners if I could sleep over, hoping to see two ghosts? That wouldn't work. I didn't want to think about any plan, I just wanted to go, to at least see the place. The plan would emerge once I saw it and remembered more pieces of my childhood. The physical things would sharpen my memories.

I squeezed my eyes tighter and scooped up more water. My face was dripping as if I had been crying and the edge of my hair was wet. I reached for the faucet and the back of my wrist hit the coffee mug. It crashed into the sink. Hot coffee splattered across my hands and a few drops hit my face. I left the water running and turned to the paper towel dispenser. I grabbed three towels and patted my face. When it was mostly dry, I opened my eyes and saw the mug was broken in two perfectly even sections. There were no chips in the ceramic, as if it could easily be glued back together.

Water continued splashing across the sink, hitting the broken mug and spraying out. I moved back and tried to reach forward to turn off the faucet without getting wetter than I already was.

The bathroom door swung open. "What was that crash?" Kate looked at the sink. "Did you cut yourself?"

"No."

"Let me help."

"I can get it." I stepped closer. Water splashed at my skirt as I reached to turn off the faucet. Dark spots of water and two stains from the coffee, creamy brown against the white, covered my left hip.

Kate stepped inside and pushed on the flap of the trash can. "Drop it in."

"I'm going to keep it."

"What for?"

"Have you ever seen anything break perfectly in two like this?" I held up a piece in each hand. The only difference between them was one half had the handle.

"Probably, I don't remember. Why would you keep it?"

"Maybe it means something. It's so perfect."

"It's a broken mug. I don't see why you'd keep it." She

laughed. "I doubt there's a message."

She was wrong. The mug was exactly like my life, broken in half when my parents were murdered. Two almost perfect halves — the fifteen years before they died, and the fourteen years since. I know that sounds far-fetched. I'd been crying and running water, splashing it across porcelain, creating a slick surface, and I shouldn't have tried to balance a ceramic mug on the edge. Of course it got knocked over. Viewing it as a message about my life was fantastical, but the perfection of the break was too strange not to view it as out of the ordinary. I've broken mugs before, but they either shattered or broke apart into several sharp fragments.

It had to mean something. I needed it to mean something.

I didn't want to tell Joe and Kate about my parents' murders. I didn't want them treating me with all kinds of knowing looks and concerned questions. I didn't want Joe to think that losing my parents to a killer had made me imagine seeing ghosts. He already thought the second half of that, so I could see how he'd pack it all into a box and think he had it figured out. I also didn't want them to start preaching at me. I don't think Kate would, especially now that we knew each other better and are more like friends than boss and employee. Especially after witnessing a ghost herself.

Aside from feeling lonely because they didn't know, and angry because they didn't think I should have time off, I needed that mug to mean something. To be a sign that I was on the right path, that this was the perfect time for putting the two halves of my life together and figuring out where I was headed.

Until now, there's been nothing solid in my life. I stumbled into being an administrative assistant because I had a part-time job as a receptionist when I dabbled in attending community college for a year after high school. I didn't stick with college because I had no idea what I wanted to do or be. Being an admin is easy in some ways because people tell me what to do. I've had two boyfriends, including JD, and felt partially disconnected from both of them, never sure if I loved them or not. I've taken pottery and calligraphy and yoga classes. When I was a child I took ballet and piano lessons, but that stopped immediately the day my parents died. I didn't know who I was, and I had to go back and try to find out why they were killed, even if it sounded crazy that I was relying on the chance of meeting their ghosts and a detective who had already told me many times they had no leads.

I turned and looked at her. "My parents died when I was a teenager. I haven't been back to that house, and I really want to do that."

Tears filled Kate's eyes. She reached out to hug me. It was rather awkward since I was still holding the broken mug.

"I'm so sorry," she said. "Why didn't you ever say anything?"

I shrugged.

"Was it a car accident?"

"I don't want to talk about it."

"Okay. I understand, although talking can help."

"Maybe."

Two

ON THE WAY home from work I stopped at the grocery store. As I wheeled the cart down the aisles, goose bumps ran along my arms. I kept shivering which made it hard to concentrate on figuring out what I wanted for dinner. I stood in front of the glass case filled with meat — all red and pink, begging to be cooked, but I had no idea what I was in the mood for.

At one end of the case was a section for pre-roasted chicken. It smelled delicious and sounded easy, but what was I going to do with a whole chicken? The butcher, a middle-aged guy with curly brown hair and a vinyl apron, I guess so splattered blood could be easily wiped off, asked if I needed help.

"I'm still trying to make up my mind."

"Take your time." He stood near where I was. I glanced around, hoping there was someone else he could offer to help, but I was the only one.

Having him stand there, watching me, made it even

harder to think about what I was hungry for. My stomach grumbled. The roast chicken was smelling better every minute. "Does the cooked chicken freeze very well?"

"Sure does."

"I'll take one of those. The smallest one you have."

Wheeling the chicken in my cart didn't get me any closer to dinner. I could make it easy on myself and buy potato or macaroni salad from the deli, but I try not to fall into that habit all the time, otherwise I'd eat nothing but food someone else made.

Finally I decided on tacos. I could cut up part of the chicken and shred it, add beans, salsa, some avocado and lettuce and cheese. Having a mission made it easier to walk around the store, instead of just blankly rolling past all that food.

At home, I sliced up the entire avocado, chopped half of it and put it into a small bowl and sprinkled on Italian dressing. The rest got stuffed inside the two corn tortillas I'd cooked quickly in a pan with a little oil. I watched *Rear Window* while I ate my tacos and ate the extra avocado. I've seen that movie twice already, but I was in the mood for the slow, quiet unease it generates and I was not in the mood to eat and let my mind wander around all the obstacles to finding out about my parents, starting with no time off.

When the movie was over, I poured a glass of iced coffee, added cream, and stirred it for a few seconds longer than necessary. I changed into jeans, thick socks and shoes, and a sweatshirt and went out onto my back deck. It wasn't quite dark, but almost. A light breeze carried the smell of stew or soup from my neighbor on the left. They're a couple with two kids. Based on what I smell coming out their kitchen window, they're always having stew or soup. My neighbor on the right is a guy who writes software code and seems to work all night because quite often when I get up for a cigarette in the middle of the night and go out onto the balcony attached to my bedroom, his light is on. He's like a nocturnal animal, holed up in there, sometimes not coming out at all during the day, at least from what I've observed. I talk to him once or twice a week, but only brief conversations about the weather, about our mutual neighbor who has his front porch piled with car parts and how the homeowners' association should make him clean it up, the neighbors who we think might be growing pot inside because they have foil on their windows, and other impersonal topics.

I sat on the wood lounge chair and looked out over the open space behind the complex. I sipped the iced coffee and tried to think about the next step in my plans, or non plans.

It occurred to me I could quit my job. I definitely need a job on a long-term basis, but there's enough money from my parents that I was able to buy the condo when I turned twenty-one, and there's still a small buffer in case I get laid off or fired. That wasn't likely to happen, so I could fire myself.

I like working at Central Avenue Church. I like Joe

and Kate, and Joe's wife, Cindee. I feel like I'm forming a bit of a family there, although I don't know if they see it that way. Is it really a good idea to view your employer and co-workers as your family? Probably not. Still. I feel at home. I suppose a church is different than working at a business, so maybe it's okay to think of them as family-like.

But I was pissed off that they wanted to know my personal life before they'd allow me take time off. So maybe they aren't family at all. If they were, I'd tell them about my parents' murders. I actually don't completely understand why I'm so secretive, whether it's only because they'll never be able to feel what I feel and yet they'll view me differently, or if there's more to it than that.

Quitting was an intriguing idea. It might be nice to have a fresh start. I'd already worked in high tech and didn't care for the pressure and long hours, so I had no idea what that fresh start would be, since high tech is the main industry in Silicon Valley. The church job is calmer, and gives me more opportunities to be creative — editing the newsletter, designing the layout, and finding fonts and images to make it look more interesting. I could go back to school, but that would make my cash stash shrink too far, too fast, and I feel secure knowing I have money right where I need it, in case my life goes off the rails. Besides, I haven't figured out what I'd study, what kind of career I'm actually interested in.

There's something exciting about quitting your job,

making a sudden change. But maybe that excitement was only in my head. It wouldn't be that way in reality. And I wasn't supposed to be thinking about my career future, I was supposed to be figuring out how to settle my past.

I was stuck having to either make up a story or break down and give Joe just enough information to let me off the hook.

The neighbor who'd been cooking stew closed the window and the smell dissipated. I got up and went inside, grabbed my cigarettes and lighter, and returned to the deck. The air was still. The leaves on the water gum trees were frozen shadows in the pale light given off by lights in the condos and the moon. Nothing moved in the greenbelt. Usually there are a few crows or jays fussing around out there. Sometimes the wild grass moves as cats or possums slink through, invisible except for the wake they leave behind.

I pulled a cigarette out of the pack and put it between my lips. I cradled the lighter in my hand, feeling its slim body that gave no hint of the dangerous liquid inside, the power it had to explode into a flame that itself could create instant destruction. Every so often, when I flick it and the fire shoots up in front of my face, I wonder about touching the tip to dry grass or fabric. It's not that I would ever come close to doing that. I wish I understood where that impulse comes from, if it's even an impulse. It's something more subtle, curiosity, or a desire to see something startling happen in the midst of the sameness of life. Maybe it's an impulse that's only found in developed countries where people have all their needs met and everything is so good, relatively speaking, our animal sides get buried and they're itching to reveal themselves, to not atrophy deep inside of us. Unless I'm over-thinking it. Maybe I'm the only one who has thoughts about fires, or driving my car off a bridge just to see what it's like. I don't think about actually doing it, the idea of doing it forms in my mind. It fades as quickly as it appears.

Before I could flick the starter on the lighter, a breeze moved across the deck and out over the greenbelt. It carried a strange odor, like food left inside a car in eighty-degree weather. Then it was gone. I held the lighter to the tip of the cigarette. My hand shook a bit, maybe because the smell made me feel lonely, with no one there to comment on it, no shared wrinkling of our noses and gagging with disgust.

Once again the night turned airless, but as if the breeze had stirred up something that had kept itself hidden before, the odor crept back. It was so faint, I wasn't quite sure if it was the memory of it or the actual thing. I lit my cigarette and took a quick drag so I could fill the space with smoke.

I can't always smoke on the deck in the summer because the stew-cooking family complains. Smoking is still allowed by my homeowners' association, but there are several multi-family complexes in the area that have banned it, even inside your own condo, which I don't do anyway. It's becoming more of a problem every year. I know there's an entire social movement that wants me to quit. And I want to quit as well. Yet we live in a very confusing world where smoking cigarettes still pops up in movies, and it's never a withered old person, hacking and coughing up gobs of mucous or blood. It's always someone hip, someone independent and maybe a little tough and confident, doing what needs to be done. I'm that kind of person. And smoking is relaxing and mind-settling and all kinds of good things. But soon I'll have to sit in my car because every other place will be illegal. And maybe when that point comes, the good parts won't be enough anymore. Although I know I should quit now, or at least try harder than casually eliminating one cigarette a day every few months. I haven't eliminated one in over a year anyway. I've been stuck at three a day for as long as I can remember.

My downstairs ashtray was on the deck. I pulled it closer. It's a low, flat bowl, glazed dark blue and pale gray that I made in one of my first pottery classes. I tapped off the ash and stared up at the sky. A few stars had winked into view and everything looked so calm, so peaceful, a perfect suburban landscape.

After a few minutes, I got up and walked to the railing. The smell had returned. It filtered up under the smoke, and through the evening air that was growing damp, making the backs of my hands and my face sticky, as if the dew was filled with pollutants. I went back to the lounge chair, picked up the ashtray and snuffed out my cigarette. I tucked the ashtray under the chair so if the wind sprang up overnight it wouldn't scatter ashes and the cigarette butt across the deck.

I walked down the steps onto the path that runs behind the condos. I was pretty sure that the spoiled food smell, worse than spoiled food, worse than rotten fish, was something dead — a possum or a small bird the crows had picked over. It was odd that it would be right out in the open. I really don't know where wild animals go to die in suburbia, but you rarely see them unless they're hit by a car. I've never seen a dead crow or rat or mouse. And the dead songbirds I've seen didn't drop from old age.

The odor was less intense on the path. I took a few steps toward the stew-cooking neighbor's house. I smelled nothing or maybe something, I was sniffing so hard, it was getting difficult to determine what was memory-induced and what was real. Sometimes pursuing something obsessively makes it seem larger than it really is.

I walked in the other direction to the software developer's house. There's a bunch of old lawn chairs on his deck, leaning against the back wall of his unit. He also has ten or twelve stacks of empty clay pots, so I guess he's a bit two-faced to gossip with me about the condo with car parts on the front porch. Four or five pairs of shoes were lined up near the clay pots — shoes he never seems to wear that were left outside because he had a *no shoes in the house* rule that was abandoned at some point. I don't think he'd had his windows cleaned in a few years, and the blinds on his kitchen window have seven or eight bent slats so they don't close all the way. Maybe he'd left garbage on his porch and an animal got into the bag and died. I wasn't sure when he'd last been out through the sliding glass door because all those pots and shoes blocked the way.

Near the foot of the steps leading from his deck to the path was an empty Corona bottle. I picked it up with my fingertips and then didn't know what to do with it. Leaving it on his deck seemed rude, but it wasn't right that I now had to carry a dirty bottle into my house to put in my recycling box or all the way to the concrete enclosure where the dumpster and community recycling bins are housed. It might not even belong to him. He may have a messy back deck, but he doesn't throw trash around. The groundskeeping service must have missed it. I thought about moving it into a more prominent location so they'd catch it next time, but that made me feel like I was littering. It wasn't even my bottle and I was annoyed that now I felt responsible for it.

I set it back on the ground. I'd decide later if I should take the high road and carry it to the recycling. Right then I wanted to see if the smell was coming from under his deck. It had grown stronger, or maybe just seemed stronger because it had taken root in my nasal cavity.

There are three steps to each back deck from the path. Walking up the stairs meant I was trespassing, sort of, but the smell was stronger near the steps. I assumed he wasn't home because he wouldn't be able to tolerate the smell. Or it was something under the deck. I decided I wouldn't mind if he walked onto my back deck, especially if there was something not right, so I climbed the steps.

The drapes were pulled across his sliding glass door and the blinds closed tightly over the kitchen window, except for those bent slats. His condo is the mirror image of mine. The smell was pretty much the same at the edge of the deck, but when I walked under the balcony, it was more intense. I put my hand over my mouth, glanced around and didn't see anything, so I hurried back to the edge and down the steps. I left the beer bottle where it was and returned to my deck.

I had no idea what to do. I could walk around and ring his bell, but that just seemed like busy work resulting from knowing I should do something and that normally if there's a problem with your neighbor, that's what you do. But it made no sense to go ring someone's doorbell when I knew he wasn't home. It wasn't possible with that smell. It wasn't coming into my condo, so I could just watch some TV, chat with my birds and let them perch on my finger, work on my crochet project, call JD. The list could become endless. In the morning, I'd see if the smell was still there. But if there was something under his deck, I didn't want it rotting further overnight, attracting bugs, rats, or something worse.

I went inside, closed my sliding glass door, walked through my condo, and out the front door. There was no smell out front. Leanne, my neighbor two units down, was on her front porch. The light, about fifty watts too much, shone on her like a spotlight. Her deck is filled with potted orchids — fifteen or twenty of them, white and yellow and a very pale green — still in the black plastic containers that come from the nursery.

She held a metal watering can up high, obviously almost empty, the spout tucked into an orchid that was filled with yellow and pale green blooms. She wore a baby blue spaghetti strap top and jeans that showed her belly, even though the temperature had dropped to jacket-weather. I tugged the cuffs of my sweatshirt over my wrists, suddenly realizing I was cold, and walked along the sidewalk until I was in front of her porch. "Hi," I said.

She moved to the next orchid. "What's up?"

Leanne is about fifteen years older than me. She's single and has three cats which never go out, but I see them sitting on the windowsill watching the world pass by. I talk to her when I see her outside and she does the same. Compared to the others in the complex, she and I are friendlier than most, although she knows more about me than I do about her, which I suppose means I sometimes talk too much.

She knows where I work, and she knows about the dead bodies I've stumbled across, although I haven't mentioned the ghosts to her.

I don't even know what some of the residents look like, much less spend time talking to them, or even saying *hi* when we pass each other near the carport.

"There's a bad smell coming from Larry's back deck."

"A smell like what?"

"Something dead. I'm not sure what to do."

"Did you ask him about it?"

"I can't believe he's home and putting up with that smell. It's bad. Really bad."

"How bad?" She smirked and put the watering can on the half wall surrounding the porch. "Did you *check* if he's home?"

"I didn't see the point. There's no way he could stand being in there."

"Well that's what I'd do."

Her voice was even-toned, as if that was the no-brainer thing to do — the one thing that seemed a waste of time and illogical to me. "You don't know how strong it was. He can't possibly be home."

"Why don't you go ring the bell."

"But then what?"

She walked down the steps. "Why are you so hesitant?"

"I'm not. He's not home, so it won't accomplish anything."

She started along the sidewalk and I followed. She walked up Larry's steps and rang the bell. I waited on the sidewalk, taking deep breaths, unsure if I just wanted to clean out the bacteria from that smell creeping inside me, or if I was trying to detect it out front.

She rang three more times before she gave up, maybe as stubborn as I am. When she turned and walked slowly down the steps, she looked past me, trying to work out if she could see the carport from where she stood. She didn't acknowledge I was right, and I tried not to smirk back at her, although I was definitely smirking inside. No one could be home with that smell.

"Well I didn't smell anything," she said.

"Come around back."

I went through the gate to the narrow ally separating my end unit from the next building. We didn't even hit the side of my back deck before she took a quick sniff of the air.

"Oh, that's vile," she said.

"I know. At first I thought it was garbage but I think something died under his deck."

"Something's dead somewhere," she said.

We walked around the edge of my deck, along the path, and up to his steps. Leanne put her hand over the lower part of her face. Her breathing was loud and rough as she pulled air in and out of her mouth. To me, that's almost worse than smelling something foul, because even though I don't smell it as much, it's still there, and then it seems like I'm getting it in my mouth which just makes me feel sick to my stomach.

I walked to his steps and knelt down. I looked under the deck but it was too dark to make out anything. The smell wasn't any less or any more. I put my cheek on the path and then bravely took a deep breath just to be sure. I stood up and brushed the grit off the side of my head and my sweatshirt and jeans.

Leanne looked at me like I was crazy. "I'm going to call animal control."

I walked up the first two steps. I don't know why I

was looking again — it was all the same, the stacked chairs, the empty pots and shoes. Maybe something small was caught between the pots. I moved to the top step and glanced at the closed drapes and the sliding glass door, a blank wall. I took another step closer. The door didn't look right.

I crossed the deck and stopped a few feet away. The door was wide open but I hadn't noticed earlier because of the drapes being closed. I glanced back at Leanne. She looked even more horrified than a moment earlier. Both hands covered her face and she'd backed up to the stairs leading to my deck. As I watched, she took one hand off her face and gestured with a sweep of her arm that I should return to my own deck.

I pushed the drapes to the side and stepped in.

The room was watery gray and the odor so strong I knew that what was dead wasn't under the deck, and I had a sickening certainty it wasn't a wild animal.

"Madison!"

Leanne's voice was faint, her mouth obviously still covered by her hand, the thick drapes behind me blotting out sound. I knew she wanted me to run out the door. I wanted to run, didn't want to see what I knew I was going to find because that smell was now so hideous, it couldn't belong to anything but a human being, lying exposed above the ground, when all the rot that he'd turned into belonged in a deep, dark hole.

Then I pictured Larry with his longish blonde hair, thin gold earrings in both ears, broad shoulders and his tall wiry body. I tried to hold that picture as I stepped forward so that it would burn itself into my brain and dominate whatever final image I would have of him.

The gray quality of the light came from a lamp with a sheet of protective film over it, presumably to keep the glare off his computer. The entire living room where I was standing had been designed around his electronics. There was a massive flat screen TV to my left and a brown leather couch facing it with a rather small space between the two, half of which was occupied by a rectangular, utilitarian coffee table. On top of the table was a large pottery plate with a half-eaten hamburger that looked so hard it resembled a ceramic model of a burger. Three French fries and a puddle of mustard lay on the opposite side of the plate. The mustard was hardened to a plastic shell.

Behind the couch was a long desk and on that sat a seventeen-inch computer display, a keyboard and mouse, and stacks of notepads and a bunch of pens. A beer bottle and a large white coffee mug were near the left side of the keyboard. The computer screen was dark.

The dining area beyond had a table and three chairs. The chandelier overhead was on but the dimmer switch turned very low, as I hardly noticed the glimmer of light except to see that three of the six bulbs were burned out.

I stood there, looking at the room, knowing I should leave and call the police, but always too impatient to do what I'm supposed to do. I was also a jumbled mash-up of terror at what horrible thing I might see, along with an insane curiosity. I tried to think when I'd last talked to Larry. The burger and fries had transformed beyond mold into a petrified meal which meant they'd been there for a few days.

I walked behind the desk and into the kitchen. The counters were wiped clean, glistening like tiles in a model home. The sink was also spotless, the faucet buffed to a shine. There wasn't a single crumb or drop of mustard. It was so clean compared to his bent blinds and his cluttered back deck it felt like I'd entered another house. I went to the fridge. A dishtowel hung on a rack at the end of the counter. I wrapped it around my hand and opened the fridge. Everything inside was packaged, so it was impossible to tell if there was something spoiled by age. Beer bottles — Corona — filled the top shelf alongside a few bottles of water. The other shelves contained organic peanut butter, jam, jars of condiments, and other odds and ends. I closed the door.

The bathroom on the first floor looked unused, so I started up the stairs, putting both feet on each step. The fear of what I would find on the second floor returned with double the force. The smell wasn't any worse, but it seemed to grow heavier, like a wet blanket settling over me, penetrating my nostrils and growing like mold inside my nose, creeping toward my lungs. I put my hand over my mouth and nose and took shallow breaths, trying to find the scent of my skin, the fresh, familiar odor of living cells so I could wipe out the stench of the other.

Just like in my condo, there are five steps, then a small

landing, and the stairs turn with seven more to the second floor. The minute I reached the top hall, I saw into his bedroom. An arm hung over the side of the bed. This would definitely be the time a normal person would back away and call the police, but I thought I would just take a quick peek because I really couldn't walk away not knowing. Being so close, knowing he was dead, not wanting to see any signs of decay which would be too awful, but wanting to see if I could get a sense of how he died. I took a step forward and paused. My inclination was to take a deep breath to prepare myself, although why we think breathing deeply provides preparation, I have no idea. I suppose it's some kind of natural thing that sends oxygen into your blood vessels and maybe releases calming hormones. It doesn't really matter because taking a deep breath would have been too sickening.

I walked to the bedroom door. Larry was on his stomach, his head at an awkward angle, his face turned away from me. His hair was spread out across his brow and cheek so I couldn't see his face, which was fine with me. His left arm hung over the side, the skin tinged with black and his fingernails almost shiny. He wore a tan t-shirt, although only the sleeves were still tan because most of it was dark with blood. He wore black jeans and black socks. The handle of a large knife protruded from the center of his back. The white comforter was covered with blood. I closed the bedroom door and went downstairs.

DETECTIVE MARTIN, WHO came to check on Larry,

Cathryn Grant

wore slacks and a white shirt. He looked more like a business executive than a cop. He had short brown hair streaked with gray. It was creeping away from his forehead, but his face looked younger than the level of his hairline. He used a smartphone to take notes, and didn't waste any time starting his lecture that I should not have entered the house and I should not have gone upstairs.

"Why not?" I said.

"It's a crime scene," Detective Martin said.

"Well I didn't know he was murdered."

"The smell should have told you that."

It's probably not a good idea to argue, or point out errors to a detective, but I couldn't help it. "The smell told me something was probably dead, but it didn't specify murder."

"Don't be smart," he said.

I smiled a very apologetic smile and he seemed to soften a bit.

"Please wait outside," he said. "I'll want to talk to you."

"I live next door, can I just go home and wait?"

"Please remain on the back deck."

He went upstairs while I unfolded one of Larry's chairs and sat down on his deck. Leanne had gone home when I called the police. She didn't want to be involved, but I told her if they asked about the process of finding Larry, I might need to mention I'd gone to her house. She insisted it wasn't necessary to provide that detail. "I'm not like you. I don't get all excited about crime," she said.

"I don't get excited about it."

"Well you like answering questions."

"Not really."

"Whatever. I want to stay as far away as possible."

I assured her I'd do my best to avoid mentioning her.

While I waited, the coroner and a uniformed cop arrived. I could see through to the front door, and they walked in without knocking.

After a while, Detective Martin came out onto the deck. "Was the bedroom door closed when you found Mr. Brighton? You didn't mention opening it."

"It was open, but I closed it when I left."

"You shouldn't have done that."

"Oh."

"Why did you close it?" he tapped on his phone and waited, his finger hovering over the screen.

"I guess it seemed more dignified."

He nodded as if he totally understood, but made quite a lengthy note in his phone.

"How long have you lived next door to Mr. Brighton?"

"He moved in about four years ago."

"Do you know him well?"

"Define *well*."

"How often do you talk to him?"

"A few times a week."

"Have you been in his home before? Has he been in yours?"

"No, to both."

"Have you met any of his friends or family?"

I shook my head.

"Do you have any idea who might want to kill him? Did he ever mention any problems? Legal? Financial? Drugs or alcohol?"

"No."

"Have you seen women over here?"

"No."

"Ever hear any fights with visitors?"

"No."

He asked a bunch more questions but they were all equally unproductive. It began to seem as if I didn't know Larry at all. How could we share one thin wall and see each other a few times a week, yet I knew absolutely nothing except that he worked on computer software and liked country western music which I heard coming out of his house when the sliding glass door was open? I knew he wanted a vegetable garden but never got around to planting it. That's it. After four years. He'd been lying in there dead for five days, the coroner had estimated. Five days and I didn't smell a thing or hear a thing and I didn't realize I hadn't seen him around. He was in my life several times a week and then I didn't see him for five days and I didn't even notice. I felt like I was self-absorbed and unfriendly.

Finally, Detective Martin told me I could go home. I went inside my condo and closed and locked the back door. I put the piece of wood in the track that hopefully prevents anyone from forcing the door open and wondered if I were being silly. Maybe someone Larry knew had killed him. The house didn't look messed up, the computers were still there, so it wasn't robbery.

I went upstairs and stood at the window that faces the front. Finally, I saw them go into the house with a gurney. It was another twenty minutes or so before the gurney emerged and they lifted it down the front steps and slid it into the back of a van.

Even after they drove away, I stood at the window and thought about Larry never coming home again, lying alone in a morgue, unable to control his coming and going, people poking over his body, and him turning into an object, not really him at all. I tried to remember what he looked like when he smiled, but I couldn't.

Three

AT TWELVE-FORTY-THREE in the morning, I realized I was not going to be able to sleep. Every time I closed my eyes, I saw Larry's arm, his hands almost black with pooled blood and the slow eating away of all the things that create a living body. I sat up and turned on the bedside light. One of the parakeets chirped softly from the cage on my dresser, as if it wanted to say *hi*, but didn't want to wake the others. I clicked my tongue slightly and it was silent after that so maybe it was looking for a bit of comfort in the darkness. I'd like to think I can tell the difference between the chirps and whistles of Simon, Sara, and Sierra, but I really can't. Maybe after I've had all three of them for a few more years I'll be able to distinguish their sounds.

The door to my balcony was partially open and I imagined I could smell Larry's body, left alone for all that time. I knew it was my imagination but I still felt more than a little ill. I got out of bed, grabbed my cigarettes out of my bag, and went onto the balcony. The sky was cloudy with only two or three stars poking through and no moon. I shivered and went back into my bedroom. I put on athletic socks and grabbed my robe.

Outside, I lit a cigarette and leaned on the rail, staring out at nothing. Larry's condo was dark, which wasn't surprising, but I wondered if it had been dark for five days and I'd never noticed. All these condos — there are sixty-six in my complex, in clusters of three, all of us leaving for work, coming home with groceries, buried inside cleaning, having friends to dinner, living out our lives, and there are only about twenty or thirty people I even recognize by sight. And of the few people I know and the even smaller amount I say hello to, or exchange more information with, I still knew nothing important about Larry, how he really spent his time, and certainly not his enemies or problems. For all I knew he was a gangster doing software code as a cover, or he owed money to someone who wanted to punish him for failing to pay it back. Although I was pretty sure people like that used guns rather than knives to deliver a message.

I bent over and picked up the ashtray off the balcony floor — another effort from my pottery class with red and golden swirls of glaze. I balanced it on the rail, and tapped the excess ash into the bowl. The smoke in my mouth and nose was more pleasant than usual, wiping out the deathly stench that had crawled into bed with me. I shivered. I put the cigarette between my lips and rubbed my arms hard. My elbow bumped the ashtray and it crashed onto the deck below.

A sharp cry came out of my throat. My eyes and nose filled with tears. It was hard to see anything except my hand holding the cigarette. I loved that ashtray. Even though it wasn't very good, it was mine, and something I worked hard to try to form into a semi-functional dish. It meant a lot for that reason, but I wasn't really sure why I was so upset, over-reacting, really. The inside of my throat tightened and I could feel huge gasping sobs trying to push up from my belly.

I did not want to stand on the balcony crying and howling for all the neighbors to hear. I inhaled some smoke, hoping it would make the tears and tightness go away. I blew it out very slowly. The ash grew longer. I didn't want to carry it through my condo because one of my rules is to not smoke inside. The rules help me stick to my plan of only three smokes a day. The ash dropped and disappeared into the darkness. I was trapped with a burning thing in my hand that I couldn't put out and couldn't get rid of.

A moment later I was gasping for air. I felt I was in the middle of the Pacific Ocean, no land anywhere in sight, my arms and legs exhausted so I couldn't move them enough to keep my head near the surface, water splashing my face and sloshing into my mouth. Instead of coughing as salty water hit my throat, I tried to breathe more, sucking it into my lungs. Is that what life is — always alone, impossible to breathe? I felt that I was the only human being in the entire complex, one neighbor dead, my other neighbor not caring. How can a man lie dead in his condo for days and no one even knows? It's so wrong.

Who would notice if I died? JD, I suppose. But how many days would it take until he thought that not responding to his text messages or phone calls meant something was horribly wrong? And if he was camping with his friends . . .

If it were the weekend, no one at the church would know I was gone. And my neighbors wouldn't notice. Surely not Larry.

Even if they did notice, would it matter? I was alone in my condo, no one to talk to but three small birds. Me and my cigarettes, as if they could give me comfort. I could call JD but what would I say? He was so far away, and I kept him that way, pushing him to stay in his own home, not sure I wanted to get closer but still feeling so alone.

I knew my mind was creating an imaginary existence that wasn't really accurate, a world where everyone but me, and Larry, had mates and children, parents and siblings and friends. Even now, they were safely enclosed in the walls of their homes, each one's breath mingling with the others, their dreams helping the others, steering away nightmares and making room for the good dreams. Husbands and wives had someone to hold. All I had was this guy occasionally in my bed, a guy I ate dinner with and talked to, went hiking with and to the beach, watched movies, but were we really connected? He kept saying we should live together, but why? Did he think I was his one and only? I wasn't sure. I wasn't sure about anything. I felt like the universe was a cold, selfish, unfriendly place that had no room for me.

My friend Renee would call this a pity party, which is cute and amusing when you're complaining about gas spilling out of the pump, or a clerk opening a new register and not taking people in the order they've lined up. That's a pity party. But when you feel like you're a solitary person in the world, a tiny part of the brain might whisper it's a pity party, but mostly it hurt. I hurt so bad, I couldn't stand without leaning on the railing.

I took a long, hard, mind-freezing drag on my cigarette. As I slowly released the smoke, I wondered if I didn't exist at all. The greenbelt was dark and silent, no birds or any other creatures. My parakeets hadn't uttered a peep since I'd been standing there. No one on the earth knew where I was at that moment in time, standing and looking into the darkness. There were no lights shining onto back decks as far as I could see. Larry's place was the darkest of all. It was hard to distinguish the outline of the railing around his back deck. The way our units are aligned, I've never been able to see his balcony from mine. That's supposed to be a positive feature — enjoy your outside space without your neighbor looking right at you.

After a few more minutes my cigarette was down to the filter, and as I stood there, it died. I held it in the palm of my hand and carried it inside. I walked through the bedroom and down the stairs. I got the trashcan from under the sink, went onto the back deck and felt around for the pieces of the ashtray. They thudded against the plastic when I dropped them into the trashcan. I let the cigarette butt fall on top, then thought about breaking my rule and having a fourth.

Instead I locked up, put the trash can under the sink, and drank a glass of water.

When I was back upstairs in my bed, I rolled to my side, facing the balcony, and pulled my knees up to my chest. I tugged my nightshirt down so it stretched partway over my lower legs. I was still wearing the socks, but didn't want to get out of bed and remove them.

I closed my eyes and of course my brain began to race even faster than it had before I'd gotten up. I'd thought smoking would lull me to sleep and instead I'd destroyed my pottery piece. I started to cry again.

Scenes of everything wrong in my life danced through my head like tiny chipmunks, chattering and laughing, but their faces not sweet like a chipmunk's face usually is. Their mouths were pulled back, their teeth exposed for the sharp, dangerous weapons they are. Their eyes glittered and bulged like they'd gone mad, and their chattering voices verged on shrieks.

I turned over but it did no good. Images of my parents lying dead, bullet holes in their foreheads, rose up in vivid color, as fully formed as a 3D movie. I remembered my first boyfriend and how he said I talked too much and was kind of an airhead. I thought about JD and how upset he was that I didn't want to move in together. At least I think he was upset. And it sounds contradictory to say I was drowning in loneliness but didn't want to live with my boyfriend. The thing is, he seemed like he wanted that not because he couldn't be without me, but because it was some sort of logical next step. Or maybe more convenient than passing back and forth between each other's homes.

After another round of images flashed by — my parents, JD's inscrutable face — thinking about how I had no career plans, no extended family, no close friends, I flipped to the other side.

It was building like a pot of steam. I wanted to scratch at the walls, but I have very short fingernails so that wouldn't be very satisfying. I wanted to scream and throw something, a lot of things. Break all my sad little pieces of pottery. I wanted to stand on my balcony and wail. I had no idea what was wrong with me and it started to tickle at the back of my mind that maybe those mad chipmunks were hinting at something wrong in my brain.

AT TWO-SEVENTEEN I decided to call JD. If he's supposed to be in love with me, why was I lying there torturing myself? If he really loved me, he wouldn't mind a two a.m. call one bit. If you love someone, you're there when they need you, even if all the trouble has been created inside their own head, even if they seem mad. Even if they actually are a bit mad. Can someone who's mad be loved? And what is madness anyway? Is it a complete raving lunatic, or are we all teetering on that line?

It took a few seconds for the cell phone to figure out what it was doing, and then his phone rang. He picked it up on the second ring.

"You okay?" he said.

"No."

His voice was suddenly crisp, deeper, as if he'd sat up in bed. Maybe turned on the light. "What's wrong?"

"I found a dead body."

"At two in the morning? Where?"

"No, earlier. It's my neighbor. There was a horrible smell and I went into his house, the door was open. He'd been dead for a few days. After I talked to the detective, I finally fell asleep, but then I woke up and I started thinking about things, and decided to call you before my brain exploded."

He laughed. "What things are you thinking about?"

"Life."

"I can see why that would explode your brain. I try not to think about big subjects in the middle of the night. Sleeping is better."

"Really? If I could sleep, I would."

"Well stop thinking so much."

I swallowed. I wanted him to make me feel better, not imply I had some defect because I couldn't turn off the rush of thoughts, coming one after another, waves on the shore, never stopping, never pausing for breath. "I feel terrible that Larry was in there all that time and no one noticed he wasn't around. He disappeared from the earth and the only one who knew he was gone was the person who killed him."

"He was murdered?"

"A giant knife was sticking out of his back."

"I guess that explains why you can't sleep."

"Yes." This was a partial lie, but I didn't want to tell him all the other stuff on the phone. I wanted him to be holding me. I wanted to smell his skin and feel the heat from his arms and chest. I wanted him to say he'd be right over. Aside from all my other bad thoughts, there might be a killer living in my condo complex, or somewhere nearby. He might have seen me go into Larry's place, he might think I knew something about Larry, some secret that couldn't get out. And even if that was all my imagination and needless worrying, I still wanted JD to say he'd come over.

"Did you try getting up for a while? Watch a little TV? Have a snack or something to drink? That helps me. I also count sheep."

"That's stupid."

"It works."

"I had a cigarette and it made me more awake."

"No kidding. Nicotine is a stimulant. That's why I don't smoke at night."

"Yes you do."

"Okay, hardly ever."

"Usually it relaxes me."

"That's all in your head."

So maybe he did think I was mad. I wasn't sure what to say. I wasn't going to ask him to come over. There was a temptation to hint around the idea, but that would just make me feel demanding and high maintenance. I wanted it to be his idea.

It was possible he was lying there, or sitting there, or maybe walking around by now, thinking that if we lived together I wouldn't need to call, wouldn't need to wake him, or if I did, he could just roll over and kiss me and stay half asleep. Maybe he thought I wouldn't be waking in the middle of the night, thinking too much, if he was sleeping with me all the time. And maybe he would be right. Why was all of this so confusing — having a boyfriend, trying to figure out love and how to be together. Although love isn't something that should be analyzed and figured out.

"I'm not criticizing you," he said.

"I didn't think you were. Or not too much." I thought I could feel him smiling in the dark, far away over the foothills, right near the coast, but connected to me by invisible particles in the air, our voices sounding as if they were right next to each other in the bed, pillows side by side, parts of our bodies touching each other.

"Do you want me to come over?"

"Why would you say that?" An even better question is why I would ask that when I was wishing he would suggest coming over. But suddenly, now that he'd said it, I felt like a helpless child.

"You sound scared. Or upset. I want to be with you."

"It's the middle of the night. You have to go to work tomorrow."

"You have to go to work too. And my shift isn't until eleven."

"It seems like too much trouble."

"Don't play games, Madison. What's wrong? You're not usually like this. And unlike most people, you've seen murdered bodies, before."

He was right, I was playing games. I wanted him to come over, called him hoping he'd come over. Now that he offered, like the awesome guy he usually is, to drive forty miles through the hills and come to my place just in time for us to have an hour or two and then have me get up, waking him again as I rattled around in the bathroom, I was backing away. I didn't know why I was trying to discourage him. Did I want him to insist? Or maybe I didn't want him to feel obligated.

I snuggled down under the comforter and turned on my side. I stared at the blackness beyond the glass door. The drapes were open, which is how I usually have them, but the door was shut tight, not half open so the breeze and night air could come into my room. "I want you to come over," I said. "I'm scared and kind of down. But I know it's a lot to ask and I don't want you to do it unless you really want to."

"That's more like it. More like you. I'll be there in an hour."

I heard scuffling from the birdcage on my dresser, as if the parakeets were noticing I'd already started to pull myself out of the gloom.

AT THREE-TWENTY, JD rang the doorbell. By then, I really regretted asking him to come over. I felt weak and needy and scared of the dark. He wasn't going to get any sleep and he would have to drive back to the coast and then be friendly and charming and alert mixing and serving drinks until nine that night when his shift ended. This was exactly why he wanted to move in together, but I kept putting him off and refused to tell him why I wasn't ready. I did tell him that he wasn't quite on the same page as me when it came to digging into my past, seeing if I could nudge the detective to work harder on finding my parents' killer. But I knew that wasn't all of it, and from his perspective, that probably sounded like an excuse.

I opened the door. He was at the far edge of the porch, outside the circle of light, staring at Larry's condo.

"He's gone," I said. "They took his body away before I went to bed."

"I know, just looking."

I stepped back and he came inside. He set his backpack on the floor, pushed the door closed, and locked it. He flicked off the light, turned, and scooped me up in his arms like a cat. I laughed. He carried me up the stairs and put me on the bed. He kicked off his shoes and stripped off his t-shirt and jeans and boxer shorts. He climbed into bed and pulled the sheet and comforter over both of us.

His skin felt cold as he rolled closer and put his arms around me. He slid his hands up under my nightshirt. I bit my tongue to keep from shrieking.

"Did I chase all the monsters away?" he said.

"Don't make fun of me."

"I'm not."

We settled down and I was glad he didn't try to make love and he didn't tell me what a pain I was for refusing to live with him then asking him to make a bedside call in that vacant space between two a.m. and dawn, the emptiest time in the world.

We fell asleep without saying another word. I heard the parakeets murmuring and then I was dreaming.

In the dream, it wasn't just Larry's hands that were black with settled blood, but his arms up to the biceps and his jaw and ear and neck on the exposed side of his head. Someone was behind me, pushing me into the room, whispering that I had to look at his face. It was important to turn him over. Doing that would make the dark stuff recede and he'd look more normal, not splotched like something dragged up off the bottom of the bay. He'd look human again. But I didn't want to look at his face. I didn't know if his eyes would be open, staring at me, the eyeballs frozen like they were made of glass, if his tongue would be out — large and too big for his mouth.

The hands pushed harder on my back and shoulders. Despite their strength, I didn't move forward but I knew I couldn't hold out much longer. Eventually I'd weaken and fall forward. If that happened, I'd land on the edge of the bed and when I put out my hands to break my fall, they would brush against his cold, possibly pulpy flesh. I tried to move to the side, tried to see who was pushing me, but no matter how I twisted, the person stayed out of my line of sight.

Then I was in a different house filled with birds. It was the living room of my childhood home, but there were no hallways or connecting rooms, just the living room filled with the furniture I grew up with. There were so many birds, swarms of them, they lost their appeal. They looked ugly with hard, mean beaks, their eyes sharp, black beads. Birds were everywhere. Sitting in huge crowds on the seats of the sofa and chairs and lined up on the backs. They were clustered on the ceiling fan and everything was coated with white sticky bird droppings. The racket was so loud I couldn't hear myself when I tried to ask where they came from. I tried to walk across the room but was afraid of stepping on a bird.

After that, I was back in Larry's bedroom but his body was gone. The bed was clean and perfectly made. It seemed as if he hadn't been killed after all, but then why would I be in his bedroom? I fluffed the pillows on the bed and turned, and there was a knife, covered with dry, crusty blood, placed on the dresser next to a hairbrush and hand mirror. The knife handle matched the handles of the other objects.

Then I woke up.

JD was snoring and I was just as miserable as I had

before I called him. A lot of good that had done. I got up, grabbed my cigarettes, and was about to head out to the balcony when I remembered my broken ashtray. I bit my lip so I wouldn't cry, and went out of the bedroom and downstairs to smoke on the deck.

I lit a cigarette, inhaled, and stared out at the greenbelt. The sun wasn't actually coming up, but the sky was growing light enough that I could make out the delicate parts of the tree branches instead of just the inky blackness of a solid object.

Connected to nothing, not my dream, not Larry's death, or my plans to go back to my childhood home, I suddenly realized why I didn't want to live with JD.

If I move in with him, I'll be choosing a path, and I'm not ready to do that. Right now, I can keep going, and everything seems possible. But the more you choose things, the smaller your life gets. The road of my life will be split in two and all kinds of things will be forgotten along the sides of the road I'm not walking down.

I probably won't join the Peace Corps, or move to Europe or New York City. I might not go back to college and I won't sell everything and travel around the world for two years. I won't be an FBI agent or a fashion model or a pilot.

Not that I necessarily want to.

It's possible I could still do some of those things, but every big decision you make erases other possibilities. And I don't want to do that. Not yet.

Four

THE NEXT DAY was one of those days when I veered into thinking I'd made a mistake taking a job in a quiet church office. All day it was like a cemetery. Pastor Joe had a full schedule of hospital and nursing home visits, and Kate had gone with the seniors' group to an exhibit called *Beyond Belief: 100 years of the spiritual in modern art*, sponsored by the San Francisco MOMA.

No one came into the office and the phone rang one time all day. I'd finished typing and printing the bulletins for the Sunday service the day before, so there wasn't much to do.

When you're trying to figure out whether you're obsessing too much about the past and when you're recovering from a night filled with dark thoughts and bad dreams, it's not a good time to sit at a desk and stare at empty armchairs and a closed office door, with the entrance to a dark, empty basement looming a few feet away. Even the gardener wasn't working that day. The preschool was in session, but unless I go outside and up the stairs to the classroom wing, I never see the teachers. I rarely hear the kids because their play area is at the opposite end of the property.

Finally I was so bored, I opened a new file on my computer and typed a list of the reasons someone might have killed Larry. It was short — *owed money, cheated on a girlfriend, stole something, lured someone into a pyramid scheme, gave someone a bad stock tip, took credit for someone's work, stole another person's software code, moved in on another guy's girlfriend.* I'm sure there were other possibilities. The reasons are probably endless, but those were the ones I thought of.

It crossed my mind that I could make a list of why someone might have killed my parents. The minute I had the thought, my hand started to shake so violently I wasn't able to control the computer mouse. I put both hands in my lap and twisted my fingers around each other. My mouth was dry and I couldn't swallow, no matter how I kept trying, which made my throat ache.

After my parents' murder, the cops had questioned three transients, but the likelihood any of them had a gun was slim. There were no signs that a stranger had broken into their house. When I came home from school the day they were killed, the front door had been locked. The detective asked me that many times. I still remember. It's one of the few things I do remember. The constant repetition of that question, and the constant repetition of questions about whether anyone I didn't know had called or come to the house in the previous few weeks. Over and over. I know it wasn't that they didn't believe me, they were trying to be thorough, to jog my memory. I was a traumatized teenager and I'm sure they thought I was burying my experiences, but it started to feel like they didn't believe me. That, or they thought I was too stupid to answer correctly the first fifteen times.

The police have no idea who killed my parents. No idea why they were shot in their bed. I don't either, but since I also had no idea why anyone would kill Larry, I decided what the heck, and made a similar list for my parents — *bad stock tip, pyramid scheme*. The little black characters raced across the screen as I typed, making it seem as if I was inventing parts of their lives. I felt terrible, as if I were suspicious of them doing bad things, but I pushed that thought away and kept going. It occurred to me that I had to start thinking about them as real people, people that had faults or might have done something wrong, if I was going to try to find out about their deaths.

Then I wrote the hardest word: *cheating*. I closed the file.

I surfed through YouTube for about two hours, then took a long lunch. I bought a copy of Cosmo and read that for most of the afternoon. At ten to four I decided to leave early. I put the phones to voice mail and told myself it was wild imagination, worrying that ten or twelve people would call in the next hour and Joe would be annoyed that I'd taken it on myself to say it was okay to leave the phones and the office unattended.

AFTER I PARKED my car, I went to my condo and stood on the front porch staring at Larry's identical front porch. There was a strip of yellow crime tape across the opening, but other than that, nothing looked different. It seemed as if any minute his front door might open. He'd step onto the porch and nod at me, or if he weren't buried in software code and just coming out for a fast food run, he'd walk over to talk for a few minutes.

Inside my condo, the air tasted stale and dry. The heat made it feel like a tangible being putting its hands on my shoulders. I opened the sliding glass door in the dining area and the window over the kitchen sink. The downstairs bathroom has a tiny window facing the back which I keep open almost all the time. I turned on the kitchen ceiling fan to draw air into the bathroom. As I stood in the hallway listening to the fan, it occurred to me that Larry might also leave the window open in his small bathroom. I wondered whether the police would notice and close it.

After dinner I cleaned up the kitchen and vacuumed the living room and watched a little TV.

When the sun was fully down, I opened the flashlight app on my phone and put it in my pocket. Even though it was still warm out, I put on my hoodie, zippered it halfway up, and shoved a pair of dishwashing gloves inside. I braided my hair and folded it up and put a second hair tie around it to keep it from swinging all over the place. I got a glass of water and went out to the back deck. I drank half the water and put the glass on the small table by the chaise lounge. I walked down the steps.

For a few minutes, I stood on the path. Once I walked up Larry's steps, I'd potentially be getting myself in trouble, but only if I got caught. And what would bring the cops to his house in the evening? They'd collected all their evidence. Now they were busy talking to people and waiting for autopsy results. I've never understood the point of an autopsy when someone is murdered. There was a knife sticking out of his back, what else could they possibly find? If he had drugs in his body, how did that matter? If he died from one stab wound rather than another, how would that help them find the killer?

I didn't know what I thought I'd find in his house that the police hadn't noticed. Maybe it was pure nosiness. Even though they surely took his computer and were analyzing the age of his uneaten dinner and most likely had taken all the other interesting things out of his drawers and closets, there might be something to catch my attention that they thought was irrelevant. I'm sure a female administrative assistant who tends to obsess over trivia looks at the world differently from a police officer trained to gather evidence. Besides that, there was the real reason hovering beneath the surface — maybe Larry's ghost was there, waiting to make itself known, waiting for justice, or something else. Waiting for me.

The bottom step creaked as I walked up onto his deck. I tiptoed close to the condo, then laughed at myself. It wasn't as if anyone might hear me. I went to the bathroom window, hoping I wouldn't be disappointed. If Larry *was* like me, and kept it open all the way, the police might not have noticed. I thought there was a good chance they hadn't, or had simply left it open because those downstairs bathrooms get really muggy really fast if you close the window.

I put on the gloves and carried one of his patio chairs over and set it under the window and climbed on. I pressed my hand against the screen. The window was open. A more difficult question would be whether I could get myself up there and through the opening and onto the toilet without damaging the screen or the toilet lid or myself.

I popped the screen out and set it on the deck. I took off my hoodie, wrapped my phone inside, and tied the sleeves around it. I dropped it through the window. I thought about taking off my tennis shoes to make myself lighter and more nimble, but decided I might need the traction and I didn't want to go in barefoot and leave toe prints when I'd been forward-thinking enough to bring rubber gloves. I don't know if they collect toe prints, or if toes even make a distinctive print, but I imagine they must.

The opening was about two feet wide and less than two feet high. It was large enough for me, but the squirming and trying to pass myself through would still be tricky. I placed one foot on each arm of the chair, grabbed the top of the window frame, lifted my left leg, and stuck it through. It took quite a bit of wiggling and some contortions, but I managed to get through fairly quickly, which made me think I should start closing my bathroom window when I wasn't home.

I flipped the switch and the light came on. I'd expected they would have turned off the electricity and water, but maybe they were waiting for Larry's relatives, or someone named in his will, if he had a will, to take over. Then I realized I was advertising my presence and flicked it off. I turned on my flashlight app and held the phone low so it wouldn't flicker through the window.

Although the entire condo beckoned with the possibility of small, telling parts of Larry's life, I decided to start with the bathroom. There aren't many personal things in my downstairs bathroom, but you never know. I opened the cabinet under the sink. It was much emptier than mine — a can of powdered cleanser and a hard, withered sponge. The shelves behind the mirror contained a disposable razor, a bottle of aspirin, and a stack of dimes. It was a strange place to keep coins, but I'm sure I have things in my cabinets that would look out of place to others. I'm sure everyone does. I closed the cabinet. There's no tub or shower in the downstairs bathrooms of the two-bedroom units, just the toilet and sink.

Next I went to the kitchen. It was just as clean as it had been the day before. I opened all the cupboards and each one contained what I expected — plates and pots and pans, spices and cans of food. He had seven different kinds of cooking oil, including sesame oil, so I guessed he liked to make stir fry.

The contents of the drawers were equally average. He didn't seem to have a clutter drawer. Instead, the narrow drawer at the top where I keep my odds and ends was empty. Maybe there had been junk and the police took it.

I was getting discouraged and started second-guessing myself. It was arrogant or naive, or both, to think I was going to offer some special insight, find something that would tell me about his life, and even more optimistic — his death. The only thing that kept me going was knowing this was better than returning home and trying to sleep, spending another night of madness battling dreams and morbid thoughts and self-pity. I hate it when people indulge in self-pity. It's one thing to feel occasional waves of it, but it's another to make it the focal point of your life, sucking other people into your drama, steering conversations to all the ways life has specifically chosen you as an object of harassment. When I start feeling sorry for myself, I try to do something, even if it's having a cigarette, which I suppose is just as damaging as self-pity.

I took all the cleaning products out from under his sink. Maybe something had fallen out of the trash, which sometimes happens to me, but there was nothing. Again, either very thorough police officers or a very neat guy. And he did seem very neat, except for his back deck. His house was super clean, almost as if he hadn't actually used it much, never used the downstairs bathroom, rarely cooked at home, just kept the supplies there in case he decided to start doing it at some point.

Maybe he had two lives, the public one downstairs that refused to reveal his personality, and, hopefully, his real life upstairs. There was nothing left from his work life, the police had taken all the computer equipment as well as the remains of his meal. There wasn't much else to look at, some framed prints on the walls, the TV, and the furniture. I got down on the floor. Sure enough, they'd swept out anything that might have been forgotten under the couch or the armchairs. The dining table and two chairs gleamed. They looked brand new.

I ran up the stairs, impatient to prove to myself that worming my way inside a home where I didn't belong hadn't been a waste of time.

The landing was open to the first floor and there were two bedrooms, just like my place, with a bathroom between them.

The spare bedroom was set up as a sitting room. There was one armchair and a second TV. Next to the chair was an antique oak end table where he'd placed a small lamp, a coaster, and a bowl littered with the crumbs of roasted peanuts. The table had two drawers with metal fixtures featuring rings as drawer pulls.

I opened the top drawer. Inside was a stack of greeting cards bundled together, secured by an oversized rubber band, and a squat jar filled with marbles. I shook the jar. The marbles clinked on the glass with a sound like they were submerged in water. I put it back in the drawer and pulled out the stack of cards. A tiny prick of awareness, a needle in my heart, told me I shouldn't be going through his things. But he was dead. And they were just greeting cards, not love letters. *And* he was dead. I assumed the police had looked at them and found them uninteresting. I put them on the top of the table, shut the drawer, and opened the bottom one. It was empty, but there was a border of dust around the edges so I guessed there'd been something of interest to the police in that drawer. By the size of the ring of dust, maybe a photo album.

I removed the rubber band and counted twenty-six greeting cards. The top card said, *Happy Birthday! Now You're Nine!* The cards up to age twelve were the same — now you're ten, now you're eleven . . . the last two were sealed inside envelopes with a return address to Peter & Michelle Sanford, 1432 Merriweather Drive, Saratoga, California.

The messages in the other cards were printed. There were no personal notes in any of them. They were signed Aunt Michelle and Uncle Peter with lots of x's and o's. The upper left inside corner was dated March 25 and the year. The dates started in 1988 and ended in 2011. The card from 2011 contained a photograph. The picture was cut so that most of the background was gone and the three people filled the entire narrow space. It showed a man and woman with a boy between them, standing slightly in front. The boy looked to be about ten or eleven, maybe twelve — I'm not very good a guessing the ages of kids. The man wore a baseball cap so it was hard to see his face and he had a dark, somewhat large, mustache. The woman had short, curly dark hair and wore sunglasses. They all wore bathing suits, although the woman had a flirty little skirt covering up the bottom half of her bikini. She was a little old to be wearing a bikini, but she looked good in it, so I could see why she wore it.

The boy had longish, tangled dirty blonde curls. He was barefoot but the man and woman were wearing slip-on tennis shoes. Even though the boy scowled at the camera, looking like he wanted to scratch out the eyes of the person taking the picture, I knew it was Larry. In fact, he hadn't changed much. Larry always had a little kid look about him, and seeing the picture made me think he'd never grown up.

On the back of the picture, someone had written in blue ink: *See how happy we were?*

That was a strange message to put on a photograph. Why do you have to insist you were happy? And the kid did not look happy. The man and woman didn't look exactly ecstatic either. They weren't frowning, but the woman's smile looked posed and the man's mouth was hidden by the mustache which made him look like he wasn't smiling at all. His right gripped the boy's shoulder, either trying to get the boy to smile, or perhaps propping himself up. I assumed they were Larry's aunt and uncle, unless he'd stuck another picture inside the greeting card so it wouldn't get lost.

Why would someone send a picture of people who didn't look one bit happy and insist they were? Why was their mood pointed out at all? It seemed like part of an ongoing conversation in which Larry said he was not happy, and had a miserable time on that vacation, or growing up overall, and the note-writer was compelled to argue with him, to send documentation that he was wrong. He was happy. *See? We were happy.* But he wasn't.

I held the two unopened cards on the palm of my hand. They felt strangely heavy, whether they contained more snapshots, or possibly a letter, or they just felt heavy because I was violating Larry's life by considering opening something he'd left closed. I wondered why the police hadn't opened them. Maybe they hadn't even removed the rubber band and didn't realize there were two sealed envelopes. In that case, was I tampering with evidence if I opened them? I thought about taking them home, sleeping on it, but then I'd be left needing to get back inside the condo to put them back. And what if the police returned and closed the window? What if his family took over the house and closed the window?

The unopened cards grew weightier on my palm. I set them on the table and got up. I walked to the window and put my hand on the cord to open the drapes. Then I let my hand fall back to my side. Of course the drapes had to stay closed. If someone were watching, they'd think the house had been broken into, or there was a ghost. It had been broken into, but not to steal anything, so that meant it wasn't really a crime. But anyone calling the police wouldn't see it that way and neither would the police. I backed away from the window.

As I turned the room grew darker. The flashlight app

on my phone had gone out. I didn't see why that would happen unless my battery died, but it had been at least half charged when I left my condo. The flashlight shouldn't have drained it that fast.

A faint bit of light penetrated the drapes, enough that I could see the outline of the chair and table, the cards still sitting there. I picked up my phone and pressed the button to wake it. Nothing. I put it in my pocket. I would be able to get out of the house fine without it. If nothing else, I knew the floor plan and could follow it without light since I did it all the time at home, in reverse.

The cards would have to wait. I opened the drawer and pushed them inside. I left the drawer open, debating with myself. After a minute, I put on my sweatshirt, zipped it closed, picked up the unopened cards, and tucked them inside my sweatshirt. I hoped they wouldn't get bent when I crawled back out through the bathroom window. I closed the drawer.

As I moved closer to the doorway, my throat tightened. It was difficult to breathe. At first I thought it was guilt over stealing the cards. Even if the police thought they were uninteresting, even though Larry was dead, they didn't belong to me. He didn't want them opened, so what right did I have to read them? But he was dead. He'd never know, or maybe he would, who knows what the dead can see. But would he care? Do we care about secrets revealed after we're gone? We work so hard to protect them when we're alive. Some people spend their whole lives and all their energy guarding their secrets, polishing their reputations. But what about after? And I wanted to know.

It was becoming more and more difficult to breathe. It felt as if fingers, or something stronger, were closing around my neck, pressing on my windpipe. I wrapped my arms around my waist, holding the cards in place, trying to give myself a little hug in the hopes that I'd stay calm. I took a few steps closer to the doorway. The pressure grew more intense. I gagged. I stumbled forward and leaned against the doorframe. The hallway was dark. I'd planned to search that next, but without the flashlight app, and without my breath, it wasn't going to be possible.

After a few minutes, the squeezing lightened and I took deep gulps of air. I pushed some strands of hair that had come out of my braid off my face. I lowered my hands and put them in my pockets. Something brushed across my face, not just the light touch of a piece of hair, but something that stroked my skin from my forehead, down the length of my nose, across my cheeks and tapped my lips. I swept my hand across my face. The minute I moved my hand, something brushed it again. It felt rough, almost scratchy, like a fistful of hay, or a thick rope. I stood still for quite a few minutes. Just as I was ready to make my way into the hall, it happened a third time.

When the sensation stopped, I looked toward the door to Larry's bedroom and saw a figure, or the faint shape of a figure. I didn't think it was a police officer, or a technician. An official person would have spoken, I think.

My hands started to shake. If it was Larry's killer, come back for something else, it was too late for me. My heart felt like someone had scooped a big hole in it, taking out all the flesh and leaving thin sides that trembled like flower petals in a violent wind.

"Hello?" My voice gave away my fear. I said it again, trying to sound more firm. "Hello?"

There was no response. I couldn't see a face, just a carved out pit like a melon scraped clean where the face would be. "Who are you?" I whispered.

The hallway and the entire condo were silent. Quieter than when I'd entered, as if all the life and air had been sucked out of it. "Larry?" I could barely hear my voice.

I took a step forward. "Who's there? Is that you, Larry?"

The figure remained silent and motionless.

I walked slowly toward it, desperately hoping I'd see the face. It was so disturbing without it, not that ghosts always have faces, but this one seemed to have more form to its body and the lack of a face was scaring me. When I was about two feet away, the figure shrank back and disappeared. My eyes were blurry, as if I'd just woken up and they were filled with sleep and I couldn't get them to focus.

It looked like the ghost might have stepped into Larry's bedroom. I'd left that room for last because it had a different intensity — the room where a life had exited the planet. I walked through the doorway. More light came into this room because the drapes had been taken down. The bed was stripped of all the linens and everything that had been on the dresser and nightstands were gone. There was an armchair shoved in the far corner.

The figure wasn't there.

I walked further into the room. It was still difficult to focus my vision so I continued blinking which was making my eyes tired and dry.

I sat on the corner of the bed. It gave me the creeps, sitting where he'd been stabbed and bled to death. I kept to the very edge hoping that I wasn't anywhere near the blood. I was sure it had mostly pooled around his body and soaked into the comforter and sheets that were now gone. Maybe being that close to where he left his life behind would open the door for his ghost to return. If it was him.

There was no way I was going to lie down on the bed and rest, or sleep, so I couldn't stay all night, but I thought I'd give the ghost time to find the courage to return. Or maybe it was watching me, seeing what I was up to, and had no interest in revealing itself again.

I'm not sure how long I sat there. My legs started to ache because I was so close to the edge of the bed, keeping my muscles flexed to prevent me from sliding off. It was unlikely I was going to be able to return to his condo. Someone would notice the open window and I'd be locked out. I really didn't want to leave without seeing the spirit again, finding out what it wanted. Inside my sweatshirt, the corners of the envelopes poked into my ribs. I shifted and felt myself start to slide as the corner of the mattress caved down. I scooted back and crossed my legs. That made my muscles jitter more.

The room was getting colder which wasn't helping the stability of my shaking quads. I stood and went to the sliding glass door. It was closed and locked but I could feel the cold air pressing against the glass, even without touching it. Cold spread out from it, grabbing at my skin, as if the glass was a sheet of ice. Outside the sky was clear, filled with stars, the moon a thin sliver.

I turned back to the room and saw the spirit just outside the door. Once again I felt pressure on my throat. Behind me the cold coming off the glass covered my back. I shivered. I swallowed hard which made my neck and throat feel worse, tight and gasping for air.

The thing still had no face and the body was now indistinct. Wisps of wavy hair fell across what should have been the forehead. It groaned and seemed to fall back against the wall behind it.

I'm sorry. I wanted to be a different kind of man. The voice sounded weepy and pathetic, as if the spirit was more sorry for itself than for whatever it was apologizing for.

"What," I said. "What are you sorry for?"

It consumes you . . . stronger than human willpower.

"What are you talking about?" I took a few steps toward the bed. The cold from the glass doors followed me. I shivered more, unable to stop, not wanting to touch the bed, and for some reason, suddenly afraid to walk around it. I didn't want to get close to the thing, and I wasn't sure why I was moving toward it. I guess it's some kind of natural inclination when you don't understand what someone is talking about to lean in, as if getting closer will clarify things.

I thought I'd find him here, but I suppose he's done with me. He was already done with me.

"Who are you?"

The place where the face should have been grew darker, as if there had been the brief suggestion of a face and now it was collapsing in on itself. I closed my eyes. I couldn't look. Some kind of decay was eating away the face. I felt sick to my stomach. Without thinking, I sat down hard on the bed. I put my hand palm down to keep myself steady. I knew instantly the blood hadn't dried. There was so much, and it had soaked in so deep. Even though it wasn't touching my skin, I could feel it slick and thick on the palm and fingers of my rubber glove. I jerked my hand up, opened my eyes, and stood. The figure in the hallway was gone.

It sure hadn't looked anything like Larry, but how could I know? It hadn't looked like anything. The things it said could have been said by anyone.

Now I had blood to get rid of. Somehow I'd have to wash the gloves completely clean and then get out of the condo. They'd probably taken all the fingerprints they needed, but I wasn't a hundred percent, absolutely without a doubt, certain, so I felt I needed to keep them on.

I went to the bathroom and used my left hand to turn

on the faucet. It took quite a while to fumble around in the dark with getting the water hot and managing the soap, the rubber gloves making me clumsy, trying not to touch anything, including myself, with the blood-smeared glove. I also tried not to think about the fact I had Larry's blood on me. I was more successful with soap management than I was managing my thoughts.

Finally, I thought they were mostly clean, they had to be clean after all that water. I rinsed the sink and then dried my gloves and the counter around it and then realized I was now leaving a wet towel. I stood there for several minutes, debating whether I should take it with me and risk someone noticing it was gone, or leaving it and risk them finding it still damp. And then I wondered what I was so worried about. It wasn't as if I'd get arrested for going into a crime scene. Would I?

Five

THE MINUTE I got back to my condo, I called JD. I told him what happened but left out the part about taking the cards. When I finished, he was quiet for a few minutes. Finally, he said, "So you have no idea who the ghost belonged to? Not even a guess?"

"No."

"Maybe the person who killed Larry? Maybe he's dead too."

"That would be a huge coincidence," I said.

"Not if Larry was involved in some kind of gang."

"Have you ever heard of a software developer in a gang?"

He laughed. "Not when you think of a street gang, but a white collar crime gang."

"Maybe."

"Well who else could it be?" he said.

"Anyone. Someone who lived there before."

"Did Larry ever mention seeing a ghost?"

"No, but it's not like we had in-depth conversations."

"Since you probably shouldn't go back, I guess you'll never know."

I opened a bottled coffee drink and took a sip. I hopped up on the kitchen counter and drank some more. "I might."

"Are you sure that's a good idea?"

"I was worried the whole time and then I realized, what would they actually do to me if I got caught?"

"Accuse you of tampering with a crime scene."

"What does that even mean? They already took their evidence. And I didn't really tamper." Well, maybe I had, but I hadn't told JD that yet.

"Breaking and entering."

"But isn't that only a crime if you steal something?"

"You know you're taking a risk, that's all I'm saying."

I swallowed a huge gulp of coffee. The icy coldness felt smooth going down, all the rich coffee and creamy milk blended so completely it was its own drink rather than coffee with milk. "I took even more of a risk."

"What's that?"

"Two of the cards I found were sealed in their envelopes."

"You opened them?"

"Not yet. I took them."

"You kill me. Why do you have to be so damn curious?"

"Aren't you?"

"I'm curious about you."

"You're curious about why I'm curious?"

He laughed. "You're cute."

"Cute and curious."

"What do you think you're going to find out reading greeting cards?"

"I wonder why he never opened them."

"Taking them isn't going to answer that question."

"How do you know?"

"Fair enough. Are you going to open them?"

"Soon."

"Why are you waiting?"

"I'm talking to you."

"I can hang up."

"I think I'll sleep on it," I said.

"Why are you so indecisive? Just open them."

"I felt bad taking them. I feel like I'm invading his life. But he's dead, so I'm really not. I don't know . . . Once I open them, that's it."

He yawned. "I'm tired so I'm gonna hang up now. Let me know what you decide."

"I will."

"I love you," he said.

"I love you."

I put the cards on the dining table, leaning against a fat, half-burned candle. I really did want to sleep on it. I thought about discussing it with Kate. No matter how much I told myself he was dead, I felt like I was prying into his life.

I realized I should have shown them to the ghost. I

wondered if it would have reacted.

THE NEXT DAY I arrived at the office before Pastor Kate or Pastor Joe, which was not unusual. They have a lot of meetings and other activities going at night, and fairly often Joe ends up at the hospital or a nursing home in the middle of the night when someone is about to leave this world and enter the next. If there is a next. I think there is, there must be, but no one really knows for sure. Joe thinks he knows for sure, everyone at Central Avenue Church operates on that belief. I wish I could be as damn sure as they are. You'd think I'd be more certain, since I've seen people who aren't from this world, but I'm not. Who knows where these ghosts come from? We think we know, but we don't. And I guess that's why they're so scary — most times, the ghosts don't look anything like you'd think someone enjoying paradise would look, and so the somewhat logical conclusion is the ghosts have come from an in-between space, and people seem to have decided that's not a good place to be from.

Based on the spirits I've encountered, they aren't particularly happy, so maybe the perception that it's not good is accurate. But then, most people on earth don't seem all that happy, so what's the difference?

I made a pot of coffee and as soon as it burped to signal that it was finished, I filled a mug — the one that's pale pink with no design on it, which I prefer because it's got a larger than average handle so I feel I have a better grip on it. I checked voicemail and wrote up the messages for Joe and Kate, read email, and added some new upcoming events to the church's online calendar.

The office door swung open hard and fast and Kate stepped inside. She was wearing her red cowboy boots with a white skirt and a white sweater, and all of that white, including her pale whitish blonde hair, made her look like she'd stepped in a bucket of blood. I'm sure I had that image because of smearing Larry's blood on my rubber gloves the night before, but still, I couldn't stop staring at her feet and sort of wondering why she'd chosen that shocking combination of white and red. I love her cowboy boots, but it was too dramatic. Of course, Kate is a dramatic person. Maybe that's why I've gotten to like her so much. That, and she listens to me. Since she had her own encounter with a ghost, she's stopped dismissing my experiences. Although she hadn't talked about what happened in quite a while, which made me a little bit nervous about bringing up the subject. I didn't know for sure where she stood on it at this point in time. But I definitely wanted to get her take on the ghost, and on whether I should open the greeting cards. Maybe. I'd see how it went and then decide.

"Nice outfit," I said, very nicely, not catty.

"Thanks."

"I love those boots."

"You always say that. Are you trying to get me to give them to you, or buy you a pair?"

"No."

She half smiled, went to the coffee pot, and filled a

mug. She dropped her bags on the floor — she always has two or three — and settled into the armchair nearest the coffee pot. "What's new?"

"I just saw you two days ago," I said.

"So nothing new in your life?"

I smiled.

She laughed. I worried her shaking arm was going to splash coffee across all that white, but she kept the mug steady. "There's usually something new with you."

"Is there?"

She nodded and sipped her coffee. She stretched out her legs and turned her feet, looking at her boots as she rotated her ankles one way then the other.

"My next door neighbor was murdered. Stabbed in the back."

"Oh my God!" She pulled in her feet and sat up straighter. "Were you there?"

"No, I found his body. He'd been dead for a while. There was a terrible smell. His back door was open so I went inside. His bed was soaked with blood and he was in the middle of it."

"When was this?"

"Tuesday. Then something else happened."

"What?" The coffee cup was in front of her mouth so I couldn't see her whole face. Her voice sounded nervous, as if she knew where this was headed.

"I snuck into his house last night."

"You broke in? What if you got caught?"

I shrugged. "I already did it, so I guess it doesn't

matter now."

She asked how I got in and I explained. With each word, her eyebrows rose higher on her forehead until it looked like her face was going to split in half. Then I told her about finding the greeting cards, but not the unopened ones.

"That doesn't sound particularly interesting."

"I think the police took all the good stuff."

"Or maybe there was no good stuff," she said.

"He was so nice. I can't see why anyone would want to kill him."

"Maybe it was random." She took a sip of coffee and put the mug on the table.

"The police didn't say that."

"You should stay out of it. There's nothing you can do."

"I saw a ghost."

"What is it with you? Do they follow you around?"

"I have no idea. I guess I'm a sympathetic listener."

"You're more of a talker than a listener."

"Not when I'm alone."

"Well no one's a talker when they're alone, unless they're mad," she said.

Her comment made me think about that horrible, long night after I found Larry's body, scared that I was losing my mind. The feeling hadn't returned, and I wondered if going into his house had kept those demons, or whatever you call them, from getting their claws embedded in my skull.

"I do wonder why they're attracted to you," she said.

"I'm very open."

She picked up her mug and took a long swallow of coffee. She half-coughed and said, "True. So tell me about your ghost."

"It's not *my* ghost."

"Okay. I assume it was your neighbor and he didn't scare you and you remained calm and open and he told you who killed him and why. Of course, that can't be true or you wouldn't be concerned with greeting cards."

"I have no idea who it was, but I don't think it was Larry, and I have no idea who killed him, or why. The cards are all I have, even though they're hardly anything. They're signed by his aunt and uncle, with one photograph. Except . . ."

"Except what?"

"Nothing. The ghost had no face and . . ."

"Do they ever have faces?"

"Sometimes. The Blue Lady at The Distillery did. But this was different. It was an empty pit, caved in or decayed or . . . It's hard to describe. It was almost more of a feeling than actually seeing anything. I asked who it was and there was no answer."

"Maybe if he's dead, he doesn't know who he is."

"Maybe."

"It sounds like you don't know anything."

"I have to go back. If no one closes the window."

"Don't you think if the ghost is in a condo, it could come through the wall and find you, if it was so eager to talk to you?"

"It doesn't know where I am."

"How do you know?" She stood and drank the rest of her coffee. She re-filled the mug but didn't sit down again. "I should get to work."

"There's something else."

She stepped closer to her pile of bags and waited.

"Two of the greeting cards were sealed in their envelopes."

"Interesting. Did you open them?"

"No."

"Why not?"

"Do you think I should?"

"Yes."

That surprised me. I expected the opposite from her. I thought she'd lecture me for not leaving them in the drawer. I expected her to tell me I shouldn't violate the dead.

"Something makes me not want to, or at least wanted me to wait."

"You're crazy. No one is stopping you and you might find out something. He's dead, the police didn't want them."

"What about relatives? They might want to see his life as it was."

"Since they're from that aunt and uncle, he mustn't feel very close to them anymore or he already would have opened the cards."

She had a point. But the more she insisted I open them, the more hesitation I felt. Almost as if I'd waited so long I'd passed the right moment and now they should remain sealed forever. As if the spirit, or Larry's spirit, unseen by me, had followed me out of the house and was pressing me to keep his confidence. But it wasn't really his confidence, he had no idea what the cards said. "Maybe he knew what was inside and so he couldn't open them. Maybe there's bad news."

"Who sends bad news in a greeting card?" she said.

"Maybe someone died, and they sent the news with a sympathy card?" Even as I said that I knew it wasn't true. I'd checked at home, the cards both came during the third week of March, one each year. They were obviously two more birthday cards. The reluctance to open them grew and my body felt heavy, unwilling to touch the cards ever again. Although I'd still have to do something — destroy them, or take them back.

"You're making a huge deal out of an unimportant decision. I don't know what your problem is. Usually you just grab something and run with it."

I shrugged.

A shadow passed by behind the drapes that cover the sliding glass door behind my desk — Joe.

Kate must have seen his shadow too. She splashed more coffee in her mug and picked up her bags just as the door opened. She said *hi* and immediately disappeared into the basement area.

I turned to my computer and started poking around with the mouse. My head was unsettled, like there was more I wanted to talk to her about, although I wasn't sure what that was. The cards, I guess. The more I waited to open them the more momentous they became, expanding in my mind, as if they were messages from beyond the grave, something that would reveal Larry's entire life, when really, they were probably just cards with the names of his aunt and uncle scribbled at the bottom.

I felt Joe watching me. I turned.

He glanced at the coffee pot. "It looks low, do you mind making another pot?"

I nodded. I got up and went to the coffee maker, turned it off, and picked up the carafe to go rinse it out.

"You seem moody," he said. "Don't hold a grudge over not getting time off."

"I'm not."

"You aren't very talkative."

"I'm all talked out."

"Why?"

I shrugged.

"You need to be cheerful if anyone comes into the office."

"I know that. When have I not been cheerful?"

"Right now."

I lifted the pot in his direction. "I'm headed to make the coffee."

"Thanks." He went into his office.

While I rinsed the pot and refilled it, I wondered why he was suddenly picking on me — no time off, ordering me to be more friendly. I'm always friendly. That's why ghosts are attracted to me. At least that's what I think.

I walked back across the basement. I wanted to talk more about the cards with Kate, but I was supposed to be working, so I decided to wait until my lunch break, hoping she wouldn't go out.

I poured water into the coffee maker, only half concentrating on what I was doing, so some of it splashed out on the coffee cart. Maybe the ghost really had attached itself to me and Joe was seeing that sunken face in me.

If that were true, and if Pastor Joe felt its presence in some way, he might be capable of seeing ghosts. A bit of a leap, but I laughed out loud. Not just a quick laugh, I giggled for several seconds.

He appeared in the doorway. "Everything okay out here?"

"Yes."

"I didn't mean you should start acting goofy."

"I'm not. Just laughing."

"What's so funny?"

I couldn't tell him. Things were already rocky and I knew he would not think it was funny. In fact, he'd be pissed off. He'd try to hide it, acting all professional and pastoral, but he'd be pissed.

"I had a dream that I was making coffee and the water was the color of coffee but didn't taste like coffee. When the coffee brewed, it turned clear and was just water. I kept making it over and over. And since I just made a pot half an hour ago, and I'm doing it again, it reminded me of the dream and I laughed."

I'd never told such a ridiculous story in my life. I don't

know where the idea came from, but it flowed right out of me as if I'd been planning it, or it was waiting there to help me when I was in a tough spot and sort of needed to lie, but not really tell a full-on lie.

Joe smiled. "That's amusing."

"Not really. I guess I spend a lot of my life making coffee."

"Well you sure drink a lot. I'll make the next pot." He went back in his office.

For some reason, I felt I needed to smooth things out between us, even though he was trying to be nicer, offering to make coffee. I could get his take on the greeting cards without telling him all the details. I shouldn't have felt as if it was my job to get us back on a friendlier, less egg-shell-walking path, but I don't like stiff relationships. The best way to get rid of stiffness is obviously to talk about the situation. Since time off was a stalemate, this was the next best thing.

When the coffee was finished brewing I poured myself a fresh mug. I filled the San Francisco Giants mug and brought it into Joe's office and put it on the desk.

"You didn't have to bring it to me, but thanks." He picked it up and took a sip.

I shivered, imagining the heat searing my lips and tongue if I drank it that fast. I held my cup with both hands. "Have you ever opened mail that didn't belong to you?"

"Of course not," he said.

"What if the person was dead?"

"Why would you have unopened mail from a dead person?"

"Not *from* a dead person. It belonged to a dead person."

"If I were the executor of the will I'd open it."

I should have known. This wasn't going to work at all and I'd backed myself into a pointless conversational corner. "Okay. Thanks."

I moved toward the door, hoping he'd let it go at that, knowing he wouldn't.

"What's this about?" he said.

"My neighbor was murdered. And I . . . have some of his mail."

"Why do you involve yourself in sordid situations like this? Can I expect you to be going off on seeing ghosts again?"

"Why are you picking on me all of a sudden?"

"I told you the other day, it's starting to seem as though you're not committed to this job, that you're just playing around, telling fantastic stories, looking to cause trouble."

"I'm not looking to cause trouble, ever."

"Maybe that was a little strong, but the impression is you're not focused on your work," he said.

"Well it's not true."

"Why do you have mail from your deceased neighbor?"

"I wanted your opinion, it's no big deal." I turned and stepped closer to the door.

"What's going on with you?"

"What do you mean?"

"You're acting strangely."

I suppose he could sense I was annoyed about his refusal to give me a few days off. I know he doesn't like that I see ghosts, but what am I supposed to do about it? I don't know why he gets so wound up, as if he's trying to convert me to his point of view. Convert me to his beliefs is a better way of putting it.

"I have a few greeting cards and I feel funny opening something a dead guy didn't want to open. That's all. I wanted to get your take, but I should have known what you'd think and I don't know why I brought it up."

"You shouldn't be involving yourself in murders. It's going to get you hurt. I'm only watching out for you."

"I don't need watching out for."

"I think you do."

"You're not my father."

"I didn't say I was."

The light forcing its way through the loose weave on the curtains slashed across the room. Dust motes danced in the beam, like tiny ghosts themselves. Joe's face was shrouded in darkness so I felt as if there was a huge chasm between us. And I suppose there was. "I don't need someone to take care of me."

"We all need people to care for us, Madison. Even a tough girl with fiery hair and tattoos and metal rings in her ears like armor."

"That's not who I am."

"Are you sure?"

"Thanks for your input on the cards. I haven't opened them." I don't know why I needed to tell him that, it's not as if I had to explain myself to him.

"I'm trying to be your friend, and I really do think you should learn to keep your distance from gruesome things. Murder and . . ."

"You mean from ghosts?"

"You know how I feel about that."

"It's not like I go looking for them."

"Somehow it finds you."

"I know."

"But that doesn't mean you have to get involved. Leave the unopened mail for his estate, or turn it over to the police. Probably the latter."

I nodded because all I wanted to do was end the conversation.

"If someone didn't open their mail, it was for a good reason. Especially personal mail. I think you can assume his relationship with the sender was not good," he said.

"I better get back to work," I said.

He nodded. I still couldn't see his eyes, especially since he was squinting to try to see past the beam of light. "Don't open the cards. You need to stay out of it."

I left the office. He had no right to tell me what to do. He surely *was* trying to act like my father. I flopped down in my chair and rolled it up close to the computer. The force of the arms hitting the depression in the desk that held the computer woke it up. It felt as if I'd woken Larry's ghost.

I should have torn the cards open on the spot. Now I was asking JD and Kate and Joe for their opinions and acting like it was a life or death decision and I had no idea why I was so concerned about it.

I worked for a while, wishing the phone would ring and Joe would close his door and get involved in a long conversation. With the door open, it felt like he was listening to me, making sure he heard my fingers on the keyboard.

AT LUNCHTIME I hurried outside and up the stairs to the street level, anxious to get away from Joe. I hoped Kate would take a break for lunch. If she'd brought her lunch, it would be in the fridge in the kitchen behind the fellowship hall.

My wish came true. My pasta was still spinning in the microwave, the pesto sauce starting to pop when the kitchen door opened. I'd forgotten the shocking look of her white clothes and red boots and was surprised all over again. "Joe doesn't think I should open the cards," I said.

"What are you doing, taking a poll?"

I smiled. "No."

"Why did you ask him? Of course he doesn't think you should. He's perfectly moral and by the book."

"And you're not?"

She grinned. "I am, but it's different."

"How?"

"He follows the rules. I'm more about the spirit of things."

"I see."

"Open them tonight. You have me curious, although I'm sure for nothing."

The microwave chimed and I took out my pasta. I went to the table. While I waited for Kate, I cut an apple into thin slices, trying to see if I could make each slice thinner than the one before until they were almost like sheets of fruity paper.

For a few minutes she talked about church stuff and I ate and drank the iced coffee from my thermos. Then I told her about what the ghost had said.

Even though she'd seen that ghost in the deacon's basement, her face crinkled with disbelief, as if her memories had faded, or her doubt had overcome them. "So you *are* going back?"

"I don't know."

"I guess you have to."

"It's scary."

"You don't usually seem scared of . . . them . . ."

"My curiosity is stronger than my fear."

"Why?"

"How should I know."

"You never think about it?"

Sure I'd thought about it. And I was pretty sure it had to do with my parents being murdered, but I still wasn't ready to give her that information. "Not really." I ran a slice of apple across the bottom of my food container and scooped up the pesto sauce. I popped it in my mouth. "I'll go back. I have to at least try. I'm sure they're investigating, but unless someone leaves fingerprints or other evidence, how would you ever find out?"

Kate ran her finger along the bone in her forearm, pressing hard, as if she were giving herself a mini massage, or surreptitiously scratching a rash. "And the cards?"

"I think Larry would want me to open them."

"I don't think Larry has an opinion one way or the other."

I smiled. Again I hoped I hadn't made too big of a deal out of it. I hated the thought of opening the cards and seeing nothing but two more scrawled signatures.

Six

THERE'S A SMALL patch of grass with a trellis covered in morning glories and a bench underneath across the lane from my condo. It's too small to call it a park, but there are several garden areas like this scattered throughout the complex and if you smashed them all together, you'd have a park. I don't know why they didn't design it that way.

When I got home, the neighbor who lives on the other side of Larry was sitting on the bench. She's a small lady, about sixty years old, with long pale gray hair and thick bangs that cover so much of her face you only see part of her eyes, her nose, and a very narrow slice of her cheeks around her mouth. She's always watching people. She sits on that bench a lot, in fact I rarely get to enjoy it because whenever I'm around, or have a desire to go outside other than my back deck, she's there with a gin and tonic in her hand, sipping and watching. I say *hello* to her sometimes when I pass by, but I don't know anything about her and we've never really chatted.

I locked my car and walked across the pavement to the grassy area. I felt like a subject approaching a queen the way she sat on that bench, watching me with a tiny smile on her lips.

"Hi, Alice."

"Hello." She sipped her drink. "What can I do for you?"

"It's so terrible what happened to Larry," I said.

"It is."

"So sad. And a little scary."

"And sad that it takes a murder to have you say more than two words to me."

I stepped back. My foot hit the curb and I slipped down into the gutter, almost twisting my ankle. "Did you talk to him much?"

"More than I talk to you."

"I suppose I get busy and don't always take time to socialize."

"You have plenty of time to socialize with that ponytail man who comes over."

I smiled. I wanted to find out about Larry, if she knew anything more about him. I was not going to let her comments provoke me into swatting back her rude comments with rudeness of my own. For instance, maybe I don't have time to sit around and drink all day and watch my neighbors, waiting for them to treat me like royalty. "Did the police talk to you?"

"Yes."

"When was the last time you saw him around?"

"Helping the police, are you?"

"No. I was just wondering. I feel bad that I didn't notice I hadn't seen him for quite a few days."

She put her drink on the bench and folded her arms. "No one around here would notice if anyone went missing. They're all locked inside, or on their private decks, or zipping out the front door and into their cars."

"People are busy."

"And standoffish."

"Maybe. The complex isn't very well designed for seeing people outside. There aren't pathways or a park," I said.

She picked up her drink, stuck her finger in up to the second knuckle, and pushed the lime wedge around.

"Were you worried?" I said.

"Sometimes he holes up in there. Or he did. I didn't think anything of it."

"So you felt bad too? When you found out he was dead?"

"Murdered."

"Yes. Did you feel bad about not noticing you hadn't seen him?"

She didn't answer.

"Have you seen the police around again? Do they have any suspects or anything?"

"They came by and took down the tape," Alice said.

I turned. I hadn't noticed it was gone. "Does that mean they're done?"

"I guess so."

"So did they talk to you again?"

"No. They got all they could the first time."

"What did you tell them?"

"That's between me and them."

"Okay." I took a few steps back. Obviously she didn't want to talk to me, even though she was peeved at me for not being friendly.

"Already leaving?"

"Well, I . . ."

"Since you didn't get your curiosity satisfied, you're done talking?"

"I don't mean to be rude. I'm tired from work. And hungry."

"I could make you a sandwich. And tell you some things."

"What things?"

"Do you want to have a sandwich with me or not?"

"Sure." I was a little nervous to go inside her house. I'm not sure why. There was something unsettling about her, maybe the drinking, but also something more. She seemed like she wanted to consume me. I don't know where that idea came from, probably the strange things she said, chastising me and at the same time wanting to be closer to me. Maybe her loneliness was so vast, she had to suck her neighbors into that pit with her, and even then it wouldn't be filled.

If someone sits and drinks all day, she must be determined to numb something inside of her. And there was the way she called out to me, and others, demanding they pay attention, then treating them badly for going about the business of their lives. No one deliberately ignored her, but she wanted to make it into that. Maybe if she did something nice for her neighbors, instead of making angry demands, they'd view her differently. But I decided to try a sandwich. I had my cell phone. It wasn't as if she was going to stab me to death or something equally gruesome. She was small and older and I'm pretty strong.

But I did wonder why I was having those thoughts, as if another part of me was whispering to watch out.

She stood slowly then made me wait, perched on the curb, while she finished her drink. And she didn't do it quickly. She put the glass to her lips, sipped, and closed her eyes to savor it. Then she took another sip. She didn't move, just kept her hand locked near her chin and took those small sips until I wanted to grab the glass and finish it myself.

Finally she was down to ice cubes and the wedge of lime. She plucked it out, her thin fingers and small hand fitting easily into the glass. She popped the lime in her mouth, rind out, and sucked on it as she took a few steps across the grass and down onto the pavement.

I followed her inside her condo, nearly identical to mine, except she had it done all in brown — chocolate colored carpet, tan walls, dark brown furniture, some brown corduroy upholstery, a brown leather chair, and wood bases on all her lamps.

She led the way to the kitchen and gave me a choice of roast beef, ham, or pastrami. No lean turkey or chicken for this gal. She liked her red meat. She checked with each ingredient before she added it to the sandwich — she even had two choices of bread and three kinds of mustard.

"Do you invite people over for sandwiches a lot?"

"Most people decline."

That made me pause for a minute. Suddenly I wasn't judging her gin and tonic and her harping at people from the bench in the green patch and telling me I was rude and selfish when she didn't even know me. I felt sorry for her. I was glad I'd come in for a sandwich. Was everyone in our complex lonely? Did that mean I was a lonely misfit too?

The same mood that had overtaken me a few nights earlier was hovering on the edge of my mind, dark thick gloom, waiting to let loose on me. Of course knowing a guy who died and no one noticed and a woman who had nothing to do but drink didn't mean the entire complex was full of lonely people. And Larry had a life — a good job, something that interested him, not just a good income, he loved writing his code. He said it was like working on a puzzle.

Alice handed me the sandwich on a coffee cup saucer, the sandwich filling the whole area, bits of meat hanging out, and lettuce stuffed too full, and the tomatoes almost sliding off. I had no idea how I was going to eat it.

I did manage, though. We ate a few bites in silence.

Alice sipped a fresh gin and tonic and I drank from a glass of plain tonic water she gave me.

"Were you friends with Larry?" I said.

"No more than you."

"This is good." I chewed slowly. "One of the best sandwiches I've ever had."

She smiled.

"I guess we all keep to ourselves," I said.

She took several bites one after the other. When she was finished chewing, she said, "He and Leanne, on the other side of you, had a thing going."

I put the second half of my sandwich back on the plate. The top piece of bread slid off, touching the table. I left it there while I stared at Alice. "She didn't mention that."

"Why would she?"

"I asked her to help me the day I . . . when I . . . when I noticed the, uhm. The smell."

"Did she?"

"She wouldn't come with me. Even onto his back deck. She said she didn't want to get involved."

Alice pushed her plate to the side. All that was left were the crusts of bread. She'd nibbled them all into neat strips, as smooth as if she'd trimmed them with a knife. "Maybe she killed him," Alice said.

"Oh, I don't think so."

I looked into her eyes, somewhat vacant, staring past me, or through me.

"Why would you think that?"

"Passion. That's what it usually is. Unless it's a gang. Right?"

"Yes. But Leanne is so sweet."

"What difference does that make? And what's sweet? Someone breaks your heart, and all the sweetness turns sour in an instant."

"I just can't see that. You'd think I would have had a hint, when I went over there. Wouldn't the smell have been horribly upsetting to her, or . . . I don't know. I just can't see it."

Alice stood.

"How do you know they had a thing?" I said.

"I asked him to help me move that plant." Alice pointed at a huge rubbery thing in the corner.

"He was busy," Alice said. "Going over to Leanne's."

"Oh."

I pushed the other half of my sandwich to the side. "That was delicious, but I really can't eat any more. I'm stuffed."

"Why didn't you tell me that before I went to all the trouble? I would have made a half."

"I didn't know it was going to be so large."

"So you're just going to throw food away?"

"You could eat it."

She curled her lip as if I'd suggested she re-use my toilet paper. "It's a waste of food."

"I'm sorry. I'm really full."

"Now I see why you're too thin. You don't eat."

That was an odd comment coming from her. She was

as thin as I was. "I can take it home."

"Whatever. I heard him moaning."

"When?"

"I think it was the night he died."

"Did you call the police?"

"I didn't think he was in pain. I thought he was with Leanne."

"Oh." I pulled out a piece of roast beef and nibbled on it. "How could you hear? There's no common wall."

"I was on the back deck. His sliding glass door was open."

"Do you feel bad about that?"

She picked up her drink and shook it slightly so the quickly melting chips of ice rattled against the glass. "No. How was I to know he was being stabbed?"

"I'd still feel bad."

"That's you. Why would I feel bad about something that was a natural assumption?"

"Just knowing you could have done something," I said.

"Are you trying to make me feel guilty?"

"No. I'm just telling you how I'd feel."

She took a quick swallow of her drink. She went into the kitchen and returned with a plastic bag that carries fruits and veggies home from the grocery store. She held it out to me without speaking.

I put my half sandwich inside. "Do you want me to leave?" I was relieved she was dismissing me. It was dark and oppressive in her condo. She was too strange, almost scary because I couldn't figure out why she wanted me inside to begin with and wasn't sure why she was talking to me after all this time of living nearby. She acted as if it were my fault we never spoke, but half of that was on her.

"It's not my fault he's dead," Alice said.

"I didn't imply that it was your fault at all."

"You want to. You think I could have somehow called the police, caught the killer in action, summoned the emergency team, and saved his life. That's a whole lot of power and *what-ifs* for little old me."

"All I said was . . ."

"I know what you said. Nice chatting with you." She backed up toward the kitchen. I stood and went to the door and let myself out. I really didn't want the sandwich, but I carried it back home instead of dropping it in her trash can. That would be rude.

THE ROAST BEEF sandwich filled me, but I had a gnawing feeling very much like hunger in my stomach, even as I put the leftovers on the second shelf of my fridge. I grabbed a bottled coffee drink — mocha — opened the sliding glass door to smell some fresh air after the dark, closed up feeling of Alice's living room, and sat at the dining table staring at the two unopened cards.

I popped the cap off the bottle and drank some. It was icy and cleared out the taste of mustard and roast beef and pickles. I picked up the first card with a postmark from March 23, 2012, slid my finger under the unsealed part of the flap and pulled it along the fold, tearing it open. I didn't stop to think. I'd over-thought it already. For some reason, the cards were there for me to take. If the police weren't interested, they were mine. A relative might have felt worse tearing into them.

The card had a photograph of a mother dog and a puppy. The puppy's eyes were full of all the things you see and read into the large round, shining eyes of dogs. Love and a bit of sadness, a longing to be assured of love from its master. The eyes of the mother dog were more knowing, but also eager for attention and affection. Written in white script across the bottom of the card were the words — *thinking of you.*

Inside it said, *Larry* — and in the center, *Happy Birthday*. It was signed Aunt Michelle and Uncle Peter by a single hand, presumably Aunt Michelle's since the spidery script looked very female. I wonder why that is — male and female handwriting appearing recognizably different. Is penmanship affected by thicker fingers, more pressure, the awkwardness of large hands trying to clench a thin pen? Or is there something deeper that comes out through handwriting, some essential part of a person? Now that all we do is text, maybe we'll never know.

On the left side, printed in very narrow letters, it said — *You owe us a phone call. It's the least you can do.*

That struck me as a terse and unfriendly birthday note. I giggled uncomfortably at the idea of writing *Happy Birthday* on one side while managing to give an order and deliver guilt in a few simple words on the opposite side. It sort of explained the unopened cards — something happened before this card arrived and Larry was no longer interested in hearing from his aunt and uncle. Since the other card was the last, I doubted it would tell me anything more, but I opened it anyway. Might as well go all in.

The second card was the same on the right side. The left had a long note, printed in the same very narrow style, but with much smaller letters. I had to get up and turn on the light to read it. There was obviously a lot to say because the entire space was filled with that miniature print.

Basically, it said that the aunt and uncle had done everything for Larry, taken him in and treated him as their own when his mother died, fed him, clothed him, and gave him an excellent education, including college — that part was underlined three times. It recounted vacation trips and laid it on pretty thick that Larry would have been in foster care and wouldn't have the career he had now if it hadn't been for his amazing, wonderful, upstanding Aunt Michelle and Uncle Peter.

It went on to chastise him for cutting them out of his life, for taking everything the wrong way.

Now my brain was bursting with questions that couldn't even form themselves. The repetitive loop that the mind can get when it runs into a wall, racing in circles on the same track, exploding against the same invisible barrier — *Taking what the wrong way? What? What? What?* And I had nothing else to provide even a hint.

I stared out the window and watched the sky darken over the greenbelt. I thought about calling JD but I knew he'd tell me to let it go, stay out of it, then tease me with questions like he often does, pulling me in further. There was a good possibility that Leanne could provide insight, but she'd talked to me, and walked over to Larry's back deck with me and never said a word about being in a relationship with him, so I didn't think she'd want to say much more. I wondered if she'd told the police, but I had a feeling she hadn't. I was pretty sure Leanne wasn't going to cough up secrets from Larry's past, if she knew them.

The only choice was to go back into his condo, hope for an appearance of the ghost, and try to find out who it was and why it was there, and what it wanted from the world of the living.

I went upstairs, filled the seed tube for the birds, and got them fresh water from the bathroom. As I attached the food and water containers to the cage, I talked to them. "What do you think? Am I obsessed? Should I let it go? Am I inserting myself where I don't belong?"

Without waiting for an answer, not that I expected one, but still, if you're asking questions out loud, you should pause, I think, I kept going — "What choice do I have? The questions are circling my brain. It's impossible to think about anything else. Maybe if I could understand more about ghosts, more about the lingering pain and rage of people who are murdered, I'll figure out why my parents' ghosts never made themselves known to me. Maybe I'll figure out something that will help me make contact with them. What do you think?"

I peered through the bars of the cage. Simon was hanging upside down from the top. Sierra and Sarah were fighting over the fresh seed — not in a vicious way, just poking their beaks in the dish, each one pushing the other's beak aside. Over and over. I realized I should get another feeder or two.

As I was changing into leggings and a tight-fitting t-shirt — the perfect outfit for squeezing through a window — JD called. I looked at his face on the screen. It was a picture of him looking out over the ocean in Australia, something he was always doing, looking out across the waves checking the surf, getting lost in his own thoughts, or possibly non-thoughts. He loves the ocean more than almost anything. If we were ever going to move in together, or be together long-term, I knew I'd be moving closer to the water.

After buzzing and chiming wildly, the phone went quiet. A few minutes later it bleeped with a voicemail. I decided to listen to it later. I wanted to keep my mind on the ghost and making sure I didn't shrink away from it this time.

THE BATHROOM WINDOW was closed and presumably locked. I stared at it, wondering why I'd been so lucky, if you could call it that, the first time, wondering who had closed it, and how I was going to get inside. Because now I knew I had to get inside.

I assumed it was the police who'd been back and

closed the place up more tightly. I hoped it was the police. If the killer had returned, that put an additional layer of fright over going inside the condo. To me, a murderer is more terrifying than a ghost.

The window stared back at me, blank, hiding things that I had to find out. I thought about the rest of the windows that were accessible — the one over the kitchen sink and the sliding glass door. When I'd crossed the deck I hadn't seen any partially open windows, but I walked back to check, just in case.

I returned to the bathroom window. Just past the window, the deck bent around to the side of his condo. It was a narrow strip, a space for the outdoor trash cans and a second faucet for attaching a hose, but there wasn't a hose. Off the side of the deck were some small flowering trees surrounded by river rock. Just past the trees was a path out to the greenbelt. The next condo over belonged to Alice. Her windows were dark, but that didn't mean she was asleep. She seemed like the kind of person who probably walked around a lot at night, sipping her drink, listening.

I walked across the deck and down the stairs. The back of Alice's condo was also dark, no flicker of light from the bedroom suggesting she was watching TV or surfing on a computer.

I bent down and picked up a rock. It was heavy, larger than my hand so that I had to squeeze tight to keep my grip on it. I dropped it and chose a smaller rock. As I went back to the bathroom window, I tried not to think about what I was going to do, focusing on what I was doing each second, stepping softly on the wood deck, feeling the cold, smooth rock in my hand. Knowing its weight could hurt someone badly. I set the rock on the deck and returned to my condo.

With a beach towel clutched to my ribs, I hurried back to Larry's, although it wasn't really Larry's any more. It belonged to someone else, maybe his aunt and uncle, if he hadn't bothered to write a will. And who does, when you're only in your thirties? None of us expects to wind up with a knife in our spine.

I put on my rubber gloves that had been tucked in the waist of my leggings.

In five quick moves, I set the chair in place, climbed on, removed the screen, smashed the rock against the glass twice, forming a good-sized hole, and put the rock on the deck. I pried out most of the remaining sections of glass and dropped them inside the window. I wrapped the towel over the exposed shards, picked up the rock and set it on the ledge in front of the unbroken side of the window and climbed through.

The rock looked silly when I set it in the middle of the tub, but I hoped with the broken glass surrounding it, anyone who observed it would assume it had been thrown through the window. I hoped the police, if they came back, wouldn't try to figure out its trajectory. It made sense that someone might throw a rock through the window of a condo that had been sitting with crime tape stretched across the front for several days. The area is fairly low in crime and vandalism, but it does happen.

Surprisingly, there wasn't a single prick of guilt in my throat, telling me to stop and ask myself what the heck I was doing. I'd already broken in, so a broken window didn't seem like a huge step over the law. Besides, I wanted the police to find out who killed him, and there was a ghost who might know quite a lot about the situation.

I went upstairs and into the second bedroom. The other greeting cards were still in the drawer. I went to Larry's room. The mattress had been removed, which was a bit of a relief. I was nervous enough without seeing his blood again.

I sat in the armchair in the corner. I was willing to wait all night because I knew it was unlikely I'd get a chance to come back a third time. Especially after that broken window was discovered.

It was completely dark. I'd turned my phone off because I didn't want to chance it even on vibrate, the screen flickering. I know that was extreme caution, but if someone saw or heard me, I'd be in a lot more trouble than I would have been the first time. I was lucky no one heard the breaking glass. That racket was enough risk for the night.

The house smelled like no one had lived there for a while, not enough oxygen and too many smells you don't normally notice taking over — carpet and dust and blank air. A house that's lived in has lingering food and soap and other smells and when they're all gone, it has its own nothingness smell.

After a while, it was hard to keep my eyes open. I was sure if the spirit was lingering there, it would appear on a regular basis. At least it seemed to work that way in other places, that once they've made themselves known, they keep showing up, longing to connect with a living being, but maybe also feeling some comfort from familiar and tangible surroundings.

I might have dozed a bit because suddenly the room was different, filled with another presence, and I didn't remember it changing gradually. The thing was much closer this time, right on the other side of the bed. Maybe it hung back before because of all the blood, and now that the remains of Larry were completely cleaned up, it was comfortable coming closer.

However, I was not comfortable, because now I could see more. Much more than I wanted and I desperately needed to look away, to close my eyes. The face seemed to be caving in on itself. Much of it was missing, the eyes, the nose, the lips, and quite a bit of the skin. Some of the bone had broken away as well. I could see the brain, and that too, was being eaten by decay, as if mold were creeping across, turning it green and gray like mold works its way across an orange until it's a pulpy, bad smelling thing you can hardly look at. Moldy fruit or vegetables disgust me and this was a hundred, a thousand times worse. I thought I was going to be sick to my stomach.

I don't know why I didn't notice how horrible it looked the first time. Unless it had simply been too far away, or hiding part of itself so it could lure me back. But if that were the case, did it want to hurt me? I had no idea who it was or what it was and yet I felt this compulsion not to run, to wait, to find out what I could about Larry's murder, and what this thing was doing in his house.

It occurred to me that I really have no idea how ghosts select their haunting spots. It's more or less the place they were wronged, or maybe around the person who wronged them. But was Kate right? Could it make its way into my place, hardly noticing the wall between the two units?

I shivered and pressed my palms against my stomach. I took a slow breath and smelled something rotten in the air. Luckily it didn't overwhelm me.

The ghost hovered on the opposite side of the bed, waiting. Just as I was waiting. We were at a stand-off. I felt nothing in the way of a connection or a sense of any emotion coming from it. The only sensation on my part was revulsion. My eyes closed on their own, trying not to look, but that was almost more frightening because then I didn't know if it was moving closer. There was an irrational fear that it was going to eat me, that it would come up to my side and whatever mold or fungus was eating away at its skin and organs would creep across my skin and eat me alive.

I opened my eyes. I forced them to stay open. I tried to blur my vision, so I could see it but not really focus. I whispered, "What do you want?"

What do you want? Its voice was like creaking wood when the floorboards are warped. The sound was strained and inhuman.

I couldn't tell if it was mocking me or truly asking. I inched to the edge of my chair. "Do you know Larry? Do you know who killed him?"

He was an ungrateful child and he grew into an evil man. He destroyed the family.

"Who are you?"

He took everything, took our whole lives. Our money, our friends. By the time he was done, we were old.

"Are you his Uncle Peter?" The voice and the shape of the figure seemed male, but maybe just because it was so overpowering and the voice was deep. I didn't want to leave any unanswered questions or jump to conclusions and miss what it needed to communicate.

A parasite, sucking you dry, leaving you worn out with no time left.

"Larry's a parasite? Why?"

Stealing my wife. My soul.

"What did he do? Did you kill him?" I knew I shouldn't ask repeated questions like that. An answer might turn ambiguous, unattached to the right question, and I'd be left as confused as ever, but I couldn't seem to stop talking. "What did he do?"

Took everything.

"How?"

Broke the family trust. The brain collapsed slightly each time it spoke.

I wondered if the thing would decompose into a pile of rot if I asked too many questions and didn't get to the heart of things, but I didn't know the right questions, the perfect question. "Did you kill Larry?"

He killed me.

"When?"

2013.

"It's 2013 now."

Thirteen. It's unlucky.

"A lot of people think that."

He shouldn't have broken the trust. The voice was almost breathless.

"What do you want?"

Him.

"Larry?"

Yes. The whisper had turned to a hissing sound, the tongue thick inside what was left of the mouth.

"He's dead."

The thing was silent.

I gave him my love, all my love, and this is how he repays me.

"What did he do?"

With hatred. Not one iota of respect or gratitude.

"And then he killed you?"

No, I took care of that.

I felt a heaving in my stomach. I couldn't look, but I couldn't look away either. "Do you mean you killed yourself? Why? What happened?"

The spirit sounded as if he were gagging. It intensified the feeling in my own stomach and I wanted it to stop. Throwing up all over the carpet would not keep my illegal entry a secret. Talk about a ripe offering of DNA. I smiled to myself, simultaneously disgusted with what I was seeing and hearing and feeling. "Do you know who killed Larry or not?" I said.

The room was silent. And in complete darkness. The creature was gone.

Seven

THAT NIGHT I didn't sleep at all. Even listening to JD's voicemail telling me to sleep good didn't help. I didn't feel the deep gloom I had the night before, but I was consumed by Larry and how and why he'd died. It seemed more perplexing than before, when I hadn't known anything.

Now I had the notes in the cards telling me he'd upset his aunt and uncle and a disgusting creature from beyond the grave, or right out of the grave since he was more rot than spirit. I gagged every time I thought of it. I was thirsty but couldn't bring myself to take a sip of water. I didn't even want a cigarette.

I know the reason I couldn't sleep was because I'd started thinking so much more about my parents, and wondering about whether their spirits would be lingering after all these years. They were always right there just beneath my other thoughts, and seeing the decayed spirit was beyond upsetting because I was thinking about them in their coffins.

I'm sure that's why zombies and horror movies are so popular. Everyone is trying to exorcise their horrible fears of the grave, trying to make light of it or get control over it or power over it. No one wants to think about it. We can't bear it. The whole thing is like a slap in the face of life. The human race invented embalming so we wouldn't have to think about it.

It might also be why I'm not overly afraid of ghosts. There are small pinpricks of fear, of uncertainty, but in some ways they give me hope. It's better to know that there's something that's not physical living on. It's better to know we aren't just our bodies, that they're just a shell and it's okay if they return to the earth. It's just the first part of the returning that's too awful to think about. Once the flesh is gone, it's clean bones.

I suppose people are afraid because they think ghosts possess supernatural power, that they want others to join them in death. And most of all, that a deceased person isn't at peace. We'd rather see angels. Happy things. But maybe the other side isn't all perfection and rainbows either. Who knows. Hopefully, it's mostly good and no one is suffering like they are on earth, which seems like one giant cry of agony if you stop and think about all the things happening at any moment in time. Which is why, usually, we don't stop to consider it, or we'd all go mad.

IN THE MORNING I took a tepid shower, which settled my stomach and my pulse enough to drink two mugs of coffee. The day ahead would be laced with coffee, saturated with coffee.

It was probably dangerous to be driving my car after only three or four hours of sleep in the last forty-eight hours, but I had to get to work. More than needing to show up for my job, I needed to talk to Kate. Most of the time I like to let ideas bounce around inside my head and I usually figure out the right thing to do in my life, but there's something nice about having a friend to add a different perspective. Of course there was JD, but for some reason I wanted a female perspective.

Since it was foggy, I wore a long, drapey blue sweater over a navy blue top, and jeans and sandals. I put my hair up in a high ponytail with a large barrette which looks more elegant and helped counter my more casual than usual clothes. I was tired, beyond tired. I needed to be super comfortable.

After I put my lunch away in the church kitchen, I went downstairs to the offices. Kate was already back in her office and the coffee was brewing. As soon as it finished, I filled two mugs and walked through the basement. I put one mug in front of Kate and sat on the wicker love seat that faces her desk. Wicker is an unusual choice for office furniture, but it's comfortable and looks lighthearted. That and all her potted plants give her office a garden-like feeling and I could see why she went with the wicker. It's calming. Every time I actually sit down in her office I think about doing something to fix up the main office and reception area, decorating in a way that would show what I like, set a different kind of mood.

Before she could open her mouth, I said, "I saw it again."

She picked up her mug, maybe to hide her expression. But she wasn't fast enough, because I saw her lower lip tremble, with fear for the ghost, or more likely fear that I was going to destroy her career now that I knew she couldn't deny the existence of ghosts, and I would be talking to her about them every day. She spoke softly. "Did you learn anything new?"

"Not too much. It seems to be Larry's uncle, which makes no sense, unless he died there. And either he doesn't know, or he wouldn't tell me, who killed Larry. He's angry. But he also seems to be searching for Larry, wanting to see him again, like Larry really hurt him."

"That's a lot of stuff. From a ghost. Are you sure you aren't projecting your own imagination?"

I put my mug on the floor and leaned my elbows on my knees. "I don't know anything."

"Are you okay?"

I yawned. "Really tired. Really, really tired. I haven't slept for two nights."

"Not at all?"

"Not more than a few hours both nights."

"That's not good."

"I read the birthday cards."

"What did they say?"

"There was a short note in one about Larry owing his aunt and uncle a phone call. And the other had a longer note about how he wasn't appreciative of all they'd done for him."

"So there was some kind of falling out."

"Obviously," I said.

"Bad enough to want to kill their nephew?" Kate picked up a pencil and started doodling on a sticky note.

"Her note criticized him a lot, it sounded angry."

"Did she threaten him?"

"Not really. The end of it seemed a little mopey that he took something the wrong way."

"If you want someone to apologize, doesn't it seem like killing them is not the way to make that happen?" Kate said.

I smiled. "Maybe the ghost killed him. Although I'm not sure how that would work, holding a knife and all. I don't know how I'm going to find out what happened. I can't go back in the house."

"Why not?"

"Because . . ."

"Because?"

She stared at me, waiting. I knew I was taking too long to answer. I was upset with myself that I'd almost blurted out that I smashed a window. I didn't think she'd call the police on me, but still . . .

"The police are working on it, you don't have to find out anything."

"I talked to my neighbor."

"The one who wouldn't go into his condo with you?"

"No, someone else."

"Aren't you getting a little caught up in chasing this down? Interviewing people?"

"I have to know. I found his body, don't I have some responsibility?"

"No."

"I think I do."

"I think you're nosey."

"That's not fair."

"It's true, a little. I'm not trying to hurt your feelings. Maybe nosey is the wrong word. Too curious, much too curious."

I picked up my mug. The coffee was getting cool fast, so I drank quite a bit of it, but it didn't make me feel any less tired. I needed to get started working. I already wanted a break and a cigarette, but I kind of had to work first since you can't take a break from not working. "I don't think I'm nosey. I care about people not getting away with murder. Or at least about someone who's murdered knowing their killer is punished."

Kate smiled, barely moving her lips to do so. More like the ghost of a smile, if that's not too goofy.

"I need to talk to Leanne again. My other neighbor, Alice, said Leanne was having a relationship with Larry. I wonder why she didn't tell me about it?"

"Maybe because it's none of your business."

"But wouldn't you mention something like that? If someone notices an odor of death and asks you to help check it out and it's in your boyfriend's house?"

"Who knows."

"Well I would. She should have been upset. And on top of that, since he was dead for several days, that means she hadn't seen him for a while."

"You're thinking maybe she killed him?"

"No. Maybe. I can't really see that, I'm just thinking out loud."

Kate glanced at the clock on the wall to her left. She kept her gaze there, as if she was watching the second hand proceed around the circle for a full minute. It almost felt like she was trying to get rid of me, hinting it was past time to start actually working. But then, Kate is not an indirect or shy person. If she thought I was screwing around on church time, she would come right out and say so. I decided to wait, in case she was ready to erupt with profound insight into the situation.

Still looking at the clock, she said, "You aren't going to figure it out sitting here talking to me. You should probably let it go."

"I can't."

"Why? Why are you so curious about everything?"

"It's normal to be curious."

"Not like you. You're obsessed."

"I like to know why things happen the way they do. I want to know why someone would even want to kill Larry. He was a nice guy."

"You hardly knew him."

"That doesn't mean I can't tell if he was nice."

She doodled faster on her pad of sticky paper. I

couldn't really see what she was doing. It looked like she was just drawing circles, which sort of felt how our conversation was going. "Sometimes, most of the time, we can't know why things happen. Part of being an adult is accepting that," she said.

"Are you telling me I'm immature?"

"You have a child-like view of the world."

"The world would be better if more people looked at it like children do."

"Have you spent much time around small children? Because I have."

I already knew that. She was the youth minister, she thought I didn't know she was more familiar with children than I am?

"Children can drive you mad with their questions. *Why? Why-why-why-why-why?*"

"See, it's human nature." I smiled. I drank the rest of my coffee, lukewarm and leaving me wanting another cup that was hot all the way to the end.

"But they grow out of it," Kate said. "*Why is the sky blue? Why do birds fly? Why do I poop?* And if you answer, it just sends you spiraling down a rabbit hole — *Because the food your body doesn't need has to be removed. Why? Because it only uses some of the nutrients.* And then again, *why?* And at some point you start to run out of answers."

"What are you trying to say?"

"That you want to know why and sometimes we don't know why. There are more unanswered questions in life than there are answers."

"Maybe people give up too soon. Maybe parents and teachers are lazy. If they don't know the answer, they should look it up."

"But eventually it turns into a philosophical debate. You can't look up why birds are the only creatures that fly. No one knows."

"That doesn't mean you shouldn't try to get answers, just because sometimes you can't."

"But you're driving yourself crazy."

"Or am I driving you crazy?"

"Maybe. A little."

I stood.

"Don't get upset."

"I'm not. But I don't want to drive you crazy." I really truly said this without being insulted. Because I thought she was wrong. It's a terrible thing if people lose their curiosity. If they give up and stop asking questions. Isn't that the whole point of life — never giving up? To keep trying to understand the world, to meet new people, to try different things?

"I didn't mean I'm tired of you."

"But I'm driving you crazy."

"It's just difficult to hear you circle around and around a topic, and see how badly you want to know the answer. You need to know. And you don't let up and it's frustrating because I can't help you. I don't know the answer."

I moved to the doorway. I leaned against the doorframe and looked around her office. Everything in there was about curiosity — shelves with bottles of paint and jars with paint brushes, books, and boxes of shells and stones she'd collected, bird feathers and dried flowers children had given her over the years. "I don't expect you to know the answer. I'm just thinking out loud, wondering. Isn't that what friends do?"

"It might be a good idea to mind your own business."

"Why?"

"Because the police will investigate the murder. And if your neighbor wanted you to know she was seeing the guy, she would have told you."

It was on the edge of my mind, the words almost caught in my throat, to ask why I couldn't ask a few questions. Why was that so wrong? Or not my business? But then she'd accuse me of being a child. Again. It wasn't fair. Maybe we all have this secret place inside where too many questions were shoved into the back corner because none of the adults made the effort to answer them. Maybe it slips out in all kinds of bad ways. "The ghost came to me, not the other way around. So it is my business."

"The ghost didn't come to you. You broke into his condo."

"Okay. Maybe I shouldn't have done that."

"You absolutely shouldn't have done that."

I felt like she was attacking me. Once again that uncertain feeling came over me, not sure where she fit in my life — boss or friend or neither. "Maybe not, but I still think it's my business. I found him, and I was the one who didn't notice he'd disappeared. Can you imagine what that feels like? He slept twenty feet away from me, he ate on the other side of the wall, we talked at least once a week. I saw him more than that and I didn't even notice he was gone. He was dead and I was going through my life thinking he was alive. It feels terrible."

"I can imagine. But it's not your fault he was killed and it's not your job to find out who did it."

"I didn't say it was my job."

"It's not like you could have prevented his murder."

"I know."

"You're young. You haven't experienced death enough. It always leaves feelings of guilt."

I waited for her to realize what she'd said, to remember about my parents, but her face remained blank, as if she'd switched into minister mode and was trying to educate one of the teenagers. Not comfort, not help along the way, educate. Like it was her responsibility to make me understand the aftermath of death and she was so intent on her objective, she'd completely forgotten the actual person she was talking to.

There wasn't a single flicker of recognition in her eyes. I wasn't going to remind her. Maybe she'd wake in the middle of the night and it would come to her, lashing across her brain — hot and punishing. Not that I wanted her to feel terrible, but I suppose part of me did want that.

I stepped out into the basement area. "Sometimes you have to get answers."

"And sometimes there are no answers."

"I better get to work."

"For your own sanity, maybe try minding your own business and see what happens."

I laughed a very fake laugh, but she didn't seem to notice it was fake.

Back in the main office, I poured another mug of coffee and sat at my computer. Talking to her made me more determined. I was not going to let it go. The guy was my friend, sort of. He died right next door to me, and the ghost appeared to *me*. It wasn't hurting anyone to keep looking for answers. Even if I didn't get them, I was still going to look.

I texted JD and got to work.

Throughout the morning, Pastor Joe came, made some phone calls and left again to make his rounds of the local nursing homes. A woman came by wanting to see him and got peeved when I suggested she should make an appointment. It's funny how some of the church people think Pastor Joe is always waiting around for them. As if he's supposed to be available whenever it's convenient for them, since they pay his salary.

It got quiet for a while and I surfed the web and wished someone else would drop by before I fell asleep in my chair.

JUST AS I was thinking about walking to the deli to get something for lunch, abandoning the lunch I'd brought because I really wanted to take a walk, Kate appeared in the main office. She sat in one of the chairs facing my desk and crossed her legs and folded her arms as if she was trying to keep herself all wrapped up.

"I'm sorry," she said. "I don't know where my head was at."

"Thanks."

"I guess you know all about survivor's guilt."

"I don't feel guilty about my parents."

She was silent. She kept her gaze focused on me as if she thought she could force me to admit that guilt was eating away inside me and that's why I wanted to go back to the house where I lived the first half of my life. Maybe she wasn't thinking that at all, but it seemed like she was.

The office was so quiet the buzz of the fluorescent lights seemed to grow louder, like a swarm of mosquitoes fighting to get out from behind the plastic cover.

"If you tell Joe what's going on, I'm sure he'll give you time off, no problem."

"I don't think I should have to explain. He's my boss. I don't want him knowing everything about my personal life."

"I'm your boss too."

"It's different."

"Thanks a lot." She smiled but she looked kind of perturbed.

I wasn't doing it to be mean. Most of the church treats her like an appendage, like she's not a real minister. It's clear to everyone that Joe is in charge, and some people equate that with being closer to heaven or something. And even Joe acts like he's my boss. He decides what I'm paid and all of that. I do things to help Kate, but general church stuff, things that aren't related to children or the youth group always come first.

"It's not good for your soul to keep secrets," she said.

"Not outlining your whole life to everyone isn't the same as keeping secrets. Besides, everyone has secrets."

"That's true, but you're keeping something important from him and it's affecting what you want and it's affecting how he views you."

"Too bad."

She stood. "I just came to apologize. I'm really sorry. And I'm not trying to tell you what to do with your life. With your neighbor's death or with Joe. Only make suggestions."

"Thanks."

The minute she walked through the doorway, I put the phone to voicemail, locked my computer screen, and grabbed my bag. It felt as if I needed a long walk to the deli more than anything in the world.

Eight

THAT NIGHT JD came over the hill for dinner. It was his day off, but he wasn't spending the night with me because the next morning he was going surfing at seven. I made chicken enchiladas that he said had a nice kick. For dessert, we had chocolate ice cream and I had coffee. We talked about surfing and Larry's murder and the ghost and how they might make JD a manager at The Distillery. He'd still tend the bar two days a week, but the other days he'd be a manager. He wasn't sure how he felt about that. So then we talked about jobs in general and what we wanted to do when we grew up, although I'm twenty-eight and he's thirty-four, so both of us better decide fairly soon.

After he left, I moved the leftover enchiladas into two plastic containers for lunches and washed the pan. I left it to dry on its own. I poured another cup of coffee and went upstairs and put on yoga pants and a tank top. I let the birds out so they could fly around the room while I read a collection of ghost stories JD had given me.

I read half a story before I started falling asleep every other sentence. Simon was sitting on the pillow next to me, watching me nod off. I closed the book and held my finger toward his chest. He climbed on and I eased my way out of bed and carried him to the cage. Sierra had already stepped into the cage on her own. It took a few minutes to chase down Sara, but eventually she got tired of fighting and climbed on the back of my wrist.

I thought about having a cigarette but decided since I was so sleepy it was kind of pointless and I could possibly have an extra one the next day. Unless I made a leap forward in self-control and will power and finally cut my daily quota. As I fell asleep I knew I wouldn't, not quite yet. Soon. But I don't think three a day will kill me. Sure they're bad for me, but people probably breathe in more carcinogens from the air every day. Although so do I. With that thought, I drifted to sleep.

At one-thirty I woke. The room was cold even though I had the comforter pulled up to my hips. I turned on my side, tugged it up to my neck, and curled myself into an oval. It didn't help. I sleep with the door open to get fresh air, and for most of the year that's fine. The birdcage is covered, so they stay warm. In the winter I only leave the door open a crack. But it was spring, and this was colder than ever before.

Then I noticed the decaying smell. Not enough to make me puke, but enough to make me feel like I was in a crypt, surrounded by cold, damp stone, with beds carved into the earth holding corpses who hadn't yet made the transition to skeleton.

Tears oozed out of my eyes. All I could think of was Kate and how she criticized me. She made it sound so easy to mind my own business. But how can I? They come looking for me. They make their business my business. They want my help, and I don't think it's arrogant to say that. It's just how it is.

The room was darker than normal, as if the moon had gone behind thick clouds and the streetlights had burned out. Still, I could make out the shadow of the ghost in the corner — along the wall that joins to Larry's condo. The birds were silent and I hoped they were okay, that they weren't scared or freezing to death. The face was dark and formless, not the decay I'd seen before and I was thankful it seemed to be hiding the worst of itself.

"What do you want?" I didn't whisper it and I didn't say it kindly. If it wanted something, it needed to stop being so vague.

Larry. Laaarrrryyyy.

I started full on crying when it said that.

He destroyed my family. The words wailed out from the corner.

I lowered my voice to a whisper, tired already. "How?"

Family business should stay in the family. Outsiders should stay where they belong. It's no business of theirs how a family lives together. I made mistakes.

The odor of decay was growing. I hoped it didn't

spoil my apartment. It smelled very much like the odor I'd followed into Larry's condo. Did that mean Larry's ghost was also here? I'd never thought of that before.

I pulled the blankets and comforter more tightly around my neck. I wanted it to get to the point, and then leave me alone.

I want him back. I need to make him understand.

"I can't help you."

He was such a sweet little boy. But he was so sad when he became my son.

"He became your son?"

I was raising him.

Maybe Larry didn't see it that way. "How did he destroy your family?"

He told secrets. Personal things. Things others don't understand.

"Like what?"

I need him back. I need him.

"Do you know who killed him?"

Why did he have to die? The spirit was wailing again. It was equal parts terrifying and driving me mad with wanting to know and not getting a straight answer. It wouldn't veer off its own agenda, whatever that was. I suppose getting Larry back. You'd think if they were both dead it might be easier rather than dragging a living person into it, but apparently not. If it had an issue with Larry and it would never be able to encounter Larry, did that mean I was going to live with that thing next door to me forever? Maybe I would reconsider JD's suggestion that we live together. Although escaping from a ghost isn't a very good reason to move in with your boyfriend.

"I don't know why he died," I whispered. "And I don't know what you want with me. I don't know what happened to your family. And I don't know who killed him."

The thing bellowed Larry's name. It was so loud, I wondered if the sound was traveling out my open door and across the balcony and around the condo complex.

"What happened?"

And then it was gone. The room was a normal temperature, it smelled like vanilla from the candles on the dresser, and the breeze coming in the door was comforting.

THE NEXT DAY was Saturday. I knew the minute I woke up that I was going to hunt down Leanne and hound her sweet little I-don't-want-to-get-involved self to tell me more about Larry.

For breakfast, I ate buttered toast with cinnamon sugar sprinkled on top and drank three cups of coffee. I went out to the back deck to drink the last cup. Seeing Larry's closed drapes, the sprinkling of dead leaves across the deck, the shoes lined up to the side of the sliding glass door, cast a bleak chill over the warm, sunny day. I angled my chaise lounge away from Larry's condo before I sat down.

I didn't really want to go knock on Leanne's door because if she even answered, the minute I told her what I wanted, the door would close with a sharp smacking sound as if she'd slapped my face. I also didn't want to sit around all day and possibly all weekend, watching her front door like a detective on a stake-out, giving up precious hours of my life waiting for something that might not happen.

Knocking was the best option. But how to keep her from closing the door in my face? I finally decided to make peanut butter cookies. Manipulative and trite, I know, but I had to have some way to keep that door open after I said, *Why didn't you tell me Larry was your boyfriend?*

I brought my parakeets downstairs and set the cage on the counter near the open back door. While I whipped together butter and flour and sugar and eggs and peanut butter, they chirped their little brains out. When I was done, I had forty-seven cookies — twenty for Leanne, twenty for JD, and seven to hang onto for myself.

I went outside again, smoked a cigarette, then took a shower. I left my hair wet and put it in a fat braid. It made a dark stripe down the center of my white t-shirt, but it would dry eventually and I was getting too antsy to stand there blow-drying my hair, wondering how to stop Leanne from pretending she was ignorant. All I could do was charge in and see what happened. Who can be stubborn in the face of a peanut butter cookie?

I lucked out. When I walked toward her place, she was on her front porch. Four tiny tomato plants stood on the wood rail. She had a ten-pound bag of dirt torn open and was shoveling fresh soil into larger pots. The shovel clanged against the edge of the clay pot with a rhythmic pattern each time she put in a fresh scoop.

When I reached her steps I said, "Hi."

"Hi," she didn't look up. Since she didn't say my name, I wasn't a hundred percent sure she knew who she was talking to.

"I made you some cookies."

"What's the occasion?"

"Nothing. I was baking and thought I'd bring you some."

"At eight in the morning?"

"I was in the mood."

She straightened. "Thank you."

She didn't reach out to take the paper plate, so I put it on the railing.

"My hands are covered with dirt, and it's kind of damp."

"Do you want me to bring them into your kitchen?"

"No, I'm almost finished."

She didn't look even close to finished. I guess the cookies hadn't paved the way as well as expected. At least she was busy digging and spilling dirt across her front porch. It wasn't likely she'd drop her shovel, grab the cookies, run inside, and close the door.

"I didn't remember you saying you were close to Larry," I said.

"Who told you that?"

"Alice."

"I wasn't close to him."

"She said you . . ."

"I can imagine what she said. We weren't a couple or anything like that."

"What were you?"

"Friends. Sort of. Friends with benefits. But without the friend part. So, neighbors with benefits."

"What?"

She put down the shovel and looked at me. Dirt had fallen on the top half of the bag and the weight of it pulled the bag forward, spilling dirt across the top step. She tugged the top of the bag back up. "We had sex. If you could call it that."

"Oh. Okay. But you weren't going out?"

"No, we weren't going out."

This was not what I'd expected and I didn't really want to start firing questions about her sex life at someone I didn't know all that well. "When we noticed the smell, you weren't worried?"

"I didn't know what it was."

Her face had a grayish tinge. I wasn't sure if it was the shadow from the overhang of her porch and I hadn't noticed because I wasn't looking very closely, or if it had changed color at the thought of Larry's body decaying. Or maybe something else.

"I just thought it was odd that you didn't mention you were close to him. When we were looking around his porch. Do you have a key to his condo?"

"I've never even been inside his place."

"So you don't have a key?"

"I said I've never been inside. What do you want?"

"It was bothering me that you were close to him and

you acted like you hardly knew him. But you were together."

"All we did was have sex."

"You didn't, uhm, talk or anything?"

"Nope."

"I'm sorry to be so personal, but how did that happen?"

She glared at me. "I came home drunk one night." She smirked. "Really wasted. I bumped his car and set off the alarm. He came out and one thing led to another."

"Right there in the carport?"

"No, he came to my place."

"Oh, so just the one time. I had the idea from Alice that you . . ."

"Not just one time. For the past seven or eight months. He came over twice a week."

"And you never talked? About anything?"

She leaned against the rail. "Why do you want to know? I'm not exactly proud of it."

Mentioning the ghost didn't seem like a good idea. I scrambled through my head to think of a plausible reason I felt compelled to find out more about his life. "I think it's a little weird, really weird, that you had a relationship with him and we went all around his condo, and we knew something was wrong, and you didn't say a word about it."

"It wasn't relevant."

"Just because something isn't relevant doesn't mean you don't mention it. That makes it seem like you're trying to hide it."

"Maybe I am."

"Why did you have sex with him but nothing else?"

"What's wrong with you? Why would you ask me questions like this? Were the cookies some sort of . . . what are you doing?"

"I guess I feel bad that I lived next door to him all this time and I didn't even know he was dead. And I really didn't know much about his life."

"Neighbors don't usually know much about each other."

"I don't understand why he was murdered."

"You're a little off your rocker, you know that? I never noticed that before. News flash — the police will figure out why he was killed."

"What if they don't?"

She shrugged. She bent over and grabbed the loose plastic on the bag and dragged it to the other corner of the porch. She lifted two of the tomato plants off the railing and set them down near the dirt-filled pots.

"Doesn't it bother you that we all live here so close to each other and we're strangers?"

"That's how the world is."

"So why did you just have sex and not an actual relationship?"

"I really don't know. It just worked out that way. Larry was weird."

"I didn't think he was weird."

"You just said you didn't know him that well, so how

would you know?"

"True."

"You never had sex with him. Or at least I assume you didn't." She laughed, a shrieking, hysterical sound. I was starting to think she was a little crazy. I guess saying *hi* to someone for a few years and exchanging occasional bits of information tells you absolutely nothing. Everyone looks normal, going to and from their cars, watering their plants, sitting on their back decks.

She sat down on the top step and leaned her elbows on her knees. Now that she was out in the sunlight I saw that her hair needed washing. A piece hung across the side of her forehead and over her brow, plastered to her skin it was so oily. Her yellow t-shirt had dark stains under the arms and her jeans were pulled down low because of how she was sitting, and her belly bulged over the waist and poked out beneath the hem of her shirt. Her fingernails were ringed with dirt, and it looked like more dirt than what she'd accumulated digging in the potting soil.

"Since you're such a voyeur, I'll tell you how it was. Maybe it'll make me feel better to get it off my chest."

I swallowed. Unless she'd killed Larry, what was I really going to get out of hearing what she had to say? Although maybe she had killed him. Maybe she lied about being in his house. Maybe she'd had some kind of breakdown from having such a sad and pointless relationship. Maybe she wanted more from him and he treated her like she was almost a hooker. Except he didn't pay her.

"That night when I was drunk, he helped me back to my place. I was completely out of it. I shouldn't have been driving. He came inside and immediately started putting his hands up my shirt. I figured what the heck, he was kind of cute. He was a neighbor, at least I knew he wasn't some freak. He took off all my clothes and tied my shirt over my face. It was dark anyway, so I don't know why he did that. Then he jerked off."

"Oh." My legs were getting tired from standing on the sidewalk, and now they felt kind of limp. I sat down on the concrete.

"When I saw him two days later he said *sorry*, and I said *whatever*. And he said, *you didn't mind?* And I said, *whatever floats your boat*. Two days later he came over with a six pack of beer. He gave me one and asked if I would mind doing it again. It was the same scenario. And that was it. For seven months. Seven and a half."

"You never talked or anything?"

"Are you deaf?"

"It's just so . . . I don't mean to make it sound like I'm judging you."

"Oh, judge away. I know it's perverted. But who really cares? I've never had a boyfriend. Don't really want that. So maybe I'm just as weird as he was."

That was sad. Part of me wanted to reassure her, but I had no idea what to say. And maybe that was condescending. Maybe she wasn't looking for my reassurance.

"I asked if he wanted me to come to his place. To

cook him dinner. Water his plants when he was out of town, but he never wanted me there."

"Why would you do that? He didn't do anything for you."

"There was something about him that made him seem like a little kid. Like he needed someone to take care of him."

"Did you kill him? Because he gave you the creeps, or made you feel used?"

"No." She stood. "I *told* you I was never in his place. It's a cold, lonely world. I figured if I could make him happy for twenty minutes a week, it didn't matter what his issues were."

"But what about you, how you feel?"

"I've lived this long and managed just fine. I'll survive."

She picked up the plate of cookies. "I don't really like sweets." She handed the plate to me. She turned and went inside, leaving dirt, and the tomato plants that were looking withered, all over the porch. I heard the deadbolt slide into place.

Nine

BY TWO O'CLOCK I'd eaten all the cookies I saved for me and had two more cups of coffee and the last two cigarettes of my allocation for the day. I never get agitated like others complain of from caffeine and sugar and nicotine. Those things don't seem to affect me much, but they weren't doing what they usually do, and what I'd hoped for, which was to calm me down and put my mind on something so my subconscious could make sense of Leanne and Larry, and the ghost, and Larry's killer.

I sat on my chaise lounge and looked out at the green belt. In a last effort to get my brain into a calmer state, I rationalized that it was okay to have a fourth cigarette because I'd sort of planned it when I skipped one the night before.

The flame from the lighter was almost non-existent against the brightness of the sunlight. For a moment, I couldn't see it at all until I moved my head slightly and the flame grabbed the paper and tobacco. I let it die and took a slow drag. I held my cold coffee drink in my left hand, the cigarette in my right, and closed my eyes, enjoying the sweet smell of smoke. I know I'm a bit strange that I find that smell pleasant, but I do, and it didn't spoil my enjoyment of the clean, fresh air at all.

I opened my eyes and took another puff. I wished I'd asked Leanne more questions. I still wasn't clear why she'd acted as if she hardly knew Larry. Shame? But she didn't seem that ashamed now, she was very matter of fact in knowing her relationship was strange and nothing to brag about, but she wasn't concerned what I really thought of it. I expected she hadn't told the police. There's really no way for the police to know you're lying or keeping information to yourself unless they find something or someone to contradict you. Or you're a bad liar.

The more I thought about Leanne's . . . relationship, the more I wondered if she'd killed Larry. She was calm if she had, but there was obviously something wrong with her, to be okay with the set-up she had with him. It also made me think of him differently. It made me sad that he couldn't enjoy a normal relationship. What he did to Leanne seemed abusive to me, although she didn't seem to recognize it. Or maybe she did, so she stabbed him.

I took four more drags on my cigarette then put it out. I swallowed the rest of the coffee, and went inside. Leanne's cookies were on the counter. I thought about eating one off that plate, but resisted the urge. I picked up the plate, unwrapped the plastic, and replaced it with a fresh sheet. I went out front.

Sure enough, Alice was sitting on the bench in the common area. There wasn't much to watch on a Saturday afternoon.

As I approached the bench, I saw that her eyes were closed and her lips parted slightly, a very soft rumble coming out every few seconds that made her upper lip quiver. A fine sprinkling of freckles covered her nose and cheeks, something I hadn't noticed before. Her usual drink was next to her on the bench. She'd obviously been there a while, because moisture had collected on the outside of the glass and slid down to the bench, leaving a dark ring. It looked like all the ice had melted.

I stood there holding the cookies. If I woke her, she might get startled, but if I just put the cookies on the bench and went away, she might toss them since she didn't know where they'd come from. The trellis cast a dome of shade across the grass and onto the sidewalk. I sat on the ground and set the plate of cookies next to me. I hoped she'd somehow sense my presence after a few minutes and wake up.

My persistence was rewarded. It felt like less than ten minutes when she pressed her lips together, made a little snorting sound, sat up straighter, and opened her eyes. I smiled and held up the plate. She didn't reach to take it. For a few seconds she stared at me as if she wasn't sure who I was.

"Madison. Your neighbor, Remember?"

"Right. What are the cookies for?"

"No reason."

"There's always a reason."

"To pay you back for the sandwich."

"You don't have to pay me back for anything."

Even though the plate was paper and there were only twenty cookies, it was getting heavy because my arm was stretched at an awkward angle to where she was sitting. "You don't like peanut butter cookies?"

She took the plate.

"What do you want?"

"To talk more about Larry."

"Of course you do."

"It seems like you know things you aren't telling me."

"I don't have to tell you anything."

"I'm just curious."

She picked up her drink and took a long swallow. When she put it down, her eyes looked filmy, as if the alcohol had seeped right up through her cranial blood vessels and spread across the surface of her eyes.

"Did you tell the police everything you know?"

"Why would I?" she said.

"They're trying to solve his murder."

"It's not my responsibility to help them."

"What did you tell them?"

"Why are you so nosey?"

"I'm just curious."

"You're more than curious."

I shifted my legs, trying to get comfortable, which is impossible when you're sitting on concrete. It would have been nice for her to offer me a place on the bench, but she seemed determined to keep it to herself. She was quite spread out, a gauzy green skirt that matched the lime in her gin and tonic covering part of the bench. "I really need to know who killed him. I really need to understand. I'm a little obsessed with it, to be honest."

"You don't have to tell me that. Running up and down the street, talking to neighbors you never bothered to meet before."

Was she really going to beat me up again about how unfriendly I was? I don't think I am. She'd never done much to approach me either. It's Silicon Valley, we're busy. The world is busy. There's a lot going on and the leisurely pace she might have remembered from her past isn't available much around here. "It's really upsetting me, and I'm sorry if I wasn't friendly in the past. I'll try to do a better job in the future."

She nodded. She plucked her lime out of her drink and sucked on the fruit. I shivered, thinking of the sour taste. Maybe the alcohol dulled her taste buds.

"So what did you tell the detective?" I said.

"I answered his questions."

"Did you ever go inside Larry's condo?"

"Once. A year or so ago."

"What for?"

"He traveled for work."

"Yeah, I know."

"He wanted me to water his plants."

"You only did it once?"

"He didn't want me there anymore, said it wasn't necessary, he wasn't usually gone long enough."

The detective seemed to think Larry was killed by someone he knew. At least his questions to me headed in that direction. Alice didn't look strong enough. And she seemed to like him. "Did you tell the police you'd been inside?"

"No."

"Why not?"

"What difference would it make that I was inside his place one time? None. Anyway, I'm not a very helpful person."

"So you don't care if his killer's caught?"

"If they need someone like me to catch his killer, with the random, insignificant things I might or might not know, then they're in trouble."

"What do you know?"

"I know his aunt tried to hit me up for a key. She drove by a few times and I was usually sitting here. One day she stopped."

"When did that happen? Did you tell the detective?"

"Why do you keep asking me that?"

"I think it's strange you wouldn't provide information like that."

"It wasn't anything."

"Why did his aunt want a key, why wouldn't she talk to Larry?" I thought about the unopened cards. I suppose he wouldn't open his door to her either.

"How should I know?" Alice peeled the plastic off

the side of the plate and took a cookie. She ate it in several good-sized bites, chewing slowly. The little smile on her face made it seem as if she was starting to enjoy answering questions, and maybe enjoy answering in a way that was unnerving, trying to keep me guessing. She thought the whole thing was a game.

"He said he didn't feel at home there anymore. He was thinking of moving."

"Really? He never mentioned that to me."

"It was recent, just a few weeks ago, I think. Besides, you're a young girl. Maybe he was intimidated by you. It's easy to talk to an old crone like me. I'm invisible, it's as if you're talking to yourself."

"I don't think that's true."

"Just wait."

That made me sad. I think it was because she was drunk half the time that she felt invisible, not because she was old. But what do I know? Maybe I would find out one day. "Why wasn't he feeling at home?"

"He thought there was a presence in his place. Or he was having nightmares — very vivid — of a presence of some kind."

I shivered.

"What's wrong?"

"Nothing. Can I have one of your cookies?"

"Didn't you make any for yourself?"

"I did, but I'm hungry right now."

She held out the plate. "You don't look hungry. You look sick to your stomach."

I shuddered even more, as if big thick clouds had moved over the sky and it was turning quickly back to an icy cold day in early spring. The sidewalk sent sharp, chilling pains through my bones.

"You look very upset. I'd say scared, if I didn't know better."

"I'm fine." But I lied. I was worried that the spirit was not only right next door, he'd already found his way into my place. How would I get him to leave? The cookie in my hand was half gone and I hadn't even realized I was nibbling on it. "I'll bring you more cookies," I said.

"That's okay. I don't have much of a sweet tooth. This is more than enough."

"Did he really think someone was inside, or he just had bad dreams?"

"He said he thought he'd seen someone on the stairs."

"So do you think he had a premonition, or a dream he was going to be killed?"

"I thought he was losing his mind. That can happen, when someone lives in this make-believe world where all they do is talk to computers."

"He didn't just talk to computers."

"Well he was a troubled guy."

"How do you know?"

She smiled. Her teeth were small, spread out a bit, and it made her smile look as if it belonged to a child. She kept smiling at me like that. "You don't think I recognize a troubled person?"

Oh. I guess I was disturbed by the ghost, the creature, and I wasn't really thinking about Alice much any more. Of course she would know. "Why was he troubled?"

"He was very angry. You can recognize that sort of person. They speak normally, but there's an intensity in their words. And they're often making comments about how life has beaten them down. As if life were harder for them than everyone else. They forget they know all their own secrets and their own troubles and they only see the surface of others' lives, and they assume everyone else has it so easy. And those little comments, casually thrown out, about trouble here or there, has this suggestion of barely controlled rage. You can feel it clawing at the glass, trying to get out."

"It sounds like you've studied this quite a lot."

"It doesn't take studying."

I wanted another cookie but figured I could exercise a little bit of self-control for once in my life, so I turned my head and looked toward Leanne's place. I thought about her creepy relationship. It seemed like several people in the complex had a darker side I'd been completely unaware of. I looked back at Alice. She was watching me, her drink untended on the bench. "Did he think it was dreams, or did he think it was haunted?"

Alice laughed. "Haunted? A condominium? That's for old houses with long histories." She picked up her drink. I watched her holding the glass, a little nervous that it was going to slide through her fingers, but she had a firm grip, despite the pickled look in her eyes. I wondered if she drank gin from the minute she got out of bed in the mornings. She sipped it, staring over the rim of the glass, looking directly into my eyes, as if she could bore inside my head. As if she were assessing whether I was worthy of her giving me any more information. Although none of her information was helping me understand anything.

"Did his aunt say why she wanted a key?"

"She had to help him with some stuff."

"Stuff?"

"Yes, stuff."

"Like packing? Or spring cleaning?"

"She didn't say. Just stuff."

"Does she live around here?" The minute I said it, I realized I already knew the answer. Her address was right on the envelopes with the birthday cards. Saratoga. Only seven or eight miles away.

Alice leaned forward. "You can't stop thinking about it, can you. You have to dig and dig until you get the answers you want. Sometimes the answers you think you need are not that satisfying after all. It's like eating too much junk food. You think it will relieve your hunger and instead you wind up with a stomach ache."

"Sort of like drinking too much alcohol?"

She leaned back. "We all have our needs. You have to know everyone's secrets, I have to keep the voices to a dull roar."

"The voices?"

She laughed harder, almost cackling. "I'm not saying I'm looney, that I hear *voices*. I just mean the voices of the past, that devil inside that whispers you should have done this or that, shouldn't have done the other thing."

"Don't we all have those thoughts?"

"The older you get the louder they are. Maybe not for everyone. Depends on how many things you screwed up along the way."

I stood.

"You should talk to Leanne," she said.

"I talked to her. It was kind of confusing."

"I can imagine. Being a whore is confusing."

"She's not a whore."

"What she did," Alice said.

"She got into a weird relationship, that's all." I wasn't defending her. But Alice made it sound so harsh. Like Leanne said, she wasn't proud of it, but something drew them together, and maybe she satisfied some dark need in him. Maybe she gave a glimmer of hope or kindness to his life.

"If you call that a relationship." Alice's voice sounded like she was issuing a warning. But she didn't add any more and I didn't really want to hear any more. Considering what I'd seen of her life, admittedly only a fragment, a microscopic corner, she wasn't one to be critiquing others' mistakes or failures.

"Are you saying she did something else? Besides having sex with him?"

"She didn't have sex with him. She was an object for him to abuse."

"How do you know all this?"

"I see things."

I found that hard to believe. Was she saying she'd been around Leanne's condo and seen them together? "What did you see?"

"I'm going to mind my own business. Maybe you should too."

That was the last thing I was going to do. Probably I should have talked to the detective whose card was sitting on my dresser next to the birdcage. But it's hard to tell a story when a ghost is part of it and official people are not inclined to believe you about ghosts. I had to figure out something if I didn't want a creepy, decaying spirit showing up on a regular basis. There was a reason I was curious and obsessed or whatever anyone wanted to say about it. Condos most surely can be haunted. Anywhere human beings live and fight and cry and love and hate can be haunted.

Ten

AT FIRST, I was going to talk to Leanne again, but then I decided she'd more or less told me she had nothing else to say. If I could find Larry's aunt, if I could manage to convince her to talk to me, both very large IFs — well the second was much larger than the first — maybe I'd have something else to ask Leanne.

I did wonder if Larry had mentioned his bad dreams. But Leanne said they never talked. Although she was very insistent, almost over-insistent, on everything. She *never* went inside his house. They *never* talked.

At the end of the day, Leanne didn't seem inclined to tell me much more, and his aunt would surely know more about him.

THE SANFORD HOME, quite small by Saratoga standards, where you see large pieces of property, sprawling homes hidden by seventy-year-old trees, gated driveways, brand new monster homes that look like they belong on a cliff overlooking the Mediterranean sea, was almost a cottage. It looked like it might have been a guest house for the property next door at some point in the past.

The front yard was un-mown grass — the kind that spreads out like sea urchins and then sort of stops growing. It was a faded yellowish color. There was a birdbath without water in the center of the lawn, surrounded by brambly shrubs with tiny leaves. The same shrubs grew along the front porch and had dropped little dried leaves all over the concrete.

I rang the bell and waited. After a few minutes, I rang again. A few more minutes after that, I knocked. There was a Toyota Corolla parked on the gravel drive, so I wasn't going to leave until someone told me to.

The curtain covering the small window in the door moved. Part of a face, the mouth and nose and one eye, looked through the opening. There was no effort to conceal the fact that someone was peering out. The curtain fell back into place and the deadbolt turned.

The woman who opened the door was taller than me, although she was standing up on the threshold. She was about sixty, and had long curly gray and brown streaked hair. Her face was pale with dark red flushed spots on her cheeks and her eyes were bluish gray.

"What can I do for you?"

"Are you Michelle Sanford?"

"Yes."

"I'm a neighbor of Larry's."

"Oh." She leaned on the door and it started to close.

"Can I talk to you for a few minutes?"

"About what?"

"I have some questions about him."

She brought her lips up into a frown and scrunched her brow. "I thought you were his neighbor."

"I am."

"You sound more like the police."

"Did you talk to the detective?" I said.

"Why do you want to know?"

"Can I come in for a few minutes?

"What for?"

"I want to talk about Larry."

"There's nothing to talk about."

"I might be able to find out who killed him. And I thought if I talked to you about what I know, you might be able to help me."

"The police are taking care of that."

"Are they?" I moved closer, just a small step, hoping she wouldn't think I was crowding her. The air wafting out her door, tickling my nostrils, was cold. "Do they have any suspects?"

"Not that I know of."

"Then wouldn't it be good if we knew something they didn't? If we could give them suggestions?"

"Police detectives don't look for help from average people."

"But they'll take it if they can get it. Besides testing evidence, what else have they got but average people?"

"What do you think you know?"

"Can I come in?" I knew it was a risk to tell her about the ghost, you never know how people will respond. Or maybe I do — there are three possibles responses — fear, disbelief, and curiosity. Okay, maybe four. Along with disbelief there's thinking I'm mentally unstable.

She took a step back, pulling the door open a tiny bit, although there was barely enough room for me to squeeze through, so it seemed as if she didn't really want me to come inside, but her curiosity got the best of her. She led the way past the living room. I had time for a quick glance inside to see a leather couch and armchair, a small window with the drapes closed, a coffee table, and a bookcase near the fireplace. The floor was hardwood. It looked charming except that all the decorations had been stripped off the walls. Pale shadows filled the space where there used to be paintings or photographs. The surface of the coffee table, the shelves in the bookcase, and the end tables were all empty.

She went into the kitchen and said, "Have a seat."

I pulled out a chair at the table. She sat across from me in the only other chair.

"It must be hard, Larry's death."

"What do you know about it?"

"I'm the one who found his body."

"Oh." She glanced at the counter. There was a six pack of Coke sitting there. I thought maybe she'd offer me one, but she looked back at me and waited.

"Is there going to be a memorial service?"

"No."

"Why not?"

"I don't know any of his friends. Maybe they'll plan something."

"Don't you and your husband want to remember him, or your other relatives?" The cards made it quite clear they were not on good terms, but if I told her I'd read the cards, I'd have to explain that I was in the house, and I was hoping to get away with telling her about the ghost coming into my room and blurring the lines a bit with the other times it appeared so she wouldn't know I'd broken in. Kind of tricky, since she might wonder whether the ghost had anything to do with Larry at all.

She pushed back her chair and studied my face, then she stood. Her hair fell over her cheeks and covered her shoulders. The curls trembled as if there were a breeze coming through the window, but it was closed. Her body wasn't visibly shaking, but still her hair moved with a life of its own. She walked toward the door that led out to the side of the house where the car was parked. The floor creaked, squeaking in one spot with a sound that sent shivers along my arms, and then resumed its creaking with each step she took.

A fly buzzed across the room and around the light above the table. Michelle swatted at her hair, then dropped her hand even though the fly continued circling.

The silence between us dragged on so long, I worried our conversation was over, that she'd forgotten I was even there.

I hoped she was planning to tell the truth, to let me

know Larry had cut them out of his life, to tell me her husband was dead, to explain something, anything. But still she remained silent. I wasn't sure if she was waiting for me to say more or didn't really care that we were floating in a void of non-communication. Maybe only I felt awkward. I wanted so desperately to get some answers it felt as if I'd been sitting there forever, trying not to pester her with a string of questions, to blurt out information about the ghost, even to tell her about Larry's bizarre relationship with Leanne. She probably didn't want to hear about his sex life, but maybe there was something wrong with him. He'd always seemed rather normal to me, but maybe everyone does when all you do is say hello and talk about the weather or traffic, what you're having for dinner or petty annoyances in your condo complex.

The fly stopped buzzing. She swatted at her hair again and put her hand on the doorknob. Surely she wasn't going to walk out on me, get in her car and drive away, leaving me alone at her kitchen table. But that's what it felt like. I put my hands on the table. I tried to think of a question, but I was still waiting to hear about her husband being deceased.

"He's dead."

I waited.

"They're both dead."

"Your husband?"

"Yes."

"Was he sick? Or a heart attack?" I was sure he'd

killed himself, at least as sure as you can be talking to a ghost who hasn't identified himself. If she said it was a heart attack, I'd be back to having no clue who the ghost belonged to.

She folded her arms. "You're a nosey little thing."

"I'm sorry. It must be terrible for you. Your husband . . . the man who was almost your son . . ."

"He was my son. My sister deserted him. She left him to us. We did everything for that kid. And he broke our hearts."

"Why?"

"How should I know. Because he's the devil, I guess."

"What does that mean?"

"Evil. He tried to destroy us." She turned and leaned on the end of the counter. She put her head down and for a moment I thought she was going to bang it on the white and beige streaked tile. "He succeeded. My husband killed himself."

"Oh. Oh, I'm sorry. That's awful."

"Hanged himself. Right there." She pointed at the corner where the fly buzzed. Part of the ceiling was discolored, a smear of patching material over a spot that was whiter than the rest of the ceiling. I put my hand on my throat. I couldn't help it. Touching that tender part of my neck reminded me how difficult it was to breathe when I'd seen the ghost. Was that why?

"Cut a hole in the ceiling, ran a rope over the beam. He put a lot of thought into it. A lot of thought into giving me the worst moment of my life, and the sight of him to carry with me forever."

"It must have been terrible for you."

She glared at me. I shouldn't have said anything. Saying something inadequate is worse than silence. It takes the other person's feelings and wads them up in a tiny ball and stuffs them in a container with other wadded up feelings so the person feels small and unimportant. They feel as if they don't exist, and their feelings are unimportant.

The corner, with the fly buzzing in circles as if it couldn't find a safe place to land, looked empty and tragic. I wondered how she could be in the kitchen at all. I wondered why she'd brought me to that room instead of the perfectly tranquil living room. Or maybe nothing in the whole house was tranquil any more. It made me more curious about the objects that created the blank spots on the living room walls. Asking about them would take me off course, so I shoved it to the back of my mind. The fly continued to circle. It upset me to think what it might be attracted to in that space.

I turned, trying not to look obvious that I was turning away from the corner with its bleak walls and the patched-up ceiling.

A man who'd ended his life like that — trying to inflict pain — would surely be restless. So he'd found his way to his nephew's. I don't know how that's possible, but I suppose if you're not bound by physical barriers, you're not doomed to stay in a single place.

"I'm so sorry you've suffered so much — with your

husband, your nephew's murder."

"Is there a point to your chatter?"

"Yes."

"Because right now you're striking me as an ambulance chaser, or one of those people who feed on the grief of others."

"That's a terrible thing to say."

"Which part?"

"Both, but especially feeding on your grief. I'm not like that at all. I feel sad for you."

"Well it's my impression. So what is your point? I don't think it's just reminiscing about Larry."

"I've seen a ghost."

She laughed. "What does that have to do with anything?"

"It was looking for Larry. In my bedroom."

"Oh. Oh, I didn't realize. Are you the woman he was seeing?"

"How do you know about that?"

"I know things that are my business to know."

"I'm not her. And I don't know why the ghost was there. It scared me."

"I imagine if I saw a ghost I'd be scared. If ghosts existed, which they don't, and maybe you running around talking about dead people, prying into their lives, makes you impressionable to delusions."

"You don't believe in ghosts?"

"Absolutely not. If there were ghosts, I'd be more haunted than most." She glanced toward the corner.

Looking at the space it almost seemed as if I could see his body hanging there. I couldn't imagine a more horrifying sight. At least when I found my parents' bodies they looked peaceful. Seeing them lifeless, stiff, is an image that stayed in my mind for all of high school and beyond. It's dimmer now. I remember more the memory of it than the thing itself. But they did look peaceful. And they were together. Larry's uncle had left his wife behind to suffer alone, whatever it was they suffered. It was the cruelest thing imaginable. It might have been less painful to tell her he no longer loved her and walk out. Instead, he told her he not only didn't love her, he was going to make sure she was miserable for the rest of her life.

Or maybe people aren't thinking about others at all when they kill themselves.

Still, I could see in every twitch of her lips or blink of her eyes, even in the tangled curl of her hair, that she was saturated with grief. I wondered how she kept going, how she managed to eat and shower and wash her plate. I imagined she didn't sleep much. "And Larry?" I said.

"What about him?"

"Does he haunt you?"

"I said I *would* be more haunted, not that I am."

"This ghost, this spirit I saw, came into my bedroom. It was looking for Larry."

"You're a nut case. I don't even know why I'm talking to you. I thought you had actual information about him. That you knew something about what was going on in his life, that you knew why he turned his back on his family.

Two people who gave up their whole lives for him. We didn't want children, and then we got him. He was already a surly eight-year-old."

It was difficult to imagine an eight-year-old being surly, but I didn't argue. There are some things, especially with people who have decided the world is a certain way, that it's not worth debating. Although I always want to. A surly eight-year-old? "I know it's hard to believe, but I did see this spirit and I think it was your husband."

"I'm done talking to you," she said. "I don't know what kind of sick person you are that you come to a grieving widow and mother, and suggest my husband came and talked to you from beyond the grave. Who the hell are you? A total stranger. Why in God's name would my husband's ghost show up in your bedroom looking for Larry?" She walked to the side door. "Go. Now."

I stood. "I'm trying to help."

"Exactly how are you trying to help?"

"I want to find out who killed Larry."

"Maybe I don't care."

"Because he stopped speaking to you? He wouldn't even open your birthday cards?"

She squinted at me. She was quiet for a long time. "How do you know about the birthday cards?"

I was equally squinty and quiet. How did she know the detective didn't tell me? Is that why the police didn't find them? The cards weren't there when I found Larry's body? Did she put them there?

She opened the door and stood back. "I asked you to

leave, I want you to go right now."

I walked to the door and the closer I got, the further she backed away until she was standing in the corner where her husband ended his life. I shivered. "I'm sorry I bothered you."

She didn't respond. I went out and closed the door.

IT WAS ALMOST ninety degrees. I could tell from the way the seat of the car burned through my jeans, making me squirm, half sitting sideways all the way back to San Jose. The outside area of my complex was deserted. No Alice sipping her cocktail. She must have decamped to her back deck, or inside, cuddled up to the AC.

It wasn't very reasonable to have thought Michelle would believe a total stranger going on about a ghost, but at least I knew for certain why there was a ghost. A man killed himself thinking he could escape whatever pain had seared his heart, but life, or the afterlife, or something, turned the tables on him and he was as tormented now as he had been when he cut a hole in the ceiling and wrapped a rope around a beam.

I sat at my dining table where the greeting cards were still propped up against the candle. I picked up the first one and read it again. Then I read the second one. As I studied her words, I could see Michelle's face. It wasn't hard to understand why she'd called me an ambulance chaser or why she didn't want to hear about her husband's ghost. I could see that a stranger showing up and claiming to know something about your husband that you didn't know yourself would be threatening. Even if you did believe in ghosts.

It seemed as though each shred of information increased my obsession with finding out more. Bits of knowledge and understanding should bring satisfaction, but when you don't know it all, it turns in on itself and becomes more consuming. Everywhere I looked all I saw were blank walls, dead ends, faceless spirits.

I spent half an hour on Google and came up with a three-sentence obituary, if you could call it that, from the San Jose Mercury News. It said Peter Sanford was the husband of Michelle, no mention of Larry. It said he worked for a high tech company doing quality control for most of his career, and he'd gone to college in Oregon. His whole existence — nothing but school, work, and the wife he'd stabbed in the heart and left full of rage, her life a gaping hole.

I Googled Larry's name along with his aunt and uncle's but nothing came of it.

I ate a cup of peach yogurt and three of JD's peanut butter cookies. I grabbed a chilled mocha coffee from the fridge door, untwisted the cap, and went out to the front porch. I took a long drink. I wondered what Alice would have to say about the suicide. I wondered what she would think of the ghost.

The sky was pale, hardly even blue. It was even hotter on my tiny front porch where the large support posts and narrow openings on each side keep out most of the wind and all of the rain, but also trap hot air. I walked down the steps and it felt more pleasant. The shadows were getting long, crossing the sidewalk and creeping up to the empty bench under the trellis.

I walked along the sidewalk past Larry's. So far, I hadn't seen anyone at the house since they'd removed the plastic ribbon, but it's not like I was out there watching it day and night. If someone else came in, the ghost might appear or it might decide to drift into my place again. I should have asked his aunt if the condo belonged to her now.

Information is like currency. I'm sure I'm not the first one to think that, but it's what I was thinking as I walked and sipped my nicely chilled coffee drink. If I told Alice about the hanging she would feel obligated to tell me what else she was keeping to herself. She seemed to like to dribble out information when she thought it might shock you, or whenever it floated across her gin-soaked brain, so maybe she wasn't holding out, maybe she just didn't remember at the appropriate time. And maybe she hadn't hidden anything from the detective — she honestly didn't remember at the precise moment he asked.

Currency might not be quite right because you don't exchange currency. It could be we're traders at heart. People used to exchange what they had for their labor before everything went to beads and shells, and then coins and cash and checks, and then credit cards. Now, money is just an illusion because it's simply numbers being moved from one computer to another.

If you tell people something interesting, often they'll

tell you something back. That might be why I preferred snooping around on my own. Cops and detectives break that rule. They want all your secrets and stories and observations, but they give nothing back. They hoard it until they have all the answers. Maybe that's why a lot of people have this contradictory respect versus resentment relationship with cops. You're in awe of how they risk their lives, you want to give them respect and listen because it's all of society trusting and depending on each other and if they don't have special authority, special privileges, then the whole thing kind of falls apart. But you do resent them — for throwing their weight around, for trying to intimidate you. For stashing secrets.

I didn't think it was gossip to tell Alice about the hanging. It was just information. I think about gossip more than the average person because Pastor Joe is obsessed with the topic. He hired me as a gossip preventer. His theory is that someone who doesn't belong to the church is less likely to get caught up in their politics and letting their curiosity run wild when a devout couple comes in for marriage counseling and the administrative assistant, sitting right there, sees it all. I really wasn't sure what the difference was between gossip and giving information. Another subject for Google.

Alice's front porch wasn't as stuffy as mine. Her place is near the end of the complex so the air isn't completely trapped. Or maybe it just felt cooler because I'd been walking in the shade. I rang the bell.

She opened the door right away. She'd changed into a

pink dress that came almost to her ankles. She'd pushed her thick bangs to the side and clipped them off her forehead. It no longer looked as if she was trying to hide her face from the world. Aside from the rearrangement of her bangs, she looked different and I couldn't figure out why. She led me into the living room and gestured toward the rocking chair. When she sat on the couch facing me I realized what was different. She didn't have a drink in her hand. I felt self-conscious with my coffee, but I took a sip, waiting to see if that prompted her to run to the kitchen and mix a fresh one. She remained seated.

"What do you want?" she said.

"I met Larry's aunt."

"Creepy lady, isn't she."

That wasn't how I would have described her. Sad, maybe. Angry. Tormented. I sipped my coffee and watched Alice, waiting for her to explain why she'd said that. But if there's one thing I should have known by now, she didn't feel compelled to follow normal social expectations. After a minute or so, I said, "What's creepy about her?"

"She's furtive."

"What do you mean by that?"

"Like she's hiding things."

I bit my lower lip and put the bottle there to cover my smirk. Was she projecting her own personality onto Michelle? "What do you think she's hiding?"

"If I knew, it wouldn't be hidden."

I laughed, glad to have something to cover my original reason for wanting to laugh. "But why do you feel that way? What gives you the idea she's hiding something?"

"I just know. She watches what she says. Never trust someone who bites their tongue. We are who we are, and if you have to always be biting back what you're thinking, what you want to say, then why even exist? Then you're not really a person at all, just a mirror reflecting back what other people want to hear." She crossed her legs and smoothed the pink dress across her knee. She lifted her hair off her shoulders and spread it across the back of the couch. It settled there like a nest of grayed twigs and threads.

"No one says everything they're thinking."

"This is different."

I guess I was just supposed to take her word as authority. I saw her point, and I agreed, but I couldn't quite make the connection between Alice's philosophy and knowing with such certainty that someone was keeping a secret. "I found out Larry's uncle hung himself."

"Is that right." Alice's face didn't move at all. Her lips spoke and then settled down into a resting position.

I was pretty sure she hadn't known, but her lack of animation argued with my assumption. "That's not what she's hiding," Alice said.

"She was pretty angry about it."

"Who wouldn't be?"

"She found him. Hanging from a beam in the kitchen.

It's too awful to think about."

She shrugged. The strap of her dress slid over her left shoulder. She left it hanging there — bright pink against the surprisingly dark tan on her arm. I waited. If she wasn't impressed with my information, maybe she wasn't going to let me in on her own secrets after all. Or maybe she had a good poker face and she was shocked, putting all the pieces together inside her mind. She remained silent.

The unspoken bargain of secret sharing wasn't working. Maybe she was too stale and cynical for such niceties. Or maybe it was the alcohol — it had fried her brain. She really didn't remember whatever it was she was holding back. I was being too coy. Playing games, even. "It seemed like there's something else you aren't telling me," I said.

"I don't know if I can trust you."

I put down my coffee. I crossed my arms and squeezed my fingers into my skin. "Trust me about what?"

"To leave me out of it. To do the right thing."

"What's the right thing?"

"I told you, Michelle asked me for a key to Larry's place. She screamed at me that she was worried about him and if he were dead it would be my fault."

"You didn't let her have it, did you?"

"She wanted a key, I gave it to her."

"Why?"

"What difference did it make? He left the sliding glass

door open all the time, even at night, and sometimes when he wasn't home. He thought no one could tell, with the drapes closed and stuff piled in front of it. He didn't think about the wind moving his drapes. These computer guys — so smart, but so dumb."

"Didn't you feel any responsibility for Larry? Why would you give out his key?"

"I don't need some crazy woman screaming at me. She was his aunt. So what if he didn't want her barging in on him. Like I said, his back door was open half the time."

I crossed my legs, so now my whole body was wrapped around itself like a caterpillar trying to form its cocoon. "Do you think she killed him?"

"I know she killed him."

"If you have information, why didn't you mention it before, or suggest that to the police?"

"I don't want to get dragged into it."

"But he was murdered!"

"They'll figure out who did it. They don't need me."

"How will they figure it out?"

"It's their job. Ask questions, gather evidence."

"Asking questions does no good if people like you don't answer them."

"Everyone else will. You will."

"Why don't you want to get dragged in? It's not like you have to do anything."

"If there's a trial, they'll make me go to court, they'll tell me I can't have a drink or something crazy like that."

"Why did you decide to trust me? And why didn't you trust me before?"

"You're a smart girl. Before I thought you were a fluff ball. Red hair. All the tattoos. The too cute car. But I misjudged you."

"Okay."

"And I trust you to find a way to tell the cops without dragging me into it."

I couldn't even figure out how to get her to give me information, how was I going to figure out how to tell the cops something that directly involved her without involving her? I could blame it on the haunting spirit, but they wouldn't want to hear that. "I'm sure they wouldn't make you go to court."

"I'm sure they would."

"Well they can't keep you from drinking."

"They could lock me up for days, force me to cooperate."

"I don't think they do that."

"How do you know?"

"How do you know she killed him?"

"He was abused," Alice said.

"Why do you think that?"

"There was something not right about him. He was damaged. The weird relationship with Leanne. The way he jumped every time you spoke to him."

"Lots of people do that."

She shrugged. "I think he finally spoke up."

"About what?"

"About what his uncle did to him. And his aunt didn't want to hear it. He told people and destroyed their lives. So she killed him."

"Well how do you know? You can't just say that."

She stood and backed toward the kitchen. "You can get going now."

"You think his uncle molested him? How do you . . ."

"I can feel it. One victim to another. Good-bye." She turned and went into the kitchen. I heard the refrigerator door open and ice cubes clink into a glass.

I wanted to stay, but she wanted me gone, so I left. No wonder she needed to know if she could trust me.

Eleven

THAT NIGHT JD came to dinner and I told him everything that had happened. He listened without commenting. When I was finished, he said, "So Larry told someone, maybe a lot of people, his uncle's secret and Michelle hated him for it."

"That's what it looks like. Maybe Michelle took the cards when she killed him and returned them later. But when, and what's bothering me more — why?"

JD popped open a can of soda and took a drink. "Everything bothers you." He winked.

It bothered me that he said that. I like things settled. I don't think that's a bad thing. His wink didn't do enough to soften his comment. "Don't you have any curiosity at all?" I said.

"I get curious, but I also mind my own business."

"I don't think I stick my nose in other people's business. Things kind of get in my face and it's hard to let go without trying to figure out what's going on."

He stood and walked to the back door. He slid the glass panel along the track to open it all the way. "If I had a ghost in my house, or tripping me up at work, I'd be curious."

"Good."

He turned. "So what are you going to do?"

"Larry spoke up and broke the family code, or whatever it was. His uncle was ashamed, or guilty, or depressed, or all of those things, and hung himself. His aunt blamed Larry for destroying her family and stabbed him. She took the greeting cards so the police wouldn't consider her. The uncle's ghost came looking for Larry, to make amends, to punish him, I don't know. I assume his aunt returned the cards, but I have no idea why. Maybe it doesn't matter. Help me think of an explanation."

"She didn't want them in her place in case the police did come calling, so she put them back?"

That made sense. I went to where JD was standing, took the can out of his hand, pushed him on the couch and sat on his lap facing him, with one leg on each side of his hips. "You don't even think about things, and a logical answer just pops into your head."

He tugged my ponytail. "It's an answer, I don't know if it's right."

"I was thinking she wanted them for memories and then changed her mind."

"You still haven't answered my first question. What are you going to do?"

"About the police?"

"Yes."

"I'll call the detective."

"And say, *I saw a ghost and I have other information but I can't tell you where I got it?*" He grinned.

I climbed off his lap and flopped down on my back with my legs across his lap. "I don't know. Can I just tell them that's what I think and not explain anything? They'd still check, if they're curious."

"Cops need more than curiosity to go on."

"That's not what I meant."

"What did you mean?"

"I guess that if they hear something, it will make them curious enough to start looking for things that will give them the evidence they need."

"Or you could tell them about the ghost. It might be easier, if you're really bent on not mentioning Alice's input."

"I think I'll sleep on it."

"Can I sleep on it with you?" JD said.

Of course I said yes.

SLEEPING ON IT did no good. I slept on it for three nights. On Tuesday morning, I was no closer to deciding how to go about it, but I knew I was going to tell the detective something. In the end, I took JD's advice and blurted out the ghost story. They treated me more seriously than you'd think. Or maybe they treated me carefully because they thought they had a wacko on their hands.

I asked them to find out why Michelle returned the greeting cards, left them sitting in the drawer, waiting for me to find them. Waiting to reveal the horrible secret of their family. Of course, she didn't know a curious neighbor would break into his condo. They never got back to me on that. It's not that I think the police department owes me an explanation, but the curiosity was still eating at me. There are a lot of things in life you never know and you have to put your mind elsewhere or the curiosity will twist your brain in knots and eat you alive.

When I got to the office, Kate and Joe were both there. They should have known I was talking to the detective, I'd called and left a message, but sometimes they can be stubborn about checking the voice mail because that's my job. I usually leave a message on their cell phones too, but I was too focused on getting to the detective's office on time and I forgot.

The coffee was already made and Joe's door was closed. I filled a mug and walked through the basement to Kate's office.

As always, she heard me coming, and was staring at the doorway, waiting for me to appear. "How'd it go?"

"Fine."

"What did you tell them?"

"I didn't bring Alice or Leanne into it."

"Why not?"

"They both wanted to be left out."

I smiled, wanting to tease her into asking more before

I mentioned the ghost.

"Sit down." She pointed at the wicker love seat.

I sat and told her about both of them. After every other sentence she said, *oh* or *wow*.

When I finished that part of the story, Kate said, "How did you manage to tell them who you thought killed him without bringing them into it?"

"All Leanne did was kind of show that he had some problems. And I told them I'd broken in, told them about the cards. Even that made them pretty interested. So when I brought up the ghost . . ."

"You told them you saw a ghost?"

"Yes."

"And they didn't open a file to keep an eye on you?"

I laughed. "Lots of people see ghosts. Twenty-five percent of Americans believe in them. I'm sure the police hear about it all the time."

"Maybe."

"I'm sure they hear even crazier stuff," I said.

"Good point. I guess a serious, average-looking, well-spoken person like you has credibility even if you say things that are beyond the norm."

I yawned.

"Still no sleep?"

"Not much." I yawned again and took a sip of coffee.

"What did they say about the ghost?"

"They didn't comment on that specifically, they just listened. I went pretty fast past the ghost part and got to what I thought and because I already gave them the cards, and obviously the cards hadn't been there when they collected evidence, they took my suggestion seriously. Although they weren't real happy I took evidence, or that I was in the condo."

"Hopefully they'll get all the answers. So you'll know what happened." Kate said.

"I already know the answers. I don't need them to confirm it."

She nodded. The room got brighter. The sun was now high enough that beams of light came in through the top portion of her sliding glass door. They fell on my face which was warming and soothing. The sunlight also made me want to curl up like a cat. I squinted and yawned again, deeper this time.

I scooted forward on the love seat. "I should get to work." I stood. "Oh, and I decided I will tell Joe why I need time off."

"I'm glad you let go of your pride," she said. "Like I said, it's not good to keep things inside, to be so protective of yourself. It keeps you from getting close to people."

"It hasn't kept me from that at all. And I don't want to get close to my boss."

"You know what I mean."

"No, I don't."

"I don't mean close like in a confidante or something, but from having a genuine relationship. You can't shut yourself up in a box and expect to interact with people around you."

"I don't do that."

"If you don't want to tell people what's going on, to explain why you need something, you sort of are."

"I don't think I owe people explanations."

"It's a fine line."

"Whatever you say." I swallowed some more coffee. The heat on my throat took away the constant desire to yawn.

"Don't be like that."

"Well it's a pointless conversation because I told you I'm going to tell him."

"I'm glad." She smiled. "Did you bring your lunch?"

"No. I was in too much of a rush to get to my appointment with the detective."

"Want to go out somewhere?"

"Sure." She suggested we go early at eleven-thirty and I went back to the main office. I put my mug down and knocked on Joe's door. He probably wouldn't appreciate the interruption for something personal, but now that I'd decided, I didn't want to wait.

He invited me in and I walked over to his desk. "I want the time off because I need some closure. My parents died when I was a teenager and I want to visit the house where I grew up."

He stared at me. For once, he didn't have any words handy.

"It's been bothering me for a while, and I really need to do it. That's all." I turned and went to the door.

"Wait."

I turned back.

He stood and walked around the desk. "I'm so sorry to hear that."

"Thank you."

"Why now?" he said.

"Because."

"I'm not asking that to stop you from going, I'm just curious."

"Well sometimes in life we're curious about a lot of things and we don't always get the answers."

"I hope it's therapeutic for you."

"Thanks." I went back to my desk. To the left of my computer was the mug that had broken cleanly in two a few days earlier. I sat down and thought about the pottery bowl I used as an upstairs ashtray — also broken in half. I remembered my dream where something I couldn't see was pushing, refusing to let up. Maybe it was my own self, that's what they say about dreams — everyone in the dream is really some aspect of yourself. I find that hard to believe, but I've read it several places, so maybe it's true.

I opened a browser window and entered "motels Novato California" in Google. A chill ran down my arms when the results appeared. It was really going to happen.

Cathryn Grant

EMPTY HOME

A Suburban Noir Ghost Story

Published by D2C Perspectives

One

PEOPLE SAY SMOKING is bad for you. Not just inexperienced people, but doctors, scientists, and people who have had a lung removed, who are attached to an oxygen tank, dragging it around like a shopping cart. And I know smoking is bad. But it feels so good. I know it can kill you, but the thing is, it doesn't always. Butter and cheese and beef will kill you. A drunk driver can kill you. A fire hydrant that explodes and hits you in the head — yes it happened. A gas line, poorly maintained for twenty years, can rupture under your house — you disintegrate without even knowing your life is ending.

You can come home from school and find your parents lying flat on their backs in their bed, blankets tucked around their bodies, peaceful smiles on their faces, eyes closed, as if they'd just made love. Although when you're fifteen, you aren't necessarily thinking in those terms about your parents. There's a round, black hole in the center of each forehead where the bullets went in.

Did they know they were going to die? Did they see who shot them? Were they surprised? Or scared? Or maybe even happy that they got to go out of this world side by side?

Okay, maybe they didn't look peaceful. I don't remember all the details that clearly. Except for those two bullet holes that shot holes in my heart.

And now, after I've lived almost as long without my parents as I lived *with* them, I'm going back to visit that house where they died. It's a long story why I've never been back inside the house. Mostly involving my very controlling aunt and uncle.

The minute they got *The Call*, they swooped in like a strike team and picked me up. I had to sit in the car with my uncle while my aunt packed up some of my things. I wanted to go back inside the house but he said, *Over my dead body*, which was a very poor choice of words.

He rambled on about bad vibes, dreadful energy. I think he even mentioned the spirit of the devil.

As best I remember, I watched police officers scurry in and out, carrying a lot of things out of the house in plastic bags, and I didn't know if they were mine, or exactly what they considered evidence. And since I never got to go through my room myself, I don't know if they have something that belonged to me, even now.

My aunt climbed into the back of the car, put her arm around me, straining her fingers to try to cover my eyes, although I don't know what she was trying to prevent me from seeing at that point in time.

I'd already seen the worst.

Later, more of my things, most of my things, appeared in the spare bedroom where they set me up. They drove me to and from school so I wouldn't disobey them and take a circuitous route home, passing by that house. They didn't speak of it so I don't know how long the police occupied it, if the house sold quickly, when it sold. Nothing.

To be honest, by the time I had my first car and the ability to pay a visit on my own, I was too freaked out by their muttered comments to want to even drive past the house. Eventually, when I was nineteen, I drove down the street on a rainy afternoon and parked a few houses away. It looked exactly as I remembered, except it was painted gray instead of white. The carport was empty and there was nothing to tell me anything about the occupants. I moved the car so I could see the wide, open backyard. The wood swing still hung from the tree.

Aunt Gloria and Uncle Paul firmly believed that, *a)* — the killer might return and try to hurt me, and *b)* — the place had a bad atmosphere that I was to be kept as far away from as possible. They never considered what kind of atmosphere they created with all their worries and rules and refusal to speculate about who might have killed my parents, and why. If the police shared information with my aunt and uncle, it wasn't passed along to me. I didn't talk to the detective, aside from the original questioning, until I was twenty-two, and living on my own.

His name was Detective Smith, believe it or not, Arthur Smith. He was nice enough, agreeing to meet with me, assuring me that driving by the house wasn't bad behavior unless I kept it up and the owners complained. He wouldn't tell me about the current owners. Maybe he didn't know much. I wondered if he thought I'd be bold enough to knock on their door and introduce myself, but I wasn't. Now I am bold enough, and I'm wondering what took me so long.

There are a lot of questions for the detective. He must be getting close to retirement and I have this *now or never* feeling about the whole thing. This time I'll ask more questions. This time, I won't give up and accept his official answer. This time, I'm going all out. Not like the other few times I called or spoke to him over the years. At the start, I nodded and listened because I was intimidated by him being an old guy who knew a lot and gave me a big story about how hard he worked trying to find my parents' killer. The second time I talked to him, I asked a few more questions, but he beat me down with a line about being *reasonable*, not *expecting too much*, and *now that I was an adult I could grasp how next to impossible their job was*.

When I think about the detective, I get kind of wound up. Which is one of several reasons I started the smoking — not because of him, but because it soothes me. I started smoking because I had to do something for *me*. I was fifteen. I had no siblings and my parents were dead. I had no living grandparents, and Gloria and Paul didn't have any children. If there were other aunts or uncles and associated cousins, I never knew about them.

In some ways I was a stereotype — a fifteen-year-old girl attracted to the *coolness* factor. A lot of people would say smoking is not cool, but it is. Watch the tough, smart people in movies, the sexy, funny people, the doers and the ones who take risks and are comfortable in their own skin. How often do you see someone smoking in a movie that is not a person you want to emulate in some way? I had nothing left in my life, my parents ripped out of my house, my bedroom wiped clean without a chance for me to say good-bye, my things looking out of place in a strange new room with a striped bedspread and a desk from a discount store that looked plastic, even if it wasn't.

My mother had home-schooled me until I was fifteen and I'd only started at a regular high school a few months before she and my father were murdered. Every single thing in my life was gone, or so different, I wasn't sure I recognized my face in the mirror. I needed a crutch. I needed a habit. I needed a ritual.

My aunt was not happy with my ritualistic habit. She told me I was ruining my voice and stinking up my mouth. She told me I was killing myself, one breath at a time. She said my mother wouldn't like it, my father would be disappointed in me. I stared at her. I didn't think she could possibly know what my mother would like or anything about my father's disappointment. And either way, they weren't there to tell me themselves, and I certainly wasn't going to let her start pretending she could make me live according to her rules by attributing all of her opinions and beliefs to my dead parents. I told her she should be glad I was going to school and studying and not getting high or living a life of crime.

She said I should be more thankful that I had a loving home.

After that, she backed down. She made faces, pinched her nostrils, coughed with loud, bloody, hacking sounds, and turned on the fan when I came into the kitchen, but she didn't say another word. Now that I'm an adult, I imagine she regretted using such harsh words. She looked a little startled at how quickly they came out, and she looked like she wasn't sure who said them, but she didn't apologize. Not then or ever.

And she didn't add in anything kinder to try to smooth it over, nothing about being glad they had a child to share their lives, nothing about how she was happy she could help her sister- and brother-in-law, and keep the few remaining threads of the family together.

Despite her aloofness, she treated me well, physically. She made sure I had a hot breakfast seven days a week and dinner every evening. I was expected to pack a lunch for school. She always had a choice of lunch meats and cheese, a few kinds of fruit, and homemade cookies. She washed my clothes and I was supposed to fold them, and she vacuumed and dusted my room, as long as I kept it picked up.

My chores were all outdoors — weeding, mostly. Sometimes pruning, and I felt a weird sense of pride that they trusted me with the deadly sheers that were sharp enough to slice through a branch three inches in diameter, like cutting a piece of hard cheese.

At first I smoked a lot — half a pack a day, sometimes more. I loved blowing thin ribbons of smoke into the air, watching it swirl and fade to nothing. I loved the rhythm and how my mind floated around with the smoke, stopped thinking and analyzing every single part of my life. When I'd been out on my own for a while, and didn't have to admit defeat to Aunt Gloria, I started cutting back.

Now, I only smoke three cigarettes a day. I haven't been able to cut further. I need those bookends and that mid-day pause. I'm not ready to let go of that habit that helped me through my grief and into adulthood. Not yet.

Two

IT WAS THE Friday before I planned to leave for Marin County. I'd decided to drive up on Sunday afternoon, scope out the house, and stalk the current occupants a bit. I didn't tell anyone that last part, not even JD. I'd asked my aunt and uncle if I could come to dinner on Sunday evening, but didn't tell them I was spending a week, getting in touch with the detective, or staking out the house. And I wasn't going to let out any of that information during our dinner either.

I hadn't seen my aunt and uncle in three years. When I'd called, Gloria asked why the sudden visit. I told her I just wanted to catch up. She said, "That's nice." Nothing about missing me, about how a family should remain more connected. But I was used to that. It's how she is.

At eleven-fifteen, Pastor Joe's wife opened the office door. Joe wasn't there, and Cindee has a pretty good handle on his schedule, so I assumed she was there to see me.

"If you don't have plans, I thought I'd take you to lunch." She smiled and tipped her head slightly so her long dark curls swung out to the side, making her look as if she were advertising detergent on TV. Her voice always has a musical quality, but right then, it sounded like it was slipping over the edge into full-on song.

"Why?"

She stepped up to my desk and put her purse down near the edge, making sure she didn't encroach on my space. "Why not?"

"What did Joe tell you?"

"Can't I invite you to lunch?"

We'd had lunch a few times over the years. Sometimes when she was around the church working on other projects or helping with food for the seniors' lunch, she'd suggest we grab something to eat. Maybe it seemed contrived because of how Joe reacted when I told him my parents had been killed — which had been a laser focus on the therapeutic value of visiting my childhood home. Or maybe I'm too suspicious. Or maybe it was that lilt in her voice, but I knew this wasn't like those other times.

The lights buzzed and the coffee maker sizzled from liquid trapped between the pot and the burner. Why it chose that moment to hiss, I have no idea. A crow shrieked outside as it moved from one tree to another, probably following up on a sighting of fast food spilled in the street.

"He told me about your parents. That you're taking time off to get closure."

Hearing her say it made me realize how mysterious it must appear to other people. That's what happens when you leave out half, or more like ninety percent, of the story. I just hoped Joe hadn't sent her on some sort of badly planned grief counseling mission, that she wasn't there to force me to talk out my feelings. Pastor Joe is big on talking out your feelings. So is Pastor Kate. And I see the value in that, but it has to be the right time. It definitely has to be the right person. Cindee could eventually be that person, one of those people, but not yet.

I suppose, as Kate accused me of, I'm a secretive person. I wanted to walk back through the beginning of my life alone. I was an only child, and then I was an orphan, and doing this alone seemed right. JD seems to know I need to do this alone. Although I think he's worried that I'll run smack into a concrete wall again, and he doesn't understand why I think this time will be any different. But how could he? I'm not sure I understand why I think it will be different. It might all be wishful thinking.

Cindee and I went to a Thai place on Forrest Street. One other table was occupied with a mom, grandma, and grandchild. But by the time we ordered our food, a few groups of business types had filled up several more tables and it didn't have that echoing where everyone hears every word you speak so you're afraid to say anything, as most conversations sound lame when there's an audience of strangers.

Cindee poured tea into both our cups. "Why didn't you ever mention that your parents died when you were so young?"

"Joe should have told you I'm not going to talk about it."

"You must be hurting a lot."

"Do I look like I'm hurting? Do I sound like it?"

Our spring rolls arrived. I filled my tiny dish with peanut sauce, dipped the end of a roll in the dark creamy ochre-colored liquid, and took a searing bite.

"You have a tough shell," Cindee said.

I eased off the harshness in my voice. "I don't like to talk about it. Okay?"

"I'm trying to be your friend."

"I know." I did know. And I believed her. But she's my boss's wife. Thinking of her as a friend at all could be dangerous territory. Working in a church isn't like a regular job. It blurs the lines between boss and employee. In some ways, Pastor Joe and Kate are my bosses, in some ways, only Joe is, and in other ways, every member of the church is my boss.

"Can I ask why you don't have closure?"

I finished my spring roll. I picked up the third one on the plate. I don't know why they do that — maybe it's some kind of up-sell thing where they want you to get two orders, so they always bring odd numbers.

"How long ago was it when your parents died?" she said.

"Fourteen years."

"Oh. That's a long time. It makes me sad that you

didn't get closure."

"Are your parents alive?"

"Yes. But I know how it feels to lose people close to you."

I shoved the rest of the spring roll in my mouth. Sort of like a plug to keep myself from blurting out — *Do you know how it feels to have someone close to you murdered?* Talking with my mouth full, I said, "Maybe you don't know how long it takes."

She looked at the empty plate.

"Sorry," I said. "Should we get another order?"

"No, we have so much food coming already."

As if Cindee's words had summoned her, the server arrived with a plate of pot stickers, followed quickly by Mus-Mun with chicken, red curry beef, rice, and pad Thai noodles. We took turns spooning steaming food onto our plates. Cindee poured more tea, and we started eating. The place was filling up and the sound of voices swelled around us, loud and insistent enough that I had the ridiculous thought we might not have to talk at all, it would require so much work to compete with the noise.

I was wrong.

"Why did you decide to go now?"

"I told you I don't want to talk about it."

"Sorry. I'm just concerned. What are you planning to actually do while you're there? Do you know the people who live in your old house? Do you have relatives there?"

I laughed. "It would take me the rest of lunch to answer all those questions."

She smiled and tilted her head to the side in that coy way again. "Then feel free to start any time."

I put down my fork. I sipped some tea and looked at her, waiting to see if she realized how pushy she was being and would lower her gaze. She didn't. She stared at me, chewing slowly. She swallowed and poured more tea for both of us.

"I really do not want to talk about it," I said.

"That's not normal."

"How would you know?"

"I'm married to a minister. I've been around a lot of people who experienced loss."

"I'm not a lot of people."

"That's not what I'm saying."

"I just don't feel comfortable talking about it."

"At all? Or to me?"

"To most people."

"Why not? Are you afraid you'll fall apart?"

"No."

"Then what is it?"

I wasn't talking about what happened to my parents or my feelings, but we sure were talking all around it. I couldn't figure out if that was her plan, if she was manipulating me or just overcome with concern. I wanted to believe it was concern, she's such a sweet person, but I wasn't a hundred percent sure. The way she'd swooped in and asked me to lunch and jumped right onto that topic. Although I suppose the fact that I was taking a week off made it a natural subject of conversation.

"How are your girls?" I said. "Are they excited for summer vacation?"

"Lily, Patti, and Michelle are. Joy isn't as excited, because we told her she needs to get a part-time job. Don't change the subject." She took a few bites of curried beef. "I think I know what it is," she said.

"Oh?" I dribbled more tea into our cups and nudged my plate away.

"Aren't you going to eat any more?"

"It's too much."

"We can take it home."

"You can. Remember, I'm going out of town."

"I think all these ghosts you keep talking about have made you think you can hunt down your parents' ghosts."

"How do you know I haven't seen them already?"

"Have you?"

"No."

She smiled. The look in her eyes had a hint of smugness, as if she'd won, forced me to crack open and reveal my secrets.

"Is that what it is? Do you know the people who own your old house?"

"No."

"No to which question?"

"I don't know who owns the house."

"Is that why you don't want to talk about it? You're afraid I'll tell Joe?"

"Why would I be afraid of that?"

She looked down. She poked her chopstick at a

noodle, swirling it around a few broken peanut pieces. "Afraid he'll get fed up with all the talk of ghosts."

"Is that what he said? Am I going to lose my job if I see another ghost?"

She looked at me. "Oh, no. He's not like that."

"Then what would happen if he got *fed up*?"

She shrugged.

"So I could lose my job."

"He really likes you. And you're a great office assistant."

"But he hates the ghosts."

"He thinks you're imagining them."

"I know what he thinks."

"He doesn't understand what your motivation is."

"My motivation? Did he tell you to come talk to me about this?" I drank my whole cup of tea and then half my glass of water, trying to slow my breathing. Then I had to pee, but it didn't seem like a good time to leave the table.

"No. I think he's just frustrated. He can't wrap his head around it."

"Because he's stubborn. And if he believed what I said, he wouldn't be looking at it that way. I just tell people what happens to me. I can't help it that ghosts seem to want to find me. What am I supposed to do?"

"I don't know." Her voice was soft. She continued dragging the noodle around the plate like she was making a finger painting.

She changed the subject then, suddenly eager to talk about her daughters, about their family vacation in June, right after school was out, so Joy could spend the rest of the summer in her part-time job. They were planning a trip to New Orleans, which I thought was pretty funny. Talk about a place known for ghosts. But I didn't point that out. I didn't think she'd appreciate it. She was trying to be nice, caught between Joe and I. She believes me, I think, although she isn't quite sure she believes ghosts are real, but she doesn't think I'm making things up, or hallucinating.

Sometimes, I'm a little surprised Joe hasn't told me to find another job. Not that he'd fire me, putting a stain on my resume, but telling me it's not working out. Maybe he's more curious than he lets on. Maybe his dogma won't allow him to listen to me or consider the possibility, but his human side is whispering from the back corner of his mind, *What if she's not making it up?*

The check came. Cindee poured more tea. "Are you going to tell me?"

"Tell you what?"

"If you're hoping to see your parents' ghosts. Is that what you mean by closure?"

"I wouldn't be disappointed if I did see them."

"After all this time, do you think that's . . . possible?"

I broke open my fortune cookie.

"How did they die?" she said. "A car accident?"

"Not going to talk about it," I said.

"Okay. And what about hoping to see their ghosts?"

"Maybe."

She smiled triumphantly.

I handed my fortune to her and she did the same.

Hers said, *You are going on a trip soon.* Big surprise. Some fortune.

Mine said, *What you hope for will come to pass.*

Three

THE MOTEL ON Elm Drive in Novato had looked like as good a place as any when I found it online. It was trying hard to be quaint but was really the old fashioned kind of motel with several small buildings, each with three or four rooms, scattered in a haphazard fashion around a parking lot. There were a lot of trees and shrubs, although I don't think there were any elms. At least it looked exactly like the photographs.

I checked in and put my clothes in the drawers. I'd brought my coffee press since I can't live without good coffee. There was a burner and kettle so I'd be able to get my water nice and hot. There was also a small fridge where I stashed a pint of half-and-half, three peaches, two pears, and a ball of mozzarella cheese. Smoking wasn't allowed in the rooms, which wasn't a surprise, but they nicely provided a bench at the back of the property and a concrete ashtray filled with sand — better than most five-star hotels would probably offer. It was a family-owned place with a tiny old lady running the front desk and I guessed they were realistic regarding the number of smokers who might be passing through.

It was only three-thirty by the time I settled in so I had plenty of time to drive by my old house before I saw my aunt and uncle for dinner. Although I was terrified of how it would feel to see that house, locked in my memory, I figured it was better to tackle it right away.

As I drove down Elm and turned onto Front Street, I found myself going so slowly I must have looked like an old lady myself, driving my Beetle five miles under the speed limit. Cars crept up close to my bumper, then passed me, a few with excessive pressure on the gas and a burst of speed to express their frustration with my sluggish pace.

When I reached the T intersection at my old street, I pulled over to the side. My heart pounded like I'd run three miles. I wiped my hands on my jeans and grabbed the steering wheel again but my skin was still damp. My scalp felt hot and wet even though my hair was in a ponytail. I studied the trail of vines tattooed around my wrist. They made me feel connected to the earth, reminded me of who I was, but I still couldn't manage to shift my car back into drive and proceed around the corner onto Whitewood Way — number 1701.

I turned off the engine, got out of the car, and lit a cigarette, my fourth already. Across from where I was parked was a small market and next to that, a strip mall, more like a strip of a strip mall because there were only three stores — a UPS drop-off, a flower shop, and a

Laundromat. As I looked at the strange combination and lifted the cigarette to my lips, my hand shook. I imagined my father buying flowers for my mother. Although the minute I had that thought, I realized it was overly sentimental because my parents had a huge flower garden with gorgeous roses and tulips, irises and gladiolus blooming every year. It wasn't likely he ever bought her flowers in a shop, if the shop even existed fifteen or twenty years ago. I put out my cigarette, got in the car, drove quickly to the corner, and turned left.

The house was in a somewhat rural, unincorporated area where there weren't any of the six-foot-high fences that enclose most California yards. The roads were wide, without sidewalks, lined with mature trees, and the grass surrounding the homes wasn't all trimmed and clipped into perfect square boxes. The houses were smaller and more run down than I remembered. The yards that had play equipment looked almost abandoned, a few bicycles half buried by un-mown grass, swing sets that were rusted to a copper color. My Bug rolled along, powering itself from the momentum of the gas I'd given it when I rounded the corner. At 1697 I drifted to the side of the road.

In my memory, my house is cheerful — white with green trim. There's no picket fence but there might as well be. I remembered the large flower garden in front of the living room window and the vegetable garden filling half the back yard. I also remembered lots of space, the length of three or four houses between each house on the street. Sure, it was small but it used to look better cared for.

Now, number 1701 was painted dark blue instead of the gray it had been the last time, and the trim was the same color as the house, as if someone couldn't be bothered to tape it off and paint with a different color. The grass was mowed, but it was mostly brown, because of the drought, I suppose. Still, that made it look sad, even though all its neighboring yards were equally brown. There were no toys in the yard, and the flower garden had disintegrated into a big, unruly patch of dirt with half-dead plants and weeds. The few lingering rose bushes were leggy.

A silver minivan was parked in the carport. All the drapes on the front windows were closed. It wasn't going to give me any hints about the people who lived there, and it sure didn't offer any suggestion of the family that had occupied it so many years ago. If it wasn't for the number, and the size of the dying garden, I might think I'd come to the wrong house, the wrong street even. It was impossible to tell if the area had changed, or people had less time or money to care for their houses, or if my memory was completely clouded by the happy eyes of childhood.

Before I realized what I was doing, I'd shoved open the door and climbed out. I closed it carefully and leaned against the side of the car, staring at the house. I didn't plan to knock on the door. That would come later, after I'd reconnected with my aunt and uncle, after I'd talked to the detective. But here I was, my feet moving deliberately around the car and up past number 1699. Anyone watching would have thought I was very determined, not hesitant or afraid in any way, and yet I felt I was in a dream, walking into the past. I stopped at the end of the driveway and stared at the concrete, as if I expected my chalk drawings to rise to the surface after all these years, giving me a sketch of my childish mind, telling me things I'd forgotten.

There was no more life to the house from my closer vantage point. In fact, there was no life in any of the surrounding houses. It was a Sunday afternoon. You'd think someone would be washing their car, or a few kids would be outside, or the smell of barbecue would be filling the air. It was hot, so maybe the entire neighborhood was indoors, watching TV, running the AC, planning takeout for dinner.

I looked toward the end of the street. Two boys were kicking a soccer ball, not back and forth to each other, but chasing it around like it was an escaped animal they were trying to corral. I glanced back to the intersection and saw a car pull into the driveway of the first house. I let out a breath. Now that I could see the street wasn't as vacant as I'd thought, I could relax a bit.

A small part of me wanted to walk up and ring the bell, wanted to be done with it. But even after all that time, all that thought, I hadn't considered what I would say to the occupants. With all those dreams and fantasies of someone opening the door, none of them contained any specific words, just feelings of recognition toward the house. And right now, there wasn't a single thread of recognition. I suddenly realized I hadn't considered what I might say because in some confused, twisted part of my brain, I expected my parents to answer the door.

I hurried back to my car, climbed in, and started it, so I could enjoy a little AC of my own. I pulled out my phone and sent a text to JD.

Madison: Drove by the house. Not ready to barge into the past.

He texted back right away. Even though he was at work, he must have had the phone propped in front of him on the bar.

JD: Take it easy. Deep breath.

I pressed the button for the phone function, but couldn't think of what I'd say to him. I didn't want to try to describe it, didn't want to talk about expectations versus reality, and definitely didn't want to talk about imagination versus reality.

There was a thud on my window. I jerked and the phone fell onto the floor. A woman stood peering into the car, her expression a little bit scared and very annoyed. I lowered the window halfway.

"Are you looking for someone?" she said. Her long hair fell forward, brushing against the window. She looked about forty, and wore a blue tank top that revealed surprisingly muscular arms. She didn't have any makeup on and her feet were bare, which looked uncomfortable on the pavement in the heat. As if she'd just realized what

I was thinking, she rose to the balls of her feet and danced around a bit. Then she lowered her heels and put her hands in her pockets.

"No, not really."

"Then why are you sitting here?"

I stared at her. I had no idea what to say.

"What do you want? Are you Ken's wife?"

"No."

"I mean ex-wife."

"No."

She folded her arms. I continued staring at her while hot air crept into my car. After a minute or two, it felt as if I'd never had the AC on at all. It must have been close to ninety degrees. The trees around us stood motionless.

"I don't like strangers lurking on our street. This is a nice neighborhood. Safe."

Up until my parents were shot in their bed, I would have agreed it was a safe area. I don't recall a moment of fear when I lived there as a child, playing wherever I wanted, never thinking about strangers. And now I looked like a stranger, somewhat threatening, based on how this woman was acting. I never think of myself as having an unpleasant demeanor, but maybe with all my earrings and tattoos, I looked like a certain kind of person that made her nervous.

"Are you going to tell me what you're doing here? Or should I call the police?"

"I'm just driving by."

"You're not driving, you're parked. Watching."

"I used to live here."

"I've lived here for over ten years and I've never seen you before. I remember everyone."

"It was before that."

She lowered her brow, assessing my age, I'm sure.

"What house?"

I bent forward to pick up my phone. She let out a little shriek and jumped away from the car. She pulled a cell phone out of the back pocket of her jeans. I guess she thought I was reaching down to get a gun. Obviously she did not think her neighborhood was as safe as she wished. I released the parking brake. "I'll get going, I was just taking a walk down memory lane."

"Well it's weird."

"Sorry."

She took another step away from my car. "I hope you won't be coming back."

I smiled. "It's a public street."

"We don't like loitering. So if you need more trips down memory lane, you can expect the police to walk with you."

I really didn't want to attract attention and I didn't want her to remember me, but it was too late for that. I should have realized the quiet outskirts of a smallish town near an exclusive community would notice every strange vehicle that turned down the street. "Bye. Sorry I upset you." I put the car in gear, pulled forward, and made an easy U-turn. When I reached the end of the street and put on my turn signal, she was still standing there, watching me drive away, holding her phone in case she changed her mind and decided to call the police.

UNCLE PAUL and Aunt Gloria lived in a large, modern house. It wasn't the house I'd moved into when I was fifteen. This one was on a hillside, all straight lines and glass, with tile floors in soothing earth tones. Every single piece of furniture announced they had money to burn. My first thought was whether any of that cash came from my parents, and my second thought was actually two thoughts — why was that my first reaction and why was it that I really knew very little, nothing actually, about what my parents had and how their estate had been settled? I got a nice amount of money that helped me buy my condo and had enough still on hold for my college education. But obviously I was a kid when all that got sorted out. I'd never once thought about it until I stepped into that entryway and looked down the main hall, out at their rock garden that formed the back yard, stretching to the edge of a cliff with a beautiful view of Marin County.

Aunt Gloria opened the door and greeted me with a polite smile. After she ushered me into the living room, she stood on the opposite side of the coffee table, looking at me, but not actually meeting my gaze. "Would you like a glass of wine?"

"No thank you."

She looked offended. She pushed her short wavy, nicely highlighted brown and silvery hair off her face and smiled. "I thought now that you're an adult . . ."

"Remember, I don't drink." I guess she didn't remember.

"Well. Okay then. Water?"

"Sure."

"What kind?"

"What do you mean what kind?"

"Sparkling or still?" said Uncle Paul. "Flavored or plain? Pellegrino or Volvic?"

"Sparkling. Lime if you have it. I don't care what brand."

"Certainly." Gloria turned and walked out of the room. Her bare feet made no sound on the sage tile. Her black dress clung to the backs of her legs, and she was busy pushing her hair away from her face again as she turned the corner.

"To what do we owe this honor?" Paul said.

"I told Aunt Gloria when I called — I haven't seen you in ages, and I thought we could catch up."

He nodded but looked confused. His head was very round, the gray hair trimmed super short, and the top bald and shiny. He had rimless glasses but because of the angle of the light coming through the windows, I couldn't see his eyes. "Anything specific you wanted to catch up on?" He sat on a large ottoman, his posture perfectly straight, his hands curled into fists, pressing on his kneecaps. "Or just wanted to see the new house?"

"I didn't even know you'd moved until I talked to Aunt Gloria."

He nodded.

"How long have you lived here? It's gorgeous."

"Thanks. Almost two years."

Gloria returned with a bottle of sparkling water and three large, delicate wine glasses on a tray. One glass was empty, a wedge of lime stuck on the rim. The other two were half-filled with white wine. She let Paul take one, then held the tray in front of me. She put the tray on the table and stood holding her own glass. She took a sip and smiled. "So what brings you here?"

They were starting to creep me out. I repeated my reason, which now sounded like a foolish desire. Their faces were both formed into pleasant, somewhat vacant expressions. These people were my surrogate parents and they acted like I'd stopped by to sell them a water filtration system. They'd always been formal, slightly cold, probably not that excited to have a teenager invade their very settled lives when they were in their mid-forties, but they'd agreed to be guardians. I'm sure it was a shock, but if they really were that set on never having a kid in their lives, why would they accept the responsibility? Of course most people who sign up to be guardians know it's unlikely they'll be called on to help, but they have to consider the possibility it could happen.

"I haven't seen you in almost three years. And not a lot before that. I feel like we've drifted so far apart since I moved out. I wanted to see how you're doing."

"We're doing good . . . very well." They spoke at the same time, but Paul said *good* and Gloria said *very well*, canceling each other out.

"That's great." I smiled. I squeezed the lime into the sparkling water and dropped the wedge in the glass.

"And how are you doing?" Gloria said. She smiled over the edge of her glass, which hadn't moved more than three inches from her lips the whole time she'd been sitting there.

I told them about my job at the church. They smiled and sipped their wine. I told them about JD and our trip to Australia. They smiled and sipped their wine some more.

"Are you going to apply for college soon? Before it's too late?" Paul said.

"Too late for what?"

"You're not getting any younger," Gloria said.

"True. But I'd rather know why I'm going instead of randomly taking classes. I've done enough of that."

"Your parents always planned for you to go," Paul said.

"I know."

"You're letting them down, don't you think?" He didn't smile or put any kind of expression on his face to soften the harsh comment. He set his glass on the table and folded his arms across his chest. He tapped his index finger on his bicep as if counting the beats until I coughed up a good explanation.

"I don't think I am. They also would want me to live life, to not feel pressured. Don't you think?"

He shrugged. "I have no idea. Their thought processes baffled me."

I stared at him. After a few minutes, when he didn't add any explanation, I looked at Gloria. Her face was the same impassive mask as his. My fingers and toes were suddenly icy and I wondered if they'd always been this cryptic and cold and I was more aware because I was older, or if something had changed.

I looked at the back patio, then turned my gaze to the enormous painting on the wall across from me — something abstract that looked like the colors had been selected to match their décor, which made me wonder how much they really liked it as a painting rather than a color enhancement — like matching towels in the bathroom.

Gloria stood and polished off her wine. "Do you still smoke?"

"Yes. But I'm cutting back." I smiled.

"That's what they all say. Excuse me." She walked out of the room, heading in the same direction she'd gone earlier, so I assumed she was ready for a refill.

"Are you ever going to attend college seriously?" Paul said.

"Yes."

"What are you planning to study?"

"That's the problem. I don't really know, and it doesn't make sense to go with no purpose."

"I suppose that's understandable."

Gloria returned with her glass and the bottle of wine. She refilled hers and topped off Paul's. She remained standing. She propped her elbow on her opposite forearm and proceeded to take tiny sips.

"So, to what do we owe the honor of your presence?" Paul said.

I felt like I was in a surreal movie, the director playing with timelines and human interaction to create an unstable, unnerving atmosphere. Why did they keep asking the same question? When I'd called, Gloria hadn't acted as if they didn't want me to visit. Maybe I wasn't as clever as I'd thought. Maybe they saw right through me and knew I was here to harass the detective and they were taking a typical parental tactic — pressing their stony façade against me until I admitted what I was up to.

"Why did you quit your job in high tech?" Paul said. "I imagine it paid a lot better than working in a church."

"It did. But I'm doing fine."

"You're not blowing through what Dave and Annie provided, are you?"

"No."

"And your college fund is untouched?" He took a long slow swallow of wine then coughed repeatedly.

"No. But I . . ."

He put his glass down and held up both hands, palms facing me, as if setting up to shove me off the cliff outside their window. "Hold on. Don't even ask. Let me save all of us some awkwardness. We worked hard for our money, and we gave you several years of our lives. Full time. Exactly what was asked. And then some." He glanced up at Gloria, then back at me. "Putting up with the smoking. But we are not loaning you any money, and we're certainly not giving you any. Your parents provided very well for you. We're done."

I stood up. Inside, I was hissing at myself. *Don't cry. You won't cry. This isn't the way it sounds.* But it sure seemed the way it sounded. "I would never ask you for money. Never."

"Then why did you suddenly invite yourself for dinner?" Paul said.

"I wanted to see you." My voice was a strained whisper.

"My mistake. Apologies," Paul said.

Gloria smiled and perched on the arm of his chair.

"Why would you think that?" I said. Now, my voice was too loud, but I couldn't help it.

"The unexpected call. Because you're under-employed."

"It looks like you haven't had a haircut in months," Gloria said. She smiled with such a gushy, maternal look, I expected her to jump up again and offer to make foster mother-daughter makeover appointments.

"I like it long. So does JD."

She smiled. She switched her wine glass to the other hand and ran her fingers through her short, silky hair, stroking it as if she were petting a cat.

I was still standing. I walked to the other side of the room and looked out at the rock garden. It was filled with cactus, including an enormous saguaro that reached past the roofline. Winding among the boulders and smaller pools of rock was a gravel path. Near the edge of the property was a gazebo and inside was a wood table and chairs with a cactus in a pot sitting in the center. I turned to face them. "Do you want me to leave?"

"Oh, no," Gloria said. "Please don't think that."

"Now that we cleared the air," Paul said, "We hope you can stay for dinner."

I'd already thought I was there for dinner and was beginning to feel more and more like a freeloading interloper. "Is that really the kind of person you raised me to be?"

"Oh, we didn't raise you at all," Gloria said.

"Part of the time you did."

"You were already a finished product by the time we got you." She smiled. "And of course, I didn't agree with Annie's child-rearing philosophy at all. Not at all."

"Oh." I folded my arms around my ribs.

"Not that we were really clear on what that was," Paul said. He chuckled and stared into his wine glass as if he might find the answer at the bottom. He looked up. "To be honest, Madison, we were surprised to get you."

"Why are you telling me all this?"

"We'd assumed that now that you're an adult, the transaction was complete," he said.

"Transaction?"

"I guess since you were a child, you weren't aware," Gloria said.

There was a buzzing feeling between my brain and my skull, making me feel as if my brain were vibrating. I wished I had a drink of water, and not anything sparkling with lime. Just a nice plain glass of water. Or a cup of coffee. I felt like I'd mistakenly walked into the home of strangers, that I really was out selling something and was invited into this *Alice in Wonderland* wine party.

Gloria stood and walked toward me. "You look pale, hon. Come have a seat." I let her take my elbow and she guided me back to the leather sectional. It felt like a very long way down as I lowered myself to sit. She arranged herself next to me and put her wine glass on the table.

"Annie and I weren't really speaking to each other when she was . . . when she . . ."

"When she was murdered?" I said.

She nodded.

"Why not?"

"I don't want to speak ill of the dead, and it's not important now. The point is, we were very surprised to get you. We assumed they'd changed their will."

I waited for a few seconds, trying to stop the buzzing, trying to breathe so my voice wouldn't come out on the edge of tears. "You never wanted me?"

"I wouldn't put it like that," Paul said.

"How would you put it?"

Gloria jerked away from me. I guess my voice was louder than I'd planned. "Calm down," she said.

"You're telling me my parents were shot in their bed and then the people who were supposed to love me in their absence didn't even want me? And you thought once I grew up I'd just disappear and leave you alone?"

"You're making it sound terrible," Gloria said. "It

wasn't like that."

"Then explain it to me."

"We were caught off guard," she said.

"That's not an explanation. Why didn't you ever tell me this?"

"We try to make the best of things."

I laughed with a harsh, ugly sound.

"Don't be upset," Gloria said.

I stood. "Thanks for showing me your new home. I'm going to head out now." I walked to the end of the couch and picked up my bag.

"Wait. Don't be upset. You're taking this the wrong way."

I didn't think I was, but I sure wasn't going to talk to them about it anymore. I held my bag in my arms like a cat to be sure it didn't swing around and break any of the glass objects sitting on tables scattered between the couch and the foyer. Neither one of them stood or tried to follow me. They called after me, asking me not to be upset, not to rush off, wondering about the dinner Gloria had prepared.

In the driveway, I tossed my bag into the car on the passenger side, got in, and drove down the narrow private road away from their house. I had three things in mind — find a place to have a cigarette, find a place that had good hamburgers and fries, and figure out what the hell had just happened to me.

Four

AFTER ESCAPING FROM my aunt and uncle's, I'd found a terrific burger place. I'd gobbled down a juicy patty and bun, trying to think about meat and lettuce and tomato and ketchup, and fat, salty fries, and nothing else. It worked fairly well because the burger place was filled with teenagers. Watching them flirt and fool around and strut and posture was like watching a live reality show.

After I'd eaten, I'd gone back to my cottage and sat out on the bench for a few hours. I smoked seven cigarettes and didn't feel one speck of irritation at myself for going way over my limit. The smoke kept my brain from exploding. At least the buzzing had subsided while I ate my burger. I'd thought about calling JD, but had no idea what I would say.

While I smoked, I thought back over the time I'd lived with my aunt and uncle and nearly every aspect of that part of my life suddenly looked very different than it had when it actually happened. Sure I knew they weren't the warmest people ever, but I didn't know they considered me an obligation. I wondered what had changed to make them spit out all that terrible information now. My other visits over the years also took on a different shape — casual conversations and questions about what I was up to. Now, all those questions seemed like efforts to reassure themselves I was fully independent. Maybe they thought moving to that new house meant a new life and they weren't expecting to ever see me again. It had been startling that they didn't bother to tell me they'd moved.

The way I remembered it, they'd arrived within an hour, maybe a little more, of when I called the police. I didn't remember calling them, so how did they know? It was something to ask Detective Smith. If I were to ask myself what I did remember, I would have guessed that a neighbor called them. But if they weren't in touch with my parents, how would a neighbor know they existed, much less that they were the named guardians?

The whole thing made my brain feel like it was full of splinters. I wondered if I was in an actual state of shock. I wasn't crying, just staring at things, random thoughts skating through, not settling down or having any impact. Part of me was angry with myself for losing my equilibrium and rushing out. I wanted to know why they hadn't been speaking to my parents when they were murdered. Now I'd have to figure out a way to see them again, to start over, if they'd even agree to a visit after my hysterical departure. It sounded like they'd already wanted to be done with me, now I'd given them a perfect excuse.

It was also surprising that although I was upset, I wasn't all that hurt. Maybe I'd felt their disinterest all along, maybe I never really loved them either.

After a while, I didn't want to think about it. All of the new information was exhausting. My main reason for being there was to talk to the detective and check out my house. I needed to focus on that. Seeing my aunt and uncle had been a sideline — it wasn't as if they knew who killed my parents. And I wasn't really interested in talking to them about ghosts and the possibility that my childhood home might be haunted. I'm sure I'm the only woman who ever wanted a house to be haunted. Usually people run from that kind of thing.

The next day, I woke before the sun came up. I'd heard cars coming and going from the little cottages most of the night. I dressed in a skirt and t-shirt and a short jacket, although I guessed that by ten or eleven, it would be too hot for the jacket. I put my hair up in a coiled braid and went the extra step with mascara and lip-gloss. I wore flat sandals. My plan was to drop by the police station as early as possible, hoping Detective Smith would be more open to seeing me before the day got going. I suppose for a detective, the day is going twenty-four-seven, but still, I thought there was probably some routine, more people coming by, more paperwork during peak business hours.

After I ate some cheese and a pear, I brushed my teeth and vowed no cigarettes until that evening. I didn't want to talk to the detective smelling of smoke, and depending on how things went with him, I was planning to go directly from there to my old house and ring the bell without pausing to think about it.

THERE WAS NO parking available in front of the police station. It was a small lot and one row was filled with official vehicles and marked police cars. In the second row, half the spots were roped off for some unknown reason. Regular cars occupied the rest, which was surprising at eight in the morning. I drove around the lot twice, and then expanded my loop and found a spot in front of an antique store with a sign that said it was closed on Mondays. I walked quickly back to the station, trying hard not to over-think my plan. I'd be flexible and friendly and sociable and all those good things that help you get what you want rather than plowing in like a rabid dog.

A cop with a blonde mustache manned the front desk. The mustache was big and bushy, but other than that, he looked crisp and cop-like.

I introduced myself and told him I was there to see Detective Smith.

"Do you have an appointment?"

"No, but he knows me."

"Is he expecting you?"

"Not exactly, but he's working on my parents' murder case."

"Did he ask you to come in?"

"He said I could stop by pretty much any time."

"Pretty much? That doesn't sound like him."

I smiled. "I won't take long. I just wanted to get an update."

"We don't give *updates*. If he has something he wants you to know, he'll be in touch with you."

"He can't spare five minutes?" I wanted more, but figured once I got in there, I could work on that part. "My parents were murdered, I really need to talk to him." Under the lip of the counter, I was crossing my fingers. It's very childish, but every so often it helps relieve tension to twist my fingers around each other when I'm hoping for the best. I was hoping he wouldn't ask when they were murdered.

"Let me check. What's your name?" he picked up the phone.

"Madison Keith."

He turned his back to me and spoke softly, working overtime to prevent me from catching his words. He put down the phone. "Detective Smith asked you to make an appointment."

"But I'm here now."

"He's headed out on an investigation."

"Right this minute?"

He nodded.

"What time can I make an appointment?"

"This afternoon. One o'clock or three-thirty."

"Oh." The clock on the wall behind him pointed to eight-ten. I couldn't go by my childhood house and introduce myself to the occupants this early. And now that I'd had a moment to think that through, I realized they'd probably left for work, unless there was a stay at home mom or someone who worked the night shift. Or unemployed.

I should have walked up to the door on Sunday afternoon when I had the chance, when the minivan was there, assuring me someone was home.

"Which one do you want? Or you can schedule something tomorrow."

"I'll take one o'clock."

He made an entry in his very old-looking computer and wrote the time on the back of a business card with Detective Smith's contact information. He held out the card. I took it, said thanks, and hurried out the door. Wouldn't I be lucky if I bumped into the detective in the parking lot? I'd seen all those official cars lined up — he'd be using one of them. It would be risky, possibly make him antagonistic, but it would be good just to see him and get a read on his mood so I could figure out the best approach for our meeting that afternoon.

When I reached the bottom of the steps, Detective Smith and another man were standing near the back of the building. The other man was talking on his phone and Detective Smith appeared to be sending a text message. Then I had a better idea. Instead of intersecting their paths right then, setting the wrong mood, I'd see what they were up to. I turned and nearly ran the two blocks to where I'd parked. I stuffed the card in my bag, got in the car, and drove back toward the police station. They were pulling out of the lot as I drove past. I made a U-turn in their parking lot and followed them. I'm sure they weren't expecting to be followed by a VW Bug, and as far as I could tell, they didn't notice I was there.

They drove about a mile and a half, passing the downtown shops, then a new housing development with a brick wall surrounding the homes. They ended up at a small apartment building. It was made of stone and looked to be about eighty years old, maybe more. Three police cars were parked along the curb and there were uniformed cops and a bunch of other people scurrying around.

I parked under a tree and watched Detective Smith and the other guy get out and talk to a uniformed cop, then disappear through the open gate into the center of the complex. I got out of my car, locked my bag in the trunk, put my key ring in my skirt pocket, and walked in the opposite direction to the end of the street. Then I turned, crossed the street, and strolled along the sidewalk as if I was out for a Monday morning walk. When I reached the area where the cars were parked, I slowed.

A female cop came up to me. "You can't be around here," she said.

"I'm just taking a walk."

"Not today." She gestured toward the opposite side of the street. "You can take your walk over there."

"What's wrong?"

"This is a crime scene."

That was sort of easy to figure out from the tape

stretched around the entrance, but I guess she thought if I were going to ask a stupid question, she'd go ahead and give an obvious answer. I inched forward. She moved to the side and blocked my way.

"I asked you to cross the street, Miss."

"What happened?"

She glared at me.

I smiled and tried to look kind, staring directly into her eyes, hoping to communicate that I understood the difficulty of her job, even though I know nothing about being a police officer. But I have a good imagination. "A murder?" I said.

"Yes."

"Who?"

She sighed. "Please leave the area."

I crossed the street and walked to the other end of the block. I rounded the corner and once I was behind a shoulder-high brick wall I turned and looked back to see if I could figure out another way in. Sometimes I get so overcome with curiosity, all my caution and every bit of experience I have about reasonable behavior gets chewed up by this burning need to know. I just have to *know*.

Studying the building and the gated opening, I knew there had to be a parking lot. They couldn't possibly have taped off the entire area. If I could find someone going to or from their car, I could soothe that little kid inside me screaming — *What happened? What happened? Tell me!* I crossed the street and walked past a hair salon and a mobile phone store. Sure enough, there was a driveway after the phone store that led to a small parking lot with a strip of trees forming the border, and beyond that, a large parking lot backing up to the apartment building.

I walked across the pavement, stepped on the grass strip surrounding the trees, and into the other parking lot. There were two rows of carports and uncovered spaces for visitor parking. The back of the apartment building was flat and bland like most of them are. Just rows of windows with molded concrete casings. There was a breezeway cut through the back of the building, but I couldn't see far enough down the corridor to make out what was going on in the courtyard.

At least two-thirds of the carports were empty. I walked slowly, trying to look down the breezeway, hoping a resident would come out before one of the cops decided to block off that entrance. I loitered for about ten minutes before I started to wonder if they were sequestering everyone, no matter if they had to get to work or a doctor's appointment or do anything to continue on with their lives. I lit a cigarette and took a few puffs. I figured since it was such a large open area, I didn't have to worry too much about smelling like smoke for my one o'clock meeting. And maybe it didn't even matter.

I was halfway done with my smoke, dropping my ashes on a pile of old cigarette butts, when a woman about thirty-five emerged from the breezeway. She wore very short denim cutoffs, a seventies-style halter top, and flip-flops. She had dark curly hair, not really long enough for a ponytail, but it was bunched up in one anyway. A lot of other hair was spilled out around her jaw. She was crying. She scrunched up her face as she stumbled out into the morning light. Her nose and lips were bright red. She covered her eyes with her hands and leaned against the corner of the building, as if she wanted to slink back into the shade.

Being the ghoulish person I am, I pulled out another cigarette and lit it, hoping it would give me a reason to linger without looking like I was staring at her. I assumed she was crying because of the murder, but you never know. And if she was that upset, why weren't the detectives noticing and questioning her? Or maybe they had and that's why the sobbing. Her cries were so loud my heart ached listening to her. I edged closer to the building. She pulled her hands away from her face and immediately stopped sobbing. She squinted at me and walked to where I stood.

"You're making a mess," she said.

"These were already here. I only dropped one, and a few extra ashes."

"Can I have one?" Her voice was clear, if a little soggy from all the tears.

I held out the pack. She removed one, and I flicked the lighter for her. For several minutes, we smoked silently, our inhaling and exhaling strangely in synch with each other. When she blew out smoke, she turned toward the building, tilting her head to look toward the second floor. I didn't want to ask a total stranger why she was crying, but she'd made the first move. I thought it over, watching my cigarette shrink, knowing I was almost out of time. "I guess you live here?" I said.

She turned back and nodded.

"I heard there was a murder."

Her eyes filled with tears, but they didn't slide down her face. She took another puff on her cigarette, tapped off the ashes, and glanced up at the building again.

"Who died?"

"A woman who lives here."

"What's her name?"

"Karen. She was only twenty-nine."

I shivered. There was no reason to, she was a total stranger, but it shakes you up when someone your age dies. It makes you realize you aren't going to be alive forever.

"What happened?"

"She was stabbed."

"Oh. Did you know her? I mean I guess you knew who she was."

"She's a neighbor."

"So did the detectives talk to you?"

"Yeah."

"And they let you go?"

"I didn't have much to tell them."

I nodded.

"All her toes were cut off," she said, looking back toward the building.

"Ew. That's awful." I started to take a final puff, then

decided I didn't have the stomach for it. It seemed disrespectful. I looked down at my feet, toes poking out of my sandals. They looked so clean and smooth, despite tromping through parking lots in the heat. "Why would someone do that?"

"I don't know."

"So what did the detectives ask you?"

"Why are you so interested?"

"Just making conversation. You don't have to tell me."

She studied the tip of her cigarette, then looked at me, squinting again, her eyes filled with tears. "Can I have another one?"

"Sure." I gave her one and started my third. I would end up reeking of smoke when I met the detective.

"They're talking to everyone who lives here. Her body is still in her apartment."

"How terrible. How many apartments are there? Twenty or more? That will take forever."

"Thirty. But they're going fast. Asking if you saw or heard anything and how you knew her. That's about it. They think it was a boyfriend."

"I guess they always think that." I took a drag on my cigarette.

"Also because of how she was found."

"How was that?"

"Arranged in her bed. Cleaned up quite a bit. They think she was bathed."

Even though it was hot, the temperature climbing into the 80s, a coldness spread across my shoulders and down my arms. "Were the . . ."

"Yes."

"How do you know what I'm going to . . ."

She took a long slow drag on her cigarette, my cigarette, I guess, but I didn't mind sharing since talking to her was not only satisfying my curiosity but passing the time. It's possible it was also helping me avoid going to my childhood home. As much as I wanted to go, and although you'd think I got the kinks out the day before with my dry run, I think I was avoiding it. I was terribly afraid of being disappointed, afraid of a dead end, afraid they'd send me away and I'd never get to see inside the house or find out if there'd been any appearance of ghosts.

She took another long, slow drag. Maybe teasing me. Maybe not wanting to tell any details. "You seem like a blunt person. I knew what you'd ask. Were the toes missing or did they find them near her body."

"And?"

"They didn't say."

I shivered again, thinking about those toes, worrying whether the girl, Karen, had suffered unbearably having them cut off while she was alive. I wondered why no one heard her screaming before she was stabbed to death, but for once, the horror of it forced my curiosity into the background. I just wanted to think about the sunshine and my cigarette. "What's your name?" I said.

She paused for several seconds, staring at the tip of her cigarette. She tapped it and let the ash fall.

"Roseanne."

"I'm Madison."

She smiled, but she didn't really look at me. "I've never seen you before. Do you live near here?"

"No."

"Well where do you live?"

"San Jose."

"What are you doing here?"

I don't know why I didn't see that coming.

She dropped her cigarette and stamped it out, which looked risky with a thin rubber flip-flop. "You aren't some kind of undercover person, are you?"

I laughed. "No nothing like that. It's kind of awkward to explain."

She folded her arms and moved her foot to the side as if she was standing her ground, letting me know she wasn't budging and was going to think I was a cop if I didn't have a good explanation.

"I'm in town to meet with Detective Smith."

"They guy investigating Karen's murder?"

"Yes."

"Why?"

"He was the detective for some people I knew who were murdered." I really hoped that would be enough information.

"So why are you here? At the apartment?"

My face was hotter than what was caused by the heat. It had seemed perfectly normal to follow the detective, thinking I could bump into him and have a casual chat.

But trying to explain to Roseanne made me realize how seriously abnormal my behavior was.

"I wanted to talk to him, and I guess I got carried away."

She smiled. "Don't be embarrassed, Karen was like that. Too much curiosity."

"Maybe that got her into trouble? Someone killed her because she interfered in their business?"

"I don't know."

"I thought you didn't really know her?"

"I don't. Didn't."

"How did you know she was curious?"

"I always saw her talking to people. Neighbors, strangers. Delivery people. Repair people."

"So you saw her around quite a lot?"

"We were neighbors. It's a small complex. Anyway, I better get going to the gym."

"In flip-flops?" I laughed.

"My stuff's in the trunk. I was headed out and then the detectives asked me to stay and answer questions. Thanks for the smokes."

"No worries."

She walked away, her rubber flip-flops slapping the bottoms of her feet. As she lifted each foot, her grubby heels were exposed.

I dropped my cigarette in the pile and walked back across the parking lot. It was time to go see my old house, no matter if someone was home or not. I could wait until my appointment to talk to Detective Smith. I wasn't sure why I'd been so anxious, thinking I had to speak with him right away. As I walked, I stared at my toes and thought about the dead girl.

Five

MY BUG FOUND its way to my old street as if I'd programmed in a route and the car had the ability to follow the path without any additional input from me. The street was as quiet and deserted as it had been on Sunday, although I supposed this time it was because most people were at work. I pulled up right in front, and unlike my drop-in visit to the detective, luck was with me. The minivan was in the carport. I reached to the floor on the passenger side and picked up the little cactus I had wedged in a box so it wouldn't tip over. I thought a plant might help soften my awkward request. But as I looked closely at the needle-like thorns, I wondered about buying something prickly to soften another person. I shoved my keys in my bag, put on some lip balm, and walked up to the front door.

The porch was barren except for a wicker chair that looked as if sitting in it would send you crashing onto the floor. It had faded grayish white cushions with a hint of a yellow floral pattern that had been gone so long, I wondered if the chair belonged to my parents. I didn't remember it, but nothing about the front porch was familiar.

The welcome mat was one of those thick things woven from recycled rubber. I stood with my toes near the edge and pressed the bell. The sound of it ringing was soft and far away. I was greeted with silence. The living room drapes were closed. On my right was the dining room window, if I remembered correctly, and I was pretty sure I hadn't forgotten that much. Those drapes were also closed. I waited longer than I normally would before pressing the bell again.

After a minute, I realized I was holding my breath, hoping that if I were completely silent, I'd hear someone moving around inside. There wasn't a sound. The street behind me was the same. It felt as if I was in a deserted town, the kind I saw once in the Sierra Mountains. The buildings were empty. When I looked through the windows, I saw tables and chairs, sometimes a refrigerator or a couch. It was slightly shocking and made me wild with curiosity to know how it ended up that all the inhabitants basically left town at once and no one came to replace them.

The door opened. Blurred by the screen, I saw a woman who looked a few years older than me.

"Yes?"

Although Novato is a smallish suburb, it seemed no one had received the directive about small-town friendliness. Of course, this was Marin County, not Kansas, so maybe it was different. I wanted the woman to open the screen so she could clearly see the cactus and so I could look her in the eye. She made no move to reach for the handle. I smiled and started in. "Hi. I have kind of a weird request."

"No thank you." She started to close the door.

"Wait! I'm not selling anything. Or asking for contributions. Or trying to get you to sign a petition."

"Then why are you holding a plant?"

"That's for you."

She closed the door further. "Do I know you?"

"I'm not sure where to start. I used to live here."

"Okay. So what do you want? We don't have any of the stuff from the attic or anything like that."

"How long have you lived here?" I said.

"About two years. But my boyfriend lived here for ten years or something before that. Which is really none of your business, so I'm going to say good-bye."

"Please don't. I . . ." I scoured my brain frantically for something, anything, to keep her from closing the door. Once she did, that would be it. Unless I came back when her boyfriend was home, and if she told him about me, he might behave the same way. Or they might not open the door at all. "Do you still have that swing in the oak tree in the backyard?"

The door moved slightly. "I love that swing," she said.

"My Dad put it up for me. I swung on it every day. Even when it rained."

She smiled, sort of.

"Do you have kids?" I said.

"No."

"I thought because of the minivan, you might."

"I'm a caterer." She shrugged. "What do you want?"

"I sort of wanted to look around the house."

"Why?" She pushed the door closed a bit.

She'd just started to warm and now she was probably thinking I might be some kind of scam she hadn't yet heard of — pretending I'd lived somewhere so I could go inside and figure out if it was worth robbing and look for easy ways to get in. I really did not want to tell her my parents were murdered there. I was betting she didn't know. A lot of people are creeped out by living in a house where there was a murder. Or any crime. I moved back a few steps. I put the plant on the railing. "I don't want to bother you. And I know I probably sound strange, or dangerous." I put my hands in my pockets and glanced to my left at the sad wicker chair. I looked back at her. "My parents are dead, and when I moved out of here, it was really sudden. I never got to say good-bye."

"To your parents?"

I held my breath for a moment. "To the house."

She opened the door and moved closer to the screen. She was thin with dark hair cut short and kind of haphazardly, but it looked cute. She had big eyes and a wide mouth and super high cheekbones, which is partially why the short hair looked so good on her. She had a long, graceful neck. She was wearing a yellow tank top without a bra and white cotton pants. Her feet were bare and her toenails were painted bright pink.

"I know exactly what you mean. About saying good-bye to a house. Or a place."

I held my breath again.

"But I feel like I should talk to Kev. He thinks I'm too trusting."

"Can I go around back and see the swing?"

"I don't see why not. But don't use it. We don't want a lawsuit if the branch breaks or something."

I laughed. It didn't sound to me as if she were at all trusting, but maybe she'd modified her perspective based on what Kev told her about her attitude. "When would be a good time to come back?"

"I guess this evening, or any evening. Not on the weekend."

"Okay." I picked up the plant. "Do you want this?"

She looked uncertain. It was a charming cactus, gently curved, and the spikes were very delicate. It looked healthy and strong. The pot was ceramic with yellow glaze. If you liked plants at all, and especially cacti, it would be a hard one to turn down.

"You could leave it on the railing. It looks good there."

"If it falls, the pot is breakable."

"I'll move it later."

I gathered she was going to check with Kev on that.

"Well," she said. She moved back like she was about

to close the door.

Inside, I saw a sliver of the living room. There was a large print on the wall, hung over a sagging blue and white striped sofa. The print was a field of sunflowers with a thin silver frame. "I . . ."

"What?"

I slammed my mouth shut. I didn't want to say anything that would make Kev suspicious. I knew that print. It was my mother's. And it had hung on that same wall in the living room as far back as I could remember. Now I wondered why she'd been so precise about not having any stuff in the attic. It was an odd thing to point out — to a stranger. And I hadn't asked for any things, hadn't even acted like there might be any things left. But if they had that print, what else did they have?

She turned and looked over her shoulder. She turned back. "What did you see?"

"Nothing."

"You looked surprised. You still do."

"Do I?"

"You look like you saw a ghost."

"Have you seen ghosts in this house?"

She laughed. "No. It's just an expression."

"I'll just walk around the side and look at the swing. If you still don't mind."

"Not at all." She backed away from the door so I had an even better look at the print.

"Wait. What's your name?"

"Gwen." She closed the door without asking mine.

She'd gone back and forth so quickly from warm to cold, now I wasn't sure how it had ended. A few minutes earlier, I thought we'd agreed I was coming back, but now I worried she'd changed her mind and I'd face an unopened door, or a very untrusting boyfriend.

I stepped off the porch, walked across the lawn, and around the side. The side of the house was nondescript, like most are, and there was nothing to jog my memory, but the minute I cleared the back corner and saw that tree, I almost started crying. It looked exactly the same. The tree must have grown over the years, but it had been huge when I was a child, and to me, it looked as if nothing had changed. The swing was attached to an unbelievably high branch, about twenty feet off the ground. The ropes were thick and long so it was easy to fly quite high in the air. The bench was wood that had been sanded until it felt like silk under my fingers. I longed to go sit on it, to start swinging, but I didn't want to disrupt the precarious situation in case she was looking out the back window. And I was sure she was.

AT ONE O'CLOCK I was back at the police station, opening the door, and walking into the air-conditioned lobby, which felt great after the quickly warming temperature outside. Between standing in the parking lot smoking, eating a huge turkey sandwich with jalapeño peppers for lunch, and the heat, I wasn't feeling like I would make such a great impression, but decided maybe that didn't really matter after all. It wasn't as if they were going to give me more information just because I looked crisp enough for a job interview.

A different cop manned the front desk. He had a buzz cut and no mustache. I told him I was there to see Detective Smith. He asked my name and told me to have a seat. I wandered toward the group of chairs arranged in a haphazard sitting area, all of them empty. I looked out the window past a few small trees that weren't doing much to keep the sun from beating through the glass.

I made three or four laps of the sitting area before Detective Smith came out. Up close, he looked about the same as I remembered. He wore frameless glasses, which I didn't remember, and his hair was thinner, still blondish-gray. He was dressed in dark pants and comfortable shoes, a pale blue short-sleeved shirt, unbuttoned and showing a t-shirt underneath. He smiled but he looked tired. Whether because it was of the girl with her toes cut off, or having to deal with me, I couldn't be sure. Maybe both. "Hi," he said. He shook my hand. "Come on back."

I followed him down a short hall and through a door into a room with four desks. They were all unoccupied, all the computers sleeping. He went to the one in the back corner near a narrow window, which I sort of remembered from the last time I was there. What I couldn't remember was what it had all looked like when I was fifteen. I know they talked to me in a room by myself, but I hadn't seen any doors leading to such a room, and I couldn't remember this area or the front desk, or the sitting area I'd just left.

He sat and gestured to a chair facing his desk, which was kind of obvious. "I thought I made it clear last time I spoke to you that there's no active investigation of your parents' murders."

If he hoped that delivering the bad news quickly would make me turn and walk out, he'd forgotten what kind of person I am. I sat down and put my bag on the floor and scooted the chair closer to the desk. "Why not?"

"I told you. We need fresh leads to do anything else. We interviewed everyone we could come up with at the time. We looked at all the physical evidence. There's nothing. I'm sorry."

"Someone walks into a house in a nice enough neighborhood and tells two people to get into bed and shoots them right in the face and you don't have any ideas? You just give up?"

He leaned back and fiddled with his glasses then folded his arms. "No one's giving up. There's just nothing we can do without new information."

"Have you looked for new information?"

He took off his glasses and studied the lenses as if he could see as well as I could they needed cleaning, but he didn't want to be bothered. He set them on his desk. "I forgot how relentless you are."

"Well I have new information."

"What's that?" He casually pulled a pad of paper toward him and picked up a pen that was already uncapped.

"I had a strange meeting with my aunt and uncle."

"And now you think they killed your parents?"

"No. Oh, no." I wasn't sure if he was mocking me. His tone was slightly off center. I felt a little queasy thinking about the possibility of my aunt and uncle being killers. It was something that hadn't crossed my mind, ever. And it didn't settle very well in my heart. But because of the things they'd said, I sure saw them from a different perspective, as if they'd been shadows before, and suddenly a more complete picture was emerging.

I wanted the detective to ask questions, not rush to instant, badly thought-out conclusions. "No. I don't think that and didn't mean to make it sound that way at all. But they weren't on very good terms with my parents when they died, which I didn't know before. And I wonder if there might be things they haven't said."

"We questioned them. Extensively."

"And what did you find out?"

"Nothing. You already know that. There weren't any other close relatives. We talked to their friends, neighbors, your father's employer. Everyone. We put hundreds of man hours into this case."

"It's not just a case." My voice wobbled. I took a deep breath.

"Don't take it personally, that's just how we refer to it."

"I can't believe you've given up."

He put the pen down and rolled it across his pad. The room was quiet, and the sound of cars moving around outside came through the windows, even though they were closed. "We have not given up. The case is still open. But there's no one else to talk to."

"I was wondering if you could talk to my aunt and uncle again."

"And ask them what?"

"I don't know. Why they weren't getting along with my parents."

"Okay. That's fair. What did they say to you?"

"Nothing."

"Did you ask?"

"I didn't have a chance."

Thankfully he nodded and let it go. "They didn't mention there was a problem when we talked to them initially."

"So they kept that a secret? Maybe they kept other secrets."

"I'd have to look at my notes. I wouldn't call it being secretive. They didn't mention it. But I know we would have asked about their relationship, and I suppose there wasn't anything to raise a flag that would make us probe further."

"Can you look at your notes?"

"Not right this minute."

"But will you? Today?"

"I'm in the middle of another case."

"Oh, the girl who was stabbed?"

He glared at me. "How do you know about that?"

I smiled. "I followed you."

His eyes widened.

"I was having a cigarette out back, hoping I might bump into you and I started talking to someone who lives there."

"I see. Well then, you know I'm busy." He pushed his chair away from the desk and stood. He put his glasses on. "But I'll look at my notes when I get time."

"When?"

"I don't know."

"I'm only here for a few days. Can you do it while I'm here?"

"If I find something, I'm not going to allow you to join our investigation. You realize, that, right?"

"Can't you at least tell me if you're going to talk to them?"

"I'll check my notes, although I know we were very thorough. A relatively young couple — things like that catch our attention."

"Some cases get more attention than others?"

"That's not what I meant. It's, well it's not like a gang killing where we know the victims were at risk, or an obvious crime. Never mind, I shouldn't have said that." He pushed his chair back under the desk.

"Like the case you have now? It's harder to deal with a younger person getting murdered?"

"That's not what I was saying. Anyway, we put a lot of time into investigating your parents' murders." He walked around the desk.

"Are you trying to get rid of me?"

"There's nothing else to say."

"I think there's something going on with them. They didn't tell you everything."

"What makes you so sure of that?"

"They acted like they didn't even want to be my guardians, that they only did it out of obligation, and they were surprised they were named. Do you know anything about that?"

He shook his head. I didn't like looking up at him, but I wasn't going to stand and give him an easier way of pushing me toward the door. I had to think of a way to keep him talking. I'd thought maybe I could get him going about the girl whose murder he was looking into now, but I should have realized that was a stupid, wishful idea. Of course he wasn't going to talk to me, to anyone, about a crime he was working on. "I think you owe me more."

"I don't owe you anything."

"I was a child."

"Yes, and you seem to have managed to grow up into a competent adult."

"Is that the goal — competency?"

He shrugged.

"You didn't try hard enough. There has to be a reason."

"Of course there's a reason. We just didn't find one."

"You don't feel bad, that you failed?"

"Of course we do."

"Then why won't you keep trying?"

He returned to his chair and sat down. His elbow bumped the computer mouse and the screen woke up. I felt as though I'd won. At least the first round. "It's hard on us, too. Do you think we like not accomplishing what we're here to do? Do you think we like running into dead ends and watching grieving families thrash around trying to find answers? It's terrible."

"Poor you."

His face sagged. He glanced at his computer.

"I do feel like you owe me. Because I was a kid and I didn't get any answers at the time, and now that I'm older, I've been thinking about it a lot more. And there are some things I don't know."

"Such as?"

"Who did you talk to?"

"Like I told you, we talked to your aunt and uncle. Clerks at all the places your parents shopped. We talked to known gang members and people with a record. Friends."

"You didn't find any other relatives?"

"Not on the west coast. There were some cousins in New York. I can go over it all with you."

"I don't want to go over the stuff that's a dead end. I want you to think of something new, take a different angle, talk to people you didn't talk to before. Ask my aunt and uncle what they didn't mention the first time."

"There is no one else, Madison. And I said we'd look through the notes and see if there are any other questions for your aunt and uncle."

"They bought a new house. A very nice house. And they didn't want me. In just twenty minutes I found out all kinds of things I didn't know before."

"I'm sorry to hear they weren't excited about their role as your guardians. That must have been devastating."

"It was."

"But are you suggesting their expensive home is somehow connected to your parents? That there's something suspect about what happened with their estate?"

"I don't know what I'm saying."

"Well if you want to talk about the estate, you need to see the attorney who handled it."

I shook my head. "Maybe I'll talk to him, but I wasn't saying they stole money from my parents and now it's suddenly appeared in a spectacular new house with an amazing view."

"Then what are you saying? I don't know what you think I can do for you."

Surprising me as much as it surprised him, I started to cry. Tears leaked out all around my eyelids and spilled over my cheekbones. He reached in his bottom drawer and handed me a tissue. I wiped my eyes and smiled, although he looked very blurry so I wasn't sure if I was actually smiling at him or at something to his left.

"My aunt and uncle are not the people I thought they were. That's all I'm saying. I'm not saying that makes them bad people, that they hurt my parents, stole from my parents . . . nothing like that. What I'm saying is it was so surprising, the things they said. I wonder if there are more things hidden that didn't come out. If you took a different angle."

"And what angle is that?"

"Not treat them like my guardians."

"We didn't take a soft touch with them. They were treated as persons of interest."

"But maybe your thoughts were clouded by . . ."

"Our judgment isn't colored by relationships."

"They were the kind and loving relatives taking the orphan into their home. That must have made you view them a certain way."

He stared at me. I knew I'd startled him and maybe made him realize he was too trusting of his professional neutrality. At least I think I startled him, because he continued staring. I was dying to know what was going through his mind. His expression didn't change, just that steady gaze, his mouth not moving. His eyeballs didn't even flick to look at anything else in the room. I wasn't sure if I'd insulted him or made him doubt himself. It's hard to believe a detective would doubt himself, but why not? They are human. They can't be perfect. No matter how hard they tried to solve my parents' murders, they failed, and he said they felt bad about that, so they must have feelings, make mistakes, do stupid things. We all do things wrong in our jobs. Why would anyone assume they're different, somehow above the rest of us?

He stood. "I'm sorry, Madison. I have a lot of work to do. I owe it to this girl . . ."

"Like you owed it to my parents?" I stood.

"Yes. Without a doubt."

"And now you don't?"

"What's happened to you?"

"I grew up."

"I've seen you since you were an adult."

"I grew up more. I guess I want to put my past to rest."

"You might need to find another way to do that. I said I'd read my notes and see if another conversation with your aunt and uncle is warranted, but don't count on our investigation to give you closure. "

"They weren't speaking to my parents. Remember that. I never knew that. They never hinted there was anything wrong. And I don't think you knew that either."

He nodded. Not giving away what I knew he was thinking. He knew I was right.

THAT EVENING I ate another burger. If this kept up, I was on my way to a heart attack.

At six forty-five, I drove to my old street. I figured seven o'clock or later meant they'd be settled for the evening, so it was better to show up at dinnertime and risk their annoyance than face the greater risk of them not even answering the door because it was too late to open the door to strangers.

The minivan and a motorcycle were cozied up in the carport. I parked in front of number 1701 and didn't waste any time worrying about my approach. It hadn't helped in any situation so far. Charging in was the best option, and it probably calmed my anxiety more than I realized. The cactus was still on the porch rail. I wasn't sure whether I should take that as a sign of rejection or if she'd forgotten about it.

The street was bathed in shadows as the sun settled low in the sky, ready to depart for the day. There were more kids outside this time. The smell of cooking beef permeated the air, so I guess someone wanted to enjoy summer even though it was a work night. Somehow everything, even work, seems more easy-going when the day lasts longer and the air is sweeter.

If the woman who interrogated me the first day was keeping her eye out, I wondered what she was thinking now, and if she'd do anything about my repeated visits, observing the neighborhood, up to no good.

I walked up the path and knocked on the screen doorframe. Knocking was friendlier. A solicitor was more likely to jam a finger at the doorbell so it made a loud, steady tone and hardly even rang like a bell. I wondered if door-to-door people knew they gave themselves away when they stabbed at doorbells. They might as well shout — *I'm here to waste your time.*

All the drapes were closed and lights were visible through the fabric. I hoped that was their normal course and not because she'd told him to hunker down and ignore me. Or maybe she'd completely forgotten about me just like she'd forgotten the cactus. I thought about picking it up and presenting it to her again, but discarded that idea. The simpler the better. I knocked again, harder this time.

The door opened immediately after my second knock, so maybe I was too impatient and they'd just been chewing and swallowing and wiping their mouths before they came to the door. And I do mean they — Gwen and Kevin were standing so close together I thought they'd joined forces to turn the doorknob. "It's her, I told you," Gwen said.

Kevin was about six feet tall. He had reddish blonde hair and pale skin. He was thin but not gaunt and stringy. He wore cargo shorts and a faded green t-shirt with a message I couldn't read.

"Hi, I'm Madison. I guess Gwen told you I came by this morning."

"Yup."

He wasn't going to make this easy. Neither was Gwen. She stood behind him now, mute, as if she'd never seen me in her life. I turned and picked up the cactus off the railing. "You forgot to find a place for this." I held it close, not wanting to appear as if I was shoving a bunch of sharp thorns in their faces.

"I'm not good with plants," Gwen said.

"You don't want it?"

"Who are you?" Kevin said.

"Didn't she tell you?"

"You used to live here. That tells me absolutely zip."

I held the cactus awkwardly in front of me. I didn't want to put it on their railing again, but I needed to be careful not to stab myself with one of its delicate quills. "There's not much else to say. I lived here since I was born and moved out when I was in high school."

"Why is it so important to get inside? It's kind of disturbing," he said.

"I just want to remember."

"Why? Why'd you move out?"

"It doesn't matter."

"Maybe it does to me."

I'd expected an odd look, some unflattering but unspoken thoughts, but not this prying. What was the big deal? If he really didn't want me inside, why didn't he just tell me to forget it and close the door?

"I'm not casing your house."

"You're not being very open either. It's a weird request and I think I have a right to know why. Gwen tells me you were in the backyard moping over the swing."

"She said it was okay."

"Whatever. It's just a weird request. I've lived in this place for years and you came out of nowhere."

I took a step back. "If it's too much trouble, never mind." My voice sounded thin and strained, hovering on the edge of tears. I hated to give up, but there was no way I was going to give him information. It was a simple request and all his questions were making it sound more bizarre than it was.

"Can I see some ID?" he said.

I laughed, which made the tears recede. "You're kidding."

"I'm not. Then I'll know your name and if anything happens . . ."

I turned and put the cactus back on the porch rail. I reached into my bag, pulled out my wallet, and removed my ID. I held it up for him. He opened the screen, reached out, and took it. He studied it, still holding the door open. He looked at it for so long, it felt as if he was memorizing it. Now I was worried about someone stalking me, or invading my life in some way, now that he knew where I lived. Or that he'd slam the door and I'd be without a license. Finally, he handed it back.

"Well, Madison. Let me think about it. Discuss it with Gwen."

"Why are you making a big thing out of it?"

"It's a very unusual request, right? You caught us by surprise. It's not like any stranger who walks up to the door gets invited inside."

"Gwen said she understood why I'd want to say good-bye."

He didn't look at Gwen, but he seemed surprised. I had the feeling she hadn't told him. "Stop by tomorrow evening."

I nodded, wanting to cry, but also hopeful. And as I turned, I realized maybe their house was a mess and they just didn't want me to see it. The answer could have been several innocuous things that weren't as stubborn as it felt. I was just too anxious.

Six

WHEN I RETURNED to my cottage, I smoked a cigarette. I went to the deli and bought a roast beef, tomato, and alfalfa sprout sandwich on some of the freshest sliced sourdough bread I'd ever eaten. I surfed the web on my iPad for a while, but in spite of the exhausting day, when I tried to sleep, I couldn't. I called JD, told him all the stuff that had happened, listened to his logical, soothing voice for a while, and still couldn't sleep.

I got up, threw on some clothes, went out to the bench, and smoked another cigarette. I was so alert it seemed as if it was eight in the morning, even though the sky was a warm dark blanket, thick with stars like the fairy lights that decorate JD's town during the Christmas season. The air was silky on my skin and I felt no need to cover my tank top with a sweatshirt. My jeans were a bit warm, but I was too afraid of mosquitos landing weightless on my legs, announcing their presence with a quick, sharp intake of blood, to change into a skirt. At least I could keep my eye on them around my arms and shoulders. It was the most comfortable the weather had been since mid-day, and although there was air conditioning in my room, I guess my longing for the cool evening air was part of why I couldn't sleep.

It was so beautiful I felt glad to be alive. That, or too many things racing around my head — the detective who had given up despite what he said, the cold blast from my aunt and uncle, the closed door on my old house, and every so often, like a tiny ghost herself, flitting through all of my problems, the murdered girl with the missing toes.

I tucked my cigarettes into my bag and got in the car. I was so keyed up, I thought for a minute about walking to the apartment building, but decided for once in my life to play it safe. I didn't know the area and it might seem like a good idea when I was wide awake, but not such a great idea when I faced the return trip of two or three miles.

The street in front of the complex was lined with cars, but empty of human life. Lights glowed from some of the windows. The police tape was gone. I found a spot on the opposite side of the street and walked to the corner. I passed the strip mall and went around to the parking lot. It was only about two thirds full.

I wandered over to the spot where I'd stood that afternoon for a smoking break and conversation that now seemed like it had taken place a week ago rather than just a few hours earlier. The pile of cigarette butts was still there, which made me feel kind of bad about littering. I usually try to pick them up, but they weren't all mine, so I justified being a slob. I looked up, wondering which window belonged to Roseanne, and which of the dark windows belonged to the dead girl.

The closer I moved to the building, the quieter the night became. I imagined that all the residents were in contemplative moods after what had happened. I stepped into the corridor that ran through the building from the parking lot to the courtyard. Looking down the length was like looking through a tunnel back in time. The rear of the building was flat dull stucco, softened only by the thick covering of vines that had wrapped themselves across it over the years. The corridor was utilitarian — a straight, narrow box cut through the center. But inside . . . It smelled of gardenias, soft and intoxicating. Each apartment had a wrought iron rail to protect the balcony, and all the balconies were crowded with potted plants, as if the residents had agreed on creating a stupendous garden. Vines dripped over the iron rails, bursting with flowers in some cases and lush greenery in others. At the center was a pond thick with water lilies and a large, multi-tiered fountain, off which the water dripped like it was dripping from a roof rather than a lively fountain, making the place seem both tranquil and neglected.

Dim lights, hardly enough to be called lights, lined the pathways. Sconces adorned the wall near each apartment door opening onto its balcony. I breathed in the perfume of the flowers and listened to the drip of the fountain. I closed my eyes, and when I opened them, I saw a ghost. It was vaporous white, draped over the balcony directly across from me. She had the faint outline of a woman, bent over, hair covering her face. I heard soft weeping and recognized that she was gazing at her feet. I knew instantly the murdered girl's toes had been brutally hacked off before she died, as I listened to the crying turn to loud wailing, an expression of unbearable physical pain.

Listening to that cry made my whole body ache. I sort of knew already that I'd come here expecting she'd be there, waiting for me. Although she didn't seem to be speaking or have any interest in speaking. I wondered whether anyone looking out their door had seen her, or if she'd revealed herself only to me. She had to help me, had to suggest something I could give to Detective Smith so he'd want to return the favor, even though it was his job and shouldn't be a favor. If she pointed to her killer, the detective couldn't use her as an excuse to keep pushing my parents into the background.

I stepped further into the garden, the aroma of flowers so heavy now I felt I wasn't getting oxygen, just a solid, steady infusion of perfume. It was darker than I'd realized at first. Pitch black, in fact. The only light now was the shimmering white of the ghost and the pale non-color of her hair draped over her shoulders and along her arms. The lights near the path that I could have sworn were giving off a faint glow earlier, were dark. I couldn't even make out the fixtures and doubted whether I'd seen them at all. Every single apartment had also gone dark.

There were no sounds except the fountain and the cries of pain. It felt as if the entire place had been emptied of human life. I wondered if other ghosts stalked the interiors of those apartments.

I stopped near the fountain. They couldn't all be sleeping. It was far too early, but not even the flicker of a TV alleviated the darkness. The sky was pale with reflected lights from the rest of the town, but that was it. I sat on the edge of the fountain and tapped one of the lily pads. This proved there must have been lamps a few minutes earlier. How else would I know the surface of the water was blanketed with flat leaves sprouting their pointed flowers? The fountain continued its anemic trickle of water, making the silence all around me seem more vast, as if that thin dribble was the dying breath of the old building.

As I sat there, the perfume from the flowers increased, seeping inside me and seeming to coat my lungs, making me feel sluggish and dreamy. The ghost continued to weep although with fewer sharp cries of pain. I waited, hoping she'd speak or somehow communicate through her tears, but I felt nothing, no sense of what she wanted. No sense that she had something to resolve and wanted to use me to help her accomplish it. Maybe she just wanted a sympathetic heart.

Still, it was hard for me to leave because having her there made me feel hopeful about encountering my parents' ghosts. Cindee had been right. I wanted that more than anything.

After talking to Detective Smith, I was hopeful that someone from beyond the grave would be more successful at solving their murders than he'd been. I didn't understand how he could be so complacent. It's not that he didn't try hard during the weeks and months after it happened, although did I really know that for sure? I was a kid. They said they tried, they had lots of files and notes and a list of people they'd talked to. They had evidence and boxes of stuff — but no answers. Not even a suspicion! How often does that happen? Maybe a lot, I don't know, but it seemed far-fetched. I assumed they tried hard because it was their job. But how could they give up? Yes, I know it's my parents. I'm slightly more invested than a few detectives who never met them and know absolutely nothing about who they were except what other people chose to say, or not say. But I would never give up.

If you become a police officer, and eventually a detective, don't you want to solve crimes? Wouldn't you have this drive that kept you from ever giving up? Wasn't that what they were paid to do? Was he really out on active, current cases eight hours a day five days a week? If he wasn't, what was he doing in all that downtime? He should be reading his notes — he should have those notes memorized — looking for a new connection in his brain every single week, not letting the details stagnate like the water underneath the lily pad I was touching.

I took my hand out of the water and wiped the moisture onto my jeans. The heavy sweetness of the flowers was starting to make me want to lie down and sleep. Now that I'd been sitting in the darkness for a while, just Karen's ghost and me, still drifting silently around that balcony, I saw there were some lounge chairs covered with thick cushions. These were high-end, from a store like Pottery Barn. I slipped off my sandals and took a few steps toward one of the chairs. I sat on the end.

As much as I wanted to stretch out, thinking about the sweaty, sunscreen-lathered bodies that had probably occupied the chair kept me upright. I closed my eyes to see if I felt anything from the ghost, but there was nothing, just a peacefulness. I had to keep peeking because there was such an empty spacious feeling, I wasn't sure she was still there. My eyes were growing more accustomed to the dark and I realized the strong, saturated aroma of the flowers was more than could be accounted for by the few gardenia plants in the garden. If the scent of flowers, syrupy and thick inside my nose, creeping into my lungs was from the ghost, what did it mean?

It seemed to me that cutting off her toes was a very intimate thing. So I guess that's why the detectives ran pretty quickly through their questioning of her neighbors. Were the flowers related to her boyfriend or lover? Or was it just a garden full of aromatic flowers and I was trying to make it into something more because there was a spirit weeping above me, but refusing to speak?

After a while longer, I felt her tears had become more sorrowful. There was no animal cry of pain from having parts of her body cut off, bones broken, skin torn, tissue full of nerves burning their messages up her legs, searing throughout her body. The tears now were softer, the mood changing from agony and rage to a defeated, weary despair. It was as if she'd given up or she was lonely, simply wanting someone with her, another presence, even if it was a different kind of matter — the slightest whisper of a being's soul or whatever that essence of each person is — a flesh and blood, talking, thinking, interfering girl like me. I suppose I should say *woman*. By no stretch of the imagination am I a girl, but somehow I don't feel mature enough to call myself a woman.

Gradually I began to feel calm. I don't know if this was in my head, or some sort of quiet, mental communication from the ghost. I was less upset that I couldn't see inside my home, and not as frustrated with the Detective. Just peaceful. Maybe it was the sweetness of the flowers.

Then, I realized quite suddenly that she wasn't just looking for my comfort, my presence. Maybe she'd come for that reason, but she was trying to comfort *me*. It was a shocking thought. Part of me worried it was wishful thinking, but a deeper part of me knew, absolutely knew, without even a prick of doubt, that it was true. She had come looking for something for herself, but she'd stayed because she felt my mood, my unfinished business with people on the other side of the chasm. She was trying to get back to this side, and I wanted something on her side.

I wondered if we'd be able to help each other.

I stood and walked away from the fountain. The sound of the water faded. She'd also stopped crying. I moved toward the side of the courtyard until I was just a few feet out from the balcony where she sat. Her hair covered her face, so all I really saw was the shadow of long hair and the dress and part of her arm.

I whispered so softly I wondered if I'd even made a sound. "Can I do something for you?" I waited.

A breeze moved across the courtyard, drawing an even heavier scent out of the flowers. I felt like my whole body was draped in moist petals, taking the heat and sweat out of my skin, making me feel clean, as if I'd just had a long bath in scented bubbles and rinsed myself under a cool shower. I looked up. She was still there, motionless. "What's wrong?"

The night remained quiet. I thought about speaking louder, but I didn't want to spoil the mood, and I sort of felt she could hear me, she just didn't want to answer. I waited for several minutes, hoping she'd speak, or do something. The fresh feeling on my skin remained and all the apartments were still in utter darkness. It seemed as if the scent of the flowers was a drug, causing everyone to fall into a deep sleep so the ghost and I could be alone. But for what purpose, beyond wordless comfort, I had no idea.

Finally, I turned. I hated to go. I felt bad leaving her alone, but I was tired. Still, she hadn't spoken, hadn't made any move toward me, except to soothe my feelings. And maybe that was good enough.

Seven

THAT NIGHT, I slept without moving an inch on the stiff, slightly crunchy mattress. When I woke in the morning, I was lying on the same side as I'd been when I fell asleep, facing the window at the back of the room, the sheet and blanket neatly folded over at the top edge, tucked under my arm. They say you dream every night, but I didn't have the faintest whisper of anything lingering from my sleeping hours, so if I did dream, those scenes were gone forever, or at least for now.

I got up and boiled water for my coffee press. Once the coffee had taken over the room with its delicious smell, I filled a small white cup and went outside wearing the yoga pants and t-shirt I'd slept in. The air was already light with that tender, pleasant feeling it has when it's going to be beastly hot. It was seven o'clock. I cut across the parking area to the bench at the back. I sat down and sipped my coffee. Trees with small leaves that looked slightly limp and waterless from the heat drooped over me as if they were begging me to pour my coffee on their roots, anything to get a little moisture.

While I'd been waiting for the coffee to be ready, I'd felt my brain was in a holding pattern. Now it sprang to life, racing past thoughts of the ghost, wondering why she hadn't spoken, wondering when I should go back, knowing I had to go back, trying to figure out how I would locate Roseanne, who had given no last name and no apartment number. I thought about Detective Smith and wondered when he'd update me on his next steps and about my aunt and uncle and I wondered when I should try to visit them again. Finally, I thought about my house. I spent several minutes mentally arguing with myself about whether or not I should find some hidden spot in the neighborhood — although I had no idea where that would be — wait for Gwen and Kevin to go out, and then hope for an open window where I could get inside. It's not as if I'd never done something like that before. Although the time I broke into my neighbor's condo, he was dead, so it was sort of different. In this case my parents were dead, but there was no way I could convince myself that house still actually belonged to them in any way.

On top of all the choices, I had four text messages from JD. I was a little surprised he hadn't started calling. All of them had come in late at night, so maybe he figured he'd let me sleep in, even though he knows I rarely do. He might have thought he'd give me space. He's good at that. But sooner or later, he'd start worrying.

I finished my coffee in four large gulps, hurried back to the room, poured another cup, and sliced up some cheese. I laid it across a few wheat crackers and called it breakfast. After my shower I took a third cup and a cigarette out to the bench so my hair could dry in the growing warmth of the sun. Standing in a tiny bathroom in hot weather, blasting a blow dryer at hair that reaches almost to my waist did not sound like a pleasant way to begin the day.

I had decided Detective Smith would be more willing to talk if I gave him some space, like JD was giving me, and that Gwen probably wasn't going to let me in the house unless I came up with some brilliant reason, so I headed back to the apartment. Possibly it could perform double-duty. I was still hopeful that if I discovered something to share with the detective, he'd be more concerned about my "case".

I felt like a stalker. Maybe I pry into other people's lives all the time and was simply more aware of it because I was in an unfamiliar place. There was no legitimate reason for me to visit that apartment complex, and if I ran into Detective Smith I had no idea how I'd explain my presence. The whole thing might backfire, and he'd consider me an interference. He'd be more determined to get rid of me. But I had to do something. I had to make him excited and passionate again about finding my parents' killers. He couldn't just toss them off while he focused on this girl, as much as I felt sorry for her. Every year my parents had slid further and further to the back of his mind, as new victims cropped up, demanding justice.

The parking lot was mostly empty. Roseanne's car was still in its spot, but there weren't any numbers over the carports so I had no idea how to figure out which apartment was hers. I'd have to hope luck was on my side. Or maybe there would be someone leaving or coming home that I could ask. Anyone but Detective Smith.

I parked at the strip mall, crossed the section with the small trees, and walked across the lot to the back of the complex. In daylight, the passageway through the building into the courtyard was somewhat more intimidating, making it obvious I was charging through into private property.

My phone buzzed with a text from JD, asking what I was up to. I texted back —

Madison: Snooping as always.

JD: Where?

Madison: At the apartment where that girl was killed.

JD: Why?

Madison: I don't even know.

JD: Are you ok?

Madison: Kind of.

JD: Yes or no.

Madison: Yes.

JD: Did you go inside your old house?

Madison: Not yet.

JD: When are you?

Madison: Soon.

JD: Be careful.

JD: I miss you.

JD: I love you.

Madison: I love you.

That's the beautiful thing about texting. You can skip part of what's going on and people don't always recognize you didn't acknowledge everything they said. I wondered if he was paying attention, if he noticed I didn't promise to be careful. Although why I had to be careful going into a perfectly tranquil suburban home, I have no idea. Unless he was worried I hadn't been very welcome, which would have been right. He was probably worried I would just go inside without an invitation.

I put my phone away and walked through the alley to the courtyard. The fountain was the same anemic dribble. The air smelled of gardenias, but not nearly as powerfully as the night before. You'd think there would be aromas of bacon or toast, but nothing, just fresh morning air and gardenias, as if the complex was still empty of life.

Up above, I heard a door close, but didn't see or hear anyone walking down one of the staircases leading to the ground floor. I waited, standing just inside the corridor, hoping I wouldn't look like I didn't belong. I couldn't understand why there was no activity from people leaving for work. It was only eight, so maybe they all started extremely early or late. I heard another door open and close but still no footsteps. Were they all tiptoeing around because they were afraid of running into the ghost? Maybe they'd all been cowering in their apartments the night before, terrified of something they'd never seen and didn't understand.

The iron gate that led from the front of the complex into the courtyard squeaked as someone pushed it open. I pressed myself back against the wall and bent my knees slightly. I hoped the move would allow me to see beneath the bougainvillea that draped itself around the posts and across a small covering over the bench near the lounge chair where I'd been sitting the night before. I saw the backs of two people as they walked out the gate. They must have come down a staircase that wasn't visible from where I stood. I'd thought there were only the two staircases, but everything was so overgrown, and there were enough nooks and crannies, I suppose there were all sorts of things I didn't know about the place.

By nine-thirty, thirteen people had headed out for work. My legs ached from standing and my shoulder was stiff from pressing against the wall. I walked over to the fountain, hoping that I looked casual, as if I belonged, and that if anyone did see me as they hurried off to work, they'd think I was waiting for a carpool or something. I sat on the edge of the fountain and looked up. The railing where I'd seen the spirit looked the same as the others. I wondered if it was the balcony for Karen's apartment or the spirit had chosen it at random. Or was it the home of her killer? Even though the police seemed to be leaning toward a boyfriend, and hadn't identified a boyfriend in the complex, that didn't mean there wasn't one living right nearby.

I turned and saw Roseanne standing at the foot of the staircase facing me. She walked toward me slowly. She wore the same flip-flops with a short tight skirt and a loose top that slipped off one shoulder, showing very white skin with no hint of a tan line. She was a bit old for the casually-falling-off-the-shoulder look, but it was hot, so I stifled my critical voice.

"Why'd you come back?" She tugged her shirt over her shoulder as if she'd heard my critical voice yammering despite my effort to stifle it. Or maybe it was just uncomfortable, sliding toward revealing more than she'd intended.

"I'm not sure. Just upset about Karen, I guess."

"You didn't even know her."

"It's still upsetting. She was the same age as me."

"You have nothing better to do than hang around a murder scene? What are you one of those psychic types and you think you're going to get a vibe and solve the crime?"

"I guess you don't believe in psychics?"

"They're just good guessers, and swindlers."

I nodded.

"You agree?"

"I've never met a psychic, I was just nodding that I heard."

She stared at me, her eyes bulging out. "Got a smoke?"

"Is smoking allowed in the courtyard?"

"Most everyone is at work. Those who are left are a

larger percentage of smokers."

That concerned me. It seemed like she'd made a point of studying it, that she thought smokers didn't quite have their lives in order, or something. But I guess I shouldn't be over-sensitive. I like smoking, it doesn't say anything about your character. It was more her tone of voice that made me feel that way. Besides, even though she was never equipped for it, apparently she was more of a smoker than she admitted. I took out two cigarettes, handed one to her, and flicked the lighter. "Where do you work?"

"I work from home."

"Doing what?"

"Copywriting."

"Sounds interesting."

"Boring as shit most of the time. People ask you to write something and then spend as much time re-writing it as you did in the first place, so you're left wondering why they hired you."

I resisted the urge to nod. "So if you think psychics are swindlers, does that mean you don't believe in anything supernatural?"

"Like God?"

"I guess. Or some alternate plane of existence?"

"What?"

I looked for somewhere to drop my ashes.

"You can just drop them on the ground," she said. "No one will notice and the breeze will move them around."

I glanced at the fountain and the surrounding flowers. There was no evidence of a breeze. In fact the back of my neck was damp. I lifted my hair and held it on top of my head with one hand while I took another drag.

"You have gorgeous hair," she said.

"Thanks."

"I love that color."

I smiled. "Do you think there are other senses that connect us to things we can't see?"

"What the hell are you talking about?"

I wasn't sure myself. I was trying to subtly force the conversation to ghosts, and maybe I should have just shot it out there, but I decided to stick with the confusing path first. "You knew I was looking for a place to drop my cigarette ash."

"That doesn't take a spiritual seventh sense. I saw the ash, you looked around."

"Sixth sense," I said.

"Whatever."

I gave up and plunged in — "Have you ever seen a ghost?"

"No."

"Do you think it's possible?"

"That ghosts exist?"

I nodded.

"Not really."

"You don't think there's anything outside of what we see and touch? You said there were other senses, so that makes me think you believe there's some sort of other dimension."

"I don't know what I think."

"Are you freaked out about the murder?"

"It's upsetting," she said.

"Are you worried the killer will come back?"

"Why would that happen?"

"If it's a serial killer. Or maybe a guy who's worried someone saw him."

She was quiet.

"I guess it's hard for the police to find killers," I said. "I wonder what percentage is never caught?" I felt I was babbling, leaping from subject to subject. But I wanted to find a way to talk about Karen's ghost. We'd both put out our cigarettes by now, so I pulled out my pack and offered her another. She seemed very willing to keep smoking mine, and I wondered if she was relapsed and didn't actually have any of her own, but couldn't resist the temptation.

"I don't know. I never thought about it," Roseanne said.

Her comments seemed stiff as if she wanted to find a way to argue with me, or she was annoyed about everything I said, but she didn't seem inclined to stop talking to me. If she was a relapsed smoker, I guess the free cigarettes made it worth putting up with me. If I kept offering, I think she would have willingly smoked her way through my entire pack.

"Why'd you say that about ghosts?" she said. "Do you think this place is haunted? Because it sure scares me at night, but I always thought it was because I'm over-sensitive, or have my head too full of scary movies."

"I don't know. Have you had any strange experiences?"

"No."

"I've seen some ghosts," I said.

She looked at me, her eyes slightly narrow, as if she wasn't sure whether I was making fun of her, or was completely out of my mind. "That's kind of hard to believe."

"I know."

"At least you're honest about it."

"A lot of people don't believe me."

"Then why would you mention it?"

I took a few puffs and didn't speak. I'd mentioned it because I wanted to tell her about a particular ghost, but I still couldn't tell how she'd react. I don't know why I even cared. Maybe I was enjoying talking to her and didn't want to shut down the conversation. Maybe I was lonely after a few days of nothing but people closing doors in my face, literally and figuratively. "I wondered what you thought about ghosts."

"I already told you, I don't think they exist."

"But then you said you had a bad vibe here." Although I imagine the bad vibe was completely unrelated since there was nothing threatening or scary about the ghost I'd seen. Unless there were others.

"That's a bit of a leap from a bad vibe to thinking I should believe in ghosts."

"But there are things we can't see, so many things we don't understand."

"Isn't that the truth."

"Do you believe me, that I've seen ghosts?"

"I believe that you think you have."

"So you think I'm delusional?"

She laughed. "I don't know. You're a little weird. What are the tattoos for?"

"To keep me grounded."

She nodded as if she understood completely.

"I saw a ghost here, last night."

She dropped the cigarette on the ground and left it burning. "If you say so."

"The girl who was murdered."

"Karen?"

"Yes."

"How would you know it was her?"

"I just knew. I could meet you here tonight, maybe she'll show up." It was equally likely the ghost would not show up and then Roseanne would have even less reason to believe me. I don't know why I wanted her to know. I wanted to talk about it, I wanted . . . something. I think I just wanted to talk about ghosts, how they all have a will of their own. How so many of them manage to find me, yet the two I want to reach haven't found me. Apparently haven't even tried. Although it's not like I'd tried that hard. I hadn't figured out a way to get into the house and I wasn't even putting that much effort into it. Maybe I needed to show a little more passion and determination.

If ghosts are energy, maybe they need similar energy to respond to. I tried to think about the details around the ones I'd seen, trying to decide if there was any merit to my thoughts, or they were simply slipping sideways.

"I have no interest in a séance."

"It's nothing like that."

"Well what do you think you saw? Some white thing howling about how she was brutally murdered and she was coming back to exact her revenge?"

I laughed.

She smiled and tapped her cigarette. Her ashes fell on the ground and she smeared them around with her foot. The squeak of her rubber flip-flop on the concrete gave me chills.

"She was sort of transparent, but she didn't say anything."

"Do they usually chat with you?"

Her tone made it sound as if she was making fun of me, but her questions sounded moderately serious, and the look on her face wasn't sneering or pitying, just curious.

"I've heard them speak. Usually they mention bits of their lives. It can be difficult to figure out what they're talking about. Sometimes there's a lot of feeling in the sound of their voices. It's not like we chit chat as if we'd met for coffee."

"And they tell you who killed them?"

"Sometimes. Sometimes they stick to letting me see scenes from their lives. That leads me to think of something to talk to another person about and when all the pieces come close to each other, I realize who the killer is."

"So you go around hunting for murderers?"

"Not really. I guess I've encountered a few, but I don't go looking for them." It took half a breath for me to realize that this time, that's exactly what I was doing.

"And what did this ghost say?"

"She was crying. At first it sounded like she was in pain, but then she just seemed sad."

"How in the hell would you know that?"

"A feeling."

The sun had moved higher. The shadows were receding and pretty soon the sun would shift enough that we'd no longer be in the shade. The heat was creeping in just as fast, and Roseanne's forehead was shiny with perspiration. The space above her upper lip also looked damp, despite the drying effect of the cigarette.

"You come here at night, think you see something, and then feel that this thing is crying? That sounds like it's totally in your imagination." She stomped out her cigarette. "Can I have one more? I really should get going, but I want to hear more about this, as crazy as it sounds. One more and then I need to go."

I didn't like her taking my cigarettes and acting like I was interfering with her day. I gave her one anyway.

"Why do you think it was crying?" she said.

"I don't know. At first, maybe the pain over her toes?"

She nodded. "You didn't get a feeling about it?"

"I'm just telling you what I experienced. You don't have to believe me."

The iron gate scraped on the concrete with a horrific screech that made me shiver. Roseanne did the same. We turned and looked past the fountain. Detective Smith stepped around the gate. He turned to push it closed. I braced for the shrill noise and could feel Roseanne tense up. It must have made his skin crawl too, because he found a way to lift it slightly as he moved it back into place. He turned and raised his hand in an unmoving wave as if he'd already known we were standing there. Maybe he'd noticed us when he was still outside the gate. Maybe he'd been watching us, wondering what I was doing there.

He walked along the path past the fountain. He stopped a few feet away from us, standing in the sun, not looking particularly uncomfortable. The twisted look on his face said the sun beating on his head was preferable to cigarette smoke. "What are you doing here, Ms. Keith?"

I turned and tried to blow the smoke away from him, but it seemed to have a mind of its own, drifting back in his direction. To his credit, he didn't wave it away or start hacking like he was going to eject half his lung. He grimaced.

"She was hanging around last night and saw a ghost. Karen's ghost," Roseanne said.

He stared, looking like he wasn't sure who was crazier. He put his hands in his pockets and looked down at his feet then back up at me. "Why are you here?"

"I don't know. I . . . I've seen ghosts of people who were killed before and I sort of wondered . . ."

"Ghosts?"

"I know it's hard . . ."

"Impossible," he said.

"No it's not." From the corner of my eye I saw Roseanne smirking. She took a drag on her cigarette and dropped the butt right near my foot, leaving it to burn out by itself.

"I want to know why you're lurking here," he said. "But wait, let me guess. You have a history with paranormal curiosity and you think you can utilize that for your parents?"

"No."

Roseanne moved to the left so I could see her face. "Your parents were murdered?"

Detective Smith actually looked upset, so I'll give him credit for that. I guess he'd assumed I'd told her. To try to recover, he pulled out a notepad and looked at Roseanne. "I have some more questions for you. Can we go up to your apartment." It wasn't a question.

"I don't mind her hearing my answers," Roseanne said. She stared longingly at the cigarette I was holding. Her lips parted as if she wanted to ask for another, then she pressed them closed.

"I do," he said. "Now that she's involved herself in this, I have to consider her a witness."

"I didn't know Karen," I said. "I wasn't anywhere near here."

"You are now. Ms. Caplan? Your apartment."

"I guess I should get going." I put out my cigarette, scooped up the butts, and carried them to a trashcan.

"I'd appreciate it if you'd wait," he said. "If you don't have anywhere to go right this minute."

"Okay."

He and Roseanne crossed the courtyard and went up the stairs, then disappeared from sight. I walked to the fountain and sat on the edge.

The whole time he was gone I could hardly think about anything else, I was so curious about what he was asking her, what he thought about the ghosts, and what he was going to ask me. Or tell me. Maybe even though he was annoyed I was hanging around the apartment and annoyed about me bringing in the supernatural, he had something to say about my parents.

After fifteen or twenty minutes he came down the stairs alone. I couldn't imagine what he'd talked to her about all that time. How many questions could there be?

He crossed the courtyard and to my surprise, he sat down next to me on the rim of the fountain. "You said you followed me here yesterday. Is that all there is to it?"

"Yes."

"You'd never met Ms. Caplan before?"

"No."

He pressed his lips together, folding them inward, and turned down the sides of his mouth. "Did she speculate about who might have killed Ms. Varstead?"

"No."

"Did she mention any of Ms. Varstead's friends?"

"No."

"Did she mention anyone else murdered at this complex?"

"Someone else was murdered here?"

"Not that I know of."

"Then why are you asking that?"

"I'm trying to find out what you talked about."

"Smoking, ghosts, just small talk."

He nodded.

"Did you have time to read the notes on your interviews with my aunt and uncle?"

"We'll get to that in a minute. Did Ms. Caplan tell you if she met any of Ms. Varstead's boyfriends?"

"No."

He went on asking me questions and the more he asked, the more I realized he had no suspects, no ideas, and so he was asking every relevant and irrelevant question he could think of, desperately hoping that he'd stumble across a piece of useful information. At least I assumed he was desperate. Maybe he wasn't. Maybe he wasn't a very good detective.

Finally he said, "I re-read my notes on your parents' investigation."

Instantly my heart got all soft and gooey and I was sorry I'd had those thoughts about him not being a very good detective. Once again I wondered how frustrating it must be to fail at your job. Maybe he was facing the possibility of another failure, and that made him want to forget my parents, and then I'd shown up and reminded him of things he didn't want to think about.

"We did question your aunt and uncle at some length about their relationship with your parents. And asked them specifically if they'd been on good terms, since their instructions for your care hadn't been touched for almost five years before they died."

"What did they say?"

"They mentioned they weren't on the best of terms, but they didn't think it mattered when it came to doing what was right and caring for you. They said there weren't any other options."

"Why not?"

"You know all this. No other relatives."

"I want to know what they said."

"Exactly that. No one else."

I put my hand in the water. The water was cooler than I would have expected given how hot the air was getting. We were right out in the sun, but I didn't want to move and have him take it as an excuse to leave. "What else? Why weren't they on the best of terms? And what does that mean? Chilly or not speaking?"

"They still had contact, but they didn't see each other. Your parents had wanted to borrow some money from your aunt and uncle. They refused. After that, they limited their contact with your parents."

I felt my face get hot, hotter than what the sun would do, hot as if I was embarrassed for them, and maybe embarrassed for myself, because now I realized why my uncle thought I was there to borrow money. I don't know why borrowing money is such a shameful thing, but it is. And it upset me to think about my parents needing money, and having to lower themselves to ask, and then being humiliated by the refusal. And after that, the isolation of being shunned. "Why didn't I know this before?"

"It wasn't important because there wasn't anything else to it."

"I guess not." I dragged my fingers through the water, trying to shift my picture of my parents to accommodate this new information. I didn't like it. My parents were careful with money, so part of me found it hard to believe. I didn't remember them ever talking about needing money. "When was this?"

"When was what?"

"That they asked to borrow money."

"I don't know the year. It was several years before their deaths."

"But you didn't ask?"

"Why would I?"

"I guess. I mean, I guess not. Or whatever."

We were quiet for several minutes. I looked up. Roseanne stood on her balcony, staring down at us. I tried to get a sense of where her balcony was in relationship to where the ghost had been the night before, but everything looked so different in daylight. "You believed them?" I said.

"Your aunt and uncle?"

"Yes. About the money."

"Yes."

"But why? Did you have any proof?"

"When we ask people to tell us their stories, if there are no red flags, and no contradictory information, we accept it at face value."

"Really?"

"Is there a reason you doubt the story?"

"It doesn't sound like my parents."

"You were a kid. And you have a very idealized view of them at this point in time. Because they're deceased, and because of the way they died."

The condescending, know-it-all attitude was insulting, but I didn't want to alienate him. I wanted him to say he'd interview my aunt and uncle again, try harder to find out more. Although if they were lying, and he accepted everything at face value, and there was no one to contradict them . . .

"There's not much else to do at this point. No leads to follow. Unless they said something definite to you that would give us a reason to go back and interview them again." He stood. "I'm sorry. I really am."

He held out his hand. I shook it and looked him in the eye. He smiled tentatively and I did the same, giving the impression I was assuring him that I'd accepted his answer, when the reality was, it was the complete opposite. I was going to talk to my aunt and uncle and find out something tangible that would force Detective Smith to change his viewpoint. He kept insisting he hadn't given up, but everything about him said that he was tired of trying. I had no idea how I would get my aunt and uncle talking, how I was going to do something an experienced police detective had failed to accomplish, but I guess I had more passion than he did. For him, it was a job. For me, it was life and death.

When he was gone, Roseanne leaned over her balcony. "One more cigarette? I promise, if I see you again, I'll bring a pack and return the favor."

"Sure."

A few minutes later she appeared at the bottom of the stairs. We sat back down on the edge of the fountain. I was so far past my quota of three smokes a day I didn't even want to think about it. But at least talking to her and being curious about Karen's ghost was keeping me from getting upset about my failure to accomplish anything I'd planned.

"Did he ask you about me?" she said.

"He asked what we talked about, whether you mentioned if you'd met any of Karen's boyfriends."

She stared at the tip of her cigarette for a minute. "That's all?"

"Yes. Why?"

"Just curious."

"Did you meet any of her boyfriends? Did she have any?"

"No. I don't know. I guess that's what they're looking for though. They seem pretty sure it's a love affair that turned bad."

"I wonder how they know these things?" I said. "Is it experience, they see the same thing over and over and there's a pattern? Or do they just have a list of likely scenarios and they follow one until they're proven wrong?"

"Good question. He's very fixated on the boyfriend thing. I guess because of her toes, they're convinced it's not a serial killer, but how do they know? I thought serial killers did lots of weird things, took souvenirs or had strange habits that they repeated."

"I don't know," I said.

"But I thought you were involved with other murders."

"Not like that. I've seen some ghosts that pointed me in the right direction, but I was never involved in any investigation. It's not like the police take me into their confidence."

She laughed.

"Are you scared it was a serial killer and they're not considering that?"

"Wouldn't you be?"

"Yes, but I'm sure they know what they're doing." Inside, I was not at all sure. Maybe the whole thing was just one big guessing game. Trial and error. "Or maybe they don't. What was he talking to you about for all that time?"

"The same things. Guys coming around, things she'd said to me. He seems to have it all mapped out in his head," Roseanne said.

Suddenly I realized I'd never asked the detective what they thought happened to my parents. It wasn't as if they just proceeded blindly. They must have had a theory. I stood.

"Are you leaving?"

"Yes."

"What for?"

"I have stuff to do."

She stood and put out her cigarette. "I guess I should get to the gym."

"Where are your workout clothes?"

She stared at me. She dropped the cigarette. "Oh, I guess I shouldn't call it going to the gym." She laughed. "I go there to have a smoothie."

"That's strange."

"Why?"

"Aren't there smoothie shops?"

She looked past me. Her eyes shifted up like she was scanning the balconies behind me. "I like theirs," she said finally.

"Do you ever work out?"

She shook her head. "I smoke."

"That doesn't mean you can't work out."

"I guess not."

"So how did you find out they had good smoothies?"

"I . . . I forget. Let me think." She put both her hands on the sides of her head. She tugged gently on her hair, then pushed her hands, hair and all, up toward the top of her head. "I . . ."

"It's not that important," I said. "It just seemed unusual."

She laughed. "No biggie."

"No, it's not, you're right." I had the feeling she really wanted to tell me how she'd come to go to a smoothie bar at a gym, but it was too much effort for a casual question.

"Do you think Detective Smith will ask you more questions?" I said.

"God, I hope not. I'm tired of the questions. I said I don't know anything, they should just take me at my word."

With that, she turned and walked to the alley cutting through the building.

I put out my cigarette. I used a tissue in my bag to swoop up our butts. There was nothing I could do about the ashes, but I always figure they're more or less biodegradable. I found a trashcan at the end of the alley and dropped the mess inside.

I drove back to the motor inn. When I pulled up to my parking spot, it was occupied. JD's SUV sat there as if it had been there the entire time. I drove around to the extra spots and before I parked my car, I saw him sitting on the bench under the trees where I'd spent so much time smoking. He was doing the same, taking a long, slow drag on a cigarette and looking right at me, as if he'd known I was arriving back at my place right that minute. I guess I didn't keep in touch with him as well as I'd thought.

Eight

JD AND I grabbed a snack and then went for a long hike at a nearby open space preserve. Then we came back and sat on the bench at the motor inn, cuddling, kissing, and smoking until it got dark and we finally admitted we were starving and would have to let go of each other long enough to eat a sandwich.

He drove to the deli where I'd eaten twice before. We both ordered pastrami — JD on rye bread, me on dark rye, JD with mustard and mayo, me with only mustard, and both of us with lettuce and tomato and onion. We sat at one of the three small tables. JD tore open a bag of chips for us to share. The pastrami was lean and salty and so delicate it nearly melted on my tongue.

Throughout the day, I'd told him everything, repeating some things, but wanting to tell him each event in the correct sequence. Of course, it's almost impossible to tell things in perfect chronological order, at least it is for me. The *who said what* weaves together like a piece of frayed fabric with a lot of loose threads. This meant I had to keep backing up and starting over, which meant even more repetition. But JD is a very patient guy. He can listen forever without appearing bored, and he doesn't insert words to hurry me along.

When I finally wound down and took a long drink of my watery iced latte, he said, "Is that everything?"

"I'm sure I'll remember fifteen other things before bed and a few more while I'm sleeping. Are you staying until I head back home?"

He smiled.

"Why are you smiling?"

"I was afraid you might be feeling like this place is your home."

"I feel like a stranger in some ways. Why'd you come up here?"

"You're finally curious?" he crumpled the chip bag and put it on his plate.

"It took me a while to get around to it. There's a lot on my mind."

He pressed his index finger at the spot between my eyebrows and rubbed gently. Until that minute, I hadn't realized I had a headache. The pressure and motion of his finger rubbed some of the knots out of my brain. It felt more relaxed, like I'd been squeezing it for two days and finally let go.

"You always have a lot on your mind," he said.

I smiled.

He took his finger off my forehead. "My life was

hollow without you around."

I grinned and took his hand.

"And I was worried about you. I don't know what you're looking for . . . Well, I know what you said you're looking for, but I don't know if you'll be able to find it, and I don't know if it will make you happy, even if you do."

"I'll be happy if the detective works harder on the case. If he finds out who killed them. Why wouldn't I be happy?"

"You've never struck me as a person who wants revenge."

"I don't."

"Then why do you have to know who did it?"

"I can't explain it, I just do. I need to know why."

"But they could find out who, and you still might not know why."

"I don't believe that."

"It happens. A lot, I think."

"Only if it's completely random."

He stood and stacked our empty plates. He carried them to the counter and thanked the guy who made the sandwiches. I swallowed the rest of my latte, picked up my bag, and we went outside. It was dark but the air was as warm as ever. He took my hand and started walking along the street, past shops that had been closed for hours. Trees threaded with tiny white lights lined the street. We walked two blocks without talking much and came to a small park. In among the trees was a pond where three ducks floated aimlessly. Every few minutes, one or the other made a quack-y sound deep in its throat, without opening its bill.

We sat on a bench facing the pond and JD put his arm around me. I leaned my head on his shoulder. Very softly I said, "I hope you're not trying to get me to give up."

"I'm not. I'm just worried about you."

"If you drove all the way up here to worry me into giving up, then maybe you should leave."

He didn't pull his arm away, but I knew he wanted to because all the muscles got tight, and the tendons under his arms stiffened, poking into my shoulder. I'm glad he didn't pull away. The echo of my words sounded horrible. It wasn't that I didn't want him to care about me. But I'd thought he was supporting me. With all my wandering into dead ends, having someone tell me they were worried didn't help. I was not going to give up.

He kissed the top of my head.

The ducks made more clucking-quacking sounds deep in their throats. They sounded like worrying sounds, all those noises most birds make as they fuss around cleaning themselves, or looking after their offspring, as if their very hearts were making concerned sounds. Maybe I wasn't used to someone worrying about me. My aunt and uncle surely didn't. Even when my aunt got mad at me for smoking, she didn't act worried, just put out. I suppose I was only starting into the worrisome phase when my parents were killed.

"After all these years, I don't think there's a lot more they can do," he said.

"If that's what you think, why didn't you tell me that before? I thought you were on my side?"

"I am. It's a long shot, and I think you realize that, at the back of your mind."

"You heard how my aunt and uncle were acting. I think there are stories that didn't come out in the investigation. I want to know everything."

"Why didn't you ask them?"

"I was too upset."

He squeezed my shoulder. "Are you going back over there?"

"Yes."

"Do you want me to go with you?"

My first thought was to say no. I was on my own in this, but having him there felt so much better, even though I was snapping at him. It made me feel less discouraged. He was pessimistic, but that seemed to be firing me up and making me more determined. "Let me think about it. I'm sure they'd treat me differently if you were there. They might be more superficial."

"Yes, they'll treat you differently, but I think you'll act differently too."

"Why would I be different?"

"I've seen groups of people at the bar who come in every week, talking, laughing a certain way. When an additional friend joins, each person changes slightly. It's weird."

"I guess you're right. I know you're right, I didn't think about it that way."

He stood and held out his hands for me to grab them. "I assume we're going to the apartments to meet up with your ghost?"

I laughed. He really is amazing, even if he was clucking at me like a Mallard.

EVEN THOUGH IT was past midnight, lights glowed through several windows at the exotic, tranquil apartment complex. The floral scent was still there, but less intense. More normal, I'd say. It was one of the small details I hadn't mentioned to JD, and now it seemed extremely important. It was hard to explain how very strong the odor had been. If I said something, he'd say, *well yes, it reeks of flowers*, and I'd say *so much stronger*, and he'd say, *this is pretty strong,* and then I'd feel like he didn't really get it. I decided to wait and see if it had something to do with Karen's spirit. If she appeared, and the odor intensified, I'd point it out, otherwise, it was a story for later.

I'd realized the balcony where she'd been sitting was her own apartment, so there was no help in figuring out what she wanted, in sensing what she was feeling based on her haunting someone else's apartment. The boyfriend, if one existed, must not have lived in the complex. If he did, she was keeping her distance from him.

We sat on the edge of the fountain. I touched the water. Without the suffocating smell of flowers, I wondered if the ghost was lingering any more. Maybe she was done with whatever she wanted. JD took my hand and placed it on his thigh. He rested his hand on top of mine. The weight of it calmed me.

It must have been close to twenty minutes that we sat there, not talking, my hand on his leg, his hand on mine, as if we were glued together, melding into a single being, turning to stone like the fountain where we sat — a lifelike sculpture, flesh for now, but slowly becoming a different substance.

The fountain trickled, keeping such perfect time with my pulse, I began to imagine blood flowing up through the center and spilling into the pool. When I dipped my fingertips in again, the water had turned a thick, almost oily texture that made the presence of blood entirely possible. I thought of the cut off toes and yanked my hand out of the pool.

All but one of the apartments was dark now. JD took his hand off mine and stood. He stretched his arms over his head and walked around to the other side of the fountain. The last light winked out and almost immediately the smell of gardenias and lilies steamed around us as if the lights had been holding them at bay. They had a damp, thick smell and JD whispered, his voice flattened by the scented air, "Those flowers reek."

"It was like that before."

I looked up at Karen's balcony.

Her spirit was there. For a moment, she was a vapor, something that could have been inside my own mind, but gradually her shape grew more distinct, becoming thicker and more full of substance at the same pace the odor of the flowers was increasing. I felt JD behind me. He put one hand on each shoulder and squeezed gently and I knew he'd seen her.

She was weeping softly. Her hair covered her face and spilled down over her shoulders and pooled in her lap. It was very, very long, past her hips, and extraordinarily thick. I couldn't see her face and could barely hear the weeping. I wondered if JD could hear. Mostly I felt it inside and I wasn't sure if he felt that as well. He was so quiet behind me, even his breath was inaudible, and I wouldn't have known he was there if it weren't for his hands on my shoulders, pressing down, keeping me firmly rooted near the side of the fountain.

I wanted to speak to her but she was so far away. I was sure she'd be able to hear me even if my voice was low, but something kept me from opening my mouth. Instead, I let her grief, whatever it was for, pour through me until it filled me up and started to feel like it was my own heart breaking into pieces. Inside, I was crying with her. After a few minutes, I began to feel they were my own tears, and it seemed again as if she was there to help me rather than the other way around. I felt like she wanted to listen to my feelings, wanted to know what happened in my life, as if I were the ghost and she was the living person.

The air was still thick and warm, but underneath, it was like a blanket that isn't doing its job, allowing my skin to turn clammy and cold. JD's hands didn't move, so I didn't think he noticed the change in my body temperature.

If she wanted me to start talking, just as I usually want them to start talking, I wasn't about to do that when she was up on the balcony with all those people in their apartments surrounding us. They seemed to be asleep, but that didn't mean they wouldn't hear me if I spoke up. I wasn't going to tell my troubles out in a public place, surrounded by a garden and fountain and the ears of strangers. I longed for her to leave the balcony and come down to the fountain where we could whisper our secrets to each other.

She lifted her head slightly and her hair fell back. Her face remained hidden in the darkness, but long waves of hair flowed around her, twining around the rails of the balcony, drifting ever so slightly as if there was a breeze wafting through the courtyard.

I wanted to talk, wanted to ask her who had sliced off her toes and killed her, who could be that cruel, who hated her that much. Maybe she wasn't the gentle, wounded spirit I thought, maybe she wasn't speaking because she'd done something terrible. Not terrible enough to deserve murder, no one does, but terrible enough to make any rational person understand why it had happened. If she directed me toward her killer, all her secrets might come out and she'd be remembered badly.

The sound of the fountain changed and I looked to the side. The water seemed to be flowing faster, the noise louder, more like a good-sized creek. It splashed and gurgled, drops of water spraying at me, speckling my skin. JD didn't say anything and I wondered if he felt it. When I turned my gaze back to the balcony above me, the ghost was gone. The water continued to splash wildly, drops landed on my feet and spattered up and down my arms. I could feel droplets on my shirt, pulling it against my skin and plastering it there. JD's hands tightened on my shoulders, digging into the muscle, coming close to pinching it to the bone. I tried to turn but his grip made it impossible. He took a deep breath and seemed to hold it. I glanced to the side and saw the ghost standing in the pond, her vague form blending into the upward spray of water. She was so close, I could reach out and stroke her hair.

I heard her cries over the water, turned to moans of physical pain like the first time I'd seen her. I glanced around to see if she was waking anyone in the apartments but they all remained dark.

JD let go of my shoulders and I stood, moving close to his side, leaning against him. He shifted his foot to stabilize himself and leaned into me.

"Are you in pain?" I whispered, quite loud, almost in a normal voice.

She wailed more. The sound was chilling. The drops of water, still standing on my skin turned to specks of ice, digging into me. Her hair was soaked and clinging to her form. I couldn't make out her face, just all that hair, draped along her shoulders and dripping down her arms.

She lifted her arm, moving it to reach toward me, but it looked as if the effort was too much for her, dragged down by wet hair, or maybe something else. Then she managed to raise it.

She moved closer. She reached out and pulled my head close to hers. JD let go of me and I felt him step back.

She stroked my cheek for a few seconds, bent toward me, and kissed me on the lips.

"Don't hurt me," she whispered. "I didn't do anything wrong. I love you. You're the only one I loved. Ever."

Her cries grew softer and her form wavered, her head dropping as if she were falling asleep. The odor of the flowers was acrid inside my nostrils and on the back of my tongue, making it difficult to swallow.

After a few minutes, she collapsed into the pond. Everything was silent but the gentle splash of water. For an instant, her hair was spread across the surface, plastered over the water lilies, thick and tangled, and then there was nothing.

Nine

JD AND I discussed the ghost and the smells and sounds that shifted with her appearance, but we came to no conclusions about what she wanted. Her attraction to me was inexplicable. Touching me, kissing me, whether it was sisterly, or something else, was unnerving and impossible to explain.

"The way her hair hangs over the balcony makes me think of Rapunzel."

"Maybe she's waiting for a secret lover," he said. "But the secret is the killer part."

I laughed. "Detective Smith seems to think Roseanne knows who he might be. He sure talked to her for a long time."

We lay awake until after midnight, whispering, repeating the things the ghost had said and the impressions we'd formed. It was fun to talk about it together and I felt that he was more into it than he'd been in the past. Of course, there were only two others he'd encountered himself — the Blue Lady and the ghost of his brother's ex-lover. And that one tried to take JD back to her world, so he wasn't exactly alert and able to observe what was happening. This time, he'd stood quietly and watched and listened and I think he felt my fascination. It seemed as if we were closer, that we were looking at the world through the same lens and it felt really good. There was a great sense of peace settling over me as softly as the cheap comforter on the motel bed.

THE SUN WAS UP when we woke. We made love but I think he knew I was distracted, more concerned over how I'd gain some sympathy from the occupants of my parents' home. Kev had told me to come back the night before, but with JD showing up, even though I mentioned the invitation to him, time had slipped past quickly, and then I'd forgotten about it. Now I was worried Kev wouldn't be there, or he wouldn't let me inside out of pure capriciousness. Maybe I didn't really want to remember his invitation to return, because I was secretly hoping for some unforeseen way to be inside the house without a suspicious guy and waffling girlfriend following me around. There was no way my parents' ghosts would show up under those circumstances.

"Are you sure I should go with you?" JD said. "If they weren't sure they should let you inside before, seeing a big guy might make them even more hesitant."

"Let's just see what happens."

"You could try being more straight-forward. Why

keep it a secret? For all you know, they're already aware of the murder."

"I don't like talking to strangers about it."

"But if they don't know about it, and you explain it, they might let you in and you wouldn't have to be twisting your brain into intricate plans about how to persuade them."

We went to breakfast and while we ate pancakes and drank coffee, I thought about what he'd said. What *was* the big deal? So what if they got creeped out, or put all kinds of syrupy pity on me. How did that hurt me? He had a point, but I didn't tell him then. I still wanted to see how it went.

The street was quiet when we arrived. A small, new-looking Honda was parked in the driveway of the vigilant neighbor. When we pulled up, the front door to her house was open, only covered by the screen. Next door, the little cactus in its orange pot sat on the railing where I'd left it. I guess they really did not want my gift. I was surprised a cat or some night creature hadn't knocked it over. The minivan and the motorcycle were missing from the carport. It had been a mistake to assume someone would be there. Did I expect them to be home every day, conversing with my parents' ghosts? "It looks like they're not home."

We got out of the car anyway and stood staring at the house. JD put his arm around my waist. "How do you feel?"

"It's hard to explain. Part of me feels like I never even

lived here, that it's completely unfamiliar and belonged to a stranger all this time, and another part of me feels as if I'm going to walk in the front door and see my Mom and Dad sitting in the living room, waiting for me."

"I guess we'll have to come back." He passed his keys to the opposite hand.

I moved away from him, toward the front path. I couldn't stop looking at the house, feeling an awkward combination of something completely foreign and something as familiar as my face in the mirror.

"You're not breaking in," he said.

I turned. "I wasn't thinking that at all."

"Yes you were."

I glared at him. "I wasn't." I turned back to the house. He walked up behind me and put his arm around my waist again. "What do you want?"

"To stop feeling like a child."

He squeezed gently. "I didn't mean to make you feel like that."

"It's not you. It seems as if I can't start my adult life because a big part of me is still fifteen, looking for my Mom and Dad."

"I know." He wrapped his other arm around me and pulled me closer.

The screen door on the other house opened and the woman who'd chased me away the first time I drove past stepped onto her porch. She let the screen slam closed. I could feel her eyes on me immediately, and within a few seconds she was stepping down from her porch and cutting across the lawn. "You're back."

"Yes."

She pushed her hair over her shoulder and straightened her back. "Why are you obsessed with a house you haven't seen in ten years?" She glanced at JD and smiled.

"I told you I . . ."

"You aren't thinking of moving back, are you?" She smiled at JD again. "If you are, you have good timing."

"Why?"

"I'm the owner. The renters are giving me a bad feeling. They're in and out at odd hours. I worry they're into something illegal. I'm thinking of raising the rent so they'll move."

"Can you do that?" I said.

"Their check is late almost every month."

"The other day you thought I was loitering and now you want to consider me as a tenant?"

She grimaced. She lifted her foot and shook a pebble out of her flip-flop. "You and your husband look stable, responsible." She grinned. "Friendly."

"He's not my husband."

"Well you still look stable. And this guy with his motorcycle and his creepy-looking friends . . ." She waved her fingers in the air to make quotation marks when she said *friends*. "I don't like it."

"He's lived here ten years and now you want to kick him out?"

"The late checks and creepy friends are recent."

"Why don't you like his friends?"

"I don't think they're friends at all. And his girlfriend running that business, coming home at two in the morning after she's supposedly catered a wedding. She leaves the lights on while she unloads pans and drops them on the ground and the two of them shout back and forth to each other."

"How much is the rent?" JD said.

"Are you interested?"

"When did you buy it?" I said.

"I suppose not too long after you lived there. It was a rental then, too, but they only kept it for seven or eight months, I think."

I watched her face. If she'd lived there, she must have known what happened. But I didn't remember her. I didn't remember who lived in that house, only the people on the other side. "Were you already living next door?"

"My grandmother was."

That sounded like something I remembered, an older lady who was usually out taking care of the community — working in a soup kitchen, volunteering at the hospital, and socializing every free minute in between.

"How big is it?" JD said.

I felt like we were playing volleyball, batting the ball from one person to another, back and forth, never quite making it over the net to the opposing team.

"Are you looking for a place?"

"Maybe," JD said.

She smiled. If I said maybe it would probably sound

evasive and difficult, but he said it in that smooth, calmly assured voice, and she went right along with it.

"I'm Jan." She held out her hand, then pulled it back before either of us could respond. "Do you want me to show you the place? It'll only take a few minutes."

I felt like melting onto the sidewalk. JD was very clever, focusing on what I really wanted while I was too interested in dates, information I could easily get once we were inside the house.

"I'd hate to upset the tenants," he said. "Going in without advance notice."

Jan waved her hand in the air. "It's my property. What are they gonna do?"

"File a complaint."

"They won't be back for hours. When she goes out with the van, she's gone for half the day, or the night. And he's hardly ever home, definitely not around much when she's not there."

"If you feel comfortable," JD said.

"Absolutely. Let me get the keys."

She trotted up the steps to her house and went inside. I turned to JD. He smiled. I just looked at him and he saw what I was feeling and smiled even more. He put his hand on the back of my neck and squeezed it gently. His fingers were cool and the pressure drained out all the stuff buzzing around my head, stuff I couldn't even name.

Jan came back outside. She held up the key ring and shook it like she was taking a dog for a walk, trying to get the animal excited by jangling the keys in front of its face. JD followed her right away, but I hung back, suddenly not sure what I wanted. I don't know if it was fear of what feelings might rise up out of nowhere, trapped in the walls all those years, or if I was slightly worried she didn't have as good a handle on Gwen and Kevin's schedule as she thought she did. I could easily imagine one of them showing up, especially Kevin, and then I'd never get back in the house under quieter circumstances, seeking my parents' lingering souls. I could imagine the sounds of their voices. At the same time, I was quite sure I'd forgotten them and wasn't even confident I'd recognize them if I heard a recording. I imagined the smell of my mother's shampoo — almond — and other smells, like vine-ripened tomatoes, which stab at my heart when I'm in the grocery store. I couldn't imagine what a familiar, pleasant odor would do to me in that house.

JD stopped and turned. He reached out his hand and waited for me to edge toward him. Jan already had the side door unlocked and was holding it open. We went to the side stoop that faced the carport. "Can we go in through the front door?" I said.

"Why?"

"I'd like to get a proper feel for it."

"Whatever." She pulled the door closed, locked it, and hopped down the steps. She wore a tank top as she had the other day, and I noticed again her muscular shoulders and arms. She was definitely in her forties, but looked younger in most ways, just a few lines around her eyes and lips. She walked across the lawn to the front porch, picked up the cactus, and unlocked the door. She carried the cactus inside. She obviously was very unconcerned about Gwen and Kev knowing she'd invaded their space. No matter how insistent she was about being the owner, the landlord doesn't get to just walk inside whenever she feels like it. Everyone knows that. It should have made me feel guilty, but it didn't. There were too many other things going on in my head.

I stepped through the doorway. Thick carpet covered the floor, giving the room a hushed sound. Nothing but the photograph of the sunflowers was the same as I remembered. The minute I recognized that fact, I was overcome with a horrible emptiness. The photograph had tricked me, suggesting the house contained the remains of their lives, but there was nothing. I felt nothing. I remembered nothing but vague images of reading in the living room or playing board games, and those were so indistinct they seemed as if they belonged to someone else's life.

Jan began talking a mile a minute. She explained how the carpet was new and the interior had been completely repainted three years ago. She stood in the center of the living room, grinning, her cheeks crinkled and her hands on her hips. "Isn't it charming? Those two don't appreciate it at all. This is such a nice neighborhood. Everyone knows each other. They could do so much with this place." She took her hands off her hips and swept her arms wide. I expected her to twirl around and start singing like the runaway nun in *The Sound of Music.* I wanted to slap Jan. If there was any whisper of the past, she was intent on drowning it out.

"Renters don't usually do a lot to fix a place up," JD said.

"It's their home! It shouldn't matter who owns it. They're living here, their lives are being spent in a place that they've managed to furnish and decorate as if they have no aesthetic desire at all."

"Not everyone does," JD said.

I turned my back to her. The sunflower photo had dust across the glass. Beneath it was a sixties-style orange couch with nubby fabric, wood legs, and thin cushions. The mantle over the brick fireplace was empty. A black and white *Pulp Fiction* movie poster hung over the mantle. There was a single armchair angled next to the fireplace, half facing the couch. It was piled with unfolded laundry. A sock had escaped the tangled bundle and fallen on the floor. The drapes were closed over the large window looking out on the front yard.

Jan led us into the kitchen, which was clean enough, but just as barren. An old, tired looking coffee maker holding a stained carafe stood on the counter, and the round oak table had a basket of tea bags in the center.

As we stepped into the hall my knees turned to liquid and I almost fell. JD had his arm around me and he felt me go limp. He tightened his grip and I managed to stay upright but my legs remained wobbly. At the far end of the hallway, the master bedroom door was closed, as it had been on that horrible day. Before that, it was never closed during the daytime. Only at night when my parents were sleeping.

Halfway down the hall on the right was the door to my bedroom. It was also closed. On the left, closer to where we stood was the bathroom, that door closed as well. What was inside all those rooms that they needed to keep the doors closed? I wasn't sure I wanted to know. It made the hallway stuffy and hot, the air thick and difficult to pull into my lungs. I looked at JD. He didn't seem to be having any trouble getting air and Jan was still chattering freely, so I guess I was the only one who felt the shortage of oxygen.

With all my heart, I wished I was alone. I didn't even want JD there. I wanted to move slowly, to stop when I needed. But the chance of getting in there alone seemed impossible, so far, and I wished I could be thankful for the opportunity that was right in front of me.

Jan went to the bathroom, flung open the door, and we were greeted with a mildew odor.

"Oh, no!" She hurried into the bathroom, unscrewed the lock on the window track, and slid it open.

"Should you be doing that when they're not here?" JD said.

"It stinks."

I didn't disagree with either of them.

"They aren't cleaning properly." She glanced over her shoulder, "See? That's another problem, and I didn't even know it." She opened the tub door and stuck her upper body into the opening. She stepped back and left the door open. "I'll leave a note that I came in to check on the place and they need to keep that window open when they're home. And put some elbow grease into cleaning the tile. Anyway, that's the bathroom. Not much to see, but it could be decorated a bit, something on the wall, a basket of flowers, even a live plant. With all the moisture, succulents do really well in bathrooms."

She moved across the hall to my bedroom. Half my life was created in that room. Even though I'd felt nothing at first, now it was a flood. No specific memories, just a feeling of familiarity, of being home.

"After the bathroom, I'm afraid to open this door," Jan said.

I was too. I held my breath, dreading it and wanting her to get on with it. She was making this far too dramatic, or maybe it felt that way because, for me, it was. She turned the knob. The door opened and she stepped away to let us enter. It was completely empty. The carpet was pale gray. Across from the door was a wide window, allowing soft light to fill the room. The closet door stood open. There were three shelves at the top, all empty. My breath echoed in the emptiness. The walls were recently painted pure white — as she'd pointed out earlier. I walked to the window, trying to avoid looking out at the yard. I touched the thin wood that framed one of the panels of glass. Next to the window were two small holes where thumbtacks had once been pressed into the wall.

JD was still in the hallway with Jan. Neither of them

spoke, as if my mood, the immense flooding of loss had seeped out of my body, filled the room, and spilled into the hallway, silencing their voices.

I took my hand away from the window. I remembered sitting on a wide chair in front of that window, reading, sketching birds that hopped around the yard, or daydreaming. I couldn't move, all of me wanting to stay, and all of me not wanting to remember anything more. I stepped away from the window. If I left now, I might not be able to come back.

"I have no idea why this room isn't being used," Jan said. "Or why they removed the window coverings." She made a tsk-ing sound.

"Can you show me where the water heater is?" JD said.

In that moment, I loved him more than I ever had. JD and Jan disappeared. All I could hear as they walked away was his voice, low and strong, taking up space so Jan couldn't squawk out any more comments for a few minutes.

I closed my eyes and waited. Waited for something that wasn't simply a lifetime of memories and sadness over what had been ripped away from me. The room smelled clean, so clean there was almost no odor at all, unlike the bathroom. I opened my eyes and stepped closer to the window again. The tree and the swing were visible from where I stood, as was the area where the vegetable garden had been. A wood fence that was in decent shape surrounded it, but all the area inside was stripped bare, dried grass covering the ground, with patches of exposed dirt. The bench at the back corner of the yard was still there. Beyond that was the shed where gardening tools and bikes and roller skates were kept. When I was small, they'd stored a little wading pool in there for me. I walked to the adjacent wall, unable to look out any longer.

Slowly I lowered myself onto the floor and leaned my back against the wall. I rested my head in my hands and closed my eyes. Inside of me there was nothing but emptiness echoing the empty room. I desperately wanted some sign, some hint, a whisper of knowing my parents' spirits were there, that they could be lingering in this place after so many years. But there was nothing. I took long slow breaths. I was trying too hard. Since when had a ghost ever appeared to me because I was demanding it show itself, straining to feel something, conjuring it up in my imagination? I needed to relax, to calm my thoughts. There was nothing I could do.

I opened my eyes. Maybe my parents were at peace. Maybe they didn't care who killed them, or they knew who it was and forgave. If there were no unfinished business, they wouldn't remain. But wasn't I unfinished business?

I stood and returned to the window. I studied the yard.

I don't know how long I stood there, staring with my eyes glazed over, not really seeing anything but the swing, dangling lifeless from the branch of the tree. I heard Jan's voice in the hallway.

"I'll show you the master bedroom."

I turned. She was just outside the doorway. I walked out and followed them down the hall.

I was equally scared when she turned the knob on the master bedroom door, but in a much different way. There was no longing but a tight pinch in my throat, as if I'd swallowed the sharp, silken strands inside the heart of an artichoke. It astounded me that fifteen years of walking into my parents' bedroom to look for my mother, Christmas mornings . . . jumping on their bed to wake them, a few times standing in front of their dresser and trying on my mother's lip-gloss and mascara — all those good things had faded to lists in my head. All I could really see was their bodies on their backs, the bullet holes in their foreheads. How could one image, glimpsed for what was probably less than ten minutes, wipe out hundreds, possibly thousands of other moments?

Jan stepped into the bedroom and waited for us to follow. I shouldn't have been afraid. It looked nothing like I remembered, and so that picture in my mind wasn't reflected back to me in all its stately horror.

The bed was nothing but a queen-sized mattress and box spring with a dark blue comforter thrown over it, puffed up at the top where the pillows were. There was a dresser in the corner. The top of the dresser was covered with receipts, a few dollar bills, and three coffee mugs. There was a framed five by seven photograph of Gwen and Kevin over the dresser. It was slightly crooked as if drawers closed with too much force had bumped it off center. The floor was hardwood. The side of the bed opposite of where the dresser was had a nightstand with a black plastic lamp on it and above the bed was a poster of the San Francisco skyline. The drapes were pulled closed over the door that led to the backyard.

I remembered antique dressers and a rocking chair, a bed with an iron headboard and footboard, and an old fashioned quilt with lots of extra pillows tossed along the top edge. I remembered the smell of lemons that my mother kept in a bowl on the dresser because she liked the fresh scent.

I quickly stepped into the hall. "Thanks."

"You could do so much with it. The door out to the yard is charming, do you want to see?"

"No that's fine. I can see it has a lot of potential."

"I suppose we should get going. Just in case," Jan said.

Now she was worried? I guess she'd realized going into their bedroom was stepping over an entirely different line.

It felt as if my skin was glued to the inside of the house. I didn't want to walk out that door, didn't want to admit that I'd felt absolutely nothing. I hadn't even felt the warm rush of memories that make a house seem like it has a personality, that the people who lived there had changed it. It was nothing but wood and plaster, wires and pipes woven with one or two images that had flashed across the screen of my mind. A pile of stuff. It was hard not to cry because it seemed as if it was saying my parents had never existed. If the house hadn't managed to hold a few pieces of them, did that mean they'd vanished from the earth without a trace? I guess you could say I was the evidence they'd lived, but right then, I wasn't feeling that either. I felt so disconnected, so unattached to anything or anyone, it seemed like I'd dropped in out of nowhere and was headed to the same destination.

On the way back down the hall, Jan closed the door of my old bedroom. We followed her into the living room and out the front door. JD thanked her several times. Her face was eager, longing for us to say we wanted to move in. She seemed oblivious to all the effort that would be required to displace Gwen and Kevin.

"I would really love to rent to you two. You seem nice, very easy-going. These two," she waved her hand toward the house, "give me the willies. Kevin is very controlling. Even when he's not there, she seems afraid to leave the house. She only goes out when she has clients to serve. Like I said, he's gone all the time, but she's in that place like a prisoner. I can't really complain that they're loud, except for the racket when she comes home late from a catering job. It's the opposite — there aren't any sounds of normal living. In summer, when all the windows are open, you hear people talking, the TV, someone laughing. Their place is like a graveyard with two ghosts drifting past the windows from time to time."

I shivered. I could feel JD looking at me, not because of the shivering, but because of what she'd said. It was tough to take. My hopeful side grabbed onto it and wanted to ask if she'd actually seen ghosts inside the house. But I knew, I absolutely knew that wasn't what she meant. I could see how much I wanted it to be something it wasn't.

"I'm sure most landlords don't complain about tenants that are too quiet, but it's unnatural. It makes me suspicious of what they're up to, and it makes me angry that he has a life, going out all the time, his buddies dropping by, and she doesn't. It pisses me off that she puts up with that. I know every relationship has its own rules, but . . . It pisses me off, that's all."

"Thanks for letting us look around," JD said.

"Of course," Jan said, maybe hoping to keep talking until we told her we wanted the place, "she's the kind who you'll read about some day, that she reached the end of her rope and butchered the guy."

"What makes you say that?" I said.

"She's so quiet. And no one likes to be shut up in a box. Claustrophobic. He's killing her spirit, I think. And maybe someday she won't put up with it anymore. Or she'll try to escape and he'll kill her."

"You seem very upset by them."

"I told you, something isn't right. You can feel it. He's smothering her. As surely as if he was holding a pillow over her face."

"That's very vivid," JD said.

"It's what I think. I say what I think. Let me give you my number. And my email." She ran back up her stairs and slammed into the house. Before I could even turn to look at JD, she was back.

"Here." She held out an index card with her name, address, phone, and email. "That's my cell. Call me any time."

I was having a hard time reconciling the person I was seeing now with the woman who'd scared me by pounding on my car window and demanding to know why I was watching the house. I guess JD had quite an effect on people. Of course, I already knew that. He'd given me exactly what I came here for. He couldn't give me my parents' ghosts, but if he could, he would have.

"NOW WHAT DO we do?" JD said when we pulled into the parking spot in front of our motel room.

"You tell me," I said.

"I have no idea what you want. I got you into the house and you sulked all the way back here. You're running around like a nutcase, not sure what you want from your family home, trying to influence a detective who's going to do whatever his procedures tell him, pursuing a ghost . . ."

"You didn't have to come up here." I leaned my shoulder against the door and tipped my head against the window to get support for it too. The angle hurt my neck and I straightened again.

"I love you." He reached across the console and took my hand.

I let my hand rest somewhat limply in his, but I didn't yank it away, which was my first instinct. "The ghost came to *me*, remember?"

"You went looking for something," he said.

"It still didn't have to reveal itself."

"Fair enough."

He squeezed gently and I gave a little pressure in return. "She doesn't seem to want to tell me anything."

"Maybe she's at peace."

"Then why is she haunting the apartments?"

He shrugged. "I thought your house and coming to terms with what happened was more important to you."

"I felt like she was trying to comfort me, instead of looking for peace."

"Really? How would you know that?"

"I just know it's true."

"You want it to be true."

"The cut off toes must mean something."

"She doesn't seem to want to give you any insight, so let it go. Are you going to call your aunt?"

"I sort of hoped she'd call me."

"Well she hasn't. And if you're going to see her before we head home, sooner is better."

I pulled my phone out of my bag and dialed her number while JD rubbed my leg. The phone rang and went to voicemail. "Hi Aunt Gloria. This is Madison. I guess I don't have to say that since I'm your only niece. Anyway, I was caught off guard the other night and I'm sorry I ran out like that. I hope I didn't leave you with lots of uneaten food." JD smiled when I said that. "Anyway, my boyfriend is here with me now, and I wanted to come by and introduce him to you. And catch up . . . like we planned originally. So give me a call. Any time works for me either today or tomorrow." I gave my number, said good-bye, and ended the call. I put the phone in my bag. "Let's go back to the apartment."

"Why?"

"Do you have something better to do?"

He turned the key. The engine roared. "What are you plotting now?" he said.

"I have to occupy myself somehow. I'm not going to sit around in a motel room all day waiting for Gloria to call, or not call."

"Yeah, but what are you going to do at the apartment?" Although he stared straight ahead at the road, I felt a small sliver of his gaze on me, even with his sunglasses covering them. It was like with the ghost. I knew he was looking at me, even if I couldn't point to solid evidence.

"I don't know. I'll find out when I get there."

"One thing I have to say about you. You're never boring." He pulled onto the main drag, inserting the SUV into a long line of traffic. I pulled out my phone, looked through it for some music, plugged it into the speaker, and leaned my head back against the seat.

When we got there, we drove around the back of the apartments and parked. Most of the carports were empty.

Inside the courtyard, the sound of the fountain splashing was louder, echoing off the sides of the building that huddled around it. I wondered if someone had cleaned it and the water was flowing with more force.

"Do you think the killer does live here?" I said.

"How would I know?"

"Just wondering what you thought."

"Right now, it feels like no one lives here."

"Like my old house."

"Is that how it was for you?" He turned and stepped around me. He wrapped his arms around my waist from the back and pulled me close so I felt like I was inside of him. He pressed his chin hard against the top of my head.

"Yes. In fact it felt like Gwen and Kevin had abandoned the place. I wasn't sure if that was because everything was so different yet so much the same, or what it was."

"You were hoping for ghosts."

"No, not really."

"Liar." He voice echoed through my skull.

"I don't think I was. Of course I'd like their ghosts to reveal themselves to me, but I wasn't expecting it under those circumstances — in the middle of the day, prowling around where we weren't invited, Jan talking nonstop. So many things were wrong."

He moved me forward, walking his feet with mine. We reached the bench and he sat down. He pulled me onto his lap. Well, not really his lap, one leg, so I was perched on an even narrower bench than he was. "It's been a long time since they were killed, Madison."

"Half my life."

"Do you really think they're in that house, waiting for you?"

"I don't know."

"What are you going to do if you never see their ghosts?"

"I'll think about it when that happens."

"Maybe it would be better to let go now."

"Why?"

"You might not get back in the house." He looked at me and I don't know what he saw on my face, but he said, "We aren't renting it. That's a bad idea. We have jobs. The drive is too far. It wouldn't work. And it wouldn't be healthy."

The funny thing was, it hadn't occurred to me that I could rent it. But the minute he spoke, I felt as if the idea had been inside me all that time, and his words drew it out toward the front of my mind. It was a strange sensation, as if he really had pulled me inside of him, or we were so tightly connected the thoughts flowing through one of our brains were making their way through our skin into the other person's head. It was a brilliant plan and the drive wouldn't be bad at all. We wouldn't have to stay forever. We could rent it, even if she had us sign a lease, we could put up with anything, even a horrendous commute, for six months.

He was staring at me, probably seeing in the shifting of my eyes how my brain was racing madly with his idea. Making plans, and realizing, without fully bringing it to the front of my attention, that all these thoughts were just assuming we'd live there together. Wasn't that what he'd wanted for some time?

"It's not an impossible idea," I said.

His eyes shifted, still seeming to look at me, but I could tell they were gazing into the middle distance, his thoughts shifting as surely as his eyes, thinking about moving in and probably considering if he wanted to do it under those circumstances. Not the romantic step of getting closer, but an agenda that had nothing to do with him. Except maybe convenience.

The sun had moved higher and the temperature was increasing quickly. The courtyard was designed to have a cooling atmosphere with its tropical plants and bright flowers and glistening, splashing water. But it was hot. And not a humid hot that was comforting and soft, but a dry, scratch-at-the-inside-of-your-nostrils and crack-your-lips hot.

"Should we get going?" he said. He lifted me off his leg and stood.

"Where?"

"I don't know, but it's too hot and we're trespassing and you're not going to accomplish anything."

As he finished speaking, I heard the sound of high-heeled shoes on the concrete stairs leading down from the apartments to my left. A woman emerged from the opening, looked across the courtyard. She stopped. She turned and headed in our direction, trying to look casual about it, but walking with a very insistent sound to her steps, her face turned like a magnet toward JD.

"Hi," she said. She stuck out her hand at JD. "I'm Lisa. Are you looking for someone?" She had long dark hair, flat ironed so it looked like a metal sheet. Her eyes had every kind of eye make-up that's available, and her lips were dark red. But she didn't look cheap, she looked very exotic, especially with her high heels and her fitted white dress.

JD shook her hand. I extended my hand but she didn't seem to notice.

"Just enjoying the fountain," JD said.

"That sounds a little suspicious." She laughed, to show him she didn't think suspicious was necessarily a bad thing. "You don't live here, why would you come sit in the courtyard? And who's your friend?" She glanced at me and looked back at JD, smiling.

"I'm Madison. I met Roseanne, apartment 7B?, the other day. We're sort of friends."

For the first time, she looked at me straight on. "Really? She's the most unfriendly person I know. Certainly the most unfriendly one here, and I would not back down from that opinion, even if she were standing right here. The only person she speaks to is Karen . . . was Karen. She's only lived here about six months. I think she moved here because she was friends with Karen. At least that was my impression. Never has any guests that I've seen, so you'd think she'd be more interested in making a friend or two." She shook her head as if she couldn't comprehend someone not wanting to be her friend.

"I thought she was nice enough," I said.

"You still haven't said why you're here." She smiled at JD. "Are you looking for a place to live?"

"Just enjoying the garden," I said.

"That's freaky, to hang out in a garden where you don't belong. And probably illegal."

"We only stopped by," I said.

"To see Roseanne," she said.

I moved my head slightly, hoping it could be taken as a nod without really lying. Which is a lie all in itself.

"Did you see her?"

"No. We should get going." JD reached out and grabbed my hand tugging at me slightly.

We quickly said good-bye to Lisa and walked through the breezeway to the parking lot. When we were back in the SUV, headed away from the apartments and the AC was starting to kick in, I said, "That was strange."

"Because she seemed like she wanted to hit on me right in front of you when you're obviously my girlfriend?"

"No. Roseanne told me she didn't know Karen very well and this girl says Roseanne moved in here because of Karen."

"She said she had that impression. I wouldn't take the impression of someone like that."

"I guess not," I said. But inside I was wondering why I wouldn't. She had no reason to lie to us, and the information just fell out of her mouth. If Roseanne did know Karen better than she'd implied, maybe she was protecting someone. A love triangle. Silly, but the most common thing in the world. Maybe there was another reason, besides just fear and horror, that Roseanne was crying so much the first time I met her.

Ten

JD AND I went back to the park with the ducks and hung out there the rest of the day. We talked and then stretched out on the warm grass and slept, holding hands with our fingers intertwined. I dreamt about work and then I was sitting by the apartment fountain, complaining to Cindee that the smell of flowers was making me too tired to think or speak.

My aunt finally called at four-thirty and asked us to join them for dinner the following evening. The invitation sounded forced to me, but JD said, *don't read into it. Maybe they felt bad.* There was a small chance he was right, but there was still no way I was going to be all forgiveness and love. They were cruel and I wasn't going to let them touch my psyche again. Not for a very long time, if ever. I only wanted to have dinner to crawl inside their brains and look for information about my parents. As far as I was concerned, my aunt and uncle were nothing more than ghosts helping to point me in the right direction.

After we went out for pizza, I informed JD I was going back to the apartment again to wait for the ghost.

"Why? She's not telling you anything."

"I have to try harder."

"How can you try harder? It's not on you to find her killer."

"Well at least waiting for her gets my mind off my parents and Gwen and Kevin and everything else."

"Fair enough," he said.

We went back to the motel and watched a movie on my iPad. After the movie, we set the alarm for 1 am and took another nap, if it's really considered a nap when it's nighttime. I'm not sure what the definition of nap actually is.

When we woke, I was as alert as if it were morning. JD wasn't so enthused, but then he wasn't enthused about dragging ourselves back to the apartment, trespassing again, and sitting around a fountain thinking a ghost was going to stop crying and tell us what she knew.

We parked on the street. We entered through the front gate, taking care not to let the iron post drag on the concrete, with its screech that could wake the dead, as they say. But the dead were already wakeful. I hoped one dead person was still out and about and ready to do more than cry on my shoulder. Part of me wondered if I should have come alone. Perhaps she wanted to connect girl to girl. I don't know why I thought that, it sounded absurd even in my own mind, but the thought was there and it lingered as we walked along the path to the center of the garden.

I stepped close to the rim of the fountain and it speckled my legs with cool droplets. We walked around the chaise lounges and to the bench. I sat up straight, determined to stay alert. I did not want to distract myself from my intention by slumping against JD and focusing on how good his body felt instead of being attentive to the whisper of a ghost.

Vines climbed across the arched trestle that was over the bench and as I turned and looked through them, I saw Roseanne on her balcony. The thick growth and the darkness prevented her from seeing us. I leaned close to JD, touched the back of his hand, held my finger to my lips, and pointed through the tangle of vines. He nodded.

The door to her apartment was open and a single light glowed softly from her living room. She placed a tall, thick candle in the center of a small patio table and pulled something out of her pocket. She held it out and a flame appeared. She lit the candle and shoved the lighter back in her pocket. The wick was deep in the center and the wax was white, making the whole candle seem alive with the steady light of the flame. All those times she'd smoked with me, she'd acted as if she didn't have a lighter. I wasn't sure of the significance of that, or if there was any significance.

I glanced at JD. His eyes were closed. He clearly was not as fascinated as I was by the scene taking place above us. While he drew close to dozing, I was gripped with curiosity over why she was lighting a candle at two o'clock in the morning.

She sat on the chair beside the table and stared into the darkness of the balcony next to hers.

Some time passed. I can't say how much. Enhanced by the warmth of the air and the quiet surrounding the courtyard, time seemed simultaneously stretched out and shrunk to a pinprick. I felt I'd been sitting on the bench, listening to JD's deepening breath for hours. And I felt I'd just sat down and watched Roseanne light the candle a moment ago. Nothing about the flame burning on her table indicated it had sunk any further into the wax, which added to the sense that time was motionless.

After a few more minutes, Karen's ghost materialized rapidly on the balcony next to Roseanne's. Their apartments shared a wall and their balconies were close enough to hand a cup of coffee over. Maybe Roseanne had heard something the night Karen was killed — the agonized weeping of a woman whose feet were being mutilated, and her life ending, not with a dramatic exit as we would all hope for, but a slow seeping out of her blood, after the sudden and brutal slices with a knife across her feet and into her chest. It was surprising that every single neighbor hadn't heard her screams.

I moved to the side so I could have a better view through the vines. JD was asleep now, his head leaning against the trellis. It was probably better, I'd be able to follow my intuition more quickly. His presence, even if he doesn't speak, influences my thoughts. Like he'd pointed out, another human being changes everything. After he'd mentioned it, I'd realized I'd seen that kind of thing all the time in the church office. There's one kind of vibe in the air, a kind of intimacy and interest when Kate and I are talking, then Joe comes in and everything changes, either to church business or to some sort of male-female or boss-employee divide. We each carry our psychic presence and they interact with each other and change the atmosphere in ways we can't even recognize.

The ghost was leaning over the rail now, weeping softly. All her attention was focused on Roseanne, sitting silently, darkness covering her face. Roseanne didn't acknowledge the white figure, or appear to be moved by her despair. This time, the ghost seemed oblivious to my presence. I sat up straighter and studied her, watching how she wavered toward the other balcony, moving in an uncoordinated dance with the flickering candle. It was all I could do to keep from shouting at Roseanne to turn and notice what was right there. She sat transfixed by the candle flame.

For several minutes, the tableau remained the same. I was watching the ghost, the ghost was watching Roseanne, and Roseanne and JD were on different planes altogether. Slowly Roseanne turned toward the balcony, but her posture remained the same, as if she were still staring into the light of the candle, refusing to acknowledge Karen's ghost.

The ghost moved away from the railing and turned toward me. Her weeping continued unbroken, like a faucet left running, only a thin stream of water coming out, but steady. I felt her pain from her missing toes, but no sense of revenge or anger or anything negative. Just a great sorrow that she wanted to share. It seemed she was turning back to me after the rejection by Roseanne. I wasn't sure if it was truly rejection, or Roseanne was so grounded in the earth she was unable to recognize a being outside of this realm.

I got up off the bench and moved out from behind the vines. I slipped off my shoes. The pavement was cool and the refreshing temperature washed up my legs. I walked across the courtyard until I was a few feet out from the balcony where the ghost stood. I looked up and shivered. Sometimes I don't stop to think what I'm pursuing, what I'm looking at. Here was a presence from beyond the grave, a woman who was dead, and a being that might have abilities I couldn't begin to imagine.

We remained there like three points of a triangle. There was some sort of connection between the three of us, but I couldn't explain what it was. All I felt was that we were in perfect balance with each other. Not that there was harmony of any kind, but that if one of us moved or spoke, it would disrupt the others.

Roseanne stood and I felt the delicate web between us tear into long strands of dissolving gossamer. She leaned over the table and blew out the candle with a vicious huff that I could hear on the ground below. She went into her apartment and slid the door closed with a hard thud. Then I realized, the candle had been her attempt to seek Karen. She didn't know what to do, but she wanted to contact her and she fell back on the cliché of a candle. Sitting only a few feet away, all that time, she'd had absolutely no awareness of Karen's presence.

I didn't know what to think about that. I always assumed that people who didn't believe in ghosts simply hadn't had an opportunity to encounter one. It never occurred to me that someone could be in the vicinity of a spirit and not recognize its presence.

BACK AT OUR motel room, JD slept as blissfully as he had before we went to the apartments. I didn't even pretend to sleep. As soon as his breathing shifted to a deeper tone, I grabbed my cigarettes and lighter and went out to the bench that was starting to feel like it was in my own backyard.

I lit the first cigarette. I knew there would be more, even before my first puff. There would be plenty of time later to deal with my slow, sad descent back to half a pack a day. The still air caused the flame to stand straight and tall. It was beautiful, the only light in the surrounding area except for the dim and distant glow of the lights over the door to each cottage.

I leaned back and thought about Karen's ghost. After a while, my thoughts drifted to my parents' ghosts. The minute my thoughts turned, tears rushed to my eyes. I'd been so tense in the house, and then determined not to think about it while it continued to scratch at the base of my skull like a pet scratching at a closed door. Keeping busy calling my aunt and trying to distract myself with

Karen's spirit, I didn't know how very badly I'd hoped to
see their ghosts. On some level I'd been sure I would see
them, despite the unfavorable circumstances. And there
was nothing. Not even a feeling. Not a suggestion or
touch of reassurance. But the minute I walked into the
courtyard of a stranger's apartment, the ghost was
jumping all over the balcony trying to get my attention.
Trying to tell me something that I now realized she
couldn't seem to speak, as if her tongue had been
removed along with her toes.

The next drag on my cigarette burned my tongue.
When I released a thin stream of smoke, the lingering
taste hinted at blood. I couldn't stop trying to understand
the spirit's seeming desire to connect but her complete
refusal to speak and the absence of any sense of what she
might want to say, whether given off by emotion or
through some sort of psychic pathway. Every ghostly
experience I've had has been completely different, so I
shouldn't have been making comparisons. Some spirits
are angry, some are gory, some are beautiful in their
vaporous presence, but they've all managed to bring me
to an understanding of why they couldn't rest.

I returned to the idea of Karen appearing simply to
comfort me, but she knew nothing about me or my life.
She had no idea who I was, just someone open to the
spirit world who happened to wander through her
courtyard. Only two things had been clear — she was in
pain, and during this most recent encounter, she wanted
something from Roseanne. But Roseanne was oblivious

to her presence.

Maybe my parents' ghosts had been in the house and I hadn't been able to see or feel or hear them. I burst into tears. I dropped my cigarette on the ground and stomped my foot on it. Maybe that's why Gwen and Kevin were cold and hostile and inconsistent. And maybe all their doors were closed to keep the ghosts from disturbing their sleep. I lit another cigarette even though I could hardly smoke, I was crying so hard.

After a while, I settled down. It began to get light, which put me in a slightly more optimistic frame of mind. I decided I was leaping to conclusions. The ghosts of my parents and Karen's ghost and Roseanne's inability to see her were not related at all. My frantic desire to know who murdered Karen was leading me to make connections that didn't necessarily fit. You can shape anything into a pattern in your head, but that doesn't make it true. I had to keep trusting that if my parents' ghosts had lingered all these years, I'd see them at some point.

When JD woke, I was sitting next to him in bed. He didn't seem to notice the fresh smoke on my clothes and in my hair, he just wrapped his arms around me and snuggled as if I'd been sleeping next to him all that time.

LATE THAT AFTERNOON we were seated across from Detective Smith. He leaned back in his chair, adjusted his glasses several times, glancing at his computer, doing everything he could to signal he only had a few minutes to talk to me.

"I just have two quick things," I said.

He attempted a smile but didn't say anything.

"What were your original theories about who killed my parents?"

He took his hands away from his glasses and folded them. He settled his forearms on the desk and coughed. "Well, statistically, people are murdered by someone they know. So first we look for love affairs, followed by money issues."

"So your theory was one of my parents had an affair?"

"It wasn't a theory, it was an avenue we pursued."

JD laughed softly. I'm sure he was as amused as I was by the mild double-speak.

"And I assume you found nothing?"

"That's right."

"So you looked into financial problems?"

"Yes. Especially since your aunt and uncle mentioned the request to borrow money."

"How much?"

"Five thousand dollars."

"And?"

"We didn't find anything. So we assumed it was for a vacation. Looking through your parents' finances, they were actually in very good shape, they had a robust college fund for you, retirement savings. They hadn't taken many vacations that we could find, so it seemed a logical conclusion."

"What was your next theory?"

"That's when we started to hit dead ends. We found nothing. No suspects, no physical evidence, no acquaintances that owned the type of gun that was used. We pursued a gang theory for a while — some sort of initiation ritual, but found nothing."

"Okay."

He nodded. "What was the other thing?" He glanced at his watch.

"I'm having dinner with my aunt and uncle. I'd like to make an appointment to meet with you one more time to talk about that." My voice must have sounded more heated than I realized, because JD reached across the arm of his chair and took my hand.

"You're starting to interfere and it needs to stop." He looked at his watch again and stood up.

"They're my aunt and uncle. I get to have dinner with them."

"Don't talk to them about the case."

"They were my guardians when my parents died, how can I not talk about the case? Not that it's been much of a case until I showed up."

He rubbed his hand across his nose, bending it slightly from side to side.

JD squeezed my hand, then let go. We stood up.

"How is your other murder going?" I said.

Detective Smith took his hand away from his face. He looked slightly sick to his stomach. "My other murder?"

I laughed. "Case, your murder case?"

"We're still trying to locate a boyfriend."

"Why are you so sure there's a boyfriend?" I said. "Because of her toes? Does that make it more personal, or something?"

His cheeks reddened and his jaw was so tight it looked like he was locking down his mouth. "What about the toes?"

"Cutting them off like that."

"How did you know her toes were cut off?"

"Because . . ."

"You need to tell me. That's an order."

I didn't think he could give me orders, but he sounded very official. I could sense JD bristling, or maybe I didn't feel anything, maybe I just knew he was bristling, knowing his ambivalent, semi-negative, viewpoint on cops. "I don't want to get anyone in trouble," I said. My mind raced. If Roseanne knew about the toes and Detective Smith hadn't told her, did that mean she knew the killer? Or had she murdered Karen? And cut off her toes? I shivered. She seemed like a fairly innocuous person — not at all vicious or cruel or capable of something so gruesome.

The tender gestures Karen's spirit made toward Roseanne the night before, a sense of longing, I now realized, was what I'd felt. Pleading with Roseanne to notice her presence. Was it possible they were lovers? Detective Smith, and maybe me, couldn't see what was right in front of us because Detective Smith was looking for a boyfriend, asking about men she knew, completely focused on a male killer.

"Roseanne told me about the toes," I said.

He looked at me and as if I could see past his skin and bone, right into the firing synapses in his brain. I recognized the same steps toward the same conclusion that had just passed through my mind.

"And her ghost . . ." I said.

He waved his hand in front of his face, as if he could brush the ghost away. "Well. Well, I certainly had blinders on." He smiled, although there was a hint of sadness around his lips. I'm sure the pleasure in uncovering a suspect is accompanied by a strong sense of grief at the state of the human heart. "Well," he said again. "And thank you for telling me. You didn't have to."

"You ordered me to."

He smiled and I felt all the irritation drain out of JD's posture. Finally, he'd met a cop who wasn't a know-it-all, throwing his weight around. It was clear Detective Smith was fully aware that he couldn't order me around in this situation. I suppose eventually he could subpoena me, or something. Or maybe not, I don't know much about the legal process. And I don't want to.

"About the blinders," I said.

Detective Smith looked at me with his brow scrolled into a bunch of lines. "Blinders?"

"You said you had blinders on. You were focused on looking for a male lover."

"Well we don't know that's the final story, just an interesting avenue to pursue. The first new angle on the case."

"Exactly."

He stepped around his chair and shoved it under his desk. He picked up his keys.

"What blinders are you wearing regarding my parents?"

"Completely different situation."

"Why?"

"Because it is."

"That's not an answer."

"You may be the one wearing blinders in that situation," he said. "And I understand, I truly do. You want answers so badly, you think we've missed something, ignored something important. Not spoken to every single possible lead. But the truth is, some cases are never solved."

"I won't accept that!"

JD put his hand on my arm. I wrenched it away. That wasn't fair to him, he was trying to let me know he was there for me, but I couldn't help it.

"We'll interview your aunt and uncle again. But we were thorough, whether you want to believe that or not. So I think it's a long shot, and I think you should prepare yourself for never having an answer. For living with not knowing."

He waited for me to respond. I wasn't going to answer him. I turned and walked away from his desk, increasing my pace every few feet until I was almost running. I hurried across the lobby. JD was behind me, not lingering to talk to the detective, but not racing to catch me either.

I slammed through the double glass doors of the station and kept going. I didn't slow down until I reached the apartment complex. It was a good three miles and I was breathing hard from running.

I turned and saw JD walking up the street. He'd managed to keep pace with me and looked like he was strolling casually at the same time.

I went into the courtyard. The sun was moving behind the buildings, casting long shadows, burying the courtyard in shade. I sat on the edge of the fountain and waited for JD.

"ARE YOU OK?" JD put his arm around my waist and pulled me close.

"I guess."

He didn't say anything else, which I appreciated.

After quite a long time, he squeezed my waist. "I think that detective is scared of you."

"Why would you say that?"

"Just a feeling."

"There's nothing scary about me."

"Oh yes there is."

"Like what?"

"You push for what you want and you come across like you're not worried if that makes someone angry. It makes you look fearless. And you see ghosts. That's frightening to a lot of people. And you said it so casually, as if you really didn't care if he thought you were nuts."

"I don't care. I just want him to do his job."

"He thinks he did."

"Well he didn't. He should never give up. People who are murdered are counting on him."

"I'm sure he knows that."

"Since when are you on the cops' side?"

"I'm not taking sides, just observing. Besides, investigators are different from street cops."

"That's where they all start out."

"Fair enough. Maybe detectives are the less annoying and less pompous ones who move on, so I can tolerate them better."

I smiled, but I don't think he was aware since I was pressed up close to him.

"Anyway, he's scared of you. Trust me."

I'm a little embarrassed to admit, I liked hearing his reasons. I don't think of myself as scary. I see myself as an everyday administrative assistant who sometimes gets ignored. It was kind of nice to hear I had an impactful presence in the world. "Why else?"

"You say what you think."

"Not always."

"Enough."

I snuggled closer. "Then why isn't he doing what I asked?"

"He is. He said he'd question your aunt and uncle again."

"He doesn't seem very enthused about it. He's just doing it to shut me up."

"He wouldn't do that."

"He said it's a long shot."

"It is, but he's doing it."

"I want him to have passion about this case. He's forgotten all about them." A lump formed in my throat as if I'd swallowed a very large, dense dumpling.

"Do you want him to get fired up and have passion, or do you want him to interview your relatives?"

"Both. He can't do it right if he's not passionate about it."

"That's not true."

"Shhh." I put my hand on his arm. "There she is." It was strange, seeing her in the half-light of dusk. Her image was more faint, and for half a second, I wondered if I'd imagined her. I stood and walked quickly to the balcony to reassure myself. She'd appeared enough times by now I wasn't worried about scaring her away. Obviously she hadn't settled her score. Or scores.

"Are you looking for Roseanne?" I said in a stage whisper that I hoped wouldn't catch the attention of anyone in the nearby apartments.

The spirit began to weep. She was there, wanting justice or her final word, so why wouldn't she communicate? I stepped closer. "Karen?"

The image faded significantly. I could barely see her now. "Was Roseanne your lover?"

The smell of flowers, decaying and sour, filled my lungs.

"I'll sleep now," she whispered. "I can't feel anything."

Her image became even less distinct, almost a wisp of smoke. "Wait. Don't leave. I need to know about you. Please don't leave."

Now she was so faint, all I saw was part of her skirt draped over the railing, and a suggestion of her hair. She was leaving and I knew she wouldn't be back. Maybe she hadn't even been there to get justice, she just wanted to see Roseanne one last time.

"If you see two ghosts, a man and a woman with bullet holes in their foreheads, tell them I'm looking for them. Help them find me. Please?"

And then she was gone. I sat down on the ground and felt an enormous wave of grief, but I didn't cry. A moment later JD was by my side. He pulled me gently to my feet and led me out of the garden. We didn't speak all the way home, but I felt his heart, close to mine.

Eleven

DRIVING UP THE hill to Gloria and Paul's was completely different with JD by my side. I drove, which isn't normally the case with us, but I knew the way, and for some reason it seemed right. The sun was going down and the trees cast long shadows over the road, making me forget how warm it was until I climbed out of the car. The heat slammed into me with the same force as those cruel, accusing words from Paul. *You're looking for money. We did our duty.*

JD got out and shut the door. I took a deep breath. Thinking of them as Gloria and Paul instead of my aunt and uncle was helping me push aside the relationship I thought I had with them. There was only one reason I was here and that was to try to find out what happened when I was fifteen. After this, I doubted we would have much of a connection. If there'd ever been a connection outside of my own mind and my own mistaken view of their feelings for me.

JD walked around the back of the car and put his arm around my waist. He squeezed gently, kissed my ear, and let go. I led the way up the path to the double front doors and rang the bell. It chimed and I closed my eyes for a second, wishing I could go back in time and replay that first visit, react more calmly, not feel my heart ripped out of my chest.

Paul opened the door.

"Hi, Madison. We're glad you could give us a second chance."

I smiled, hoping my face looked as phony as his voice sounded. "No worries. This is JD."

Paul shook JD's hand. He looked like he wanted it to end quickly, but JD kept a tight grip, forcing it to go just a few seconds longer than expected. I loved him for that. I loved how he was in my corner and how subtle, yet not, he could be.

We went inside and Gloria appeared with a tray of glasses, two already filled with white wine, and two with sparkling water.

"JD might want a glass of wine," I said.

"Oh. I thought . . ." Gloria set the tray on the long, low table that ran between the sofa and the armchairs.

I picked up a glass of water and sat down.

When we were all settled, including JD with a glass of wine, Paul said, "We really are so glad you gave us another chance. We didn't mean to shock you or seem rude."

"You did. Shock me."

"It was our pleasure to have you live with us all those

years," Gloria said.

I sipped my water.

"Why didn't you see eye to eye with my Mom?" I said.

"Oh, that." Gloria laughed. "It wasn't *that* big of a deal."

"You sure made it sound like a big deal the other day. You said you were surprised you were still my guardians."

"Mostly because we hadn't seen your parents in a while," Paul said.

"Why not?"

"You're very direct," Gloria took a sip of wine. "I'd forgotten that about you."

"Are you going to answer my questions?"

She laughed. "Well one at a time, let's slow down, shall we?"

JD put his hand on my knee. I wanted to flip it off like a horsefly, but I swallowed some water and pictured my hurt and anger going down with it. He was trying to help me, soothe me. I'm sure of it. Or maybe he just wanted to make sure I didn't blow it. If I let my emotions swallow me again, Paul and Gloria might not invite me back and I'd be dependent on whatever Detective Smith managed to extract. And since he was coming at it from the perspective of assuming he'd already asked every possible question, I wasn't optimistic. Too bad he wouldn't allow me to tag along.

I smiled, this time actually attempting to look genuine. "You seemed so tense about my Mom and now you're saying it wasn't a big deal. What happened?"

Gloria leaned forward and put her wine glass on the table. "It's hard for me to talk about, actually. It was very painful. And I felt it damaged our relationship."

Paul nodded. He looked slightly nauseous.

I put my glass across from Gloria's, as if I was checkmating her chosen position.

Paul stood and put his hands on Gloria's shoulders. "My sister could be blunt. It's clear to me where you get it." He smiled, still looking queasy. "She accused Gloria of having a drinking problem."

"Accused?"

"That's how it felt," Gloria said. "I still choke up when I think about it."

"We're God-fearing people," Paul said. "We enjoy the gifts God has given — financial resources . . ." He swept his arm out from him and ended the gesture with his hand pointing at the view beyond the living room. "We enjoy good food and the fruit of the vine. Music . . ."

"And that ended your relationship?"

"She didn't want you over here without her supervision. So you understand why we were a little surprised when she handed you off like the baton in a relay race." Gloria laughed. She looked as if she was dying for a sip of wine but her determination to prove my mother wrong was stronger.

"I think she just forgot to change her instructions for your care. Got busy with life. It happens," Paul said.

"Maybe she just realized Madison was old enough to take care of herself and only needed you for legal purposes," JD said.

"Madison required a lot of guidance when she came to us." Gloria smiled. She grabbed her wine glass and took a long swallow.

Her constantly changing view of reality made my head spin. Before, she'd insisted I was a "finished product", now she was taking credit for raising me? I shook my head slightly, then pushed my hair away from my face. "How did you know they'd been killed? How did you find out so fast that you were able to show up at my house in less than two hours?"

"It was a long time ago, I don't remember all the details." She stood. "Why don't we go into the dining room. Dinner is ready."

Since I hadn't seen her do anything to make dinner ready, I wasn't surprised when it turned out the meal consisted of cold cuts, sourdough rolls, potato salad, and coleslaw. It was delicious, though, and helped ease the knots that had formed themselves all across my brain and throughout my intestines.

While we ate, Gloria and Paul chattered about their social activities, and their newfound interest in "keeping their heritage alive" by attending an "unorthodox" Episcopalian church. They asked JD about surfing and me about my job at the church, and they drank wine. I couldn't believe how much wine they drank. They never brought the bottle to the table, Gloria just kept disappearing through the closed kitchen door and reappearing with filled glasses. I stopped counting after a while, but I think they had about three glasses to every one of JD's. It was like they had a faucet dispensing wine. There was no evidence they were drunk, not even tipsy. It was unnerving.

Usually if JD has more than three glasses, he's sleepy, and talks more slowly. Paul and Gloria chattered steadily, words tripping over each other. Maybe that's how the wine affected them. They'd been more careful in the living room, and now they kept interrupting each other, eager to tell stories about their lives before me and with me.

Listening to them talk, I started to get confused. Despite their cold cruelty a few days earlier, their stories sounded as if they'd enjoyed my company. They talked about taking me to the circus, an event I remembered not at all — how I loved the trapeze act, adored the animals, and pronounced the clowns the stupidest things I'd ever seen.

It summed up how I still feel — loving the grace of anyone who has control of her body and becomes adept at a sport, even an unconventional one. Especially an unconventional one. I love animals, and I detest clowns. I hate the floppy shoes and the baggy clothes. I hate the disgusting paint and the stupid noses and the faces designed to look smiling or crying, paint so thick it makes me itch just looking at it.

Paul and Gloria sounded as if they'd had some great times with me, that they enjoyed welcoming me into their lives. They talked about trips to the beach, which I did remember, and playing monopoly, which I also remembered. I started to wonder why they'd never had children.

Their incessant chatter numbed me. I lost my determination to dig deeper. They were obviously lying about why they'd had a falling out with my parents, but maybe that was something for Detective Smith to address. After all, he was looking for a solid reason, and now he had one — figuring out the truth — whether it was an accusation of alcoholism, a request for money, or something else.

The room grew darker and the sounds of their voices became slightly distorted. I felt as if I'd had too much wine to drink. I don't really know what that feels like, but it was what I imagined it to be. Outside the long narrow windows along one wall of the dining room, tiny lights blinked on along the edge of the cliff that was too close to that side of the house for my comfort.

They kept talking. Even JD was talking a lot. Then my mood shifted in the opposite direction. I wanted to scream at them to shut up. I wanted to quit the sham and find answers to questions I couldn't even fully form in my mind. So maybe they hadn't spoken to my parents for years because my mother accused Gloria of being an alcoholic. Well she did seem like an alcoholic. Maybe her words were crisp and her eyes were focused and it was just wine, but she drank a lot of it. I wondered if that's where I got my dislike of alcohol. I wondered how much she'd consumed while she was raising me. I remembered her drinking wine, but not such huge quantities. I also remembered her being quieter and now she couldn't seem to shut up.

"Don't you ever wonder who killed my parents?" I said.

It was like tossing a beating heart into the middle of the dining table, slimy and oozing blood, with strings of fat dragging across the silky white pine. They all stared at me, JD most of all. Maybe he had a plan for how to chat them up, but as far as I could see, it wasn't going to happen.

No one spoke for several seconds. Paul coughed. "Well . . ."

I waited.

"Well . . . What makes you think we don't wonder?"

"You never talked about it. Everything seems like it's hidden behind an iron door with a metal bar across it and ten padlocks."

"They never identified a suspect," Gloria said.

"But don't you wonder about it? Why don't you talk to the detective, push him harder? Why don't you . . ."

"There's no point. Some things, you never get to know in this life," Paul said. "Some things belong in God's hands."

"That's bullshit," I said.

Gloria stood and hurried out with her wine glass. When she returned, JD pushed his away. He took a sip of water and I could see that he was trying not to look in my direction.

"What do you want, Madison?" Paul stood. "Whatever it is, I don't think we can give it to you."

The answer was simple. I wanted to know who killed my parents. I wanted to know why my aunt and uncle took me in, even though she obviously didn't think much of my mother, maybe even hated her. And maybe that's why they weren't curious. They were glad my parents were gone — at least they were glad my mother was gone. I pushed back my chair.

"We should get going," JD said. He stood immediately, as if he'd felt me push away and didn't have to check to make sure his assessment was correct.

"You're a strange girl," Gloria said. "You always were. Just like her."

"I'll take that as a compliment."

JD put his arm around me. I wanted to ask them more, I wanted to say more, but I also wanted Detective Smith to catch them by surprise. Hopefully, he'd do a better job than I would of peeling away their lies. If I kept talking and pushing and prying, maybe I'd take away his power.

I knew exactly what I wanted. I wanted to know who killed my parents, and I wanted to know why. I wanted to know why no one could seem to find any leads whatsoever, and I wanted to know what Gloria and Paul knew that they weren't saying.

THE NEXT MORNING we slept until ten-fifteen. When we woke, we cuddled for a while, and then JD got up and made coffee. I went outside and had a cigarette right in front of our room, not caring much if the manager came over. There were cars backing in and out of parking spots, blowing exhaust at the doors and into the windows if they were cracked even slightly, so I figured cigarette smoke from one little cigarette wasn't that much worse.

We checked out and went to breakfast at a Denny's. I had two orders of bacon with an omelet and hash browns. JD had the same. We both had three more cups of coffee. That's one thing I have to say about Denny's — despite serving unremarkable food, they have decent coffee.

"Why did I even come up here?" I said.

"You're closer than you were. You found out Paul and Gloria aren't telling the truth about something. You got some answers about where they stood with your mother. You went inside your house. Wasn't that the main thing?"

"I suppose."

A server dropped a tray of food on the tile floor. The crash echoed through our section. When I went to pick up my coffee cup, my hand shook.

"It's okay. It'll all be okay," JD said. He took my other hand and kissed each knuckle.

At the police station, the guy with the huge mustache was back on desk duty. He recognized me and picked up the phone before I said anything. He informed us Detective Smith would be right out.

We stepped away from the desk and as the door to the

back area swung open and Detective Smith strode through, leaving it open behind him, I saw Roseanne slumped over in a chair, leaning her elbows on the edge of the desk. Another detective stood behind the desk. He was bent over too, dragging the mouse across the pad, then pausing to type with his left index finger.

Detective Smith stopped a few feet from us. He looked confident and in charge. He almost seemed taller, younger, more fit. "Thank you for telling me about Ms. Caplan's knowledge of the severed toes. I don't know how you extracted that information without even trying. It's a little scary."

JD nudged me gently with his elbow.

"Just to give you a little bit of background, since you pointed me to a new line of thinking — the two women met at the juice bar in the Get-Fit Gym. A few weeks ago Ms. Caplan went to get a smoothie. She saw Ms. Varstead flirting with some guy. Ms. Caplan was overcome with jealousy. She got it into her head she could prevent the victim from ever working out again. I haven't asked yet why she passed that information on to you. I expect she thought she'd never see you again. Severing Ms. Varstead's toes didn't satisfy her desire to inflict pain, so she kept going." He shuddered.

It was something — seeing a man that large shudder so uncontrollably. I was glad to see he had some feelings. Maybe he'd try harder after all.

"How awful." I glanced at JD. His face was pale and his lips had lost all their color. They were separated slightly and his eyes looked unfocused.

The detective didn't seem to notice JD's face. He went on, "The toes were lined up in their proper order on the nightstand. The body had been washed and her feet were covered with thick socks. So we knew right away it was someone who cared for her, despite the brutality."

"Did anyone hear her screaming?"

"I asked Ms. Caplan about that repeatedly each time I questioned her. Since her apartment shares a wall with the victim's. She insisted she heard nothing. No one else had either. I couldn't figure it out."

"It must have been unbearable pain," I said.

"I just learned Ms. Caplan gave her a mixture of belladonna to sedate her."

"Doesn't that kill you?"

"The berries are deadly. But the rest of the plant can have some usefulness. There was an oppressive odor in the apartment that we couldn't identify. When we questioned her earlier, Ms. Caplan claimed to be unaware of it, but it was impossible not to notice."

Finally, I understood the heavy odor of the flowers, laced with that sour, almost decaying stench. Karen's ghost had been trying to tell me part of the story every time she appeared. Maybe I hadn't asked her the right questions. "Why didn't Roseanne just kill her, instead of torturing her like that?"

"At the beginning, she only wanted to prevent Ms. Varstead's mobility. Evidently, she lost control and couldn't stop."

JD put his hand on my shoulder as if to steady himself. I put my hand over his, amazed that my usually matter-of-fact, and kind of tough guy was so sickened by the description of what had happened to Karen. It's not that I wasn't feeling slightly ill, but I was also curious, and wanted to understand everything. I didn't want to shrink away from knowing the truth, and sometimes, the truth is sickening and painful. Curiosity trumps nausea. "I never understand a person who kills someone they love."

"I have to agree with you." Detective Smith studied me as if he was seeing me in a new light, or maybe he was just surprised by my ability to listen to the gruesome details without being overcome with nausea. "You can say all you want about love and hate being two sides of the same coin, and jealous rage, and the possessiveness that gets tangled up with love, but to end the life of the person you say you can't live without . . . it shows how complicated and senseless human beings can be."

We stood quietly for a few minutes, each of us pursuing our own line of thinking about love and jealousy and murder.

"Anyway, that's the gist of it. I think she's relieved. People usually are, once they confess." He stepped back. "Thank you for letting me know your thoughts."

"And you'll talk to Paul and Gloria?"

"I said I would. Although we'll be asking the same questions as before."

"It's been a long time. Maybe you'll get different answers."

"Not likely, but I suppose it's possible. Do you actually think they know who murdered your parents?"

"I don't know. But they're lying. They told you they had a falling out because my parents asked to borrow money, but last night they told me the falling out was because my mother accused my aunt of drinking too much."

"Is that right? Well, I'll do my best."

I wanted to argue with that, but decided I had to take him at his word. We said good-bye and he said he'd be in touch. He didn't know me very well, even then. I'd be in touch much faster than he would. Or maybe it was just a meaningless way of saying good-bye.

JD AND I decided to drive home along the coast. He used his trailer hitch to attach my Bug to the back of his SUV.

Once we reached the highway, he turned on a playlist of 80s tunes and when he put his hand back on the wheel, I turned up the volume so I could creep inside my head and let the music build a cocoon around me.

I remembered the message from my fortune cookie at the Thai restaurant. It said that what I hoped for would come to pass. Nothing that I'd hoped for had happened. I didn't get to spend any significant time in my childhood home, and I still wasn't a hundred percent confident Detective Smith was going to go out of his way to really dig in, looking for things he might have missed with my parents' investigation. Despite never considering that

Karen's killer was female, he still didn't seem to recognize that there might be angles he hadn't considered with my parents.

Of course, I don't really believe in fortune cookie messages, or any kind of foretelling of the future. For a woman who talks to ghosts, you'd think I'd be more open. Most people are like me, I think. We crack open the cookie, and when it's something that fits what we want, we're excited. When it seems random, we toss the slip of paper aside. It really is meaningless. A generic promise is printed and stuffed into the cookie to offer a bit of fun. That's all. I doubt there's anyone on the entire planet that thinks a fortune cookie is actually going to provide direction to her life. But still, when I read the message, as foolish as it sounds, I'd felt a tremor of excitement.

After five or six miles, I turned the volume down slightly. Adjusting the knob acted like a signal to JD that maybe I wanted to talk because the minute the music faded to the background, he said, "How're you doing?"

"I honestly don't know."

"A lot of shit happened in the past few days."

"Yeah."

"It wasn't what you'd hoped."

"All these ghosts have shown up in my life, they've given hints about the person who killed them, people who were total strangers. So if I have this great ability to see and understand people in another dimension, what about the people I care about the most?"

"Maybe it's been too long."

I pulled my legs up so my shins were pressed against the dashboard and let my flip-flops slide to the floor. I leaned my forehead against my knees.

"I know you don't want to hear that." He reached across and grabbed my ankle. "But you have to think about it."

"It's not just the ghost thing. It's that the detective gave up."

"He said he'd talk to your aunt and uncle."

"But that was all me. I know it's been a long time, but doesn't he have any curiosity? Even if he doesn't care about my parents personally, doesn't he want to know? How often does a couple get killed in their bed like that? It should be driving him nuts."

"He said they exhausted all possibilities."

"He should get outside input."

"I don't know how that works."

"Neither do I, but he should do something. I can't believe it's been left hanging all these years."

"Maybe he'll turn up some new thoughts when he asks about their conflicting stories."

I lifted my head and looked at him. He was staring straight out at the road, his sunglasses blocking any glimpse of his eyes so I couldn't see whether there was a crinkle of disbelief at the corners. I turned and looked out my window and thought about Roseanne and Karen. A woman found killed in her bed, just like my parents, her body cared for despite the brutality with her toes.

The murder scene seemed a little like my parents'. I

didn't want to say that to JD because I was afraid he'd dismiss the idea and I'd get upset. But even though it was very different, it was people in a place that's supposed to be safe — your bed, and the absolute worst happens. And my parents were lying there as if they were sleeping. It always seemed as if they'd submitted to the killer in some way. Otherwise, wouldn't they be splayed across the comforter, not all tucked in?

I thought about the things Paul and Gloria seemed to not be saying, and the couple living in my house, and the emptiness I'd felt walking through it, sitting on my bedroom floor. As I stared out at the dark blue water, I said, "You know I'm going back. You know I have to get inside the house again."

"Of course." He put his hand on my leg and we rode in silence with the endless Pacific Ocean companionably by our side, equally calm. I realized I hadn't had a smoke since that morning and I was still calm, not wanting one at all.

Letter From Cathryn

CATHRYN GRANT IS the author of Suburban Noir novels, ghost story novellas, and short fiction. Her writing has been described as "making the mundane menacing".

Cathryn's fiction has appeared in Alfred Hitchcock and Ellery Queen Mystery Magazines, and anthologized in The Best of Every Day Fiction. Her short story, "I Was Young Once" received an honorable mention in the 2007 Zoetrope All-story Short Fiction contest.

When she's not writing, Cathryn reads, and plays very high handicap golf. She lives in Northern California with her husband and two cats. Visit her website at CathrynGrant.com or sign up for her new book mailing list at CathrynGrant.com/contact.

www.ingramcontent.com/pod-product-compliance
Lightning Source LLC
Chambersburg PA
CBHW022233020726
47496CB00004B/889

* 9 7 8 0 9 9 1 6 6 0 5 6 8 *